THE WICKED

THE
WICKED

JAMES
NEWMAN

Apex Book Company
Lexington, KY

Previously published in limited edition hardcover by Necessary Evil Press and trade paperback by Shock Totem.

This edition has been revised and expanded.

Cover art and illustrations by Jesse David Young
Cover layout by Yannick Bouchard

www.apexbookcompany.com

ISBN 978-1-937009-51-9

PRAISE FOR THE WICKED

"You might expect the work of a young Southern writer to show some roots, and you'll see that clearly in James Newman's writing. There's a little bit of Davis Grubb and Joe Lansdale twisting into that dark earth, and a strong straight spike of Robert McCammon digging deep. But the story tree that grows above ground belongs to a tale-spinner who can raise one mean hunk of nightmare all on his own. *The Wicked* is a well-honed blade."

—Norman Partridge
Author of *Mr. Fox and Other Feral Tales* and *Lesser Demons*

"*The Wicked* is a good old-fashioned, unabashed *Horror* novel. James Newman remembers when horror used to be fun, and he's recaptured it here in all of its gory glory. A terrifying page-turner in the tradition of Graham Masterton, J.N. Williamson, and Richard Laymon. WICKEDly good reading from one of horror's new heirs!"

—Brian Keene
Author of *The Rising, City of the Dead* and *Ghoul*

"Demons, depravity and despair, oh my! Reminiscent of the best of 80's horror and Bentley Little at his most grotesque and unrelenting, *The Wicked* is the kind of horror we don't see enough of anymore. This is one wild and bloody ride, and in the capable hands of James Newman, it's one worth taking."

—Kealan Patrick Burke
Bram Stoker Award-winning author of *The Turtle Boy* and *Kin*

"James Newman looks like he's far too young to be the bastard lovechild of William Faulkner and Flannery O'Connor...but still, I wonder. In years to come, when we talk about great writers of the Southern gothic, we'll be mentioning Newman alongside Massie, McCammon, Crews, Farris and the aforementioned. You can smell the magnolias, the kudzu and the blood..."

—John Pelan
Author of *The Colour Out of Darkness*

INTRODUCTION
by Mark Allan Gunnells

I am a child of the 80s. Big hair, Member's Only jackets, Rubik's cubes, Ronald Reagan and George Bush (the first one)—I grew up with it all. And as a full-fledged horror geek from a very young age, I also was brought up on 80s horror. I was at the local theater for each new *Friday the 13th*, *Nightmare on Elm Street*, and *Halloween* movie that was released. That also meant I was snapping up all the horror mass-markets I could find in the paperback rack of the drugstore down the street from my house.

Man, how I loved those paperback original horror novels from the 80s. Complete with garish covers, ads in the back, lurid summaries. These books were of varying quality, but for the most part I could always count on them to be *fun*. Exciting, fast-paced stories with colorful characters and juicy violence. Over the years my taste in fiction has expanded and evolved, but I've always retained a warm affection for those old horror novels and have lamented the fact that publishers don't seem to put out that kind of fiction anymore.

At least, until I found James Newman's *The Wicked*.

I first discovered Newman with his novel *Midnight Rain*. While *Midnight Rain* isn't really horror, it is an excellent coming-of-age mystery very much in the tradition of McCammon's *Boy's Life* or Lansdale's *A Fine Dark Line*. A rich novel full of complex characters, it made me an instant fan and I quickly sought out more by this talented author.

When I got my hands on his novel *The Wicked*, I suppose I was expecting something that matched the tone and subject matter of *Midnight Rain*. I was pleasantly surprised to find something totally different. I was immediately impressed by Newman's ability to be more than a one-trick pony, writing the same story over and over. I could tell he had the goods to tackle different types of fiction with equal skill. With

The Wicked, he succeeded in crafting a novel that paid loving tribute to those paperback horrors of my childhood. And like those books, I found Newman's story to be engaging and undiluted *fun!*

What he offers us here in *The Wicked*, is the tale of a family moving to the small town of Morganville, North Carolina. At first, Morganville seems peaceful and idyllic—until an ancient supernatural evil infests the town and its inhabitants.

Now, I could not even begin to count the number of novels from the 80s that had a similar premise. This is not to suggest Newman's work is at all derivative, however. While working within that framework, he makes *The Wicked* completely his own. And he brings something else to the table that many of those novels I grew up with lacked—massive amounts of talent. He gives us more than just stock characters, but instead complex individuals that spring from the page in three-dimensional glory. The situations are otherworldly, yet layered with a realism that makes suspension of disbelief effortless.

After reading *The Wicked*, it was obvious to me that Newman is also someone who grew up scouring the paperback racks for those lurid covers. The book does not come across as parody; it is a fully formed story in its own right. You could almost believe you had laid hands on one of those 80s classics, one written by an author on top of his game.

Some may consider this novel as less "serious" than *Midnight Rain*, but I find *The Wicked* just as serious and equally as impressive. It proves that Newman is a master storyteller who can write different types of tales with equal skill.

With *The Wicked*, James Newman pays tribute to the fiction of the past while proving that he is also going to be a major player in the future.

PRELUDE

On the evening of August 12, 2002, a fire raged on the outskirts of Morganville, North Carolina. Into the early hours of the morning it raged, higher and higher, as if the flames fought to devour the moon itself along with everything else. Because of the *Morganville Daily Register*, the tragedy of that night would come to be known as "The Great Fire of '02," and its casualties would haunt the citizens of Morganville for the rest of their lives.

Neither ghosts nor spirits were these haunts, but instead the collective *disbelief* that such a thing could happen to the town's innocent.

It happened at the Heller Home for Children, out on Pellham Road.

Initially the Morganville Youth Home, Heller Home was erected in October of 1952, ninety years to the day Morganville was officially established on paper. Founded by Joseph and Irene Heller (a retired Episcopal minister, he was known as "Uncle Joe" to the kids, she as "Aunt Reeny"), the place began as a modest two-story farmhouse, by all outward appearances little more than the quaint country home of a typical Southern family. Inside, however, one would find a house full of love and tolerance, a bustling home for children of every race and creed. No less than a dozen kids usually roamed Heller Home's hallways, playfully roughhousing under Mr. Heller's watchful eye while less rowdy teens nurtured their artistic talents with brush and easel. Within this makeshift haven for runaways and the like, Mrs. Heller cooked for her young wards nutritious meals which they might otherwise lack, and eventually the kind-hearted couple would convince these prodigal sons and daughters to return home to their families.

Within a year or two the Morganville Youth Home evolved into an unofficial hospital for neglected and abused children. Mr. and Mrs. Heller were not licensed medical professionals, but thanks to their close relationship with the Morgan County Department of Social Services they were granted funds enabling them to hire several qualified bodies eager to aid them in caring for poor children with nowhere else to go.

Although the official licenses and such did not come until a year after their deaths (Mr. Heller died of a heart attack at the age of seventy, Mrs. Heller four years later of natural causes), the Hellers' dreams were nonetheless posthumously realized. Six months after Mrs. Heller passed away in the first days of Spring '79, Morganville dedicated the new "Heller Home for Children" to the couple. It officially opened its doors as a government-sanctioned hospital to not only victims of abuse but also to children from needy families, particularly youth with chronic illnesses. Due to its historical value, the powers that be resolved not to raze the house and begin anew; instead, volunteers and county workers donated their time and money toward adding several new wings onto Heller Home. A local land developer, claiming the Hellers were the only family he'd ever known, dedicated three acres to the hospital and its young wards. There, the children could run through the grassy meadows bordering Morgan County, wade in the creek or climb the grand oak trees that lined the property.

It seemed as if every person in town did all they could to support the Home, be it through donations or by contributing toys or clothes, and Morganville's citizens did this not out of pity but from the goodness of their own warm hearts.

Uncle Joe and Aunt Reeny would have been proud.

But on the night of August 12, 2002, two months shy of its fiftieth birthday, no one could have expected that the Heller Home for Children would suddenly ignite.

And burn.

And burn.

Until there was nothing left.

The Morgan County Fire Department received the call at approximately ten-thirty p.m. The caller: one Marietta Rude, an eighty-year-old widow who had nothing better to do, according to most who knew her, than track the whereabouts of others so her bridge club might have ample fuel for gossip every third Saturday of the month. Mrs. Rude had lived across the street from Heller Home for decades, and many could remember the days when she had branded the Home a haven for "no-good runaways." Of course, to hear the old woman after The Great Fire of '02, it had been her duty to watch over those poor children since Heller Home's inception. Things had been slow for Fire Chief Randall Simms and his crew that evening—"like the calm before the storm," they would later tell their friends and family. Frank "Beanpole" Deon was kicked back on a sofa in the center of the firehouse, chomping loudly on a meatball sub while flipping through the latest issue of *Popular Mechanics*; Jack Deese and Ricky Friedman entertained themselves with some late-night Cinemax softcore on the Department's 13" Magnavox, occasionally making off-color comments about the women on the screen out of extreme boredom more than any desire to be vulgar; Chief Simms, meanwhile, was engaged in a game of chess with Hank Keenan (who, in addition to volunteering much of his time at the firehouse, also served as a Deputy Sheriff and president of Morgan County's Dads Against Domestic Violence chapter), both of them too bored to admit that neither could beat the other no matter how hard he tried, so why bother?

Simms had just taken Keenan's bishop, the only move of any significance to occur in their half-hearted charade for the last hour, but the Chief never had time to gloat about it or even remove the piece from the board as the station's ear-piercing bell suddenly announced it was time to move. Its shrill ring echoed throughout the halls of the firehouse, shattering the calm. A sleepy female voice on each man's two-way radio informed Simms' crew of their destination.

"Move your asses, boys!" Simms yelled, already sliding down the tarnished brass pole in the center of the room. While rookies Deese and Friedman were half his age, Simms could hustle twice as fast as either man; experience had taught him every second was precious. "Move, move, *move!*"

Chief Simms and his men responded in record time, sirens screaming and lights flashing over the sleeping gray houses of Morganville in their wake. But Heller Home could not be saved. The house's main supports had already collapsed by the time they arrived, and no matter how many gallons of water they used to douse the place, Chief Simms and his men found their efforts were ultimately futile.

Simms cursed himself more than once that night.

He realized, before long, that they could do little more than stand there.

Stand there, watch the place burn...and pull out all the bodies.

The final death toll was sixty. Thirty-seven children dead. Eleven more seriously injured. Six of Heller Home's care-supervisors who were on shift that night perished in the fire; the others were in critical condition. Of the twenty-odd residents who did make it out of Heller Home alive— be it through the aid of Chief Simms and his men or their own iron will to survive—seventeen of them later succumbed to their injuries.

The Great Fire of '02 was the worst tragedy Morganville had ever witnessed.

Several days later, after the mass funeral that saw Morganville citizens shed more tears in a single afternoon than they ever thought possible, Chief Simms and a couple professionals called in from the state capital determined that The Great Fire of '02 was no accident.

Someone had caused all that death, all that destruction, on *purpose.*

They caught him, eventually.

The arsonist's name was Robert John Briggs. He was seventeen years old, a dropout from West Morganville High.

The investigation revealed that sometime before ten p.m. that night, Briggs had broken into the basement of the Heller Home for Children, placing a series of homemade bombs (i.e., newspapers folded into makeshift "pockets," each filled with a pinch of fertilizer, topped with cotton-ball masses soaked in diesel fuel) about the earthen floor of the basement. Satisfied, he lit their lengthy fuses, made his escape...then presumably stood nearby to admire his hateful handiwork.

Bobby Briggs was arrested two weeks later, after his own mother reported to Morganville authorities that she had stumbled upon a notebook in her home that outlined in explicit detail her son's part in The Great Fire of '02. Indeed, the young man's bedroom revealed a virtual workshop for an arsonist-in-training.

Briggs said little during the whole ordeal, adamantly refusing to answer questions posed by those in charge of the investigation. Throughout it all, Bobby Briggs' only official statement was a single murmured phrase: "I wanted to show them that bad things happen to good people. Even to the little kids."

None of it made any sense. The grieving citizens of Morganville wanted to know: *Why?*

Briggs never showed a shred of remorse. The teenaged mass-murderer seemed *proud* of what he had done, in fact. Throughout his trial he stared straight ahead with glazed eyes, and the expression on his face was that of someone privy to a secret that will forever change the world. During the proceedings, in all of the pictures snapped by Simon Short for the front page of the *Morganville Daily Register,* the teenager just kept smiling. Sometimes he would scribble words on his palms with a pen, eyewitnesses later recounted on the steps of the Morgan County Courthouse. Nonsensical words like "MOLOCH," "LOCHIE," "MO-MO," and "MR. M."

When it was over, the judge remanded Bobby Briggs upstate to the sanitarium in Fleetwood. Prosecutors fought for the death penalty, but Briggs' attorney succeeded in convincing the jury that his client suffered "...severe mental problems, the result of unimaginable childhood abuse."

Right up to the end, Bobby Briggs kept smiling.

Smiling.

As if the troubled teenager knew all along that Morganville, North Carolina would never be the same.

PART
1

"Later, folks would look back on The Great Fire of '02 as the single worst thing that ever happened to our town. They would remember those whose lives were lost, and they would think nothing could hurt Morganville the way our souls were shattered that fateful August evening.

They were wrong.

Because The Great Fire of '02...that was just the beginning."

—George A. Heatherly
Excerpt from *Evil in the Tarheel State: A True Story of Demonic Manifestation* (Eerie-A Press, 2004)

CHAPTER 1

Kate Little woke with a start. She pulled the old afghan her grandmother had made for her twenty-first birthday up over her shoulders. She shot furtive glances at her surroundings, temporarily unable to recall where she was or even the time of day. Slowly the images from her nightmare faded, but her brain was still foggy, muddled with the memories her dream had conjured. Sweat beaded her brow, yet she trembled as if she were freezing.

Her husband glanced over at her, taking his eyes off the road for only a couple seconds. He turned the Allman Brothers' "Whipping Post" down to a dull murmur on the 4Runner's radio.

The clock on the dashboard displayed 6:13.

"You okay, baby?" David asked. Genuine concern painted his face as he blinked at his wife with those big blue eyes, *childlike* eyes, she'd always thought, those eyes that had attracted her to him more than anything else years ago.

"I think so." Kate sat up in her seat, but never let the afghan slip below her shoulders. It was her temporary barrier against the world, a warm shield she held tight to her chest like the chain-mail those muscle-bound warriors always wore on the book covers David painted. Kate's hand went to her swollen belly for a second as she thought of the life inside her, but then it fell back to her thigh like some tired old bird no longer able to fly.

"Bad dream?" David asked.

"Mmm," Kate replied, fondling the gold crucifix dangling from her neck. She rarely told him about her nightmares anymore, as doing so usually led to yet another argument. A fight about *that*. Again.

Kate glanced in the backseat at Becca, reassuring herself that their daughter was still back there. As if, along with her peace of mind, the blank-faced shadow-man from her nightmare might have also whisked away the seven-year-old while she slept.

Becca was snoring softly. The child appeared so tiny beside the mountain of cardboard boxes crammed into the back of the 4Runner. Kate could not see her daughter's face through her curly blond hair (save for one small patch of cheek stippled with those adorable freckles inherited from Kate's own side of the family), an impossibly large wig of gold for such a tiny girl. Lying there in the backseat, in her pink felt jacket and blue jeans with the pink piping, the Beach Blast Barbie dangling from her little hand...she was so precious the sight of her brought tears to Kate's eyes.

Kate turned back around to gaze out her window at the houses set closely together along the highway. Each house was so different from those on either side of it, yet at the same time so uniformly *alike* in their small town simplicity. For some reason Kate found that oddly comforting. Few houses along this street were more than a single story; most were stucco, painted in safe, soft earth colors mirroring the vibrant tones of the countryside around them. Not a single skyscraper in sight. Nothing more breathtaking than the foggy-blue mountains in the distance, the lavender-pink skies behind them. Kate smiled as she took it all in. Several homes along this particular road were already draped with rainbows of lights or vibrant green wreaths upon their doors for the upcoming Christmas season, bright bulbs blinking rhythmically like multi-colored eyes watching Morganville's streets. Garland twisted around light poles like vines of silver and gold everywhere Kate looked. A half-dozen or so plastic Santas waved from a half-dozen or so snowy lawns. Western North Carolina had seen its first snow of the season several days before. Kate tried to focus on a single spot outside her window as the 4Runner cruised along, the thick muddy chunks of snowy slush piled along Morganville's sidewalks blurring into a fat gray stripe a few feet away from her.

"We're almost there, aren't we?" Kate asked her husband, yawning.

"Welcome to Morganville, babe," David replied. "Shouldn't be long at all now."

David glanced at her again, then back at the road. He'd always been a very careful driver, never taking his eyes off the road more than a second or two. *That's how accidents happen*, he'd explained to Kate on more than one occasion. *If people would realize that, instead of looking for a CD or gabbing on their cell phones when they should be paying attention to the road, there wouldn't be half as many damn accidents.* At which point Kate would inevitably scold him: *"Language."* Still, she had to agree with his little credo, however hard it was to believe such words of wisdom came from a native New Yawker. She had been so surprised when he decided to haul everything down in the 4Runner, considering how all those boxes in the back made his visibility practically nil.

Kate fidgeted anxiously as she continued to gaze out her window. So this was going to be home. She nearly pinched herself, fearing it might all be a dream. It was too perfect. This was exactly what she needed. She couldn't remember the last time she'd seen so much *grass!* So many trees, a multitude of colors even in the first days of North Carolina's winter. What happened to all the concrete, the stone-gray monochrome and ugly dried-blood brick, the only scenery she had known for the past thirty years?

So perfect.

Kate looked back toward her husband, and he quickly looked away. He had been stealing glances at her every few seconds, so concerned, but she could tell he didn't want to make it obvious. Now came her turn to stare at him, to consider the hint of unease in his face. He really *was* doing this just for her. It certainly was *not* what *he* wanted. David Little could have gladly remained in New York City until the day he died—he probably would have requested, in fact, that his ashes be scattered from the top of the Empire State Building when that day came.

The Littles hoped that moving to Morganville would herald a new beginning for them, for their family. Here at last was a chance to rebuild what had been so abruptly devastated, to repair what had been shattered in one unforgettable evening. They had needed a change for quite some time, as far as Kate was concerned, but especially after what had happened.

She could barely sit still as the 4Runner drew closer to their new home. An image of a mighty phoenix came to the forefront of Kate's mind, a majestic creature rising from the ashes of its old self, rejuvenated and reborn.

Like David, Kate had been born and raised in New York. She had lived there all her life with no complaints. Not that she could ever really say she *liked* living there—New York was simply all she had ever known. The thought of leaving the "Big Apple" never occurred to her, was never an option until she and David married and started a family. Then she began to ask herself, on those long nights when she sat up nursing baby Becca while the sounds of police sirens and screams and gunshots and an all-around sense of *hopelessness* echoed off the outer walls of their apartment building mere feet from where she sat, *do I really want to raise a family in this place?*

She had known the answer for quite some time, but never admitted it to herself. And she knew why.

Because of David.

Since the day they met, David had stressed how he loved the *excitement* of the place—there was never a dull moment in New York! The place was "one big roller-coaster ride," in her husband's words, a ride he never wanted to get off (Kate had refrained from reminding him that she'd never been a fan of amusement parks). Not to mention the fact that, as a book-cover artist, New York City was the ideal place for David to be. They practically lived next door to all of the major publishing houses. Not a bad place to call home, if one wished to rub shoulders with all the right people. Kate had agreed with David's reasons for staying in New York, as he was the sole breadwinner in their family, but with Becca's birth things changed. Kate found that her opinions on the city gradually morphed into less-than-favorable once a child figured into the equation. After Becca came along, Kate found herself craving life in an environment where, well, where nothing happened. Perhaps even somewhere...*boring*. What was so wrong with that?

For the first time since they were married, Kate found herself asking David if the thought of raising a child amidst all that crime—did it not frighten him in the least? It didn't seem to bother him at all, that constant threat of violence lurking like a toxic mist in the New York City air, and Kate never understood why. Though he rarely talked about it these days, David's own father had been seriously injured by a mugger shortly after Becca's first birthday. The old man had never been the same after the attack, yet David's eternal outlook, always spoken so nonchalantly that it could be rather sickening depending on Kate's mood, was: "Crime's everywhere, babe. You're gonna find that wherever you go." End of discussion. David loved the city. *His* city, he had called it more than once, and Kate had been quite sure that nothing would ever change his mind. He was a native of the Big Apple, for goodness' sake, and still he owned one of those stupid "I LOVE NY" tourist T-shirts.

Of course, all of that changed on May 3.

After that night, seven months ago, Kate decided her only option was to leave New York City. She could not—*would not*—continue to live there. So she had given her husband an ultimatum: He could come with her, if he chose to do the right thing, or not. But after what happened, *she* could no longer live in that vile place.

"Should we grab a bite to eat before we find the house?" David said, startling Kate from her melancholy reverie. Again he reached to turn down the radio. This had always been a somewhat annoying habit of his, the radio thing, but one Kate had long ago grown to live with. Got something to say? Turn down the radio. Done? Back up goes the volume until the conversation begins anew.

"You're kidding, right?" She gestured toward the uneaten half of a vanilla Moon-Pie on the seat between them and a warm bottle of Dr. Pepper from which he had taken only a sip or two since their stop at that Seven-Eleven in Virginia.

"I'm still hungry," he lied. "Maybe we could turn around, grab a late dinner at Brunhill's one last time before we say good-bye to New York forever?"

Say good-bye to New York forever. God, how she loved the sound of that.

"Brunhill's is a loooong way behind us, hon," she said. It had been their favorite restaurant back home. "And it's 'supper' now, by the way."

David didn't get it. He glanced over at her several times, still keeping his eyes on the road. That was another thing she had always loved about him—that dumb yet adorable expression that came to his face when he was oblivious to what was going on. Or pretended to be.

"You're in the South now, darling," she explained. Mock-slowly, as if to a child learning how to read. "It's not 'lunch and dinner' anymore. It's '*dinner and supper.*'"

"Ah." David mulled that over for a few seconds. "And who filled you in on that little tidbit of intellect? Brother Joel?"

Kate grinned. "He's an expert now, I guess. The only native New Yorker I know who says 'y'all' on a regular basis."

"No way."

"Last time I spoke with him, he told me he's even developed a taste for grits."

"*Grits?*" David grimaced as if she were trying to convince him of the culinary potential of fresh roadkill. "Please tell me we're not gonna turn out like that."

"I don't know," Kate said, though her sing-songy *you-never-can-tell* tone gave her away. Obviously Kate wouldn't mind turning out like that at all.

"Anyway," David said, "I was thinking—"

"Hurt much?"

"Cute. Very cute."

She winked at him.

"I figured we could stop," he went on, "grab a burger at Mickey D's before we move in." He pointed, and Kate spotted a McDonald's coming up on their left in a shopping center called West Park Plaza. "Maybe let

Becca run wild on the playground for an hour or two?"

"Honey, she's fast asleep. Quit joking around—you know I'm dying to see the house!"

He shrugged. She slapped him lightly on the shoulder, and he chuckled mischievously. Even after they passed by the McDonald's, he kept it up.

"What's the hurry? We have the rest of our lives to see every inch of the place."

"I know," Kate said, beaming. "And I don't want to waste another second."

Everything was going to be okay, she told herself for the umpteenth time. A new home, in a new town, as far from New York City as she could get...and on top of everything else, she would get to see her baby brother soon, for the first time in three years! *Could things get any better?*

The only problem now was the matter of the child inside her.

Her smile faltered. It always came back to that, didn't it? The baby. Something that should make their family so much stronger, a gift from God, was slowly tearing them apart instead. And the child wasn't even here yet.

How was *this* little dilemma going to end?

Kate did not want to think about that. Not yet. Not *now*.

David steered the 4Runner to the right, past an abandoned apple-packing warehouse and onto a road identified by a small green-and-white sign as Honeysuckle Lane. He glanced down at the odometer and reset the bottom counter with a tap of his middle finger. "Almost there. We're exactly a mile-and-a-half from this point."

"I can't wait," Kate said, forcing her thoughts back to the moment at hand. She held her belly as they drew closer to their new home, as if the baby inside of her might somehow experience their arrival through her trembling hands.

"Honeysuckle Lane—sounds like a great place to live, doesn't it?"

"It sure does." With a sad little smile, Kate admired the other houses on Honeysuckle Lane as they passed: split-level, middle-class homes belonging to folks with fine WASP-ish names on their mailboxes like Smith and Gray, Robinson and Rose. "It sounds...absolutely perfect."

Kate absentmindedly began to curl her husband's shoulder-length hair around her fingers as he maneuvered the 4Runner through a deep curve. She couldn't wait to see the house again. David had driven down to North Carolina several times since they decided to buy the place, taking care of all the paperwork, but Kate had only seen it once. That had been enough, however, for her to know that—like the first time she saw her future husband—it was truly "love at first sight." She sat up, peering through the windshield like a child on Christmas Eve searching for Santa's sleigh on the horizon.

"I love you, Kate," David said softly.

His hand went to her thigh. Tentatively, but it was there.

She covered his hand with her own. "I love you, too."

In the back, little Becca began to stir, as if she sensed they were almost home.

"It's alive!" David said, grinning at his daughter in the rearview mirror. "Howdy-ho, sleepyhead."

Becca gazed out her window, already wide awake as she took in this new world around her. "Are we there yet, Daddy?"

"Just about."

"Yay!"

"Excited, are you?"

Becca nodded, golden curls bouncing every which way. "This place doesn't look *anything* like New York!"

David glanced at Kate. "It sure doesn't, sweet-pea. Not at all."

And then suddenly Kate had to hold herself back from squealing with delight as the 4Runner rounded a curve and their new home sat before them. In its sycamore-lined cul-de-sac at the end of Honeysuckle Lane, painted with a mosaic of crisscross branch-shadows and pinkish tint from the late day's dying sun, Kate would have known even if she hadn't seen the house before that this was it. This was home. She could feel the place calling to her: *Welcome, Kate Little. I've been waiting for you. So glad you're finally here...*

"Wow." She could say nothing else for those first few minutes. As far as Kate was concerned, this was the most beautiful house on the block. Even if it wasn't the largest, or the fanciest—she could already spot several things about its outer facade and the property that held ample room for improvement—none of that mattered. 31 Honeysuckle Lane was perfect.

Kate could barely sit still when she noticed the shiny new mailbox out front. David must have put it up the last time he came down. 31 LITTLE, big blue block letters spelled out on its side, and that cinched it. They were home.

Home.

"This is it, isn't it, Daddy?" Becca squealed. "We're here!"

"We're here."

"Neato!"

They couldn't have stopped little Becca if they tried from flinging

open her door and jumping out before the vehicle came to a complete
stop. In her excitement she almost hit their new mailbox, a millimeter
away from leaving a nasty silver scratch through the 4Runner's teal
paint. David hissed through his teeth as he witnessed the near-miss.
But he stayed silent as he watched his seven-year-old daughter sprint
through patches of half-melted snow in the yard, heading for the tire
swing he had hung from the oak tree out front just for her.

"Awesome! Mommy, look!"

Jackpot. He had known she would love it.

"I take it Little One approves," David said, before exiting the vehicle
himself and coming around to Kate's side.

"She's not the only one. Wow. Oh, David...wow." The scene before
her blurred as tears filled Kate's eyes.

"I'll get those boxes later," David said, helping her out of the
4Runner. "Let's go inside."

His arm went around her as she waddled through the yard toward
their new home. He led her patiently up the concrete walkway to the
front step, mindful of any lingering slabs of late-winter slush or ice in
their path. Kate's belly seemed to lead the way for both of them, and she
was gleefully aware of it even as she admired the house.

"Ooo...oh!"

"What is it?" David's hand clenched her own a bit too tightly. He
halted in mid-step. "Kate, what's wrong?"

She placed his hand on her stomach. "The baby! He...it kicked! I felt
it! I think the baby's excited about the house too!"

David's hand fell from hers. His smile faltered. It was back less than
a second later, though now it was cold. Forced.

As it had been so many times before, the moment was ruined.

"Daddy! Come push me!" Becca's musical laughter echoed across the
yard as she twirled around and around upon the tire swing. Her skinny,
blue-jeaned legs kicked in the air below the old Michelin, too short for
her feet to reach the ground.

David did not hear her. Or perhaps he chose to ignore his daughter
completely. At the mention of the baby, his mood had changed once
again.

Kate felt her own emotions darken like a sunny day spoiled by
approaching thunderclouds. *Why, God? Why does he have to be like this?
Doesn't he realize that I know...*

David avoided her eyes as he took her hand again and led her to the
front door of their new home, more interested in his shoes now than
anything before them.

In her belly, Kate felt more movement. *Hello, Mommy...just letting you know I'm in here,* those gentle flutters seemed to say. *I'll see you soon, okay?*

But the joy she wanted to feel would not come this time.

Why does Daddy not want me, Mommy? the baby seemed to ask, and this new thought transformed Kate's tears of joy into tears conjured from anything but bliss.

Why does he not love me?

"I'm sorry," Kate whispered, sniffling. Though she spoke to the child inside of her, David reached for her, trying to make peace. Too late. Kate walked on ahead of him, ignoring his offer to help her up the steps onto the porch. She refused to look at him.

"Come on, Becca," David said, clomping across the porch, shoulders slumped, in that sulking way of his that Kate loathed. Like a child admonished for running in the house—that's what he always reminded her of when he acted like this.

David's voice echoed hollowly in her head as it entwined with Kate's own troubled thoughts. "Hear me, Becca? In the house. You can play later."

God, how Kate wanted David to share her joy, to feel this soul within her as it made its presence known. How she wanted to share those intimate moments with him, to hold his head to her belly—like he had so many times when she carried Becca—as he listened for his child's gentle movements inside of her and they felt like three blissful souls merged as one.

But that was not to be. She knew that already.

David didn't want this child, would never accept this child.

"Becca!" David said again. Louder, this time. "*Now.* It's cold out. Don't make me tell you again, hon."

Kate said nothing, just sniffled softly as they made their way inside.

CHAPTER 2

Their first meal inside the house consisted of burgers from McDonald's. A far cry from Brunhill's, but by the time the Little family was settled in for the night it hardly mattered. They were all famished.

"I could eat a horse," David joked, mere minutes before his mood darkened for the second time that evening.

"Ewww, Daddy. That's *grrr-oh-dee.*"

"Not if you put lots of ketchup on it. A touch of mayonnaise. In fact, it's quite tasty."

"What*ever*, Daddy," Becca admonished him. "But I still think you're full of it."

"Becca!" Kate scolded. "Where did you ever hear such a thing?"

The child's only reply was a tiny finger pointed David's way.

"Uh-oh," David said beneath Kate's glare. "Thanks a lot, short-stuff."

All was fine until after dinner. Becca had devoured nearly all of her Happy Meal by the time her parents started eating, and moved on to play in the living room amidst the labyrinth of cardboard moving boxes. After their daughter left the dining room, Kate and David ate in awkward silence at the table. At one point, for a few minutes at least, David's mood did seem to brighten a bit as he gazed upon their new home, and he reminded Kate of an excited little boy as he boasted of his plans to turn the extra bedroom at the rear of the house into a studio. Kate opted not to remind him that the room would soon require conversion into a nursery. Following that, they'd discussed the possibility of getting out the next day to meet their neighbors. David had met most of them the last time he came down, but now it was Kate's turn. Guy next door was a retired Marine who made peashooters that were detailed replicas of real guns. Fellow in the next house over was Randall Simms, the Chief of Morganville's Fire Department. At the mouth of the cul-de-sac lived

James and Jenna Robinson, a middle-aged couple whose son Larry had recently recorded a country album in Nashville. Plenty of other nice families on the block, too, from what David had heard, kids with whom Becca could play and attend school if they ever decided she could return to public.

As always, though, the subject soon turned to darker things. A topic neither of them wished to discuss, but one they could not avoid these days.

May 3. And the ramifications thereof.

"Kate, I know we've been through this hundreds of times. But I can't stop thinking...*what if?* What if the baby's not...?"

He trailed off, biting at his lower lip, though Kate understood what he meant. She always did, and every time their arguments grew more bitter.

Here we go again.

"What's that?" Kate pretended to be oblivious to the direction in which their conversation had veered. Her attempts at imitating David's own clueless expression at times like these, however, made her feel stupid for even trying.

Please, God, give me the strength to handle this, she silently prayed. *Why does doing the* right *thing so often make you feel as if you've done the complete* opposite?

"I really think we should discuss this some more," David said. "Please?"

Kate shook her head. "There's nothing to discuss." Instantly, an invisible wall seemed to erect itself around her. Shutting David out. Shutting everything out. Just like always.

"You know that's not true, Kate. There's plenty to discuss. We can't go on ignoring this. What if you're wrong? What do we do if things *don't* turn out like you think?"

She turned away from him, but David never gave up easily. She knew he was right—they *did* need to talk about it. But that didn't mean she had to like it. She began to fondle her crucifix pendant, rubbing at it so furiously David suspected the thing would erode away into nothingness right there between her fingertips.

"Kate, come on. Let's talk about this, sweetheart. Please."

"What's to talk about?" A single tear spilled down her cheek. "It's too late for what you've wanted all along anyway, right? You would've been perfectly happy *murdering* this baby, without even knowing for sure—"

"I never said anything about that, and you know it."

"Oh, but don't tell me you never thought about it."

"Kate, please—"

"I know how your mind works."

David ignored that. He reached for her hand, covered it with his own. "There are other options. And I think we need to talk about those options in case you're wrong."

Her hand lay stiff beneath his. "I'm not wrong."

"How do you know?"

"Why do you do this to me, David? It's not healthy. For me or the baby."

"I'm *scared*, Kate. I can feel it. In here." He removed his hand from atop hers, placed it on his chest. "Things *aren't* going to turn out the way we want. It's going to be *his*, not mine. And what will we do then?"

When she did not answer, he said: "I just want you to tell me, before it's too late, that adoption isn't out of the question. That's all."

"And what would Becca think, David? Your daughter is looking forward to being a big sister in a couple months. What are you planning to tell her? 'Oops sorry, sweetie, we changed our minds, decided to give it away.'"

David didn't know how to answer that one. He stared at a crumb on the floor, started biting nervously at his bottom lip again.

Kate stood, trembling. "No matter what happens, you will *refuse* to love this child, won't you? Because you've already made up your mind how things are going to turn out, when the baby's not even *here* yet! You think you know everything, but I wish you could trust *my* instincts just this once."

With that, she stormed from the room, the scent of her perfume trailing behind her like the scent of rain after a heavy summer storm.

"Godammit." David said it out of spite because he knew how she felt about such language—using the Lord's Name in vain was especially frowned upon—but even before the curse was out of his mouth he cringed, hoping she was far enough from the kitchen that she would not hear.

No need to make things worse than they already fucking were.

CHAPTER 3

David Little had always considered his family a happy one, for the most part. Their problems were few, and what qualms he did have with his marriage were petty. He made good if not spectacular money, got along well with his wife, and had a beautiful healthy daughter. Sure, he and Kate bickered now and then, but that constituted a happier marriage as far as David was concerned. Couples who never argued kept everything bottled up inside and, like a boiler running hot, one day it would all explode, destroying everything within its vicinity.

After what happened on the night of May 3, though, David Little found himself wondering more and more if his family would survive. That evening had irrevocably changed their lives, and he knew they would never be the same even if their marriage made it through this ordeal intact.

While he had not wanted to move to North Carolina—or anywhere else, for that matter—David knew that their decision to sever old ties, to buy this place down south, was for the best. If it offered Kate peace of mind, David would give his wife anything she wanted.

Even if it did mean moving to Bumfuck, Egypt, leaving his favorite city behind like a jilted lover.

David sighed as he sat at the kitchen table. Rubbed his temples. Listened to his wife trying her damnedest to laugh and play with little Becca in the other room as if nothing had happened between Mommy and Daddy in the kitchen. On the television, in the background, Oscar the Grouch was grouching away about something or other on *Sesame Street.*

If David had been a praying man, now would be his turn to offer up prayers to God, to ask for help in dealing with this terrible problem before them. He felt utterly helpless, swallowed by a black hole that had opened up in his perfect universe on that terrible night in May...

Two months from now, David Little's wife might bear a child fathered by someone else.

Seven months later, David still blamed himself. He always would, he feared. For the rest of his life.

On the evening of May 3 they had planned to meet for dinner at Marianne's Italian Bistro, as Brunhill's had been closed for renovations that week. David had been contracted to design several new dust-jackets (for pulp horror novels with names like *Lilith's Spawn* and *Warlock Moon*, work he had gladly taken for the easy cash), so he and Kate had found little time for one another during those last few months. While this had not been entirely unusual, things were twice as hectic in those late spring days due to Kate's new schedule conflicting with David's workload. Kate had begun a series of classes at a local community college, claiming that she wouldn't mind one day getting a job as a kindergarten teacher when Becca was older. Where such a goal originated, David hadn't been sure—after all, his salary was more than enough for the family to survive—but he always supported his wife in whatever she chose to do.

That night, David had stayed too long at a bar with some friends after an important meeting. He had downed a few too many beers, and was over an hour late for his date with Kate. After waiting at Marianne's until well past nine o'clock, after calling home several times in hopes that David had merely forgotten her and might be back at the apartment sacked out on the sofa, Kate paid for the glass of wine she had ordered and left in a huff, wondering what had happened to her husband.

Everything would have been fine—the argument that would have ensued when David arrived home notwithstanding, of course—if he had taken care of the Saab they owned back then. Darn thing had been making funny noises for a month or so, but David could never find time in his busy schedule to take it in for repairs. No big surprise then, after Kate left Marianne's, that the Saab would not start. The car's only reply when she turned the key was a sick grinding sound, like an ornery old man wheezing his last breath. A couple of clicks, the vehicle's final death rattle, followed by...nothing.

Once Kate realized there was no hope for the family lemon, she decided to walk back to their apartment, since it was only three or four blocks from the restaurant.

The chill in the air that night had seemed like something more than the weather, she would tell David the next morning from her hospital bed. He chalked it up to the drugs she was on, but she insisted that the icy breeze lapping at her face and arms had seemed like some malicious presence, a sentient *awareness* in the air around her. An omen that something bad was about to happen.

She wrapped her scarf around her neck and began to whistle the first few chords of "Amazing Grace" as she made her way down the sidewalk. She remembered feeling little fear, if any, at the thought of walking alone late at night. It was only a couple blocks. She had walked this distance every day to and from her old job as a hostess at the Pancake House on 37th. Never in a million years did she expect anything bad to happen so close to home.

She would later ask herself, countless times, how she could ever have been so stupid.

Kate had barely walked far enough for the lights of Marianne's to no longer be visible, for the carefree clink of wine glasses and the busy murmur of multiple conversations within the restaurant to audibly fade, when she was jumped from behind and pulled into a dark alley. Someone kicked her in the kidneys and knives of white-hot pain shot through her back and into her groin. Her lips and gums began to bleed instantly when her face struck the cold sidewalk, a coppery taste filling her mouth. She could taste the tangy bite of wine she drank earlier, mixed with her blood, and that taste would forever symbolize the taste of her own fear on that horrific night.

"Get up!" a voice barked in her ear, and she could smell her attacker's sour breath, a hint of cheap whiskey and boiled eggs. He jerked her to her feet, his grip so tight it would leave hateful bruises on her forearm in the shape of his fingertips for weeks to come.

"Don't you fuckin' move, bitch," said the skinny black man in the purple skullcap as he held to Kate's throat the biggest knife she had ever seen. He kept it pressed tight to her jawline as he ripped at her clothes, tore down her panties and hiked up her skirt.

God, no...please God, not that...

He threw her to the ground, unzipped his fly and pulled himself free.

His laugh was heartless, colder than the icy asphalt at her spine, as he pushed his way inside her. "You might just like it, white girl."

"David," she wept the entire time, and continued to weep long after her rapist disappeared into the night. She could still see the ghostly afterimage of his wide, yellow junkie-eyes hovering in the air before her, could still smell for several long minutes after it was over the lingering odor of his breath, could feel the sweaty film from his hands upon her skin.

"Oh, David...David, please," Kate cried, as she lay in that trash-strewn alley.

But her husband did not come. No one came. David would find her later, passed out in the bathtub as the showerhead doused her with its cleansing spray, the water so hot it brought blisters to her flesh. She would tell him what happened through a flood of tears, and even before the embraces, before the moist shoulders and the anguished apologies that continued into the morning, long after the sun had risen and masks of strained normalcy were worn by both of them to hide their pain from innocent Becca...David would leave the apartment, hunting in the night with the only gun he had ever owned, a .38 Special, looking for the *goddamn sonofabitch* who had done this to his wife.

It had been one of those rare moments when she did not scold him for his profanity.

All the same, David did not find him. Nor did the police.

The only thing that remained of Kate's attacker—if David's fears were correct, and the baby was not his own—was the child that grew inside of her.

In the weeks following Kate's ordeal, David seriously began to doubt whether his wife was going to make it. Her entire existence seemed to consist of little more than lying around all day, crying. Always crying.

Finally, though, he'd had enough. With the help of a friend of a friend, one Father Eric Harding, David convinced Kate that she had to make it through this for her daughter. Becca needed her mother to be strong. The Catholic priest had not been of Kate's chosen denomination, but she accepted the rosary he offered her like a life preserver, and held on to it every second of the day.

After a month or so, it appeared things were going to work out. Kate's depression lingered, but at last she started eating again. She stopped lying around their apartment in a perpetual, tear-soaked daze, sleeping for ten or twelve hours at a time. The color began to creep back into her pale, drawn face. She was going to make it.

Or so David thought. Until, six weeks after the rape, they discovered she was pregnant.

"Congratulations," Dr. Melznick told them on that stormy July afternoon. "It appears as if Becca is going to be a big sister."

Kate had smiled at David, reached for his hand. So happy.

But David just stared ahead, his numb gaze fixed upon a series of cheap Norman Rockwell knock-offs on the wall behind Melznick's desk.

"How..." David licked his lips. His throat was suddenly very dry, and his voice seemed very loud in the confines of Dr. Melznick's modest office. "How far...along...is she?"

The doctor glanced down at his files. "Six weeks. I'm setting February third as your due date. Again, congratulations, Kate. Mr. Little." For some reason, Dr. Melznick had never warmed toward calling David by his first name. Not that David cared, or invited the doctor to do so. At that moment he wanted nothing less than to pound the guy's face in. Sure, Melznick was only the bearer of bad news, certainly not the cause of what had happened, but David did not care. He wanted to see someone—anyone—bleed. He *needed* to see someone pay for this travesty.

It wasn't fucking fair.

After all he and Kate had been through...and now this.

Kate had been right about one thing. Though David never voiced the exact word to his wife, would not have dared, the subject of abortion lingered constantly in his mind those first couple months after the appointment with Dr. Melznick. It was all he could think about.

Kate firmly believed that the child inside of her belonged to her husband. She reminded him that they had made love the evening before her assault. David, however—contrary to what Kate called her "motherly instinct"—felt one hundred percent *sure* that her rapist was the father of this baby. It should have been a gift, this child, a gift from the God Kate followed so unconditionally (and rather blindly, David often thought after what happened, but he soon learned it was best not to voice that opinion unless he wished to make things worse). David viewed it as an ugly curse. He could look at her swollen belly with nothing but contempt. Revulsion. This was no gift. It was a cruel reminder of Kate's ordeal, a malicious memento that would never allow them to forget what happened that awful night in May.

They had discussed with Dr. Melznick the various tests which could be done to determine who was the father of Kate's child, but Kate insisted she would rather wait. "There are risks involved, of course," Melznick explained as David looked on, a sick feeling in the pit of his stomach, "as there are with any procedures attempted *in utero*. I can promise you that the chance of any harm coming to this child is slight. But I must warn you."

Wonderful. David had known immediately what Kate's decision would be.

He had tried everything in his power to convince Kate to go through with those tests. Melznick obviously grew tired of reiterating the same assurances over and over at David's request, but in the end none of it worked. Kate read books on the subject every chance she got, did her own research to be sure, and the remote possibility of miscarriage made up her mind. They would wait. Pray. And hope for the best.

Kate was a devout Christian, had been since childhood. Her father was a Baptist preacher in Rochester, New York, and she continued to follow his beliefs as an adult. Approximately a year before they moved to Morganville, Kate had talked David into removing Becca from the public school system (which she considered a place capable of teaching their daughter only "worldly wickedness," whatever the hell that meant), and Becca had been in home-schooling ever since. But the subject of abortion was the one upon which Kate felt the strongest, and her opinions regarding that controversial topic would never falter. Kate believed that abortion, no matter the circumstances, was a grave, unforgivable sin. If God hadn't wanted that child to exist, He wouldn't have created it to begin with. According to Kate Little.

David did not understand such reasoning, *could* not understand such foolishness, no matter how hard he tried to see things from a devout Christian's point of view. Several times, he nearly brought up the subject of Kate's brother. What did her precious Bible say about *that* situation?

Alas, he had refrained from such an underhanded attack. He'd been tempted, sure. But he did not wish to hurt his wife, only to make her see things from his side of the fence.

All he could do now was wait...wait, and pray to a God he wasn't even one hundred percent sure he believed in. Pray that the day he saw Kate's baby for the first time, in the delivery room, it would not be a mulatto.

Even though he knew, deep inside, that it would be.

CHAPTER 4

Kate had called her brother earlier to let him know they made it down to Morganville without any problems, but since it was getting late and he hadn't expected them until the weekend anyway they agreed to reunite first thing in the morning. By the time she and David were finished for the evening, Becca had long since fallen asleep on the sofa. After what seemed like the longest day of their lives, the Littles finally had most of their belongings unboxed and put away. Now, after tucking Becca into her new bed amongst her colorful jungle of stuffed animals, it was at last time for Mommy and Daddy to turn in as well.

In bed, David reached for Kate, touched her shoulder. Her back was turned to him. She drew away from his hand. Razor-stripe shadows lined her shoulders where the moon's soft glow squeezed through the Venetian blinds like a voyeur watching the couple's private troubles.

"Kate?"

"What."

"I'm sorry."

"Yes, you are," was her only reply.

Gently, he ran his hand down her side, where seven months ago he could feel her ribs but now felt soft, pudgy flesh. He remembered how he had adored her plump body when she carried Becca (nothing "grotesque" about it in the least, as she had always been so worried), and now he wished he could feel the same way he had back then.

God, she had been so beautiful. With Becca.

"Mmmm," Kate moaned as his hand glided over her love handles.

"That feels good?"

"Mm-hm. But that doesn't mean you're out of the doghouse."

"I'm trying to apologize here."

She did not move. David could hear her heavy breathing. For a moment, he thought she had fallen back to sleep.

"I am so tired of fighting about this," she said finally.

"So am I."

"Then why don't you drop it, David?"

"I love you, Kate."

"And I love you."

"It's just that...I'm so scared. I don't understand why God would do this to us. To *you*."

"Bad things happen, David. But God never puts more on a person than he or she can handle. He promised us that, in the Bible."

"But you've never hurt a soul, Kate! You're the perfect Christian—"

"No one's perfect."

"I thought God was supposed to look out for His people. Keep them safe. So what did you ever do to deserve what happened that night?"

"You can't blame God."

"I'm not. Really. It's just...I guess I'm trying to understand why He does some of the things He does."

"God has a reason for everything, darling. We may not understand that now, here, but we will. One day."

"Hm." David rolled over. "I don't want to understand it 'one day.' Nevermind. I don't know what the hell I'm trying to say. I'm just confused. I'm scared. I'm sorry for being so difficult."

"No, listen," said Kate. "We have a beautiful baby on the way. You're right. I—*we*—have been through a lot this year. And I agree, it doesn't seem fair. But God has a plan for everybody, David, and He's about to bless this family more than you know."

"How do you figure?" David said, staring through the wall on his side of the bed.

"I'm talking about this baby, David. It's *yours!* I don't know how to explain it, I can just feel it. Mother's instinct. And God told me."

"God told you." David tried not to sound sarcastic.

"Yes. I never mentioned this to you because I knew you'd think I was silly, but He spoke to me, David. He said we were to have another perfect child, if we only left things in His hands." She began to play with his hair, smoothing it down in the back where those natural curls sprang up against his pillow. "A beautiful baby with his father's gorgeous blue eyes."

David wiped moisture from his eyes. "'His?'"

"What?"

"You said '*his* father's.'"

Kate smiled. "Or her." She seemed to suddenly spry up at the tiniest hint of enthusiasm in David's voice as they spoke of the baby's gender. "What do you think, Daddy? A boy or a girl?"

But David had already lost interest. His next reply was little more than an apathetic grunt: "I dunno." He pulled the covers over himself and tilted his head away from her playful hands.

Kate sighed. "Contrary to what you may think, David, God does not break promises."

Against his back, David felt a gentle kick from the baby through Kate's belly. Then another, as if the baby wished to punish him as well for any doubts regarding its genealogy.

"We'll see." David slid forward in the bed, away from the touch of Kate's belly. Away from the baby. Shortly before he dozed off, he muttered: "I hope to hell you are right."

To which Kate replied, "I am."

But as the words fell from her lips, she touched her belly, prayed she was not wrong.

CHAPTER 5

Less than twenty minutes after the Littles drifted off to sleep, a single gunshot boomed in the night, echoing down Honeysuckle Lane like an explosion.

David sat up. "What the fuck?"

Kate's belly did not allow her such speed in rising, though she came awake just as quickly. "Language," she scolded sleepily, but she did not dwell on it. "What was *that?*"

"Sounded like a gunshot," David said. "Jesus."

He leapt from the bed, peered out the window, but could see nothing. Just trees on this side of the house, a portion of their closest neighbor's split-level home next door. A birdhouse dangled from one of those trees, its glass walls catching the moonlight and winking at him like a cube-shaped eye in the night. He rummaged through the closet until he found a rumpled bathrobe to throw on over his pajama bottoms.

"David? Where are you going?"

"I think it came from next door."

"We should call the police."

"Yeah. I'm gonna check it out, though."

"Maybe you shouldn't," Kate pleaded. "Maybe you should stay here."

"You know me, babe," David said. "Curiosity killed the cat."

"That's what I'm afraid of."

"I'll be fine. Go back to sleep."

"Not until you come back to bed."

He leaned over her, kissed her forehead.

"We're in North Carolina now," he whispered. "What's the worst it could be?"

As David came out on his front porch, looking around for the source of that single gunshot, a voice called out to him from the darkness: "You heard it too?"

David's head jerked to the left. His eyes were still adjusting to the darkness, and at first he could see only a ghostly white shape through the trees. Finally, though, he recognized his neighbor, the ex-Marine, standing on his own front porch.

Somewhere down the block a dog began to bark. A big dog, from the sound of it.

"It woke me," David said, walking down the steps to stand in his yard beneath the night's full moon.

His neighbor nodded before crossing his own yard to approach David in the darkness. "Sounded like it came from next door, didn't it?" The man tilted his head in the direction of a house two down from the Littles' home.

"That's what I thought."

David extended his hand when the man stopped a few feet from him. "Heatherly, right?"

The old man's grip was firm, sincere.

"George. I believe we met before, first time you were looking at the house?"

"Right. You're the one who makes the peashooters. The Marine?"

"Retired. Good to meet you again, Mr...Little, is it?"

Despite the obvious unease in his eyes, the old man offered David a friendly grin—a grin missing one front tooth—and David knew already that he liked this man. George Heatherly had one of those faces that was impossible not to like. David estimated his neighbor's age to be somewhere around seventy, give or take a couple years. Other than a slight potbelly typical of men whose best years have passed, George's frame hinted of his days as a military man, of a body once rippling with muscles. He was without a doubt one of the tallest men David had ever known, almost freakishly so. His face was a vibrant sunburn-pink, but the rest of his skin was very pale. What little hair he had sat atop his head wiry and snow-white. Beneath his open robe he wore nothing but boxers, and the old man's thick forearms and former barrel chest were covered with more tattoos than David had ever seen on a man this age. Most were faded variations on the Marine Corps logo and its motto, *Semper Fidelis*, though David also spotted two or three cartoonishly-endowed nude women upon his neighbor's biceps. Staples of an ex-tough guy.

George turned and walked back to his own yard, gesturing for David to follow. Down the street, the dog continued its persistent barking, as if refusing to shut up until someone acknowledged its presence.

"I hope Simms is okay," the old man said.

"Simms?"

"Randall Simms. Guy next door. Morgan County's Fire Chief."

The wind swept through the leafless branches of the surrounding trees, rattling them together like bones in the cool night air as the men made their way toward the yard adjacent to Heatherly's. David crossed his arms and shivered.

"Simms is a good guy, but I worry about him," said George. "He hasn't been the same since what happened."

"What do you mean?" David asked, but then George never had time to reply as a muffled scream came from the very house toward which they were walking.

"Jesus!" George Heatherly's stroll through the grass became a quickened trot. "Martha!"

David followed, but found himself wishing now that he had stayed in bed. He wasn't sure he wanted to see whatever had caused that scream.

Something was wrong here. Something was very wrong.

That dog down the street must have sensed it, too. Its pesky barking grew more furious than ever, a mad yipping as if the thing was being beaten.

George led the way to Randall Simms' house, a quaint brick home surrounded by a low picket fence that had once been white but was now somewhat weathered and yellow. Against the curb at the front of the property a late-model Dodge Ram sat bumper-to-bumper with a blue Cadillac. Octagonal slabs of smooth concrete spaced a foot or two apart led visitors from the curb, through the yard, and up to the patio of the middle-class home, where a wooden sign hung from the awning. WELCOME, it proclaimed, in cursive script.

With the athletic grace of a man half his age, George Heatherly leapt over the picket fence. He motioned for David to follow.

George took the patio steps three at a time, knocked several times fast upon the door of the Simms' house. David stood at the foot of the porch, shifting his weight from one foot to the other, feeling horribly out of place.

In the distance, the dog continued to bark, almost as if to spite the ex-Marine. It took everything David had not to turn around and scream down the block for the damned thing to shut the fuck up.

"Godammit, Sparky, would you *shut the fuck up!*" George suddenly shouted, his head tilted in the direction of that mad barking as if he had read David's mind. He appeared to be genuinely perturbed, and David couldn't help but emit a nervous chuckle at that. The guy really looked like he might take off down the street if his demand went ignored, strangle the wretched thing where it stood.

Just as quickly, though, George reverted back to an air of seriousness, back to the business at hand.

"Martha!" he shouted, knocking on the door again. "Martha, open the door!"

He waited a minute before knocking a few more times, harder. "Martha, what the hell's going on?"

David couldn't help but notice that Sparky had stopped barking. Silence assaulted them on all sides. David almost wished for the barking to begin anew, as the night's unnatural quiet seemed *alive*. Even the sound of crickets chirping in the night was conspicuously absent. The silence was almost smothering.

David was quite sure he could hear his own heartbeat, could feel his pulse in his throat.

Finally the two men heard the sounds of a chain being undone, a lock disengaged. The door swung inward.

George jumped back with a start as a large form spilled from the foyer of the Simms house and fell upon him.

An obese middle-aged lady in a flowery nightgown cried, "George! Oh, George!"

"Martha, calm down, honey. What's the matter?"

"You gotta help him, George," the woman cried. "He's hurt. Randall's hurt. It's bad. Please help him!"

George pried Martha Simms' arms from around his neck with considerable effort before motioning for David to follow. A stranger, David at first felt wary about entering this couple's home, but when Mrs. Simms disappeared inside with George in tow, he sensed he might be needed. He entered the dark house, where no lights burned save for a single bright glow toward the rear of the home.

"This way, George!" Martha Simms' voice called to them from the blackness. "He's in the bathroom!"

David barely had time to register the appearance of the home— nothing fancy, the typical living quarters of a couple slipping from middle-age into their golden years, spotlessly clean and tinged with the smell of last night's dinner (beef stew, David thought)—before George let out a loud gasp. The old man stopped walking, and David collided with his neighbor in the darkness.

"Oh my God."

"What is it?" David asked.

Heatherly turned to David, whispered, "Keep her out of here." In Mrs. Simms' direction he shouted, "Martha, you'd better call 911." He motioned for David to enter the bathroom behind him. "911's not gonna do much good, though, I'm afraid."

David stepped forward into the brightly lit bathroom, peering over George's shoulder.

"Jesus Christ..."

Randall Simms lay crosswise in the empty bathtub, his legs splayed over the side. The back of his head had been blown off, a Rorschach Test pattern of bright red blood and chunky gray matter splashed upon the wall behind him. Some of it had collected between the tub's shiny tiles like pulpy red-black grout.

Randall Simms' right hand still grasped the .44. His other hand, open atop his knee, seemed to beckon to the men standing over him, a pose that reminded David of the homeless contingent by whom he'd been accosted so many times in New York. A crumpled, handwritten note was safety-pinned to the man's gore-spattered pajamas above his left breast, but that too was drenched with blood and was therefore illegible.

Never in his life had David seen so much blood. He gagged, tasting bile in the back of his throat. He covered his mouth and quickly looked away from the corpse.

"I feel so stupid," said George Heatherly, shaking his head. "I should've known it would come to this. Should've fucking known."

"Why?" David asked, though his question was more rhetorical than anything. A mindless reaction to the gore that assaulted him everywhere he looked.

"Poor sonofabitch," George mumbled out of one side of his mouth. "I'm sorry you had to get involved in this, Little. Jesus, I'm sorry."

He shook his head again before turning to look past David.

"Martha?" He shouted down the hallway. "Martha, you call the cops now, honey, you hear?"

CHAPTER 6

"I've never seen a dead body before," David said the next morning. His mouth watered at the aroma of bacon and eggs filling the kitchen, conflicting with the gory sights and smells he recalled from the night before. Dark bags underlined his eyes from lack of sleep.

David sat at the dining room table, sipping at a steaming cup of coffee (#1 DAD read the logo on the side, a gift from Becca last Father's Day) while Kate toiled over the stove and Becca watched Saturday morning cartoons in the living room. Kate had been asleep when he returned from the Simms' place at four a.m., so he had decided to wait until morning to tell her what happened.

"I've been to funerals before, I mean, but...God, Kate, I've never seen anything like that."

"It must have been awful," she said.

David sipped at his coffee, made a sour face.

"We're about to eat, though," she said. "So no more explicit details, please."

"I didn't tell you about the note, did I?" David mumbled, as if he had not heard her request. "That was pretty strange."

"Note?"

"Guy left a suicide note. We didn't touch anything, of course, but the sheriff told us about it afterward." David looked in his wife's direction as he spoke, though he seemed to stare right through her. "It said, 'I can't live with it anymore. Knowing I couldn't help those kids.'"

"What did it mean?"

"Mr. Heatherly told me about it later, said there was a place a couple miles from here used to be a hospital for abused children or something. It burned down a few months back. Arson, apparently. A bunch of kids died, and Simms couldn't handle it."

Kate winced as she carried a pan full of hot grease from the stove to the sink. "What did Simms have to do with it?"

"Simms is the County Fire Chief. *Was* the fire chief. Heatherly said sixty people died in the fire. Maybe Simms felt guilty because he couldn't save them, I don't know."

"That's awful."

"Yeah."

"Those poor children. How could someone *do* such a thing?"

David shook his head. "Even worse, George said it was a *kid* who did it. Can you believe that? Some teenage punk. They've got the asshole locked up in the loony-bin now."

"Language, sweetie."

Several minutes passed before either of them spoke again. The sound of bacon sizzling upon the stove filled the kitchen, mingling with the din of Bugs Bunny and Elmer Fudd duking it out in the living room. In the sunlight that bled through the window above the sink, dust motes danced like tiny punctuation marks upon the couple's halted conversation.

"Did you see Joel?" Kate asked. "I'd assume he would have to be there last night."

"I left before he got there," David replied. "The place was a fucking madhouse."

"I'll bet," Kate said. "*Language.*"

"You wanna hear the weirdest thing of all, though? About this guy, Simms?"

Kate's eyebrows rose inquisitively as she set David's plate before him. Quickly, before David could respond, she called out, "Becca! Breakfast is ready!"

"This is too creepy...in his suicide note, Simms claimed he could still hear them."

"Them?" Kate's eyes darted toward the hallway as Becca's footsteps approached.

"He said he could still hear those children," David said. "That's why he blew his brains out. Because he couldn't take their screams echoing through his head anymore."

CHAPTER 7

Saturdays were still awesome, no doubt about that. Maybe not *quite* as awesome as they had been before, but any day that wasn't a school day was pretty rad. Billy Dawson just no longer considered them *magical* days, the extra-special times they had been before what happened last August.

Ten-year-old Billy Dawson had always enjoyed playing in the vast meadow behind Heller Home, and before the hospital burned down he had forged great friendships with many of the children whose health allowed them to venture outside. At times, such friendships could meet a rather depressing end, as Billy found himself growing close to this or that child only to never see him or her again once the patient was released from the hospital. Such had been the case with Jason Bayne and Randy Musser. Billy had hated to see them go, but of course was very happy to see them get well. Even worse, though, were those patients whose health quickly plummeted after a period of hope and recovery. That had happened with Sarah Smith, same for Gary Cho and the Plemmons kid, Robby.

Sometimes, Billy thought, God could be so freaking unfair.

Most of all, Billy would never forget Anthony. Anthony Leoni. Man, they laughed until their sides hurt whenever Billy would nudge his friend, call him "Tony-Leoni-All-Skin-And-Bony." Anthony had been a ward of the state, a temporary patient of Heller Home until the powers-that-be could find a suitable foster family for the boy. He used to tell Billy stories of his abusive father, of smoldering cigars pressed to his shoulder blades as punishment for the slightest disobedience, of black eyes and broken arms that were the consequences of forgetting to take out the trash or clean up poop when the dog messed on the floor. Anthony had been his best friend. So many times that summer, they had played Cowboys and Indians—along with Susan Brown, Brian Ritter, and the Dolsenberry twins, Cody and Colby—frolicking through the high grass behind Heller Home as if it had swallowed them whole.

Billy remembered that awful day, one of the last Saturdays before the school year began anew, when his mother and stepfather awakened him with the terrible news. He and Anthony had planned a tadpole-hunting expedition that morning, down in the creek along the far edge of the Heller property.

Instead, Billy woke to find that his friends were dead. All of them.

Billy wiped his eyes with the back of one hand as he walked, refusing to cry. Anthony wouldn't want that. Anthony would want him to be happy, to remember the great times they had shared together. Even with his fading yellow bruises and various scars he carried to remind him of hateful old Anthony Leoni Sr., "Tony Leoni" was never one to feel sorry for himself.

As Billy wandered now across his next-door neighbor's property, sneaking from tree to tree like some short, stealthy ninja (didn't take much for that old Rude heifer to call parents and complain about a child's slightest infraction against her, and trespassing on her precious property might as well have been a capital crime as far as she was concerned) he wiped tears from the corners of his eyes. He could see in the distance where Heller Home once stood, and it resembled little more than a dilapidated graveyard now. Billy's tennis shoes scuffed at the gravel as he crossed Pellham Road, his windbreaker making gentle *whisk-whisk* noises in the day's pleasant breeze. Morganville's mourning citizens had placed flowery wreaths all about the old Heller property, their radiant colors drained away by the elements months ago, along with dozens of stuffed animals that now lay soggy and dirt-caked. Numerous weathered, off-white crosses were also erected in memory of the children whose lives were lost in the fire.

But none of it could hide the ugliness that would forever remind Morganville of what transpired on these grounds: the charred ruins of Heller Home. Like rotten teeth, dozens of jagged, blackened boards pointed skyward from the debris. Half of one wall still stood on the old west wing of the site, but that was all that remained of the original structure. It almost seemed as if Heller Home had never even existed here. Even that stubborn wall which had somehow made it through the blaze partially intact appeared ready to crash to the ground at any moment should a strong wind come along to finish it off. Broken glass littered the ground everywhere Billy Dawson looked. Splintered crossbeams straddled broken bricks, concrete blocks, and unidentifiable hunks of warped metal like refuse in some post-apocalyptic wasteland. High weeds had usurped the property since Heller Home's demise, and now it was their domain. Huge piles of ashes swelled above the ground like memories reduced to thin gray flakes and scattered to Mother Nature's mercy; scraggly tufts of crabgrass stabbed through those grave-mounds of soot and crumbling black embers.

"I miss you, Tony Leoni," Billy said as he stared at the debris. He sneezed, the smell of soot and ash tickling his nostrils. Even after all this time, that smoky odor still lingered over the place. It was not an *un*pleasant smell, really—it reminded Billy of the rare camping trips he had taken with his father in summers past, before Fred Dawson quit coming around anymore. But here, now, it brought visions of different memories to mind.

Again Billy wiped his eyes, trying not to cry. His voice sounded oddly hollow inside his own head as he whispered into the day's gentle breeze, "That guy who did this got put away, Anthony. I want you to know that. They put him in Fleetwood, and he ain't never getting out."

The only reply came from the weeds, the brown crabgrass whispering as if in agreement: *Yes, Billy, he was a really bad person. But they locked him up and threw away the key, didn't they?*

Billy picked up a rock from the side of the road, tossed it as far as he could. It sailed high above the remains of Heller Home before dropping to the ground in a thick gray cloud of disturbed ash and soot somewhere in the center of it all.

"It's not fair," Billy said, gazing at the sky. "Why?"

Once again, only the weeds cared to answer. As Billy made his way closer to the ravages of Heller Home, they licked and lapped at the legs of his jeans as if warning him to turn back.

He didn't listen. He made his way through those hungry weeds now, past where the front door of Heller Home once stood and into the heart of the debris. The cloying after-stench of the blaze again forced a harsh sneeze from him, but Billy did not stop. Even when his foot struck a blackened teddy bear halfway through his trek—the thing's plastic eyes were melted across the length of its furry face, hardened into long taffy strands—he did not stop. He felt as if he were walking some strange gauntlet, and would only succeed in properly saying goodbye to Anthony when he had ventured through the entire ruins of what had once been Heller Home. As he made his trek through the ruins, Billy was careful to take long, high-stepping strides instead of lazily shuffling through the debris, so as not to kick ashes all over his pants and onto his shoes. Mom would kill him if he ruined his new Nikes. Plus, she would know where he'd been. She had warned him to stay away from here.

Suddenly Billy stopped when he spotted a multitude of strange golden-brown objects scattered behind Heller Home's charred foundation. In the weeds, ten feet or so from the pile of ash and broken two-by-fours farthest from the road.

"What the heck?" Billy wondered aloud, making his way past the black ruins and into the weed-choked property beyond.

His breath caught in his throat. His eyes grew wide and he blinked stupidly, unable to believe what lay there in the trampled weeds.

Carcasses...

At least thirty of them, scattered haphazardly throughout the meadow.

They were the color of dead autumn leaves, and resembled some unnatural hybrid of insect and human infant. Curled into tight fetal positions where they lay, none of the things were more than three feet in length. Their alien heads were what caused Billy to think of babies, round and enlarged, their texture sort of a *bark*-like material with huge eyes slit in death. No ears, no noses. Those puckered brown faces reminded Billy of the Egyptian mummies he had seen on the History Channel this past Halloween. Tiny beards dangled from their thick brown chins like miniature goatees. The hair there looked very soft, and Billy oddly enough found himself wanting to reach out and stroke it. He refrained, but just barely. Their vestigial wings were veiny and transparent, bee-like and closed flat against their bodies. Their limbless, segmented bodies appeared chitinous, like the hard shells of beetles, tapering off into hard, fat points the color of fresh shit.

Billy did not know why, but he found himself thanking God that these alien creatures were no longer alive. He didn't think he would want to be around if these things had been stirring about.

What had happened to them, he wondered?

Somewhere in the woods that bordered the property, a cicada began its high-pitched chitter, the sound echoing through the meadow as if there were a million more out there. Billy jumped backward. His hand went to his chest. He knew why the sound had startled him so, because such was the song these creatures would sing in life. He knew this to be true, although he did not know *how* he knew.

Billy turned, glanced about the ruins of Heller Home. Looking for something...

A rusty pipe. That would do.

Pipe in hand, he slowly approached the creatures in the weeds, his makeshift probe spilling copper-colored water onto the ground. He didn't know what he planned to do, really—perhaps he wanted to make sure the things were truly dead, so he could take one to school for Show-and-Tell. Wouldn't that be a heck of a prize? He'd be willing to bet that none of his fellow students in Ms. Ellis's fourth-grade class had ever seen *anything* like this.

Billy grinned mischievously. He poked at one of those bizarre insect/baby things with the end of the pipe, flakes of rust snowing down on its prone form as he did so. He could already imagine the wide eyes, the amazed gasps that would emit from boys like Nathan Guice and Scotty Hogan when he stood before the class and showed off his newfound trophy. Perhaps even the class bully, Carl Bowen, might want to be his friend when he witnessed Billy's discovery!

Billy wondered if these things were from some other planet. They sure didn't look like anything he'd ever seen that might have been born here on Earth. As he poked with the pipe at one of the creatures' infant-like skulls, its dead flesh made a crinkly sound that reminded Billy of a brown paper bag being stepped upon. Its skin was tough. It gave a bit but did not burst beneath Billy's curious probe.

"Weird," Billy said, jabbing at the thing's sharp butt. The tip was gooey, covered in a gray, mucous-like substance.

"Yuck."

Billy let out a surprised yelp as the thing moved.

As *all of them* moved.

He stumbled backward, barely catching himself from falling flat on his ass, as the creature closest to him rose into the air. Its alien brethren immediately followed, as if on strings attached to the one he'd been prodding. Together they moved, like a single entity.

Before Billy had time to run, they were upon him.

The sounds they made as they lit upon the boy were not unlike that cicada he had heard in the meadow minutes ago, but beneath that high-pitched chirp their wings cut the air around him in a horrific sort of *non*-rhythm, a low choral droning like furious bumblebees. Billy flailed about, swinging at them with his rusty pipe. He struck two of them, but they only bounced back for a second, bobbing jerkily in the air, before rejoining the fray. The sun shined golden on each of their hard carapaces as they surrounded him. Their eyes were huge, encompassing the entire width of their infant *non*-faces now, but were completely black, like obsidian pits reflecting Billy's own aghast features as he fell beneath them. They blinked curiously at the boy as they swarmed around him, almost human-like; otherwise, those alien eyes hinted of no life, no clear comprehension of anything but their own hunger. Their long gray goatees swished in the air with their movements, dancing upon the breeze created by their frantically vibrating wings. Billy squealed as those wings batted his face, his arms, his legs. He could see nothing but those terrible *things* blurring about on all sides of him in a dark cloud.

Billy's screams grew louder as the things suddenly exposed their stingers. Bursting forth with sprays of thick mucus, those horrible barbs burst from the creatures' insectoid rears in a grotesque sort of *emerging* that made Billy think of birth.

Their chittering song grew louder as they drew closer.

Billy shrieked when the first one stung him in the side of his neck, in the crook of flesh between his throat and collarbone, its barb plunging into him and then ripping back out just as quickly. He batted that one away, but four more came at him in its place.

Another sting, and another. One fleshy hook in his cheek, another near his left nipple, and before his body registered the pain two more plunged violently into him, one in the soft web of skin between his left thumb and forefinger, another deep into his right buttock.

Billy screamed for help. But none came.

The pain from their stings was at first little more than a pins-and-needles tingle, a numb sensation no worse than that of a limb falling asleep. But then that sleepy-limb sensation soon morphed into jabbing needles of white-hot pain, agony beyond anything Billy could have imagined before today.

Billy screamed. Screamed until his throat grew sore and his voice was hoarse. He tried to run, but fell beneath their assault. He tried to stand again, rolling about in a pile of ashes, but they stung him again and again, on the palm of his hand and behind his left ear and on his chin and in his thigh, brushing wetly across his right testicle. Billy cried, begged for them to *stopstoppleaseGodnostop*, and still they came, plunging their needle-sharp hooks into him again and again and again.

"Please," Billy pleaded. He swatted at one of them with a limp right hand, the only remaining part of himself that he could truly *feel* now, but the thing just landed upon his hand, slamming it down onto the ashy soil. It sat there for a moment, seemed to watch him almost sympathetically with those coal-black eyes before bringing its stinger around and plunging it through the boy's skinny wrist.

It had Tony Leoni's face, that one. Billy would recognize his best friend anywhere.

The last thing Billy saw before his life ebbed away, before the poison sluicing through his body stopped his heart completely, was the old man with the beard. The things suddenly ceased their assault and hovered a few feet in the air above him. Waiting patiently. Obeying. Their long goatees swished back and forth like hairy pendulums ticking away the last few seconds of Billy Dawson's life. In one perfectly straight line they floated, like some unholy phalanx of trilling insectoid soldiers.

The old man was nude. He was taller than any person Billy had ever seen. His flesh was gray, like something long-dead, and covered with leaking white sores. His nose was beakish, vulture-like, and his beard coiled around behind him, trailing back into the meadow from where he had come. His eyes were black as sin, and far older even than the rest of him.

He smelled like something burning.

As Billy Dawson died, he saw those ghastly winged creatures disappear one by one into the old man's matted, infinite beard. It parted for each of them with a low rustle.

The old man opened his mouth wide, and the darkness inside was as deep and black as the impenetrable void of his eyes. His sigh of unholy ecstasy flew aloft upon the day's growing breeze, traveling through the town common and beyond, as he digested the boy's sweet, warm soul... and the taste was so exquisite.

CHAPTER 8

Shortly after breakfast, Joel came to visit. David and Kate heard his arrival before they saw his black Mustang screech to a stop alongside the curb out front; Kate's younger brother was fond of showing off his ridiculously expensive stereo system.

They walked out on their front porch to meet Joel. Kate was barely able to contain her excitement as he approached them. Becca, meanwhile, was too young to bother with subtlety. She burst through the screen door, a blur of golden tresses, and leapt upon her uncle, smothering him with hugs.

"Whoa!" Joel said beneath the assault. A wide smile stretched across his tan face. "Death by seven-year-old!" Giggles filled the air between them as he hoisted his niece into the air, spinning her round and round until she grew dizzy.

Joel was Kate's only brother, her junior by four years. They had been quite close throughout their childhood, but several months after graduating from NYU Joel moved to North Carolina. That had been five years ago, after his own terrible ordeal in the Big Apple. Joel loved it down here, and he had been trying to talk Kate and her family into joining him for several years. His smile said it all as he stared up at his sister on the front porch, his arm stretched as far as it would stretch as Becca's tiny heels dug into the soft ground and attempted to drag him toward the tire swing in the corner of their yard.

"Uncle Joel! Uncle Joel!" Becca chanted. "Will you push me?"

"Wait a minute, sweetie—"

"It's been a long time since Mommy and Uncle Joel have seen one another," Kate said. "Give us a few minutes to catch up before you kidnap him, okay?"

"Awww," Becca fussed. She followed her uncle onto the porch, never letting go of his hand as if he might disappear.

"Wow," said Joel. He stood back, eyeing Kate's massive belly with mock-amazement. "I guess calling you my *big* sister is truer than ever these days."

David laughed. "Careful, man, you'll give her a complex."

Kate rolled her eyes, dismissed Joel's joke with a wave of her hand. "Come here, you."

"God, I've missed you so much," Joel said. He embraced her, his voice muffled as he buried his face in her neck.

"Easy now," Kate reminded him beneath his tight squeeze.

For a minute David wondered if the two would ever stop hugging. He popped his knuckles, fidgeting as he watched their exchange. Not that he minded their show of affection. He knew how long it had been since Kate had seen her brother, and he was glad to see Joel as well. For the most part.

"Hey, David," Joel said, at last releasing his sister. "It's good to see you, man."

He moved to hug David then, but David stuck out his hand. A harmless gesture, albeit a bit too quick. Still, Joel's arm went to David's back, pulled him into a sort of half-hug as they shook.

David cleared his throat, took a step back once he was free. "It's been a while. You, uh...you look good, man."

"Thanks, David. So do you. Both of you. You look fantastic."

"Oh, Joel." Kate moved to hug her brother again. Her eyes were moist. "If you only knew how much I've missed you!"

"The feeling's mutual, sis." He returned Kate's hug, then reached down, and Becca jumped into his arms. "How's my little bug-a-boo?"

"Fiiine," Becca said bashfully, looking everywhere but in the three adults' faces as she again became the focus of attention.

Joel's hand came up before his face, his index finger and thumb extended a half-inch apart. "Do you realize the last time I saw you, you were only this big?"

"I'm seven now, Uncle Joel!"

"I know. Growin' like a weed. Before you know it, Daddy's gonna be fighting the guys off with a stick."

David raised an eyebrow, grinned mischievously.

"Did you bring me a present, Uncle Joel?" Becca asked.

Kate gasped.

"Becca!" David scolded. "That's not a very polite thing to ask, now is it?"

"Oh, it's okay," said Joel. "As a matter of fact..."

Becca's grin stretched from ear-to-ear.

"I made a new friend on my way over, guys." Joel winked at David and Kate. "I know you're not supposed to pick up hitchhikers, but this guy was so cute I couldn't help myself. Why don't you help him out of the car, Becca?"

"Really?"

"Yeah. He's in the passenger seat."

"Yayy!" Becca sprinted off across the yard, and the adults laughed as they watched her go.

With Becca out of earshot, Joel turned to his brother-in-law and said in a low voice, "Heard you had a bit of excitement last night, David."

"Yeah. You could say that."

"It's a shame. Simms was good people."

Witnessing the uncomfortable look on his brother-in-law's face, Joel trailed off. David obviously didn't want to talk about the scene he had witnessed with George Heatherly.

"How are things?" Kate asked her brother. "Do you still like your job?"

Joel nodded. "It's not bad. Since Dr. B passed away, I'm basically all the county has 'til they can find a replacement."

"Ah. I forget, what did you say happened to him?"

"Heart attack. It happened two nights after Heller Home burned down."

"That's terrible," Kate said.

"Hell of an opportunity for me, though," Joel said. "I know that sounds terrible, but shit..."

"Language," Kate said.

"Anyway...I'm sorry you had to see that on your first night in Morganville, David."

"So am I," David said.

"Oh, coooool!" Becca shouted a few seconds later, her high-pitched voice echoing across the yard as she found her prize inside Uncle Joel's shiny Mustang. "Mommy, Daddy, look!"

She pulled a huge stuffed animal from the passenger seat. A pink bunny, nearly larger than herself. It took the child some effort to carry it, but in her excitement she hefted the stuffed animal in the air proudly, waddled across the yard with it. The adults laughed as they watched the seven-year-old struggle under the massive bunny all the way to the porch. She nearly teetered over backward beneath its weight as she ascended the steps. Joel moved to help her, but Becca's body language made it obvious that she wished to do it all by herself.

Joel stood back, out of her way, then informed his niece that this particular bunny's name was "Lucky."

"Lucky," Becca said. "I like that. He's so cool, Uncle Joel!"

"What do you say, honey?" David asked.

"Thanks, Uncle Joel, you're the greatest!"

"Yeah, well…" Joel blushed slightly as he pushed Becca's golden curls back behind her shoulders. "I'm glad you like him, sweetie."

"Lucky," Becca said again, lost in her own little world now as she and the bunny moved to one side of the porch to carry on some imagined conversation.

"They don't get much cuter than that, do they, guys?"

"They sure don't," David agreed.

While Joel was in no way a big man, in comparison five-foot-nine David seemed much shorter than his true height when the two stood side by side. Joel had always been tall, Kate remembered, and one of the skinniest kids in school. These days, however, he had become quite the fitness freak, and his body showed hints of newfound muscle definition since the last time the Littles had seen him. Today he wore a sleeveless white GOLD'S GYM T-shirt. His knee-length shorts were black denim, very tight. He kept his sandy-blond hair neatly styled, short on top but clean and wavy past his ears, just shy of his shoulders. A neat five o'clock-shadow around his jawline. Joel wore glasses, the transitional kind, so in today's light their lenses were dark brown. Around his neck he wore a thin gold chain. A small black pager was attached to his belt.

David couldn't help but notice the new tattoo Joel had gotten on his left bicep since his last visit back home. It was his only one to date, which made it all the more conspicuous although it was no more than an inch or so wide and just as tall. The tattoo consisted of a thin black "M" framed within a five-pointed star.

David was quite sure he knew what that single letter stood for: MICHAEL.

Cute.

David quickly transformed his frown back into a smile. Joel hadn't seen that fleeting expression of distaste anyway—he glanced out over the yard, shielding his eyes from the sun as his glasses grew lighter in the shade of the porch.

"Man-oh-man, it's gonna be a beautiful day," Joel said.

"No kidding," said Kate. With a tilt of her head, she gestured toward a mound of gray slush at the corner of their property, against the curb. "Hard to believe it's December. It feels like spring! And to think you guys had a bit of snow just a few days ago."

"That's North Carolina for ya, sis," Joel said. "The winters are always unpredictable. But that's a good thing. One day it's snowing, next day it's nice enough to wear shorts out." He ran a hand down one of his bare legs, fingering the material of his own short pants. "You guys are gonna love it here."

For a minute or two, no one said anything. Kate and Joel just stared at one another, so glad to be reunited.

Kate said, "There's so much to talk about, I don't even know where to start."

"Jeez, I know," said Joel. "It's so good to see you, sis. You too, David."

"Well, hell," David said, turning at last to open the screen door. "What are we waiting for? Come on in and see the place, Joel."

"Uncle Joel! Come see my new room! Come see my Barbies!" Becca exclaimed, running into the house ahead of him. As was typical of a child her age, she had already forgotten Lucky in favor of another favorite plaything of the moment. The rabbit crumpled behind her on the corner of the porch, one fluffy pink ear drooping across one shiny black eye, as if disheartened that his new friend had already turned her back on him.

Joel pretended not to notice. "A bundle of energy," he laughed, and the Littles nodded in agreement.

"Care for a beer?" David asked his brother-in-law as they made their way inside.

"Brother, I thought you'd never ask."

CHAPTER 9

They sat in the living room, the men drinking from frosty bottles of Bud Light, Kate sipping at a glass of iced tea. Joel and Kate sat side by side on the sofa, while David relaxed in his favorite recliner. Becca sat nearby, watching Saturday morning cartoons, oblivious to everything around her except for her Barbies on the floor. According to the child's quiet conversation with her dolls, Barbie had just found out she was pregnant and Ken was none too happy about it.

"So," Joel said to his sister. "You seem to be holding up well."

"I'm alive," said Kate. She offered her brother a sad little smile. "I thank God for that. I think I'm going to make it."

"We take one day at a time," David said.

"I hear ya," Joel said. "That's how you gotta do it." He gazed proudly at Kate, smiling. "You *are* gonna make it. I know. You've always been strong. Remember when Mom died? I honestly don't think I would've survived if it hadn't been for my big sister."

Kate rested her hands upon her big belly, stared down at them self-consciously. She knew he wasn't just pulling her leg—she had been strong, back then. Of course, that had been more than a decade ago, when they were teenagers. She had been so sure that life would always be easy, as long as she had God on her side. But God never promised His children a rose garden, she discovered. A lot had happened since those days.

David said, "Need another beer, Joel?"

"I'm fine, thanks. Gotta drive home, you know."

"So how are things with you, little brother?" Kate asked. "Details!"

"Things are good, really good. I'm staying busy. Working. That's about it."

Kate feigned a sick grimace. "Personally, I don't see how you do it.

I'm proud of you, don't get me wrong...but you've got guts, lemme tell you."

"That goes with the job," Joel laughed. "Guts."

It took her a second, but Kate got it. She slapped him on the knee, and her hands went to her belly, as if to shield the ears of the innocent child inside of her from her brother's twisted sense of humor.

David shook his head. "I don't think I could last a day in a job like that."

"I wouldn't last an *hour*," Kate said.

"Doesn't it get to you?" David asked, raising his bottle for another cool swallow of beer.

"I'll be honest with you," said Joel. "It bothered me those first couple of months. You guys wouldn't believe some of the nightmares I had. But you get used to it, ya know? It's not bad at all now. Just another job. And like I said, there's great opportunity for advancement. I'm just waiting for the county to make a decision."

"Wow," Kate said. "My little brother, a coroner. Who woulda thunk it?"

Joel's hands went out before himself in a gesture of false modesty. "Actually, it's still 'Assistant Medical Examiner,' for now. I'm working on it, though."

"I am so proud of you, Joel," Kate said again. "You've really done well for yourself."

Kate shot a quick glance toward David then, before turning back to Joel. Normally this would be the point at which she gauged her husband's mood, debating internally whether she should bring up this next topic, but she decided to dive right in.

"And how is Michael?" she said.

David stared at his shoes, cleared his throat once, but said nothing as his brother-in-law answered Kate's question.

"He's good. Said to tell you guys hi."

"He was working as a paralegal last time we spoke, right?"

"Yeah. Though I'm not sure how much longer that's going to last."

"Why do you say that?"

"Well, Michael likes his job, but he's been keeping an eye open for something else since the Bobby Briggs thing."

"Oh? What happened?"

"Cutler, Cutler and Greene—that's the firm Michael works for? They defended Briggs at his trial."

"I know that name," Kate said. She snapped her fingers, digging through her memory.

"The guy who burned down Heller Home," David said.

"Right," Joel said. "Michael enjoys the work. It pays well. But he doesn't feel right, working for the people who defended that asshole."

"Language," said Kate, her eyes darting toward Becca on the floor.

"Sorry."

"It's okay."

On the floor, Becca continued to puppeteer her dolls through their troubled scenario. Barbie was sick and tired of fighting with Ken. He could either do the right thing, or he could "talk to the hand."

"Well," Kate said after several minutes of silence between the three adults, "maybe Michael can find something else. I hope he does, if that's what he wants."

"Maybe," Joel said. "He's looking."

Joel shot a glance David's way a few seconds later, said to Kate in a low voice, "We've discussed taking our relationship a step further, you know."

"Have you really?"

"Yeah, you know..."

"Oh, my gosh," Kate said. "You're talking about...marriage?" She smiled as she said it, but it was obvious by the look in her eyes how such a thing still conflicted with her own beliefs.

"It'd be nice," Joel said. "Just to...consummate it, ya know?"

David stood suddenly, no longer interested in Elmer Fudd's endless pursuit of that wascally wabbit on TV. He grabbed his empty mug, mumbled, "I need another beer." To Kate: "More tea?"

"No thanks." Kate glared at her husband as he stalked off toward the kitchen.

Meanwhile, on the floor, Barbie and Ken continued their fighting as parental ears lay deaf to their dilemma. She slapped his plastic face and, in the voice of a seven-year-old girl, he called her a dirty whore.

CHAPTER 10

Two days later, the Littles attended Randall Simms' funeral. While Kate didn't understand why David wanted to go, considering they'd never known the man, he convinced her by explaining that they were now citizens of this town. David felt obliged to attend, not only because he had been one of the men who found Simms' body, but also due to the fact that—if only for a few hours—Randall Simms had been their neighbor.

Becca wore her best Sunday dress, a teal ensemble she often wore to church on those occasions Kate took her. Becca hated the dress, always complained that it was "itchy-scratchy," but it was the closest thing in color and style that might be considered suitable for the occasion.

David had to admit Becca's complaints were valid. He hated dressing up himself, even when doing so was a necessary evil for attending important meetings and the like. David's idea of comfort was a New York State T-shirt and sweatpants (both stained with a rainbow of paint splatters as he tooled about the house, working on various projects for the publishing companies with whom he had contracts). For Simms' funeral, however, he opted for his best navy blue suit. On the drive across town he kept pulling at his collar, cursing beneath his breath about how the damn thing was chafing the hell out of his neck ("Language!" Kate scolded him several times, and even Becca chided in once). Still, it had been his decision to take the family to the services, as Kate was quick to point out, so he kept his bitching to a minimum.

Kate wore a long black dress she had picked up just a few weeks before for church, once she'd found a suitable place of worship in Morganville. It was the only outfit she owned for such occasions that fit her in this latter stage of pregnancy. David had to admit that, even with her swollen belly, the dress looked very nice on her. Even, yes, *sexy*. It was cut low in front, and as he drove he raised his eyebrows more than once Kate's way, becoming aroused from those occasional glances at her sun-dappled cleavage. God, did she ever smell good, too. Her scent kept wafting over his way, the Liz Claiborne perfume he had purchased for her birthday last February further exciting him at the most inopportune time.

"Mmm," he said, "I didn't realize till now just how big those things are getting."

The corners of Kate's mouth turned up in a sly grin. "What?"

"Your boobs," David said, licking his lips with exaggerated lust.

Kate's reply was a playful slap at his leg. She shot a glance at Becca in the back of the 4Runner, whispered, "Stop it, you. We're going to a funeral."

David composed himself. Kate was right. Respect for the dead and all that.

By the time the Littles arrived at the church, they could already tell this event was going to be big. *Very* big. Every emergency vehicle in Morgan County's arsenal, it seemed, was parked in the church's vast parking lot, awaiting the beginning of the procession to come. Fire engines of every size and shape glistened beneath the morning sun, as well as an ambulance or two, and more than a few Sheriff's Department patrol cars straddled the bright green grass bordering the church property.

Morganville First Presbyterian was the town's largest church. The sign out front, beneath the church's name, declared in bold black letters: EXPERIENCE THE POWER OF PRAYER—COME WORSHIP WITH US. Beneath that, in smaller letters: DARRYL RHODES/ PASTOR.

"Uncle Joel!" Becca squealed from the back seat, as David steered into one of the few parking spaces still available amidst the chaos.

David and Kate turned to see Joel walking toward them from the next row of cars. He wore a black suit with a speckled yellow tie—a tie that seemed a bit loud for this occasion, David thought, but kept it to himself—and his hair was pulled back into a tight little ponytail.

David brought the 4Runner to a stop between a white Suburban and a blue Volvo with a crumpled rear end. It was a tight squeeze. "Becca, I want you to behave yourself in there. Okay?"

"Okay, Daddy." Eyes wide, she stared out the window at a massive fire truck parked about fifty feet away. Like some sleeping beast, it was silent, though the lights atop its roof rotated in a swirl of crimson, reflecting off the dozens of smaller cars around it.

David said, "Look at me."

Becca looked at him.

"We're going to a funeral, sweetie. To pay our respect for the dead. This isn't fun-time."

"I know."

"She knows," Kate said. "She's been to church before."

"Right," said David, as he exited the 4Runner.

Kate and Becca followed, Becca jumping into her uncle's arms the second she was out of the vehicle.

"Hey, sweetie," said Joel, nodding a silent hello Kate and David's way. He ruffled Becca's hair playfully, but then, realizing it had been meticulously prepared for the services at hand, fixed it back the best he could. "Oops."

David headed for the church. Kate and Joel followed a few feet behind him, Becca's hand now in her uncle's, and Kate felt overwhelmed by the crowd already gathered beyond the church's open doors. David straightened his tie, replaced his expression of discomfort with his professional *glad-to-meet-you* face. It always came forth in large numbers such as this, Kate knew. Meanwhile, she felt awkward surrounded by so many strangers.

"Daddy, wait for us," Becca said as they ascended the steps of the church. David did not hear her, however. He was already shaking hands with a very tall, older gentleman who had turned to greet them.

David introduced them. The man's name was George Heatherly, he explained to his family, and he was their next-door neighbor.

Kate caught a glimpse of a dark tattoo beneath the old man's sleeve as he reached for her hand. She hid her slight distaste when the old man's eyes flicked over her cleavage as he bent to offer the back of her hand an old-fashioned *how-do-you-do-ma'am* kiss. Oh well. The old fellow looked harmless enough. He *was* rather charming. Still, Kate was perturbed when David abruptly followed George Heatherly into the throng of their fellow citizens without waiting for his family, forcing her and Becca to fend for themselves.

Kate felt her cheeks grow hot beneath the eyes of strangers as she stepped into the church, as she ventured deeper into the cloying fog of other folks' perfume and too-strong cologne, and began searching for an empty seat among the pews. Her neck reddened with nervousness beneath that trademark look men tend to give pregnant women, a look of admiration married with a bizarre sort of near-contempt for what has already been conquered by another.

Feeling like an antelope surrounded by a pride of hungry lions, Kate clung to Joel's arm, her other hand in Becca's. She hoped that her brother, at least, would not leave them behind to drown in this sea of nameless mourners.

Brookside Hills, twelve sprawling acres in the center of Morganville, was the final resting place of nearly every citizen who had died within the town since the beginning of the twentieth century (the others were laid to rest in the older, weed-choked graveyard behind Trinity Baptist Church on Spruce Road, provided the deceased had been a member of that church, as it was the county's only place of worship with its own boneyard out back). Its name was derived from the fact that the cemetery was bordered by a flowing brook. Social stature meant nothing in Brookside Hills, as those who were interred in the grounds of this cemetery rested beneath fancy marble sculptures and modest tombstones decorated only by time-worn names, wilted flowers, and carpets of dark green moss. Everyone had a place in Brookside Hills, eventually, assuming he or she had planned ahead and purchased a plot.

After the initial services honoring Randall Simms, the Little family followed the hearse-led procession across town to Brookside Hills. Becca's eyes seemed wider than humanly possible as she watched everything going on around her, her tiny blonde head peering over the front seat or out her window. The fire department's largest truck, Engine Number Five, followed behind the hearse like a loyal dog at the feet of its fallen master, and it seemed everywhere the Littles looked as they traveled down Brookside Boulevard a swirling cacophony of emergency lights painted the town red, white, and blue. Sheriff Guice and his two deputies escorted the convoy in twin patrol cars, their sirens belching out harsh *whoops* every time someone neglected to get out of the way.

A soft drizzle began to fall over the cemetery several minutes after Reverend Darryl Rhodes—a middle-aged gent with the largest, bushiest eyebrows David had ever seen—began the eulogy above the open grave. This lent the proceedings an even more morose bent, the day suddenly turning gray and gloomy to mirror the proceedings at hand.

David wished he had stayed home and worked on his latest project, a dust jacket for a nerdy sci-fi novel called *Black Star of Tyrinnak*, instead of coming here. He bent his head, rubbed at his temples to sway the pain of a dawning headache, and Kate—perhaps mistaking his discomfort for genuine sympathy for Randall Simms' widow—placed one arm around her husband. Little Becca looked at him, whispered, "You okay, Daddy?" and grabbed his hand.

David offered his daughter a weak smile and a nod.

The cold drizzle had upgraded to a soft rain by the time Sheriff Sam Guice's radio interrupted through the somber proceedings. Reverend Rhodes paused his monotone eulogy as Guice muttered, "Sorry," turned his radio down and held it to his ear.

"Yeah?" Guice said into it, as softly as possible. He walked away from the grave and the crowd surrounding it as he spoke, paced toward a mass of marble tombstones several yards away. When the radio's only reply was a belch of static, he said, "Guice here. Come in. What is it, Mavis?"

"Sheriff," said the radio, "we got a Code Twenty-Seven on Pellham Road." Another bird-like squawk of static, then: "It's bad, sir. Possible Fifty-Five from last night. Over."

"Ten-Four," Sheriff Guice said. "I'm on my way. Get Keenan for me, would you? And Ten-Three, Mavis."

"Ten-Nine, sir? Please repeat?"

Sheriff Guice shot a glance over his shoulder, toward the curious civilian faces watching his every move.

"Ten-Three, Mavis. Cease transmit."

With that last bit he looked back again at those gathered around the grave, found Kate's brother in the front row. When they made eye contact, Guice offered Joel a barely perceptible nod. Joel nodded back.

"Roger," squawked the radio. "Sorry, Sheriff."

"It's okay, Mavis. Ten-Three. Over and out."

With that, Sheriff Guice returned his radio to its place upon his shiny black belt and jogged to his patrol car beneath the watchful eyes of Morganville's mourning citizens.

All the while, Reverend Rhodes droned on like the distant thunder mumbling in the dark sky.

"Code Twenty-Seven means they found a dead body," came a whisper from the crowd, but it was a whisper loud enough to be heard over the falling rain and Reverend Rhodes's solemn monotone. Kate Little turned toward the direction of that voice, but could not tell who had said it. She thought it sounded familiar, however, and the closest person whose voice she could have heard so clearly was that Heatherly gentleman to whom David had introduced her earlier. George Heatherly's attention was captive to Sheriff Guice and his men as they sped off toward town, lights flashing.

Joel leaned over toward Kate and David and whispered, "I'd better go. I'll catch up with you guys later, okay?"

Kate and David nodded. Joel patted little Becca on the head before making his way through the crowd, trying to be as inconspicuous as possible. But after Sheriff Guice's sudden departure, it was too late for that.

In the crowd, Kate leaned into David. He looked back at her with raised eyebrows.

"I wonder what's going on," she whispered.

"Shh."

Reverend Rhodes continued his bored eulogy even as those gathered to pay their respects no longer gave him their full attention. Murmurs of murder and whispers of gory gossip passed through the crowd like a bad flu as the rain left tiny puddles atop Randall Simms' sleek gray casket.

Only the cold rain and the fire chief's widow seemed to remember the dead man now.

CHAPTER 11

"Jesus H. Christ," Sheriff Guice said as he stood above the corpse. Goosebumps stippled his forearms, and he felt cold all over. Not because of the rain, though.

"What do you think happened to him, Sam?" asked Deputy Hank Keenan. Wet sprigs of his fiery red hair stuck up beneath his Smokey-bear hat, and crescents of sweat darkened his uniform beneath the deputy's muscular arms. He looked as if he might lose his dinner at any moment.

"I don't know." Guice pulled a handkerchief from the back pocket of his khaki uniform, covered his mouth and nose with it, and Keenan followed suit. "My God."

The child had been dead for a couple days, the sheriff estimated from the look of the corpse, though he would not know for sure until Joel Rohrig arrived. Guice shook his head as he stood above the boy's body, sniffled once. Never in his life had he seen *anything* like this.

"Is it him, Sam?" Keenan asked. "Is it the Dawson kid?"

"I think so," the sheriff replied, looking off toward the woods at the far end of the meadows. The metallic staccato of a cicada's song began somewhere in the distance, and the sound startled the sheriff, jerking him back into the real world and away from whatever dark thoughts swam through his mind. He sighed. "Hell, we know it is, Hank. Donna said he was wearing a red windbreaker, blue jeans. Look at him. Whether we want to believe it or not, it's the Dawson boy." Another sigh. "*Shit.*"

"You want I should tell his parents?" Hank asked. "I'll do that if you need me to, Sam."

"No. Let's wait. We'll cross that bridge when we come to it."

Keenan nodded.

"Fucking-A, Hank, how the hell *do* you tell a mother her son is dead two weeks before Christmas?"

Keenan did not have an answer for that. He hung his head, said nothing.

Saturday evening, the department had received a call from Donna Evanson, who explained that her ten-year-old son, Billy, had not returned home after walking just several blocks to a friend's house to play Nintendo. Mavis, the Department dispatcher, had taken the call at approximately eight p.m.; Mrs. Evanson told Mavis she had spoken with the other boy's parents, but her son had never arrived. For that matter, they knew nothing of Billy's alleged visit. Sheriff Guice then spoke to Evanson himself, explaining that her fears were probably unfounded— Morganville was a decent place, he assured her, stuff like this happened all the time and it always turned out okay—but he would look into it. However, he did tell her that, while this would not yet be an official search, he would gladly patrol Morganville in hopes that Billy might turn up. Evanson, an old high-school girlfriend of the sheriff's own brother, agreed to place her faith in Guice and his men. They *would* find her son.

By Sunday night, however, the search had escalated into the real thing. Guice and his entire crew combed Morganville with the help of several volunteers.

Guice's attention returned to the child's body once again, and Deputy Keenan was quite sure he saw tears in his friend's eyes. The sheriff made an animal-like grunting sound—perhaps just clearing his throat, perhaps something more—as he looked off toward the woods, not wishing to stare at that little corpse any longer.

God, it was *awful*.

Thick red blisters, comparable to bee stings or maybe mosquito bites, stippled nearly every inch of the dead boy's flesh. Even now those fat welts seeped a greenish, bile-like fluid long after the child's final breath; it trickled down onto the ground with the falling rain, collecting in miniature puddles beneath the corpse.

The boy's eyes were open, cloudy and distant.

"Who found him?" Deputy Keenan asked his superior.

"Rudy Reznor. Claims he spotted the kid from the road while picking up aluminum cans. But I wasn't born yesterday. He was out here scavenging for shit to sell in his junkyard."

"I'm sure," Keenan said softly.

"I told him I'd throw his ass in the drunk-tank for a month, I caught him messing around out here again."

"Good."

"Nobody's got any business here."

"Right."

Sheriff Guice and his deputy turned then, flinching slightly at the sound of a short, sharp honk. Joel Rohrig, the county's acting medical examiner, had just pulled up in a van the color of fresh vomit. He had apparently driven from Simms' funeral to the lab to trade his loud black Mustang for the trusty old meat-wagon (along with his suit and too-loud tie for a pair of blue jeans, a light green smock, and a navy-blue windbreaker with MORGAN COUNTY printed on the back in yellow).

Sheriff Guice welcomed the young medical examiner with a nod of his head, a curt "Afternoon." Today was not a day for pleasantries. Even the normally friendly Rohrig said nothing as he went to work. The young man squatted beside Billy Dawson's corpse, his expression pained as he saw the dead boy for the first time. But Rohrig did nothing to betray his air of strict professionalism. He took a long, precursory look at the corpse before pulling on a pair of latex gloves and removing from his bag some sort of thermometer that reminded Guice of the kind his wife, Darlene, stuck in the turkey every Thanksgiving.

Sheriff Guice turned away as Joel raised the boy's shirt and pressed down upon his stomach. The skin blanched, dark crimson turning to pale greenish-white, before Rohrig stuck the thermometer in just below the corpse's ribcage. Sheriff Guice allowed the medical examiner to work for several minutes before interrupting with his questions. That was the way things had always been done with Dr. Bonansinga, Rohrig's late mentor, and so he respected the tradition. Finally, though...

"How long do you think he's been dead?" Guice asked, kneeling in the weeds beside the young M.E. His middle-aged joints cracked and popped as he did so.

Rohrig scratched at his forehead, thinking, and Sheriff Guice couldn't help but notice the speck of bloody matter that the young man's latex-covered fingers left stuck in one blond eyebrow.

"Notice the reddish-green tint to his flesh?"

"I couldn't help it," Guice replied.

"Rigor mortis has resolved." Joel grasped one of the boy's swollen arms, raised it several feet from the ground. It went slack in his grip. "Note the flaccidity."

The sheriff nodded, though Joel seemed to be pointing out these details more to himself than anyone else now. Thinking out loud.

"Body temperature's equivalent to that of the environment," Joel said, removing the thermometer at last from the corpse's stomach. It slid out with a grotesque *slurp*ing sound that reminded Sheriff Guice of someone sucking on an ice cube. "A little under forty-eight hours would be my guess. Estimated T.O.D."

The sheriff turned toward his deputy, winced. Keenan just stared at the ground. The acting medical examiner's estimate placed the boy's death at sometime Saturday evening.

"Shit." Guice turned back to Joel Rohrig. "Cause of death?"

"It's too early to tell for sure, pending a post-mortem. But I'll get right on it, let you know as soon as I can."

"Please do." Sheriff Guice slapped the ponytailed young man lightly on the back, stood. "I'd appreciate it, Doc."

"Not a problem." Rohrig offered the sheriff a weak smile, remained in his squatting position beside the corpse. "However, you know as well as I do, Sheriff, the tests are gonna show those stings are what killed him. I'd bet money on it."

"What the hell do you think it was?" asked Guice.

"I don't know. I'll draw the toxin, send it off to the lab in Raleigh. Could take a couple weeks."

"That's fine. Do the best you can."

Joel turned to the sheriff then, and it was his turn to ask a question. "Honestly, Sheriff, do those look like any kind of bee stings you've ever seen?"

"No." Guice shook his head. "They don't."

"If so, that was one fucking monster bee," Joel mumbled.

The medical examiner closed the corpse's eyes then with two fingers, and Sheriff Guice couldn't help it—a sigh of relief escaped from his tightly-pinched lips.

So much better, when their eyes were closed. So much easier to handle when they weren't staring off into nothingness like that. Staring at things the living could not see.

Guice closed his own eyes, dreading the days ahead of him. Dreading the tasks to come.

CHAPTER 12

Curiosity had been eating at Marietta Rude for the past hour, like the arthritis that nibbled constantly at her tired old bones, and she couldn't take it anymore. If she didn't find out what was going on over there at the old Heller Home property, she feared she would go stark raving mad.

Rude had lived alone ever since her husband's heart attack in '81. They had purchased the property across from Heller Home long before the hospital ever came to be, and had witnessed its rise and fall (at least, Mrs. Rude had seen the latter—A.J. had been in his grave for the better part of twenty years by the time the place burned down) from the swing on their front porch. Since Arnie Jack died, though, Marietta refrained from going outside, as one never could tell what kind of hoodlums hung around Morganville these days. Things weren't the way they used to be, thirty years ago, when a person could go outside and work in the garden without fear of those teenagers racing down the highway with their loud music and their litter flying out across your lawn, back when a senior citizen like Marietta Rude could take a trip to the store for some Ex-Lax or a bottle of Carter's Liver Pills and just leave the front door unlocked with nary a concern. Now Marietta Rude was resigned to watching the comings and goings of those in the neighborhood from *inside* her home, from the big bay window facing the street. She'd pull back the curtain and sit there for hours on end, sipping at a glass of warm milk or nibbling at a piece of her homemade blueberry pie as she watched the neighborhood ne'er-do-wells sneak through her yard like little rodents when they thought she wasn't looking. She knew, oh yes— Marietta Rude hadn't been born yesterday. Or the day before that, even.

As Marietta sat watching the scene across the street through that rain-stippled window, she found she now felt more than contempt. For it was not kids that she saw, playing over there at the ruins of Heller Home where they weren't supposed to be playing...but something else. Something that filled Marietta Rude with the closest thing to true fear she could remember having ever felt.

The police were over there. The Sheriff's Department. Sheriff Guice and his men had roped the place off with that yellow tape they used on shows like *America's Most Wanted*. Marietta knew darn well what that meant, and she could not deny the fear that crept into her veins like an injection of ice water.

Heller Home was an official crime scene.

For the second time this year.

That thought sent goosebumps across her old-woman flesh, a chill down her spine and through her legs. Marietta could not rest until she knew what in tarnation was going on over there. She squinted, pursing her wrinkled lips as she stared out the window at Sheriff Guice. He spoke with a tall, skinny youth with too-long hair, a young man Marietta thought looked vaguely familiar but couldn't quite place. A couple patrol cars were parked along the side of Pellham Road, as well as a dark green van.

Something *big* was going on over there. God, how it drove Marietta crazy not knowing what.

Marietta knew Sheriff Sam Guice fairly well, as he or one of his deputies had been out to her house many times since he'd been sworn in to his position. Guice had made so many visits out to the Rude place, whether to coax Marietta's fat Persian cat, Bernadine, out of the massive oak tree in front of her place, or to assure her that there had been no prowler stalking outside of her house in the wee hours of the morning, only raccoons digging through her garbage cans out back. Yes, Marietta Rude and Sam Guice went back several years, and she knew he would tell her what was going on. He'd better. She'd been one of the voters who had elected that man into office—he'd best not forget—and she had a right to know. She decided she would give him time to get back to his desk, but that would be the extent of her waiting. And Mavis, that hateful old biddy who answered the sheriff's phone, best not give her any lip either.

My-oh-my, there'd be plenty to talk about come Saturday night's bridge club meeting. Nan and Lucy and Helga and Gay would be so envious of her! Marietta grinned, and her wrinkled reflection in the rain-streaked window leered back at her, all large yellowed dentures beneath heavy pink lips.

Marietta stood now, slowly, and her arthritic joints creaked like ancient doors opening onto musty, forgotten places as she headed for the single bathroom at the back of her house. Her bladder had been acting up something awful lately, and before the day was over she planned to call Dr. Whitman again. Sure, it would be the fourth time he had seen her in the past couple weeks, but if he didn't like it she'd just take her business somewhere else. Nothing he prescribed her seemed to help, and she sure as heck wasn't paying him to look handsome (although, Marietta had to admit, that young whippersnapper sure would've earned every bit of her money and then some if that had been the case).

Marietta gave a dry chuckle as she crossed the living room. But then she moaned as her knees began to pain her too, along with everything else. Her knees bothered her the worst when the weather got like this. She moaned again, no longer sure she could make it to the bathroom before she was forced to sit. She would definitely call Dr. Whitman today, look up his number and call him at home if she had to—*after* she had spoken with Sheriff Guice, of course. Her hands trembled like liver-spotted branches on some scrawny, weatherworn tree, and she cursed her failing body as she stumbled down the hallway toward her bathroom, past faded pictures of her friends and family who had long ago gone to be with Jesus. Somehow, Marietta Rude had outlived them all—even her granddaughter, poor naive Kitty who was killed in that wreck ten years ago, thanks to a good-for-nothing boyfriend Marietta had warned her about—though she was quite sure none of them had suffered as *she* was suffering in these, her last few years.

"Golden years, my ass," Marietta grumbled when she at last stood before the bathroom door. Her hand went to the knob, and she stood there for a few seconds before opening the door, offering a question to the stale air around her: "Lord, what did I ever do to deserve such misery?"

The only reply Marietta Rude received when she stepped into the bathroom was her own horrified scream.

Floor to ceiling, wall to wall, Marietta Rude's lavatory was covered in a dark, roiling mass of *flies*. Chrome-green bluebottle flies, the kind Marietta had seen on Bernadine when the cat was struck down by some sadistic bastard on Pellham Road a few years back...millions, *trillions* of metallic-bodied filth flies usurping the room, leaving not a spot of linoleum or porcelain uncovered by their twitching, furiously-buzzing bodies. A veritable *carpet* of the nasty things seethed wherever Marietta looked, an undulating sea of black and gray and shiny metallic jade. Their buzz filled the room, filled Marietta's head, a persistent drone that seemed almost musical in its fervor. It sounded louder, in that moment, than anything Marietta Rude had ever heard before, louder than the rumble of thunder directly above her home now, louder than the groan of a Mac truck passing by on the highway outside.

And it grew louder with every passing second.

Flies. Hideous, infernal things, everywhere Marietta looked. So many of them, more than the old woman had ever seen.

That carpet of flies covered everything, even the shower curtain, which jiggled and jerked beneath their collective weight like something alive in itself. Even in the center of the room, in the void of space surrounded by the mass upon the wall, ceiling, and floor, more bluebottle flies swarmed about as if looking for a place to perch where there was no more room amongst their brethren.

They came from the toilet, Marietta saw, as she stood there paralyzed with fear. More of them. And still more of them. Like a pulsing mass of solid waste from a septic tank backed up beyond repair, they rolled forth from that porcelain mouth in an almost *liquid* rush, pushing up and into the air as one to join those already filling the room. Still more. And more.

The old woman clutched at her chest as pain like a thousand needles shot through her eighty-year-old heart. Her left arm tingled, her legs gave out beneath her, and by the time she fell backward and hit the floor Marietta Rude was already dead.

A single bubbly fart escaped from beneath the old woman's flowery gown...and, as if answering some beacon call, her buzzing, chrome-bodied visitors lit upon her corpse like miniscule vultures hungry and ready to feast.

Within the space of several seconds, every inch of Marietta's dead flesh was covered in quivering black.

Thousands of the feverish green-black bodies gathered to form a single word—*MOLOCH*—on the floor, next to Marietta's body. Then they dispersed, joining the pulsing sea atop the wrinkled corpse, and the word was gone as quickly as it had appeared.

CHAPTER 13

The night following Randall Simms' funeral, David Little rolled over in bed and reached around his wife's big belly to cup her left breast in one hand.

"Are you awake?" he whispered.

"Mmm. Barely."

He rubbed at Kate's nipple in slow circular motions with the tip of his index finger. It grew hard beneath his touch.

"I can't sleep," he said.

"I'm sorry," said Kate. "Something the matter?"

"I don't know. I was just...thinking."

"About what?"

"About the last time we made love."

"It has been a while, hasn't it?" Kate said.

"Too long."

Kate snuggled up to him, her butt against his crotch.

"Do you think..." David cleared his throat, pushed her thick brown curls away from her neck and kissed her there. He swallowed loudly in the quiet of the room, cleared his throat again before making his request: "Do you think we could...um...mess around a little?"

Kate was silent for a few seconds, but finally she answered, "Do you really think that's a good idea?"

"I think it's an excellent idea."

"Of course you do. But you know what I mean."

"It's not going to hurt anything," David said.

"You can't be sure."

"No...but remember what Dr. Melznick said?"

"I don't know, honey," Kate said. "I still feel funny."

"You don't want me to touch you. I understand."

"No. It's not that."

"Because of what happened."

"No, really," Kate said. "It's not that." But she didn't sound so sure.

"I'll be gentle."

"I'm sorry. Can't we just wait?"

"I've waited for eight months, Kate."

"I'm sorry," she said again.

"I have needs."

"So do I, David. But we've waited this long. Can't we wait one more month, until after the baby's here?"

"I thought I could. But I'm not so sure anymore." He snuggled closer to her, and she could feel him stiffening between her buttocks. "You know I would never hurt you, Kate."

She rolled over then, grunting with the effort it took her, and met his eyes in the moonlight that crept through their bedroom window.

"Please, David," she said. "I know it's not easy, but please try to understand. I'm just not ready."

David's hand slid down her belly...slowly...lower, working its way beneath her girth with some effort until his fingers brushed through the wiry thatch of hair at her groin. He extended his middle finger, massaged her there. So gentle. Trying to prove to her that he would take it slow. He would never hurt her, not for anything in the world.

"You looked so sexy in that dress today," he said.

"David, no..."

"I'll be careful," he promised again. "Just relax."

For those first couple of minutes, she moaned softly. Enjoying his touch. And then he gasped as her left hand found his hardness, gripped it through his pajama bottoms. But she did not stroke him. Only clutched him in her palm. Scared.

"Oh, Kate," he said. "I love you."

"I love you..."

Their lips found one another; their tongues worked together. Kate breathed heavily into David's mouth, and the taste of her was exquisite. God, how he had missed it.

His finger eased inside her, found her clit and massaged its hardness.

"Oh, David," Kate moaned.

He felt as if he might burst at any minute. Before he ever got the chance to enter her. His penis felt hard as steel in her hand.

"David..."

"It feels good, doesn't it?" he whispered. "I told you."

And then the moment was shattered. She slid away from him,

released his cock. His finger withdrew from her.

"Kate, what is it?"

"I'm sorry, David. I'm just not ready."

"But—"

"I'm sorry." Once again she rolled over, her back to him.

"Did I hurt you?"

"No."

"Then...*why?*"

"I don't know. I just can't. Not yet. I'm sorry."

"I *love* you, Kate. I would never make you do anything you didn't want to—"

"I'm sorry," she said again.

David rose from the bed, left her lying there.

He said nothing else to his wife as he stalked into the bathroom, where he masturbated in the darkness, stroking himself to an almost painful release on the spotless linoleum.

CHAPTER 14

Two weeks after Mrs. Marietta Rude died of a massive heart attack, on December 20, David Little sat beside his daughter in her bed, reading to her from *The Big Book of Children's Bible Stories*. It had been a long day for the Littles, as they had finally found a suitable obstetrician in Morganville and Kate had visited him for the first time that afternoon. They both warmed right away to Dr. Frank Bullard, a British gentleman with longish salt-and-pepper hair and a jovial attitude that—had the doctor not been such a natural extrovert and genuinely likeable sort— might have seemed out-of-place in the examination room. Even Kate laughed at his frequent jokes while her feet were up in stirrups, and David stood there chatting with him as if the two stood in a bar over drinks. When all was said and done Kate seemed satisfied that Dr. Bullard would offer her the best possible care for the last six weeks of her pregnancy, that he was the best replacement for Dr. Melznick that they would find in Morganville.

At last, after night's cloak swallowed the day and it was time for bed, Kate claimed to feel a bit under the weather after all that poking and prodding, said she planned to turn in early. She asked David if he would tuck Becca in for the night.

Though such things were fiction to David—or, at best, mere parables toward teaching children basic values—he had no problem reading to Becca from the book of Bible stories. Becca always enjoyed them, and he would do anything to make his daughter happy. Truth be told, he enjoyed the stories himself, for what they were worth.

Tonight, however, Becca seemed to have other things on her mind. They'd already read the story of Joseph and his Coat of Many Colors, but Becca seemed only partially attentive. David moved on to the tale of Jonah and the Whale, but was just a few paragraphs into that story when he stopped and stared at his daughter. He closed the book, but kept his thumb in the middle to keep his place.

"Okay, Becca," he said, "What's the matter?"

"Nothing," the child replied, but she had never been a very good liar. The truth lurked in her troubled expression.

"Come on, Little One. Something's bothering you. Fess up."

A minute or so of silence, then: "Daddy...why don't you love Mommy's baby?"

David stopped, speechless, and just sat there staring at his daughter for several seconds. God, how he loved her, and her question stabbed into his soul like a million daggers. Her golden curls spread out on her pillow as she looked up at him from beneath the soft glow of her bedside lamp, waiting for an answer.

"What makes you say that, Becca? Did Mommy tell you that?"

"No."

"Tell me the truth, sweetie. I'm not going to get mad."

"I am telling you the truth, Daddy."

"So why would you think that?"

"I can just tell, Daddy. You don't love Mommy's baby."

David bit at his lower lip nearly hard enough to draw blood. He took a deep breath. "Becca, listen. There are...things that happen when you grow up that you can't control. But you have to make the best of the situation. Mommy and Daddy, we want a baby, but this baby..."

David shifted his weight on the bed, feeling very uncomfortable beneath her innocent gaze.

"Is there something wrong with the baby?" Becca asked.

"N-no," David faltered. "It's not—" He took a deep breath. Swallowed a lump in his throat. "You'll understand one day, sweetie. I promise. This baby...that is, your mother and I—"

"You sound like you're trying to make up a fib."

David almost laughed out loud in spite of himself. No fooling Becca. She said, "You still haven't answered my question."

"You're right, honey. I haven't. And I'm sorry. It's something that—"

Becca's eyelids grew heavy even as she continued to play her role of pint-sized interrogator. Still, she did not let up. "I'm gonna have a little brother. And you don't love him, do you? You never have."

David felt warm tears in the corners of his eyes, and he quickly rubbed them away with two fingers. God, this was hard. What do you say to a seven-year-old about matters such as this?

He opted to stall some more. "You're so sure you're gonna have a baby brother, are you? How do you know it won't be a baby *sister?*"

"Because you and Mommy already have a girl," Becca explained. "Me."

David smiled. "That's right. And there will never be another like Miss Becca. But you could still have a little sister, you know."

"Maybe," Becca said, and the tone of finality in her voice seemed to indicate the conversation was over. She closed her eyes, rolled onto her side, away from him. *So* like her mother it was positively mind-blowing.

"Don't you want to finish reading about Jonah and the Whale?" David asked, placing one hand on her side. He could feel her tiny ribs through her skin, and in that moment he wanted to hold her forever and never let her go. For perhaps the millionth time since Becca came into his life, he found himself thinking about how helpless children were. Entirely at the mercy of their guardians. Empty little vessels waiting for their bodies to be nurtured, for their minds to be filled with knowledge. Perhaps that was the most terrifying thing of all—the fact that parents could fill that tiny mind with anything they wanted... with love or hate, kindness and tolerance, or with hate and bigotry. Or anything in between. It was up to him and Kate to mold this precious child into a levelheaded young woman. Pretty fucking scary, when you got to thinking about it.

"Becca, honey?" David whispered when she did not answer. She had either begun to drift off or was in deep thought. He did not expect her to let this go so easily. He raised the book in his hands, said softly, "Don't you want to finish reading the story? It's your favorite."

"No, Daddy." Becca pulled her Barbie covers up tighter around her shoulders. "I'm sleepy. Will you turn out the light?"

"Sure."

"And turn on my nightlight, please?"

"You got it." He walked around to the other side of her bed and clicked on her Lion King nightlight.

"I love you, Daddy," Becca said.

He kissed her behind the ear.

"I love you too, sweetheart. More than anything."

"Oh, my God!" Kate sat up in bed as fast as her pregnant bulk would allow. "David!"

Her hands went to David's shoulders, and she shook him violently. "David, wake up!"

"I'm awake," David groaned.

"Something's wrong with Becca!"

David heard it too, now. A frantic bawling from the room across the hall. Once his sleep-fogged mind registered the source of that awful wailing, his parental instinct kicked in. His heart skipped a beat. *Jesus Christ.* He jumped up, gasped when his toe jammed against the leg at the foot of the bed, but ignored the pain as he limped to his daughter's room.

He turned on the light as he entered her bedroom behind Kate. Becca was sitting up in her bed, squeezing the pink bunny Uncle Joel bought for her so tightly the poor thing appeared ready to come apart in her arms any second. The seven-year-old's eyes were red and swollen, and her crying persisted as David and Kate sat down beside her on the bed. Snot ran in tiny rivers down her quivering chin.

"Mommy...Daddy!" she cried.

"We're here, baby," Kate said. "What's the matter? Did you have a nightmare?"

Becca crawled from beneath the covers and fell into her mother's arms, bawling into Kate's soft pink gown. Kate stroked her hair, kissed her head, and stared at David with concern in her eyes.

"What is it, baby?" David asked. "We're here now. Talk to us."

After several more minutes of trembling and quiet sobs, Becca leaned away from her mother, looked at her father. "It was awful, Daddy... just awful."

With that, she broke into a new fit of crying, a frantic spell that brought tears to Kate and David's own eyes.

"It's okay, sweetheart," Kate said. "Whatever it is, you can tell us about it. Was it a nightmare?"

"Talk to us, baby," David said.

Becca sniffled long and hard. She leaned away from Kate again, rubbed at her eyes, and David couldn't help but notice the glistening mass of snot she left behind on Kate's new maternity gown.

"It was terrible. He wanted to get me!" Becca could barely talk now, her chest spasming with her frantic sobs.

"Calm down, baby," David said. "It's okay. Mommy and Daddy are here now. Nothing's going to hurt you."

"Would you like to tell us about it?" Kate asked.

"He...wanted to get me."

"Shhh," David said, gently stroking his daughter's back. "*Who* wanted to get you, sweetheart?"

"The bad man. The man with the really long beard."

"It was a nightmare, baby," David said, taking Becca in his own arms now. She felt like a limp doll in his arms, and only when Kate took her hand did she speak again.

"It was just a nightmare," Kate echoed her husband's assurances.

"I know," Becca said. "But it was so *real*, Mommy. He was *here*."

"No one was here, Becca," Kate said. "Remember the nightmares you had before we left New York? We explained how you were scared to leave your friends behind, but everything would be okay?"

"Yeah. I 'member."

"That turned out just fine, didn't it? There wasn't anything to be afraid of."

"Nothing to fear at all," David said. "Remember Teddy Chandler, and the Tar-Heels?"

Becca nodded, smiled weakly up at her father, though she didn't seem to understand the relevance of Teddy Chandler at the moment.

Teddy Chandler was the nine-year-old brat who had lived down the hall from the Littles in their old apartment building in New York. Seemed the kid was never happy unless he was trying to frighten Becca. Kate had spoken with Teddy Chandler's mother about this on more than one occasion, but it hadn't done a bit of good. The last thing the boy told Becca before the Littles started moving out all their stuff was that North Carolina was where all the monsters lived. They were called "Tar-Heels," according to the creative genius that was Teddy Chandler, and they crawled out from under your bed at night to eat you. They were really slow, though, so you could try to run. Problem was, these slobbering, kid-hungry beasts had planned ahead: they used brushes made from the hair of little girls to smear tar all over the floor, so your feet would get stuck and you couldn't run away. Within seconds, he told Becca, they'd gobble you whole and you'd never have a fighting chance of being anything but eventual Tar-Heel poop.

Teddy Chandler's story had given Becca nightmares every night in a row for almost a week. Finally, Kate had sat the child down with a book she rented from the local library (*Abridged History of the 50 States*) and read to her the story of how North Carolina came to be known as "the Tarheel State." Becca brightened as she discovered that this had nothing at all to do with monsters or brushes made from the hair of little girls. She had even let slip a giggle or three as Kate explained to her that they would soon be Tarheels themselves.

Tonight, however, Becca's nightmares had returned. Even in those days when Becca felt threatened by those mysterious, little-girl-eating North Carolina Tar-Heels, neither she nor David had ever seen her so terrified. She had awakened them in the middle of the night several times in the past, but more often than not such occasions had been nothing more than teary-eyed requests to sleep with Mommy and Daddy. Never had the child woke up screaming before. *Never* had they seen her like this.

"You understand that nightmares aren't real, right?" David said. "You're a big girl."

"This was *real*, though, Daddy. He wanted to get me. He wanted to *eat* me. He said he came from the Land of Tears, and...and you and Mommy couldn't stop him."

"We'll see about that, won't we?" David said, thrusting out his chest with mock bravado. He balled up his fists, twisted his features into his best Monster-Fighting-Father face.

"You know we would never let *anything* happen to you, Becca," Kate said.

"Never ever," David said.

"Never in a million trillion years."

"He was old," Becca said, as if she hadn't heard a word of that. "Really old. And he had this big gray beard that went on and on forever. His eyes were black. He looked like Santa Claus, kinda, but he was really really skinny. He was all gross-looking, too, like the belly of that frog you found that time and tried to put on Mommy's shoulder."

"Yuck," David said. "But it was just a dream, baby."

"And he was naked."

"Naked?" Kate and David said at the same time.

"Yeah. But I couldn't see his...wee-wee...'cause his beard was so long and dirty."

Everyone was silent for the next minute or so while it all soaked in. Quite a disturbing nightmare, whether the dreamer was a child or not. Finally, Becca broke the silence with more unsettling imagery from her dream.

"He killed that boy, didn't he?" she asked suddenly, her words all running together as if she had been contemplating that topic all along but hadn't really wanted to know the answer till now.

"What?" Kate said, stunned.

"That boy who died. The man in my nightmare...he killed him, didn't he?"

"How did you know about that?" David asked.

"I saw it on the news."

Kate and David glanced at one another, gave simultaneous sighs of relief. So that was it. They worried about Becca witnessing anything so graphic, so disturbing, on the local news—or on any television program, for that matter—but they could accept such a reasonable explanation. The child's subconscious had merely stored away a quick report she had seen on the news, they realized, in order to dredge it up later while she slept.

"Plus, he told me about it."

"Who told you about it?" David asked.

"The man in my dream. He told me about Billy Dawson. He said he killed that boy."

"Oh, baby," Kate said.

"He said he ate his soul."

Kate held her daughter tighter than ever. "Sweetheart."

"Becca," David began, opting to tell his daughter the truth when all else failed. "You're right, honey, a boy did die a couple of weeks ago. A boy from Morganville. But no one killed him. It was an accident. It's tragic, but sometimes things like that happen."

"I guess," Becca said, though she did not sound convinced.

"It's true, baby," Kate said. "This meanie, he was what we adults call a 'figment of your imagination.' He had nothing to do with that boy dying. Because he's *not real.*"

"Are you sure?"

"Of course we're sure," said David. And Kate added, "Absolutely."

"He smelled like something burning," Becca said. "Like when we used to go to Pappaw's house, and he burned leaves in the back yard?"

"That was real," David said, lifting his daughter in his arms to carry her to bed with them, "But the man in your dream wasn't. Mommy and Daddy would never lie to you. You know that."

As he pulled the covers up around her shoulders, Becca said in the softest, most delicate voice, "He said his name is Lo..."

She seemed to search for a word just beyond the borders of her memory, for the right pronunciation. Struggled for it. Then, finally, she found it.

"Moka...no. Moh-loch. Mr. Moloch. Yeah. I think that was it. Moloch. But he said I could call him Mo-Mo."

David frowned. As if on cue, thunder rumbled in the distance, another storm approaching in the wee hours of the morning. And with it came a furious hurricane of jumbled thoughts...

Moloch.

Where the hell had he heard that name before?

He had. He was sure of it. But he hadn't the slightest idea *where.*

"Becca, where did you hear that name?" he asked, though the only answer Becca supplied for him was that it was the name of the man in her nightmare, and she really wished she could sleep with Mommy and Daddy tonight.

Moloch.

Even after they carried Becca to bed with them, tucked her in between them, and long after Kate and Becca began to snore lightly beside him, David lay awake, unable to sleep because of that name. He stared up at the pale expanse that was his bedroom ceiling, tried to dig deep inside his brain...but that word kept tormenting him.

No matter how hard he tried to conjure up where he had heard it before, David couldn't figure out why it sounded so goddamn familiar.

CHAPTER 15

"Daddy," Becca said, a couple days after her nightmare, "my head itches."

David looked over at his daughter and grinned. He nodded, though he hadn't even heard what she said. They sat in front of the television together, David on the sofa thumbing through a catalog of graphic-arts supplies, his daughter on the floor before him watching an old *Scooby-Doo* rerun. Kate, meanwhile, was fixing a light lunch of tuna sandwiches and Doritos in the kitchen.

Becca's tiny hand disappeared into her thick blond hair. She scratched loudly at her scalp and said, "It itches really bad."

"Well, honey," David said, "what do you want me to do about it?"

"It feels like something's crawling in my hair."

David made his best *yuck* face, laid his catalog down on the lamp-stand nearby. "Come here, sweetie." He patted the empty space on the sofa beside him. "Let me see."

Becca obeyed, leaning her head back in his lap.

"I don't see anything. What am I supposed to be looking for?"

"I don't know," Becca said. "But it's been all scratchy ever since that scary man tried to hug me in my dream."

David smirked at her. "Now, Becca, I thought we agreed that wasn't real." His fingers played through her hair, and he squinted, looking closely at her scalp as he moved her curls aside one by one. Searching for what, he didn't know. But he knew it was best to humor children when their unfounded worries got the best of them.

And then he saw something.

Something moved. Something tiny. Black. Fast.

"Kate! Come here!"

"What is it?" Kate's voice came from the other room. "I'm busy!"

"What *is* this?"

Kate came into the living room, a butterknife smeared with mayonnaise in one hand. There was a spot of it on her chin, too. "What's the matter, David? I'm trying to fix lunch."

"There's something in Becca's hair."

"What do you mean?"

"Look!"

Becca reached up, tried to scratch at her scalp, but David pushed her hand away.

"Stay still, Becca."

Kate stood over them, stared down. "What is it?"

"Get that." David's hands were busy spreading Becca's hair apart. With a tilt of his head, he gestured toward a tiny black thing that wiggled beneath one of Becca's curls. As if to hide.

"Ugh." Kate's hand went to Becca's scalp. She pinched the thing between two sharp fingernails, brought it up before her. A tiny insect, slightly fatter than an eyelash. Its miniscule legs kicked between Kate's fingers. Its body was gray, yet at the same time oddly transparent.

"Oh, no."

"What the hell is that?" David said.

"Lice."

"Ah, shit."

"Language."

"Look. There's another one. And another one. Jesus Christ, Kate, she's crawling with them."

"Mommy, what is it?" Becca whined.

"Stay still," David said.

"It'll be okay," Kate said, with a little shrug. "We'll take care of it."

"This sucks. I feel like white trash."

"Why?"

"Our daughter has lice."

"It's not a big deal, David. Kids get lice all the time." Kate said it in her best *stop-being-silly* voice as she walked to the bathroom. Seconds later David heard the toilet flush. Bye-bye, little bug. "It doesn't have anything to do with a family's hygiene. Joel and I both got lice once or twice when we were kids. It's easily passed along in places where children are in close contact with one another. Schools, playgrounds, whatever."

"I never got lice when I was a kid."

"Consider yourself lucky."

"How do we kill them?"

"There are special shampoos you have to buy. Medicines to kill the insects and their eggs."

"Wonderful." David took another long look in Becca's hair before patting her on the leg, indicating she could return to her cartoons. He turned back to Kate. "You mentioned that children can get lice at school, church, whatever..."

"Yes."

"Well, don't you see a problem with that theory? Becca hasn't been around any other children. So where could she have gotten them?"

"I don't know," Kate said. "But you're right. That doesn't make much sense."

"I mean...Jesus...you saw for yourself, Kate." David's voice dropped to a whisper, and even as he spoke they watched Becca on the floor, vigorously scratching again behind her ears, at the nape of her neck. "She's *infested* with the damn things. Crawling with them."

"It's not the end of the world," Kate said. "We'll fix it."

Becca turned to them then and her hand was outstretched toward Kate, her fingers pinched together. "I got another one, Mommy."

Kate stood, took the tiny, wiggling thing from between Becca's fingernails. This one, too, was doomed for the toilet.

David made a sour face, swallowed.

"Another one," Becca said. "I bet I got them from that dirty old man."

"We covered that already, Becca," David said sternly.

Becca did not acknowledge that fact. She stared at her father and said in a quiet voice, "Yeah, Daddy, but you should have seen some of the things that were crawling through his beard."

"Becca—"

"I'll bet that's where I got it. When he put his yucky beard on me."

The Littles wasted no time in taking care of Becca's problem. That evening they drove to Frank's Grocery across town and bought three bottles of specially-medicated lice shampoo (100% EFFECTIVE! boasted the red and white bottle with the stop-sign logo on the front, KILLS LICE AND THEIR EGGS WITH ONE TREATMENT!). David felt embarrassed taking the product up to the front counter, though, and—in a rare moment that hardly suited Kate's personality—she jerked the bottles out of his hand, frowned at him, and claimed she didn't give a damn what people thought.

David shrugged, walked away to thumb through an issue of *Sports Illustrated* at the magazine rack while Kate paid for the stuff.

They followed the directions inside the box upon returning home.

There was much more to the procedure, though, than just washing Becca's hair with the special shampoo. Per the instructions, they also had to go through the child's curls strand by strand with a special comb (included in the package) in order to pick out all of the unhatched nits. It was a very tedious process. Kate lost count of how many times she had to tell Becca to sit still, and at one point when the little girl threw a temper tantrum, crossed her arms and roughly slammed herself back against Kate's belly, Kate lightly slapped her daughter several times on her naked legs, something she later regretted and apologized for despite the motto which had been her upbringing: spare the rod and spoil the child.

Finally, David went to bed before their task was complete, citing extreme boredom.

Kate frowned, shook her head as he walked off. She didn't appreciate his turning in early, but she chose not to argue with her husband. *A mother's job is never done*, she figured.

The whole procedure took nearly all night. David had been right— Becca's head was *crawling* with the things.

One thing Kate didn't tell her husband, however, was that lice were never this big. These things were at least five times the size of normal adult lice, some as big as baby cockroaches.

Becca *had* to have contracted the vermin somewhere. But where?

Kate refused to entertain the possibility that her daughter might have been correct. That she had contracted the lice from...*the old man in her nightmare*, for God's sake?

That was nothing short of ridiculous.

Still, she couldn't help but wonder...

No. Such a thing was impossible.

Impossible.

CHAPTER 16

"Sheriff," Mavis said from behind her desk. "Phone call."

Mavis Ledbetter was sixty years old, a shrewd old woman with hair the color of storm clouds and a bosom larger than any Sheriff Guice had ever seen. She was the best dispatcher he'd ever employed, and if sometimes Guice's high opinion of her was influenced by the fact that Mavis baked one hell of a batch of chocolate-chip cookies, then so be it. Mavis had been described as "grandmotherly" by more than one Morganville citizen, but such comparisons ended with her appearance. She *could* be an ornery sort sometimes—that was one hell of an understatement, actually, as Mavis favored off-color humor and politically-incorrect jokes over talk of bake sales and church get-togethers any day—but Guice loved her like one of his own relatives. She had been with the department far longer than he had been Sheriff of Morgan County, and Sam hoped her frequent threats to retire on days when things weren't going well were only that, idle threats. He didn't know what he would do without her.

"Tell 'em I'm busy," Sheriff Guice grunted. He'd been in a foul mood all week, and he saw no need to break the cycle now. Hell, it was Friday—might as well finish out the week the same way it started. As an afterthought, though, he supposed he should ask: "Who is it, Mavis?"

"Joel Rohrig. Says you're expecting a call from him."

Guice's eyebrows rose with curiosity. "Right. I'll take it in my office. Thanks."

"No problem."

Sam Guice walked past the dispatcher's desk—briefly frowning at the sticker on the side of her PC monitor: I'D SLAP YOU BUT SHIT SPLATTERS (he'd asked Mavis to remove it time after time, citing how unprofessional it appeared, but Mavis had ignored his demands thus far, so he rarely tried anymore)—and entered his office. He pulled his squeaking swivel chair up to his desk, a desk that normally remained so clean and tidy but over the past few weeks had become covered with paperwork. Things had changed in Morganville of late, and Sheriff Guice longed for the days when his shift dragged by, when the peak of his day meant pulling over some out-of-towner with lead in his foot out on Brookside Boulevard.

He glanced at the Dawson report, which lay open on the desk before him, before picking up the phone. "Guice speaking."

"Sheriff. It's Joel Rohrig."

"You got something for me?"

"I sure do. But when all is said and done, I'm afraid it'll raise more questions than it answers."

"Wonderful," Guice groaned.

"The toxicology results are back on the Dawson boy," Joel said. "Are you ready for this?"

"Shoot."

"Billy Dawson definitely died from some sort of poison. Question is, what sort of poison was it? This was no spider bite, no bee sting, nothing we've ever seen before. Even the boys in Raleigh are stumped."

"So what exactly are you telling me?" Guice asked.

"There's the rub, Sheriff. I don't *know*. The results were one hundred percent conclusive that the boy died from those stings. Hell, you and I knew that the first time we looked at him. But we've never seen anything like that toxin I drew from his veins. It's some new strain, apparently, and I've got to be honest with you: frankly, I'm clueless."

"Snakebites, maybe?"

"Negative. Like I said, I've never seen anything like this."

"Homicide?"

"No," Joel replied. "I don't think we're looking at a homicide here. A freak accident of nature, if anything."

Guice sighed.

"Any other ideas?" Joel said.

"How about a new sheriff?" That thought had crossed Guice's mind more than once since he and Deputy Keenan paid their awful visit to Billy Dawson's mother. It was never easy informing a parent that his or her child was dead. Never easy at all. And now they couldn't even offer the poor woman the consolation of answers to the questions the whole town was asking: *What happened to Billy Dawson? How did he die? Was he murdered?*

Both men knew there was nothing much else to say. Softly, Rohrig said, "I'm gonna go now, Sheriff. I have lots to do. I'll call you if I find anything else that might be helpful, okay?"

"Please do," Guice replied. His voice was weak. "Thanks, Joel. Thanks for everything."

"It's my job."

"Merry Christmas to you and yours, son."

"Same back at you, Sheriff."

Sheriff Guice hung up. For several long minutes after the connection was severed, he just sat there staring at the paperweight upon his desk—a scorpion preserved in a rock-hard crescent of amber, with ARIZONA inscribed upon the label at its base. It was a souvenir Mavis had brought back for him when she vacationed there several years before.

Ugliest damn thing he'd ever seen. Guice frowned at it, wondered why he even kept it around. But then he remembered why...because there were a hell of a lot more papers on his desk to keep weighted down these days.

CHAPTER 17

Only two days until Christmas, and the Littles were just getting around to shopping for the holiday. With everything they needed to do since moving to Morganville—settling in, their search for a new obstetrician for Kate, getting back into the swing of things with Becca's home-schooling—they had been unable to find enough hours in the day to add Christmas shopping to their already exhausting list of things to do before the end of the month. David finally finished his latest project, the cover to that sci-fi novel he'd been working on ever since they left New York but he could never seem to get just right, and as soon as he was done (or at least satisfied that the painting was the best it was going to be) he cleaned up and announced to Kate and Becca that they were going out.

Immediately Becca began to enlighten her parents on everything she wanted Santa Claus to bring her for Christmas this year. Kate and David eyed one another, their mouths turned up in excited little grins of their own, as Becca described in vivid detail the new Barbie bicycle she had seen in the Sears Wish-Book and *had* to have or she would just *die*, about the Barbie Sing-Along Radio and Just-4-Kidz Kitchen Set with a real working microwave—she couldn't *wait* to cook Daddy some of those oatmeal raisin cookies he loved so—and the Baby Bouncy-Bear that danced and jiggled spastically across the floor when you gave him a really big hug. Kate and David nodded the whole time, unable to get a word in edgewise. The little girl's sentences all ran together as she insisted that she'd been a really good girl this year and hopefully Santa would bring her so many toys she wouldn't know what to do with them all.

"That's up to Mommy and Daddy to decide," David said as they packed into the 4Runner and headed for the Morganville Mall across town. He offered Kate a sly wink. "Santa confers with us *very* closely, you know."

"Really? You told him I've been a good girl, didn't you, Daddy? Didn't you?"

David looked at Kate, and she turned to gaze out the window, hiding her own smile. "That's for us to know and for you to find out."

"Daddy!" Becca giggled. "I have been a good girl. A *very* good girl. Mommy, tell him!"

Kate's shoulders shook with the laughter she attempted to hold inside. She glanced back at Becca, shrugged.

"There's something you've got to understand, Little One," David explained. "Santa doesn't just confer with us a couple days before Christmas."

"What do you mean?" Becca asked.

"He confers with Mommy and Daddy *all year.*"

"Uh-oh."

Kate and David laughed.

Finally, though, Kate let Becca off the hook: "I think you're going to have a wonderful Christmas, baby."

"Yay!" Becca squealed.

After several more minutes of excited jabbering about all the things she couldn't wait to open Christmas morning, Becca's tiny face took on a look of severe concentration.

"Mommy, Daddy...what's Santa's telephone number?"

"What?" David laughed.

"You said you talk to him all year. So what's his telephone number?"

Busted. David desperately tried to keep a straight face. "That's, um, privileged information, sweet-pea. I'm afraid it's against the law to give out Santa's phone number."

"*Really?*" Becca was astounded.

"Really."

"Wow," Becca said. Another minute or so of deep, freckle-faced introspection, then: "What would they do to you if you broke the law, Daddy? If you gave out Santa's number, would you go to jail?"

"Depends on the circumstances," David said. "I doubt it. I probably just wouldn't get any Christmas presents for the next thirty years or so."

"Oh, no! That would be awful!"

"Awful indeed."

"So what's the verdict on Mommy and Daddy?" Kate asked. "Do you think *we've* been good all year?"

Becca seemed to ponder that one for several seconds. "Yeah...yeah, I do."

Both Kate and David sighed with mock relief.

"Mommy's been very good," Becca said. "You, Daddy...you've been okay, I guess."

David gasped. "Just 'okay'?"

"Yeah, you've been pretty good. I think you'll do fine this year, too."

They all laughed together, long and loud, as they entered the parking lot of the Morganville Mall.

CHAPTER 18

As his truck neared the Morganville Mall, Fred Dawson wished he was fuckin' dead. He was scum. Dirt. He didn't deserve to live.

Back when he had first met Billy's mother, the world seemed like a sparkling diamond in the palm of his hand. He and Donna had fallen in love so quickly, and so *young*—Donna had dreams of attending college, one day becoming a lawyer, while he worked toward getting his GED after dropping out of West Morganville High—and they were so sure nothing could ever go wrong. Their love seemed the answer to all their problems, the cure to the world's every ill.

Then Donna got knocked up.

He hadn't meant for it to happen, neither of them had, but sometimes Fred Dawson thought God brought him into this crummy world just to laugh at him every time he tried to do something right. Like his old man used to say when Fred was growing up: "shit happens." So true, those ingenious words of Dawson intellect: *Shit happens, and ninety-nine percent of the time it happens right in the path you're walkin'*...

Many times since then, Fred had wondered how the hell she had gotten pregnant. Of course, he knew *how* it happened—*ha-fuckin'-ha*—but he never understood what went wrong the night Billy was conceived. He'd worn a rubber, something Fred Dawson hated to do with every fiber of his being. On the night in question—a warm August evening down in Greenville, South Carolina—Fred had been driving a truck for AutoZone and Donna had traveled with him that weekend, as they were inseparable at that point in their relationship. Fred had tried just once in his life to do the responsible thing, to try and prevent another inevitable Dawson fuck-up *before* it happened. And still God pulled the rug out from under him and laughed like a fucking hyena when Fred fell flat on his ass.

For the first year of his son's life, Fred had tried his damnedest to play the role. At least, he fooled himself into *thinking* he had tried. Fatherhood was never something Fred wanted. He dreamed of spending carefree hours with Donna on his days off like teenagers struck with puppy love, their imaginations their only restriction. He had plans, plans to make something of himself, as well as allowing Donna to do the same. But all of that had been tossed out the window thanks to one tiny hole in one Extra-Large Ramses condom.

It wasn't fucking fair.

Fred began to drink, shortly after Donna told him the news. Heavily. And where he had never harbored any desire to cheat on her before, he began to flirt with other women while out on the road hauling this or that to here or there. Once he even picked up the clap from some lot lizard at a truck stop down in Alabama—Donna had never let him live *that* one down, even though Fred saw it as just another honest mistake. Then she had told him nine months after Billy was born that she just couldn't take it anymore. She told him to get out, and Fred had to admit that it had been a long time coming. He was not upset when it finally happened, not even angry, really; in fact, he felt a great weight lift off of him. No more living a lie. No more futile efforts toward playing that impossible role. It had been, in all honesty, what Fred wanted all along.

They had spoken, weeks later. Donna had assured him that every child needs a father, and if he decided to do the right thing she would never prevent him from seeing his son.

He had tried. At first. Fred tried to do the things with Billy fathers are supposed to do: taking the boy camping on cool summer nights, picking him up to go to the movies on those rare weekends when he wasn't working, even just dropping by Donna's place to toss a softball back and forth with Billy despite usually being too drunk to catch half of his son's gentle throws. But he had known all along that he was merely going through the motions. Fred Dawson was a nomad, a traveler lured by the freedom of the open road, with no ties to home, family or responsibility. He had never wanted a life that fit snugly into the strict borders defined by 2.5 squalling kids, the white picket fence with the peeling paint, and the Golden Retriever with the gimp leg.

Gradually, his visits with Billy grew more and more infrequent. In those early years, Fred would drop by at least once every few weeks to see his son, but then as Billy saw his fifth, sixth, and seventh birthdays, those visits dwindled to once every two or three months...until, eventually, Fred Dawson saw his boy only a couple times a year.

Fred tried to rationalize his icy attitude toward his son, had denied time and again to himself as well as Donna that he was just another deadbeat father. Shortly after Billy turned seven, he tried to blame it all on Donna's marriage to another man. Problem was, Fred knew she owed him nothing. As much as he hated to admit it, Donna had every right to move on. And Fred actually *liked* her new husband. Joe Evanson was good to Donna, *fantastic* with Billy, so Fred ultimately recognized his excuses as nothing short of pathetic.

He was scum. Dirt. He knew it. And he didn't deserve to live.

Fred cursed himself now, wished he was dead for what felt like the millionth time since he first heard the news a little over two weeks ago. God, how he wished he had it all to do over. If he had really tried, dedicated himself toward doing what he knew deep in his heart was right, he *could* have been a father to Billy. He could have given up the booze, the life on the road, and he could have been there for his son.

Coulda have, shoulda have...

For Chrissake, he'd even been too much of a pussy to go to his son's *funeral.* Too scared of what Donna might say. Too scared of the awful things she might call him (and deservedly so), afraid she might slap his pathetic face in front of all those people.

Too scared that he would never be able to live with himself, when he saw his only son lowered into the ground like yesterday's trash at the Morgan County landfill.

Fred tried to quit drinking the day after Billy's funeral. He quit cold turkey, as the saying went, although such a cutesy euphemism couldn't have been less appropriate for something Fred would best describe as pure agony. His body had been bathed in a constant film of hot, stinking sweat, his clothes plastered to him as if he'd just stepped out of the shower fully-dressed. He thought he was gonna die if he didn't get a drink. He hadn't been able to sleep at night, no matter the remedies he tried. And when he *was* able to catch a few minutes of shut-eye, it had been a restless sleep filled with nightmares like something out of a bad horror novel—especially after he started driving out to the old Heller Home place every few days, parking and just sitting there for hours, wondering what had happened to his son. There were the hallucinations too, things lurking just out of sight in the corners of his eyes. On top of that, he hadn't been able to stop shaking. Dr. Whitman had called Fred's condition the D.T.'s, *delirium tremens.* The quacks always had some sort of fancy name for it.

Finally, he'd been unable to take it any longer. He had failed again— failed *Billy* again—but what else was new? Two days ago he'd fallen off the wagon. Hard. The death of his only son notwithstanding, Fred knew there was no way he could quit drinking with those terrible nightmares plaguing him night and day. Hell, no. Nightmares of a very old, old man with a long, filthy beard that went on into forever. Couldn't do it, no matter how hard he tried. So he'd driven down to the liquor store on Somerside Drive, picked up a couple bottles of Jim Beam and Wild Turkey. And ever since he'd been trying to wash it all away.

Fred made a maddened hissing sound through his teeth now as he took another hard swallow of 'Turkey, as he thought of all the things he would never be able to say to his son. His vision wavering back and forth, he pulled his dilapidated Chevy pickup into the back lot of the Morganville Mall. The thing belched and farted, the ailing transmission grinding sickly as he jerked it out of second gear and put it into park.

Fred checked his costume as best he could in the Chevy's shattered rearview mirror one last time before exiting the truck. Swollen, bloodshot eyes rimmed with dark circles stared back at him above a fake beard as white as newly-fallen snow. He briefly wondered why he had even bothered coming to work at all today.

Being a mall Santa was easy work, but it barely paid the bills. Especially when you owed the gas company two-hundred and seventy bucks before the end of the month—either that, or freeze to death this winter. When you owed your landlady, that hateful old cunt Mrs. Rude, two months' worth of back rent you still hadn't paid and you knew any day now she was gonna throw you out. When you still owed back child support to the government for the better part of the last four years.

But what could you do, when you'd long ago lost your driver's license to multiple D.U.I. convictions?

Sure as hell couldn't expect to drive an eighteen-wheeler for a living anymore.

"Ho-fuckin'-ho," Fred Dawson belched as he stumbled across the mall's vast parking lot. He headed toward the doors that would open on the court between K-Mart, that hair salon where all the fags worked, and Kay-Bee Toys. This was the site of Fred's own personal North Pole, where he would spread cheer to all the kiddies before sending them on their way.

"Ho-cocksuckin'-ho," he mumbled, wincing as his own bitter liquor breath wafted up to meet his nostrils, "and to all a good goddamn night."

Fred Dawson chuckled, scratched his balls through his itchy red suit with one hand while adjusting his strap-on beard with the other. He licked his lips, grimaced at the taste in his mouth, and entered the Morganville Mall with more curses beneath his breath.

Wouldn't be such a bad job if he didn't hate kids so damn much.

And if he were allowed to keep a bottle of hooch by his side while he was on the clock.

CHAPTER 19

They hadn't told Becca they were taking her to see Santa Claus. That part they kept a surprise until their shopping spree was complete, as the child could barely contain her excitement already.

The Littles split up once they arrived at the Morganville Mall, Becca and Kate going off on their own to buy David's Christmas presents while David began shopping for Becca. Then, after meeting at a previously agreed upon rendezvous point at the mall's Food Court where they devoured a quick lunch at Sbarro's, David took Becca off to shop for Kate. Meanwhile, Kate finished up with the last half of their Christmas shopping for Becca.

When all was said and done, the myriad of bags in Kate and David's arms were so full they appeared ready to burst like huge white ticks. Becca was in for a wonderful Christmas. Perhaps the best ever. They all were.

After ice-cream cones at Baskin-Robbins, they walked with Becca to the west wing of the mall, where Santa Claus waited. This area of the Morganville Mall had been decorated to resemble Santa's home at the North Pole, complete with frolicking elves and animatronic reindeer whose heads jerked this way and that as if in anticipation for their upcoming midnight flight. Nearby, various bunnies and other curious creatures peeped out from the huge masses of cotton snow smothering their faux forest home, and icicles of transparent plastic dripped from the leafless winter trees of papier-mâché scattered throughout Santa's domain.

Becca's eyes grew impossibly wide as she took it all in. Her mouth hung open.

"What do you see, Becca?" Kate said, handing David several of her bags. Her breaths were heavy from carrying them around all day. "Who is that, sweetie?"

"Wow!" Becca said. "Oh, cool!"

"Do you want to sit on Santa's lap?"

Becca nodded, stunned by everything before her, and then suddenly she squealed, "Daddy, there he is!" She pointed toward the makeshift cabin in the center of that wintry diorama. "Santa! It's Santa Claus!"

As soon as the Littles looked his way, Santa let out a loud "ho-ho-ho," holding his considerable belly as he did so. David couldn't help but feel that warm, nostalgic sensation inside, a longing for the days when he idolized Santa as intensely as his precious daughter. Oh, to be a kid again, to feel that *magic* again.

A line of eager children was already gathered down the walkway leading to Santa's velvety throne, their excited conversation and anxious giggles filling this wing of the mall with a chorus of high-pitched echoes. Becca joined the throng, and could barely stand still as she waited for the line to move forward. She shifted her weight from one foot to the other behind two twin brothers who traded playful blows to quell their own impatience.

David waited outside the manmade North Pole, leaning against the wooden railing that surrounded the Events court. Kate handed him the rest of their bags before moving to stand with Becca in line. He watched as his wife made idle conversation with another mother, a black lady who was also very pregnant. They were like some secret society, David sometimes thought upon witnessing such interaction between pregnant ladies, a group of likeminded, like-bodied women who shared their thoughts and emotions telepathically.

After about ten minutes, Becca was at the front of the line.

"Mommy! Daddy!" the little girl giggled, waving to her parents as she finally climbed onto Santa's cushiony lap.

Santa waved their way too, before devoting his attention to the child in his lap.

Becca's expression became one of utmost seriousness now, her tone all business as she leaned into Santa and tried not to forget any of her requests for the upcoming holiday.

The first thing Becca noticed was Santa's weird smell. Santa Claus didn't smell right.

But this was Santa! The real thing! It didn't matter if he smelled like freshly dropped reindeer poop, as long as she could prove to him that she had been a good girl all year and not forget anything she wished for this Christmas.

As soon as she was comfortable in his lap, Santa reached somewhere into his thick red suit and pulled out a small candy-cane wrapped in cellophane. He offered it to Becca with a fat hand that trembled slightly.

"Ho, ho, ho! And what's your name, precious?"

Becca stared at his quivering belly. Shyly, she replied, "Becca. My name's Becca."

"What a pretty name. *Hmpfh*. Why don't you tell Santa what you want for Christmas, Becca?"

"Okay..."

"Go ahead." His huge right hand went to her knee. The other played gently with the golden curls atop her head. Becca couldn't help but notice how rough Santa's hands were. And his fingernails, so *dirty!* Mommy would never ever let her fingernails get that dirty before making her sit still while she took a nail file to them. That was just *gross with a capital G.*

"Well..." Becca began. Again, the man's odor assaulted her as he leaned in closer to hear what she had to say. With every passing second she sat upon his hard knee, that smell of his seemed to grow stronger. Mommy and Daddy always said it wasn't nice to talk about people, but Becca assumed that since she was just *thinking* about the way Santa smelled, and would never tell anybody, that was okay, wasn't it?

Unless Santa could read minds. Was Santa like God? Could he know what she was thinking? *Oh, no.* That would not be good. That wouldn't be good at all.

Becca tried to block her thoughts from smelly old St. Nick, tried to envision nothing but the colorful wall of presents he would surely bring her this year, but she couldn't help it. Though she would not consciously make the connection until later that day, Santa's odor reminded her of that stuff Daddy drank sometimes whenever he'd had a really bad day ("Typical Monday," he'd say, even if it was Wednesday or Thursday or Friday, which Becca never understood but she thought it was funny anyway), the stuff Daddy kept in the cabinet over the refrigerator that he always sipped at slowly like it didn't even taste good. The stuff that was the same color of Becca's own favorite drink, apple juice. That's exactly what Santa smelled like.

And sweat, too. Santa Claus smelled like really bad B.O. In fact, he was sweating so bad he smelled like he'd just flown in from the desert instead of the North Pole.

Something that looked like dried boogers was smeared on Santa's pants. Perhaps that was the grossest thing yet. Becca scooted away from that spot in his lap, as far as she could.

"Stop squirming," said Santa.

"I want..." Becca began again, trying to push all that from her mind, but her train of thought was interrupted when she looked into Santa's eyes.

Santa's eyes looked like they had itty bitty blood veins in them, all pink and scary-looking.

Becca shot a glance toward her Mommy and Daddy, but neither was paying attention to her predicament. Mommy was talking to another mommy who was gonna have a baby soon too, and Daddy appeared to be watching some woman with big boobies walk by.

But that was okay. Because nothing was wrong...yet. *Was it?*

She didn't understand the feelings of fear that nibbled at the corners of her mind. She knew she was doomed, if Santa could read kids' minds, knew that her Christmas was gonna be a real bummer this year, but she couldn't help it. Becca just felt...weird. Kinda like the feeling she somehow sensed she might feel if someone ever touched her in a BAD PLACE. Mommy and Daddy had warned her about that, about talking to strangers and how to know the difference between Good Touches and Bad Touches.

Even though Santa hadn't done anything to her (*yet*) Becca felt *icky*. Like he *wanted* to Bad-Touch her, but he just hadn't done it yet. Yes, this was the way a Bad Touch must feel, like a spider or a snake just crawled across your belly.

Becca shuddered, looked again toward Mommy and Daddy. But their attention was still elsewhere.

"Maybe you don't deserve anything for Christmas," Santa hissed, and Becca could not even respond at first because she felt frozen where she sat. "Maybe you've been a bad little girl all year..."

"No, Santa." Becca said. "I've been good. I promise!"

"Maybe Daddy tries his hardest to love you even though he can never live up to society's goddamn expectations of fatherhood. Maybe he can't give up drinking and one day he's gonna fucking wish he had."

"Santa!" Becca gasped. "You said a dirty word!"

"You don't know how good you got it, angel-face. A mommy and daddy who love you. You were probably born with a silver spoon in your pretty little mouth, weren't you? You never had a father who was a worthless fucking drunk."

Becca squirmed on Fred Dawson's lap. "I don't want to talk to you anymore, Santa. I want my Mommy now."

Santa's grip tightened on her knee. Not enough to hurt, but enough to insinuate *You're not going anywhere until I'm through with you.*

"Santa, please, I want my Mommy..."

"My son is six feet under, Becca. You know that? He's fucking *maggot food* now. And I don't know why that matters to me, because I never fucking cared when he was alive. Why should I start now?" Santa gave a sick little giggle that sent a chill down Becca's spine. "Something got my boy out there at Heller Home...and if you don't watch out, Becca, it's gonna get you next!"

"Santa Claus, why are you being so mea—" Becca started.

"*Moloch*," said Santa Claus.

And then it dawned on Becca what she was supposed to do in situations like this.

Scream. As loud as you could. No matter what.

She opened the floodgates. Began to wail, began to scream like Daddy taught her to if someone ever tried to grab her or touch her the wrong way, screamed and screamed longer and louder than she had ever screamed in her life.

David's head jerked toward that high-pitched screaming, a distinct shriek he instantly recognized as belonging to his child.

"Oh my God," he heard Kate say, though her voice was distant and did not seem entirely real beneath the stronger sound of Becca's terrified wail. "Becca!"

David leapt over the railing that separated Santa's makeshift North Pole from the mall around it. He nearly tripped over an animatronic bunny in his way; sprinting through all of that cotton proved nearly as difficult as trying to run through real snow, but he had never moved so urgently in his life.

"Becca!"

Santa's hands went in the air like a bank robber dropping his smoking gun as the police corner him. Becca fell out of his lap, slid down his legs, and just sat there on the hard floor at his feet. Tears streamed down her face.

"I didn't do nothin', man," Santa said. "I swear! I don't know what's wrong with that kid!"

"You sonofabitch!" David spat, his hands balled into fists. On all sides of him, parents and mall employees alike stared with wide, curious eyes at the scene in Santa's cottage. But David was oblivious to their existence. "What did you do to my daughter?"

Kate bent, picked Becca up and held the crying child tight in her arms. "Becca, what happened? What did that man say to you? What did he do?" She turned to Santa, cried, "You scared her...*what did you say to my daughter?"*

"Please...I don't know...I don't know what came over me," the Santa with the bloodshot eyes stammered. He was shaking uncontrollably now.

And then before Kate could stop her husband, even as he saw in his peripheral vision a chubby security guard running toward them from the entrance of the nearby K-Mart, David reared back and struck Santa Claus with a loud, smacking right hook that echoed through the west wing of the Morganville Mall like a small-caliber gunshot.

Santa crumpled to the floor. The crowd released a collective gasp.

From all around the Littles came the moaning, ghost-like sound of several dozen children weeping at once.

"Santa!" a skinny black kid cried out from somewhere at the back of the line, his face a mask of terror.

David Little stood over St. Nick, his hands balled into tight red fists, his shoulders trembling with anger.

CHAPTER 20

The Littles returned home that evening with Becca calm and no longer crying, though for Kate and David the whole thing proved to be a stepping stone toward yet another argument. They were able to refrain from getting too nasty with one another until Becca fell asleep on the living room sofa, but then David carried her to her bed and returned to the kitchen where he and Kate resumed their bickering.

"Just tell me one thing," Kate said. "Was it really necessary to punch Santa Claus?"

David shrugged. "I thought so at the time."

"Well, I hope you're happy. Those poor children, seeing Santa Claus get laid out like he was up against some kind of..."

Kate was floundering. Against his better judgment, David threw her a line: "Mike Tyson?"

"Don't flatter yourself. My point is, you've probably traumatized those poor kids for the rest of their lives."

David couldn't help it. He laughed at that, trying to hold it in at first, but his efforts were unsuccessful.

"It's not funny," Kate said.

"Yes, it is. When you exaggerate like that."

"David, I'm serious."

"'Traumatized?' 'For the rest of their lives?'"

Kate shook her head, though she could not hide the faint smile that stretched her own tightly drawn lips in the wrong direction. Okay, so her choice of words *was* a tad melodramatic. Still, her eyes blazed with contempt as she stared at her husband. "Don't change the subject."

"Okay," David said. "Maybe you're right. Maybe I did overreact. Just a little."

"A little?"

"Maybe. But I couldn't help it, Kate. Jesus. All I saw was my daughter, terrified of that man who's supposed to make children happy—frigging *Santa Claus*, for God's sake! During those first few seconds, I saw red. And yeah, maybe I did overreact. Because I had to protect my daughter."

"Our daughter," Kate corrected him.

"I did what I felt had to be done at the time," David said. "I'm sorry."

"Understood. Still...you didn't see me running across the mall to slap Santa across the face."

"I guess it's just a father thing."

"A macho thing."

"No. A *father* thing. Don't patronize me, Kate. You know I hate it when you do that."

"You looked like you wanted to *kill* that man, David!" Kate burst.

"Nah," David said, smirking. "Just break his arms and legs."

"You're incorrigible."

"And you're not being fair! I can't believe you're making me out to be the bad guy, when all I wanted to do was protect our daughter from some fucking drunk who shouldn't have been working with kids in the first place!"

"There's no need to curse," Kate said. "You need to calm down."

David stood, his chair scraping loudly against the linoleum like a third party adding its own two cents to their argument. "I'm through arguing about this. Maybe you're right. Maybe I did overreact. But the owners of that mall are lucky I don't sue their asses for everything they have! Hiring some alcoholic who's hardly better than a fucking skid-row bum to work with children? It's bullshit, and I'm sorry you don't agree."

They had asked Becca what Santa said to her on their way home from the mall, but she wasn't able to explain anything other than the fact that Santa scared her. Something about how he thought she had been naughty, and her Daddy didn't love her.

Poor kid. David had wanted to beat the guy within an inch of his life—frankly, he had surprised himself even more than he surprised Kate, as he was normally a man who tried his best to avoid conflict—but saner minds prevailed. Kate had pulled him away from the center court of the mall's west wing, assuring the overweight, out-of-breath security guard who ran onto the scene that they were leaving. Somehow they had walked away from the whole thing without David ending up in jail.

Kate flinched beneath her husband's fury now, her hands covering her pregnant belly, as David turned to leave the room.

As she watched him go, she began to cry.

What was happening to them, Kate wondered? What was happening to their family?

It was all falling apart. Crumbling, piece by piece, every day.

Maybe David had been right. Maybe they would have been happier if they had just stayed in New York.

The subject was eventually dropped. No more was said about the incident at the mall. David couldn't get anything out of Becca no matter how hard he tried, so he realized he'd better not push her into getting upset about the Santa thing all over again.

Finally it was time to turn in for the night. Kate retired to their queen-size bed, David to the sofa where he drifted off in front of the David Letterman show on T.V.

David considered sneaking into the bedroom and attempting reconciliation with Kate, but ultimately decided to hell with it. He was sick of trying. And he was still infuriated that she had made him out to be the villain in the whole thing.

What a wonderful Christmas this is going to be, he thought with a smirk, mere seconds before the clock on the DVD player atop the television clicked over to midnight.

It was Christmas Eve in Morganville.

CHAPTER 21

A few minutes after two a.m., David Little woke abruptly, sitting straight up on the sofa with a single hoarse word on his sleep-crusted lips: *"Moloch."*

He did not know how it came to him. But out of nowhere it materialized, after he had pursued its origin so desperately over a week ago, that night Becca mentioned the name of the terrifying man in her nightmare.

"Holy shit."

It hit him.

That name again...*Moloch*.

Suddenly, David knew exactly where he had heard that word before.

"Of course!" he whispered as he rose from the sofa. "Why could I not remember it before?"

He tiptoed out of the living room and into his studio. At first, the moonlight was the room's only illumination, its pale glow shining through the big bay window that overlooked the back yard. David pulled the cord in the center of the ceiling, dousing the room with light.

He walked past his cluttered desk, around the empty easel in the center of the room, and stood before the bookshelf that ran along the entire length of one wall. Here were 137 books, at last count, neatly shelved paperbacks and hardcovers David had arranged in chronological order according to when he had done the work; here he had stored every book for which he had designed and painted the cover art since the beginning of his career. The spines of sci-fi serials such as *Galactic Renegade #47: Dominion Quest*—a sci-fi novel which had been his first paid gig and the one painting in his portfolio which still made him cringe every time he gazed upon its amateurish style—stood alongside sword-and-sorcery epics like *Reign of the Dark Mage* and *Elvin Thieves of Shandakk* as well as mainstream thrillers such as *Liar's Game, Protocol 99,* and *The President's Decoy.* Not to mention their bottom-of-the-barrel horror brethren, books David had illustrated for no other reason than the quick, easy cash—titles such as *Hellbeast, Lucifer's Hammer,* and *Kiss of the Vampire,* all with equally lurid covers.

David's lips worked silently as he read each title, searching for a specific book.

Where could it be...?

"There," he said, pulling a book from the shelf. "A-ha." A thin paperback from an independent outfit called Bloodstone Press, it sat between a Stephen King reprint that was one of David's finest professional moments (not to mention his sweetest paycheck to date) and a lesser-known hardcover work from an author David had never heard from again after illustrating that particular piece, something called *Vamprey: Bloodfeast 3000.*

David stared for a moment at the book in his hands, the novel he was quite sure had been the source of that word which so stubbornly evaded him the night Becca woke up screaming:

Moloch.

Its title was *The Feasting,* by a fellow named Andrew Holland. The cover in question depicted some small country town being swallowed by a beast with humongous needle-fangs. A bone-white full moon was the tentacled thing's single eye, and as it leaned from the black sky toward the reader in an embossed effect designed to suggest three-dimensionality, it dwarfed the close-knit houses below with their tiny yellow windows of nocturnal life.

David couldn't stop a nostalgic grin from spreading across his face. Like most of his covers, he could remember painting this piece as if he had just finished its final stroke the day before.

He turned the book over and read aloud the synopsis on the back (called "selling copy" in the jargon of the biz, though David could never imagine such purple prose convincing *him* to buy a copy):

"In the small town of Scuttley's Corners, Maine, people are dropping like flies.

Good people, God-fearing people...
people with nothing to fear.
All that has changed, now.

For Scuttley's Corners is no longer a good place to live.

In fact, Scuttley's Corners is an evil place.
A place of death. A place of darkness.

And now there is much to fear.
For Scuttley's Corners is now a place possessed...by an unholy being named
MOLOCH."

"I knew it!" David flicked the back of the book with one finger. His fingernail made a hollow little *pop* sound as it hit. "Fucking-A."

That cinched it. Becca had seen the word "Moloch" at some point when she had been in her father's studio, messing around where she was not supposed to be messing around. Perhaps she had seen the book on the shelf, pulled it down and glanced at its back cover with wide-eyed wonder, as children are wont to do when confronted with visions of things that go bump in the night, terrified of such nightmare images yet at the same time morbidly fascinated and unable to turn away. Perhaps she had spotted that word while helping Mommy and Daddy as they were moving in, unpacking the contents of the boxes that had lain about the house for several days.

David nodded again as he left the room, turning out the light as he went.

Absolutely. That explained everything. Becca had heard about the Dawson boy's murder on TV, and she had seen the word "Moloch" in that synopsis of Andrew Holland's literary masterpiece, *The Feasting.* Her imagination had then taken the ball and run with it, and even if the child had not been consciously aware of reading that word somewhere in Daddy's stack of books, there was no doubt in David's mind that she had seen it. Her subconscious had stored it away, dredging it up again when the time came for a harmless, perfectly explainable nightmare.

"Damn, I'm good," David said.

He closed the studio door behind him then, quite sure that he would sleep soundly for the rest of the night with this mystery solved at last.

CHAPTER 22

Reverend Darryl Rhodes wept.

Ever since that awful night in August, he felt as if the guilt had been eating him alive. Now it had all "come to a head," as his dear old father used to say. Now there were more, more than just those who had passed on in The Great Fire.

Reverend Rhodes felt haunted by them all.

He had let them go; he had allowed them to leave this world without proper reconciliation with their Lord. Rhodes was quite sure he would answer for that come Judgment Day.

A pastor's job did not begin and end on Sunday mornings, as many believed. The sermons were only one small part of it. There was so much more to being a Man of God. When Darryl Rhodes had answered the Lord's calling, he knew he had taken it all upon himself. Not just some of it.

The Heavenly Father was a boss who wanted all or nothing.

Now, as Rhodes sat at the foot of his pulpit in the heart of Morganville's First Baptist Church, he wondered if he could continue. Never before had he doubted himself or his choice of profession, until these last few months.

In fact, Reverend Rhodes had recently begun to wonder if he even wanted this job anymore.

Perhaps the time had come to give the Lord his notice. Cut his losses, hope for a halfway-decent severance plan, and get out while he still could.

Maybe.

Rhodes shook his head at that, gave a sad little chuckle in spite of his tears as he gazed upon his surroundings. Most of the chapel's lights had been turned off for the night, only the soft illumination of those yellow bulbs around the preacher's wooden podium basking him in their somber glow. Rhodes sat with his head in his hands, trying to pray. But the words would not come to him. When they did, they felt hollow, empty of meaning. As if someone had written them down half-heartedly, a cold script written by a talentless hack minister, and now he recited them to a God who was far too busy to listen to Darryl Rhodes' problems anyway.

Rhodes shook his head again, stood. He would pay for that blasphemous thought, he knew. The bones in his knees cracked and popped like those of a man twice his age as he descended the steps of the church's main stage. He wondered why he hadn't just retired by now. He would probably be better off. Not just his own peace of mind, but the whole church. Maybe the congregation would be happier, more folks would attend Sunday services if he just gave it up. The crowd had thinned significantly of late, and Rhodes had wondered for quite some time just what he'd done wrong. Yes, perhaps it was time to step aside, let some handsome young pastor come in and turn this place around. That'd probably change a lot. Attendance would skyrocket.

Sure.

"To hell with your self-pity," Rhodes said to himself. His voice was low, but it echoed unnaturally through the empty church as if the building itself were mocking him.

Rhodes turned and stood in the center of the teal-carpeted stage. He felt so small and insignificant as he stared out over the dozens of empty pews. Bathed in the soft pink glow of the day's setting sun as it pierced the stained-glass windows on all sides of the chapel, the wooden benches appeared soaked in blood. So many sermons he had preached from this spot—surely they numbered somewhere in the hundreds, if not thousands—but had they meant anything at all? Like his prayer, had they merely been random notes, words scribbled by a man who loved God but wasn't quite sure if the Lord still loved him? Did anyone take those words home anymore? Or did they forget everything their pastor said the second those doors opened and they were back on Morganville's streets?

Perhaps, Rhodes thought, it was the dreams getting to him. Influencing him to think such thoughts. Those horrible dreams he'd been experiencing ever since Heller Home burned down.

No, he tried not to think about that. *Wouldn't* think about that. Because thinking about them made them real. Thinking about them gave his nightmares credence. *Power.*

And the things in his nightmares could *not* be real.

The preacher turned, stared toward the back of the stage. Here was where the choir normally gathered before the Sunday services, where they sat behind him, during his sermons.

Reverend Rhodes' stubbled jaw dropped.

It couldn't be.

It wasn't *possible.*

He rubbed his eyes, opened them again.

"Oh, Lord..."

At the rear of the church hung a massive wooden cross, suspended from the ceiling by several steel braces bolted behind it. It was a beautiful thing, backlit by a fiery orange glow where the arms of the holy symbol met. It was a sight that never failed to lift Reverend Rhodes' spirits any time he started feeling down. Any time he felt short of divine inspiration.

But not today. Not now.

Now the sight of that thing...*floating* there...sent chills down his spine, his legs, his toes.

"No, no, no, no, no," he babbled.

It was the man from his nightmares, up there.

Hanging from the cross—or, rather, not touching it at all but bobbing in the air several inches in front of the holy icon—was a very old, old man. The bearded one. His mottled, skeletal arms were outstretched, and he wore only a filthy yellow loincloth as if in mockery of the Savior. The ancient thing's foul gray beard dangled from his bony chin like rivers of corruption, coiling onto the floor of the stage beneath him. Fat bluebottle flies swarmed around his emaciated form, in and out of his long beard, and the stench that met Rhodes' nostrils as he stared at the man and the man stared back at him reminded Rhodes of something *burning.*

"Hello?" said the preacher. He was frozen. Couldn't move. Couldn't think. A persistent buzzing filled his mind.

The thing shot down from the cross then, descended upon Revered Rhodes in the blink of an eye as if suspended on invisible wires.

The man's cold, cold fingers—fingers that were unnaturally long and spider-like—embraced the preacher's head. Gently, like the touch of a lover.

Rhodes came in his trousers as the ancient thing's mouth opened, and the darkness embraced him.

Contrary to what he had been told all along, contrary to what he had preached to Morganville's faithful from this stage every Sunday, contrary to what Darryl Rhodes had believed in and worshipped his whole life...the dark was good.

So good.

He entered it, willingly.

The thing called Moloch whispered sweet secrets to his soul.

And, at last, Reverend Darryl Rhodes realized his true calling.

He realized he had been lied to. All of his goddamned life.

CHAPTER 23

As if God knew they deserved it above anyone else after everything their family had been through the past eight months, the Littles experienced one of their best Christmases ever. Becca was wide awake by five a.m., poking and prodding her parents like some giggling, organic alarm clock that could not be silenced no matter how hard her sleepy-eyed parents wished to snooze. Finally, Mommy and Daddy gave in. David hadn't gone to bed until well after one a.m., as—just like every year—he had played Santa Claus in the wee hours of the morning. Stalking quietly through the living room, he ate several of the chocolate-chip cookies Becca had left out for Santa, emptied most of the glass of milk in the sink, and took a minute to write his daughter a quick thank you note in an altered style of penmanship which he imagined might resemble Santa's merry scrawl. Afterward, he laid out all the presents he and Kate had kept hidden in their closet since their shopping spree, arranging them around the Christmas tree, so sure that Becca would hardly know where to begin.

Becca declared it the greatest day of her life. For the most part she had gotten everything she wanted for Christmas: the Barbie bicycle, the Barbie sing-along radio, the Just-4-Kidz Kitchen Set with the Real Working Microwave, and the Baby Bouncy-Bear. Now Kate and David felt as if their house had been flooded—not by heavy rains, but by ragged pieces of gift-wrapping and fat crumpled bows of every size and shape and color.

Joel arrived a few minutes after they finished breakfast, bringing with him the new dress and hairdryer Kate had been wanting for Christmas. For David he brought a set of new paintbrushes and a sign that said DO NOT DISTURB: GENIUS AT WORK for his brother-in-law's studio. Becca, meanwhile, did not even know where to begin wading through her sea of toys, which grew even deeper once Uncle Joel arrived.

Things could not have gone better. For once, a day passed for the Littles with no arguments. No awkward moments between David and Joel, no tension between Kate and David, and no psychotic Santas smelling of sour sweat and scotch.

Once, David even placed his head upon Kate's huge tummy, smiled up at her before kissing a line down to her belly button. The baby didn't kick, but he kept his ear there for several minutes, winked at Joel and holding his wife tightly like he had in the days before Becca was born.

For one day, at least, the Littles seemed destined for happiness.

The dawn of the New Year came and went with little or no fanfare for David and his family. Joel dropped by with Michael in tow, and despite David's slight unease around his brother-in-law's partner, the men emptied David's liquor cabinet in record time and enjoyed one another's company.

Before long, though, all of Morganville's holiday bliss would pass like the brightness of day into night.

CHAPTER 24

"What do you want to watch first?" Joel asked his boyfriend, turning down the obnoxious rasp of static on the television. The New Year was only a couple days into its infancy.

"Doesn't matter to me."

"Just pick one," Joel said, smiling. "Don't be difficult."

"Refresh my memory," said Michael. "What'd we get?"

Joel read off the titles of the DVDs they had rented earlier from Blockbuster Video. A drama, a couple comedies. As he picked up each of the discs from the stack atop the television, the blinking lights from the Christmas tree in the corner painted the DVD cases varying shades of red and green and orange. None of the titles Joel held had struck either of the men as movies they were *dying* to see, but for lack of anything better to do on a Thursday night they had decided to spend some much-needed time together at home, a quiet evening with popcorn and movies and maybe a bit of lovemaking afterward if they were both in the mood.

"That new Jim Carrey movie looks like it might be a good one," Michael said.

"Good call." Joel slid the disc into the player before plopping down next to Michael on the sofa. He decided he probably did need a silly comedy flick to help him wind down. For the past couple of weeks, with the Billy Dawson thing and all, his life felt like one sick, gore-filled horror movie. A few laughs would be just what the doctor ordered.

As the previews played, Joel thought back to how he and Michael had met, how they had beaten the odds, and for what must have been the millionth time in the last few years he thanked God for sending him "the one." Just a little over five years ago, Michael Morris had been no more than a faceless name, "Dragon25," on the information superhighway. He and Joel had struck up a friendship on one of AOL's many chat channels, specifically one for gay males between twenty-one and thirty looking for the same. Gradually their friendship progressed to more than just idle chatting on the Internet, and they exchanged phone numbers. Several days after Joel's ordeal outside the bar back home, he had flown down to North Carolina to meet Michael face-to-face, and they had spent a week together. That week had been enough for both of them to know they had found true love.

One month later, Joel moved in with Michael.

Michael's hand went to Joel's leg now as he handed him the bowl of popcorn that had been sitting on the coffee table. Neither man could remember a time when he had been happier.

Of course, they were not surprised in the least when Joel's pager went off on the dining room table.

"Aw, shit, Joel," said Michael, "Please don't get it."

"I have to."

Michael held Joel's hand for a minute, wouldn't let him go.

They stared into one another's eyes. Finally, though, Joel's hand slipped from Michael's grasp. He leaned over, kissed his boyfriend on the forehead. "I'd better see what's up."

"Let it go. Just this once."

"I can't."

"Please. Just tell them you dropped your pager in the toilet. It hasn't been working right since."

Joel shook his head, laughed. "Creative, hon...but you know I can't do that."

"I was hoping we could spend a quiet evening together," Michael said.

"I'm sorry." Joel walked to the dining room table, grabbed his pager. He was still smiling, hoping that his own pleasant attitude, in spite of the circumstances, would prevent any ensuing argument. He chewed at his bottom lip as he read the numbers on the pager's quartz display.

"What is it this time?" Michael asked. He sat the bowl of popcorn back on the coffee table then, slamming it down a bit too loudly.

"I gotta go," Joel said, reaching for his denim jacket on a nearby armchair. "I'm sorry, Michael."

"What's going on?"

"Sheriff's Department. They've found another body."

"Shit." Michael sat up. "Joel, wait—"

Joel waved goodbye as he rushed out the door. "Gotta go! I'm sorry. I love you."

"Whatever."

Michael Morris said nothing else as he propped his feet up on the coffee table and glared at the television. He shook his head, exasperated, as Joel's Mustang roared to life outside, and Jim Carrey tried to elicit a smile from a man who once again played second fiddle to his lover's stupid job.

CHAPTER 25

"I think this case is pretty much cut-and-dry," Sheriff Guice said as the younger man walked with him across Marietta Rude's overgrown lawn. "But, just to be safe, you know..."

"Don't mention it, Sheriff," Joel replied. "It's not a problem."

Sheriff Guice glanced back, offered Joel a grin as they walked up the steps of the porch and through the front door of the Rude house. Guice and his men had placed several arc-sodium lamps about the premises, and now the shadows of those in attendance—Hank Keenan, another Sheriff's Deputy whose name Joel did not recall, as well as several Rescue Squad first-responders who were useless here—flickered about the house's foyer. Behind them, across the road, the yellow tape strung across the Heller property flapped and popped in the evening breeze, and the white crosses all over the property seemed to glow beneath the new moon.

The second they stepped inside the house, Joel winced.

"Agh, God."

He covered his mouth with a handkerchief quickly plucked from his back pocket. Joel didn't think he would ever get used to that smell. There was nothing like it. Death was one thing. But then there was the smell of death that had been sitting. *Waiting.* Death that had festered in the heat of a lonely house for weeks. This was a rank, bitter smell that was undoubtedly hideous, yet at the same time oddly *sweet*. Perhaps that was the worst part of all. That putrid *sweetness* stayed with you.

"Sorry I forgot to warn you," said Sheriff Guice. "It's bad. Really bad."

"Mm-hm," Joel said beneath his handkerchief.

Joel was already familiar with the situation at hand. He had been required to help Dr. Bonansinga on similar cases in the past, such as in the winter of 2001 when a hunter accidentally shot himself in the woods on the edge of town. The guy's body had been found a month later. Fortunately, the man had met his demise on frost-hardened ground, not in a house whose furnace had kicked on and off hundreds of times, filling the house with stale heat that slowly roasted the body like a Thanksgiving turkey. That man's body had been relatively well preserved, considering the circumstances. But this was different. Joel found himself wishing, as he made his way through Marietta Rude's home, that he had stopped by the lab to pick up one of those painter's masks, or at least a pair of the nose-plugs he often wore in situations like this.

"Who found her, Sheriff?"

"Vern Nicholson's the mailman on this route," Guice explained. "He's been on vacation the past couple of weeks, otherwise I'm sure this would have been reported long before now. Younger fellow—guy by the name of Hewitt—has been filling in on Vern's route. He must've realized something wasn't right when he kept stuffing envelopes into Mrs. Rude's box 'til there wasn't any damn room left. I guess he finally put two and two together."

"Smart kid," said Joel, though he had seen Vern Nicholson's replacement around town, and Zack Hewitt was not much younger than himself.

"Friggin' genius," Guice said. "Anyway, we respond to the call, nobody answers the door, and this is what we find."

Sheriff Guice stopped walking halfway down the main hall of Marietta Rude's home, and gestured toward the floor. He did not look down himself, though, turning away as if to study something toward the rear of the house. He brought out his own handkerchief now and held it to his mouth and nose.

Joel knelt beside Marietta Rude's corpse and tried his damnedest not to gag. "Jesus, Sheriff. Looks like she's been dead for a year."

"I know." Guice made a retching noise in the back of his throat. "Wouldn't be so bad, seeing how it's winter, but the old lady must have kept the thermostat set to damn near as high as it would go all day."

In spite of the warmth that spread through the house, he shivered. Goosebumps spread across his forearms as he stared at the sticky black figure lying prone on the carpet before him. A brief image of the "Tar Baby" from those old *B'rer Rabbit* storybooks his mother used to read to him flashed across his mind.

"Natural causes, you think?" Sheriff Guice asked him.

"Probably. Mrs. Rude was, what, eighty years old?"

"Something like that."

The two men stood over the body for several more minutes, saying nothing. Finally, the sheriff moved past Joel, back the way they had come, careful not to step anywhere near the leaking black thing at his feet.

"You okay, Sheriff?" Joel asked, hurrying to catch up with him.

"I'm fine," Guice replied. "Just...keep me updated, would ya?"

"Will do," Joel said. And then he went to work.

CHAPTER 26

This was no conclusion Michael had reached overnight. It had been a long time coming, really. For quite some time he had pondered whether he was being silly, whether it was childish to feel jealous over something that should have made him so proud.

It wasn't that he didn't respect Joel's career and where it was going. He understood the concept of upward mobility, and he certainly strived for it himself. But things had never been like this. There had been so many nights over the past year when Joel did not come home at the promised time, so many nights working late because "the county needed him." When Joel first got the job with Dr. Bonansinga—or "Dr. B," as he had called the older man—three years ago, Michael had even considered the possibility that his lover might have been having an affair. That perhaps "Dr. B" might have been a horny old queen himself. But then he realized the silliness of such a notion, not only because he had heard Joel speak time and again of Bonansinga's loving wife and three daughters, but for the simple fact that he knew Joel would never do such a thing to him. He thanked God that he had never mentioned such suspicions to Joel. Things had grown worse, however, since the medical examiner's heart attack. Joel now put in twice as many hours at the lab, and sometimes it pissed Michael off so badly he thought about walking away from their relationship altogether.

He cursed himself. He knew he was being silly. What it all boiled down to was this: Michael Morris was jealous of a bunch of *corpses*. It was ridiculous, and Michael would be the first to admit it was ridiculous.

Still, he could not deny his true feelings.

Michael had seriously started wondering whether or not he wanted to continue with this relationship at all. There was a time, as recently as three or four months ago before this dilemma hit its peak, when he thought he might want to marry Joel. Now, though, as he accelerated along Highway 102, his emotions boiled within him, and Michael thought about what their future might hold. Could there be any real future for them at all? Could love survive when hindered by a career that constantly assumed precedence over everything else?

Michael didn't think so. Not anymore.

The Charger's headlights illuminated the houses along the side of the road as Michael drove faster and faster through Morganville. Speeding out of the town common and onto Pellham Road, he occasionally glanced in his mirror for the strobe-sign of bubble lights, one of Sheriff Guice's deputies out cruising for speeders, but this was secondary in his mind. Background worry. For now, his mind swam with a thousand other thoughts, conflicting emotions concerning what he planned to say to Joel the next time they spoke.

Michael didn't like conflict, never had. Confrontation was something he tried to avoid at all costs. Perhaps that was why he went through life feeling so *scared* all the damn time, so terrified of being alone, facing middle age like some dried-up old hermit queen who has forgotten long ago how to love. But he had always been like that. And now he knew he shouldn't have waited until it got this bad. He should have mentioned his concerns to Joel earlier.

The Charger zoomed on down Pellham Road, rapidly approaching the outermost edge of Morgan County. Soon, Michael would pass completely out of Morganville, and maybe that would be for the better. Maybe he *should* go far away from here. As far as the highway would take him.

Maybe.

He reached down, turned on the radio. "You Shook Me All Night Long" filled the car. Cool. Michael normally didn't care for that heavy metal shit Joel blasted every time they went for a drive together, but he could handle AC/DC. He smiled, tried to leave his worries behind him as his foot eased down on the gas and he turned the volume up even more. He bobbed his head to the music, tightened his grip on the steering wheel.

"Rock 'n' fuckin' roll," he said.

Michael looked up from the glowing green lights of his radio just in time to see a naked man with a long gray beard standing in the middle of the road.

The thing's arms stretched out toward Michael, unnaturally long and skeletal.

Beckoning, like Jesus.

CHAPTER 27

When Joel at last returned home from dropping off the Rude body at the morgue, the house was dark. The television was off, and Michael was nowhere to be found. At first, he thought nothing of it. He assumed Michael had just stepped out for a breath of fresh air.

But then he saw the note on the dining room table. He squinted, holding it close to his face in the darkness. Scribbled on a piece of notebook paper, in Michael's trademark microscopic scrawl of all-capital letters:

> *JOEL,*
>
> *GONE OUT FOR A WHILE. NEED TO THINK A LITTLE.*
>
> *DON'T WAIT UP.*
>
> *M.*

Joel stared at the note for a minute before he let it fall to the table.

More than anything, he felt confused. Unsure of what was going on. Was Michael angry? Hurt?

He'd been getting that signal from his lover lately, but neither of them had confronted the problem head-on. Not yet.

He scratched his head, stared at the empty apartment before him.

He didn't get it.

What was Michael's *deal?*

CHAPTER 28

"Gaaaa!" Michael cried, jerking the Charger's steering wheel violently to the right.

Already, the man he had seen standing in the road—*what the hell was some asshole doing standing in the middle of the road anyway?*—had passed out of his line of sight, and now all he saw as the tires squealed and he fought with the steering wheel was a fat horizontal stripe across his windshield, bold black letters on a stark yellow background:

CRIME SCENE/DO NOT CROSS

The banner flapped away in the night then like some frightened, lemon-colored bird. The Charger jostled and rocked and bounced like a tiny boat caught in a frenetic storm. Michael cried out as his head hit the car's ceiling, stammered "shitshitshitshit" as he realized where he had run off the road—on the old Heller Home property—but his mind barely had time to register his predicament as the Charger struck dozens of those off-white wooden crosses in his path. Charred hunks of debris and broken two-by-fours pounded against the undercarriage of the car, thumped across its hood and roof. Thick crabgrass swished and slapped against the car's body like angry hands batting the intruder away, but still Michael could not stop. Fat gray clouds of ash ballooned in the wake of the Charger as it stirred up mounds of soot and black ember-chunks, and then there was nowhere else to go. The end of the meadow approached in the Charger's headlights, a dark wall of trees that seemed to step forward like a crowd of curious bystanders wishing for a closer look at Michael's dilemma.

A crash, the sound of exploding glass—the loudest sounds he had ever heard in his life, other than his own hoarse scream a second before the collision—and then Michael saw only black.

CHAPTER 29

He moaned as he came to. A great weight pressed against his chest, a boulder of tightness that restricted his ability to breathe.

That weight, he realized, was the steering column. The dashboard. And everything behind it. He was pinned, couldn't move.

"Fuck. Oh, fuck..." Michael saw that the Charger's entire front end was crumpled, devastated, a thick spume of steam wafting up from under the hood and into the overhead leaves of the largest oak tree he'd ever seen. A giant spider-web of cracks spread through the windshield, and the whole thing drooped down toward Michael like a thin film of melted wax. Diamond-like pieces of glass lay on the dashboard, in his lap, in his hair.

His head felt cracked in a million different places, too. He hadn't been wearing his seatbelt.

"Agh, God," he moaned. One hand went to his forehead. The movement caused his ribs to scream in agony. He winced, knew instantly that some of them were broken.

His hand came away from his forehead sticky with blood.

"Shit."

And then he frowned.

"What the—"

Michael's pain-fogged brain had not registered it before, but now he felt a wet, warm sensation at his otherwise numb groin. A pleasant, rhythmic feeling that came and went in gentle waves.

Like a blowjob.

He looked down, and his jaw dropped.

A man's head was buried in his crotch, bobbing up and down. The rest of the man's body knelt on the weedy ground next to Michael's seat, as the driver's-side door hung open like a crooked mouth.

"Who...what..."

A throb of pain in the center of his chest caused Michael's vision to waver in and out again. He thought he recognized the man who was lapping at his cock so eagerly...but then it was gone.

"Who...are you?"

The man looked up at him, and Michael's semi-flaccid penis slid from between his lips. Michael could barely feel himself down there. It must have felt good, damn good, whatever the guy was doing down there. If only the pain would go away, he might feel *something*...

It was Joel down there, in his lap. A grinning, pale-faced Joel, holding his lover's cock in one hand as if it were the greatest prize he had ever known. He stared at it. Kissed it. Licked its purple tip.

"Mmm," Michael moaned, in spite of himself.

But this wasn't right...it couldn't be. What was Joel doing here? Hadn't they been in an argument earlier? Michael wished he could remember, but it would not come to him.

Only the pain stayed with him.

Through Michael's fog of pain, the man in his lap suddenly looked not like his boyfriend at all. Now he had transformed into the first man with whom Michael had ever made love. That gorgeous public defender down in Georgia, ten years Michael's senior, the same fellow who had given him that nasty little AIDS scare in the weeks following their affair.

Yes, it could have been him too.

Maybe.

What the hell was happening here? Michael did not understand, but he did not try to fight it. He arched his back, licked his lips as the attorney from Atlanta devoured his hardness once again. Even through his pain, through the steady, snake-like *ssss* of steam gushing from beneath the Charger's hood, Michael could hear the steady lapping sounds, the low moans of hungry passion as the man took every inch of him inside his mouth.

This wasn't right, though, Michael knew. Something was very wrong here. Still, he could not fight it. He felt as if he were in some surreal dream world. Everything was jumbled, confused.

Now his vision blurred again, and for several seconds the man resembled Michael's own father. Impossible as such a thing could be— Michael's father had been dead for a decade—it was true. The bobbing salt-and-pepper head in his crotch belonged to his *father*, the man who had hardly said two words to his son, just stared at him all the time like the teenager's presence sickened him, since that fateful day six months before his death when Michael told his father he was gay.

No. No. This could not be.

Michael could even feel his father's harelip on him, that slight cleft palate Dayton Morris had carried all his life because he'd claimed "that's the way God made him so that's the way he'd stay," could feel it scrubbing at the flesh of his penis every time the man's lips traveled down his shaft and back up again.

As wrong as Michael knew this all was, he welcomed those faint strokes of moisture sliding up and down the length of his penis. They broke through the wall of his pain, dulling the agony of his many cuts and bruises for several seconds at a time. He moaned, arched his back even as his body protested, as something cracked and popped inside of him. He ran his blood-smeared hands through the man's filthy gray hair, pushed that head which now looked not like his father's head at all further into his groin. *Yes.*

"Oh, God," he said. "Please..."

He pushed himself deeper...into the man's ice-cold mouth, into that scaly, disease-ridden throat.

"What the—" Michael looked down, and then he began to hyperventilate as the skeletal old man with the beard that went on into forever looked up at him with eyes as black as the deepest abyss. His cheeks were sunken, mottled and gray, and his wiry beard of filth and pestilence encircled Michael's jutting cock like a muddy nest of sticks and leaves and vermin. That unnatural beard trailed out through the door, beneath the man's bony, naked ass, and—somehow, Michael knew this terrible truth—back out into the meadow, past the ruins of Heller Home, and down Pellham Road for many miles.

The man paused at his sloppy work long enough to smile at Michael—a crooked, unholy smile—and Michael saw that his tongue was as black as his eyes. His teeth were yellow, broken and rotten, and stained with smears of bright, bright blood.

A smell like something burning filled the air. A droning buzz, like a swarm of angry bumblebees, cut through the night all around the car.

Michael's hands grasped at his groin, trying to push the man away now—this was *wrongwrongwrong* and Michael did not understand how he could not have seen that before—but his movements seemed so slow, too slow, like syrupy movements in a dream.

Gripping himself, he screamed and screamed, yet even as his shriek cut through the night, his mind registered that the man was gone. Suddenly gone. As if he had never been there at all.

Only the pain remained...

...as Michael's shriveled red penis came off, still jerking wetly, in his hands.

CHAPTER 30

Kate was awake when David finally joined her in bed. He had been working on his first project of the new year, a high-paying gig he still couldn't believe he'd scored which entailed designing the dust-jacket for Dean Koontz's latest novel. But his eyes had grown too heavy to continue. He would begin anew tomorrow, perhaps with some newfound inspiration for the piece.

The clock on the nightstand showed 2:19.

Kate's voice came to him from out of the darkness, giving him a start as he pulled his half of the covers around himself.

"Making any progress, sweetheart?" she asked.

He rolled over, stared at her large, pregnant form in the moonlight. Her back was to him, and she did not move at all.

"David?"

"Go back to sleep, baby," he said. "I didn't mean to wake you."

"It's okay," Kate said. "Working late?"

"Yeah."

"Making any progress?" she asked again.

"Hell, no. Not only am I having trouble finding my muse, I think she's permanently skipped town."

"I doubt that," Kate said sleepily. "You'll get it, baby. You always do."

The only sound between them for the next few minutes was the hum of the electric heater kicking on, warming the house.

"David?"

"Yeah?"

"It really bothers you, doesn't it?" she asked. "That we haven't made love in so long."

David stared at her back, at the way the covers drew tight around her body but still did not cover every bit of her these last few months.

At the way her unwashed hair spread out upon the pillow like tangled strands of thick brown yarn.

"I'd be lying if I said otherwise," he finally replied.

"I'm sorry I'm such a pain to live with," Kate said.

"You're not. I love you, Kate." David rolled over then, closed his eyes, hoping for several uninterrupted hours of sleep. "Goodnight, sweetie."

"If you really want to," Kate said. "If it means that much to you, I mean, we can do it."

David's eyes shot open in the darkness. He cleared his throat. "What did you say?"

"I said...we can make love, if you want."

"You mean it?"

"I want you, David."

They rolled over at the same time, to face one another.

She stared at him in the darkness, and her eyes seem to glow in the moonlight. "I know how hard it's been hard for you. I haven't been thinking about your feelings. I want you to make love to me."

David offered her an uneasy grin. "Honey, it's late. Go back to sleep. I think you're half-asleep."

"No," said Kate. "I'm perfectly aware of what I'm saying. What's the matter, you don't want me now?"

"I do," David said. "You know that." He slid closer to her in the bed, kissed her forehead. "You know I would never hurt you, Kate."

"I know."

He kissed her lips, tenderly at first, and then trailed wet kisses down her neck. "I love you."

"I love you."

"I'll be gentle," he promised, returning to her lips. They kissed, and before David realized the sincerity of his wife's passion, their tongues began to battle feverishly. His hand went to Kate's breast, and he squeezed. She flinched, drawing back from his touch, but only momentarily.

"Oh, Kate..."

"Make love to me, David."

Kate slid away from him long enough to pull off her nightgown, and her massive belly came between them bolder than ever. David pulled off his pajama bottoms, threw them to the carpet. David did not wish to rush things, but he felt as if he might lose it at any moment. It had been so long. He was sure he would not last for more than a minute or two.

Kate got on her hands and knees. It had always been David's favorite position, back in their younger, wilder days.

She moaned gently as he slid into her.

He had only pumped into her eight or nine times when Kate said, "David...David, wait—"

"Oh, God, that feels good," he groaned. "It's been so long..."

"David!"

It was over as quickly as it had begun.

He climaxed, hissing through his teeth, "Jesusss." And then he slid out of her, collapsed onto the bed.

"I'm sorry. I knew I wouldn't last long, but...I'll make it up to you, Kate, I promise—"

"Oh, Lord." Kate's rolled over, onto her back, and one hand went to the shiny cleft between her legs. A single tear spilled from her right eye, dampening her pillow. "Ow."

"Kate, what is it? What's the matter?"

"Oh, no. The baby. David, I think my water just broke!"

PART
2

"And sullen Moloch fled
Hath in shadows dred
His burning idol all of blackest hue
In vain with cymbals ring
They call the grisly king
In dismal dance about the furnace blue..."

—*Paradise Lost*
John Milton

"Take, for example, the recent events in Morganville, North Carolina. I would stake my professional reputation on the fact that this was nothing more sinister than a case of mass hysteria.

Wake up, folks—it's the twenty-first century. If 'demons' ever existed, we can rest assured this world's pollution killed them off a long time ago." (audience laughter)

—from *Haunting or Hoax: Investigations into the Paranormal,* PBS, hosted by Dr. Lucius Van Dorne

CHAPTER 31

The Littles agreed that it was far too late to wake Becca unless they had no other choice, so David called Joel and asked if he would mind coming over and watching her for a few hours. Joel had seemed preoccupied with something, his voice a little shaky, but he promised he would be right over. David asked if everything was okay, and Joel said something about he and Michael having a bit of a spat; David barely even heard him, though, caring very little about his brother-in-law's problems while his wife prepared to give birth any minute.

With that taken care of, David only had Kate to worry about. She pulled on a wrinkled pair of sweatpants and a maternity blouse, while he threw some of her clothes in a small suitcase. After that was done, David stuck his head in Becca's bedroom to check on their daughter. Satisfied that she was fast asleep and blissfully unaware of what was happening, he and Kate decided they could go ahead and wait in the 4Runner. With everything ready to go, they would take off the second Joel arrived.

David helped Kate into the passenger's seat with a tight, worried expression on his face.

"You okay?" he asked. "Easy. Easy."

"I'm fine. As long as we get to the hospital soon."

"We'll get there, don't worry."

David ran around to the other side of the 4Runner, started up the vehicle, letting it idle for a minute.

"What are we going to do?" Kate said.

"He should be here any minute."

"Maybe we should just take Becca with us."

"No. Maybe. Hell, I don't know. Maybe you're right." David glanced back and forth between Honeysuckle Lane, his wife, and the house.

Fidgeted nervously. He started to open his door.

"Dammit, where the hell *is* he?"

As if on cue, Joel's Mustang at last entered the cul-de-sac, his bright lights temporarily blinding the Littles.

David quickly rolled down his window, put the 4Runner in gear and rested his foot on the brake, preparing to zoom away the second things were squared away with Joel.

The Mustang screeched to a stop. Joel got out, jogged up to David's window.

"I'm on this," he said. "You guys get outta here. I've got Becca."

"Are you sure you don't mind?" Kate said. She winced as a sharp pain hit her.

"Go!" Joel said. "Just go!"

"Becca's fast asleep," David told him. "Help yourself to anything you want."

"Will do," Joel said. "No sweat. Now would you get the hell out of here and make me an uncle again!"

David released the brake and the 4Runner took off.

They arrived at the hospital in record time. David turned on the 4Runner's hazard lights, ran stop signs and red lights, broke the county's posted speed limits and passed slower cars ahead of him as if they were standing still, finally pulling into the Emergency Room parking lot of Cecil C. Purdy Memorial Hospital less than ten minutes after leaving the house.

Kate had already begun the soft, steady *hoo-hoo-hoo* breathing exercises she knew would help ease her increasing labor pains. David ran around to her side of the 4Runner, threw open her door, said "Yeah, baby, that's good, you just breathe, breathe, hang in there, we're here," in sharp little exhalations of his own. She slid her legs to the side, hanging them out her door so she could easily lower herself to the ground, but then David told her to wait. He ran inside the hospital. Kate watched him through the big bay windows; she could not hear what he was saying to the nurse at the front desk, though it was obvious her husband was taking control of the situation. Giving orders. Seconds later, David came back out—the automatic doors opened with a soft *whoosh* not unlike Kate's own harsh little gasps—with the nurse and an empty wheelchair in tow.

"Here we go," said the nurse, a thin woman with scraggly brown hair. Her voice was too calm for David's liking; her nonchalant tone might have indicated she brought the Littles cups of warm tea and the promise of pleasant conversation out here on the brightly-lit front walk of the hospital.

David looked perturbed. "Let's go," he said.

"Easy, Mr...?"

"Little," Kate grunted, answering for her husband as she slid from the 4Runner's passenger seat and down into the wheelchair.

"Take it easy, Mr. Little," the nurse continued. "No need to rush your wife. Everything's going to be fine."

David frowned at the old woman's back. *I wasn't rushing* her, *bitch,* his expression seemed to say, and in spite of her pain Kate was forced to stifle a chuckle.

"Come on, baby," David said, raising Kate's swollen feet one at a time with both hands. He eased them onto the wheelchair's footrests, stood and offered Kate a reassuring smile that was not entirely convincing. "There you go."

"Mr. Little, if you'll follow us," said the nurse. She all but pushed David aside in order to push Kate's wheelchair herself. "We'll get Mrs. Little checked in right away."

David said nothing, but followed, his knees weak. The adrenaline flowing through his body fed his anxiety even more than the crystal meth he had tried one time back in college.

This was too much. Everything was happening too fast.

Kate's baby was almost here.

And David—strangely enough—found himself trembling all over with excitement.

CHAPTER 32

If given a choice in the matter, Joel would have preferred to accompany his sister to the hospital, but he knew it was best he stay with Becca. There wouldn't have been very much he could do for her anyway, except wait in the lobby thumbing restlessly through dog-eared copies of *Newsweek* and *Time* as if the words before him meant anything. Becca didn't need to be outside in this chilly weather, this late at night, and besides, he had all the time in the world to visit with his sister after the delivery, to fawn all over the new addition to the family.

After checking in on Becca, Joel sat on the Littles' sofa and pulled the television remote from out of the cushions. Before long, though, he grew bored. Nothing worth a shit was ever on this time of night. Just infomercials and old *Three's Company* re-runs. Or *Jerry Springer*, which Joel was only half-watching now. He picked up the cordless phone atop the coffee table, decided to call and see if Michael had returned home yet. While the phone rang on the other end, purring softly in his ear, he punched a button on the remote. Jerry Springer went mute. Joel wondered why he'd been watching that trash anyway—something about drag-queens and the multiple partners who loved them was tonight's subject, and frankly it sickened him to see those flamers making fools of themselves up there—but then his attention was directed toward the recording in his ear.

Michael's voice, short and sweet: "We can't come to the phone right now. Please leave a short message after the tone and we'll get back to you. Thanks." And then the beep.

Michael still wasn't home. Or else he wasn't answering the phone.

But he *had* to be home by now. It was three in the morning!

Joel frowned, hung up the phone.

"Michael, where the hell are you?"

He all but leapt off the sofa when his pager started beeping at his side.

CHAPTER 33

On the morning of January 3, at the exact moment Joel Rohrig called the number on his beeper and Sheriff Guice informed the younger man that his assistance was needed at the old Heller Home property, Kate Little gave birth to a beautiful baby boy.

They named the child Christopher James, and he was perfect.

Perfect.

Both Kate and baby Christopher came through the whole thing wonderfully, and though the infant was a tad small considering the circumstances—five pounds, eight ounces and 19.5 inches, not unexpected for an infant born a few weeks early—Dr. Bullard assured the Littles that everything was "as fine as fine could be."

But most important of all, perhaps—at least for David—their questions were finally answered.

They knew the first time they saw the child, as soon as the umbilical cord had been snipped and Dr. Bullard placed the infant upon Kate's chest, the moment that purple, pinched little face stared up at them both with those wide, ocean-blue eyes.

Any fool could see: those were *David's* eyes.

David dropped to his knees right there in the delivery room, on its cold, blood-specked floor. He clasped his hands, and pressed them to his forehead, softly whimpering his gratitude toward God.

He was Christopher's father.

He knew it at last.

Christopher James was *his son.*

CHAPTER 34

David stood by Kate's bed, staring proudly at their new son as she breastfed little Christopher for the first time, when a young nurse they had not seen before opened the door to Kate's room. SANDRA C. read the hospital ID card clipped to her uniform.

"Knock, knock," said the nurse.

David turned to her. "Yes?"

"Mr. and Mrs. Little? Please pardon my intrusion. You have a call on line one-oh-one, Mr. Little. Says it's urgent."

"Oh," David said. He looked at Kate, frowned. He walked toward the nurse, preparing to leave the room. "I hope everything's okay—"

"You're welcome to take it in your room, if you'd like," the nurse offered. "Just dial one-oh-one."

"Oh, okay," David said, sounding dazed. He reached for the phone by Kate's bed. "Thank you."

"Don't mention it." The nurse exited then, smiling over her shoulder toward Kate and the baby as she closed the door behind her.

David picked up the beige phone beside Kate's bed, punched 1-0-1 on the number pad.

"David Little speaking."

"David," said the voice on the other end. "It's Joel."

"Joel!" David said. "Hey, buddy. I was gonna call you soon, tell you the good news. Everything's been very hectic, you know."

"I understand," said Joel. "So are you gonna tell me already? What's the good word?"

"Well, Uncle Joel, you have a beautiful nephew by the name of Christopher James."

"Fantastic! I'll bet he's perfect."

"Oh, he is. Wait till you see him, man. Five pounds, eight ounces. Nineteen and half inches."

"That's great, David. I'm so happy for you two."

"Thanks. You'll see him soon."

"I can't wait."

"Anyway, what's up? Lady who gave me the message said it was urgent."

Joel cleared his throat. "Yeah. I've got a problem. I hate to do this to you, David, but I don't have a choice."

"What is it?"

"There's been an accident out near the old Heller Home property. I have to take it."

"Ah, shit."

"I'm sorry, man. I feel terrible. I told you guys I would watch Becca, and now this."

"Nah," David said. "It's your job. You gotta do what you gotta do."

"Well, what do you suggest we do? Should I drop Becca off on the way?"

"No, no," David said. "You don't have to do that. Kate's fine, the baby's fine. He's eating. I'll come pick Becca up."

"Are you sure?"

"Absolutely. It's not a problem at all."

"Hey, man—I really appreciate it. And again, I apologize."

"Just sit tight. I'll be there in about twenty minutes, okay?"

"Okay," Joel said. "Thanks, David."

David hung up, turned to Kate. He offered her a reassuring smile as he pulled on his jacket and reached into his pocket for his keys.

"Everything okay?" Kate asked, as the baby's mouth made gentle sucking noises upon her right nipple.

"Joel has to respond to a call," David said. "There's been a bad wreck near where that children's hospital used to be."

"Oh, no. There's never a dull moment out at that place, is there?"

"Apparently not." He kissed her on the forehead, did the same to his son. "I'm going to pick up Becca. Shouldn't take more than a few minutes."

"Hurry back, Daddy." Kate's proud grin stretched from ear to ear as she gazed down at baby Christopher.

"Count on it," David replied.

CHAPTER 35

Joel wasn't sure what to do. He paced back and forth on the Littles' front porch, peering down Honeysuckle Lane for the sight of David's 4Runner.

Still nothing. It had been over thirty minutes since he had spoken to his brother-in-law on the phone, and he had to go. Soon. His job depended on it.

Once, he saw headlights and began to descend the porch steps before he realized the vehicle in question was a Chevy pickup. A very loud, ugly Chevy pickup. Someone turning around in the cul-de-sac, that was all.

No 4Runner. No David. Not yet.

Joel shot one more glance down the road before heading for his Mustang at the curb.

He figured he would wait in the car. No harm. He'd keep an eye on the house, but the second David arrived he would take off.

Surely he'd be here any second.

Chapter 36

Fred Dawson smirked as he watched the little faggot prance across the lawn to that fancy Mustang of his, start it up. He had seen Joel Rohrig around town, and knew all about him. Maybe he kept it well hidden from the rest of the world, but Fred Dawson could smell a cocksucker a mile away.

From his vantage point in the bushes between the Little house and George Heatherly's yard, Fred wondered why he had waited. He could have taken the fairy down. Rohrig was half his size, and with those limp wrists he probably fought like a woman, too.

Oh, well. That hadn't been the plan. To bring unnecessary attention to himself, Fred knew, would ruin the whole thing.

Fred tipped back his fat bottle of Pepe Lopez tequila, finished the last few swallows in one loud gulp. It no longer burned going down these days. It was like liquid ecstasy. Fred moaned, gave a satisfied smack of his lips, and tossed the bottle into the yard behind him.

He knew what he was doing was wrong. Sneaking around in the middle of the night, watching a little girl through her bedroom window like some sicko pedophile.

But this wasn't like that. Not at all.

Fred Dawson assured himself for the umpteenth time since he first started watching the Little house a couple weeks ago that he wasn't no fuckin' pervert. He had no desire to touch the little girl.

The kid wasn't for him anyway.

Fred wasn't doing this for himself.

He was doing it because he *had* to. He was doing it for the old guy with the really long beard.

The nightmares had grown worse since that day at the mall when Fred lost his job because of that little bitch and her bastard father. He still couldn't believe that motherfucker had the nerve to punch him! Oh, if he'd been sober, if he'd been just ten years younger, he would have shown him who was the better man. He had just been talking to the kid, hadn't even known yet that the man with the beard had plans for her. If the kid's fuckin' father hadn't caused such a scene, Fred's boss wouldn't have known he'd been drinking, and wouldn't have fired him on the spot.

The child had been *right there*, in his grasp, and he had blown it.

But that was okay. Because Fred hadn't known back then what was expected of him.

Finally, just a couple days ago, the old man in his dreams had told him what to do. And now that Fred knew, he would obey.

As he stared at his own sweaty, trembling hands in the darkness, Fred tried to remember the last time he'd felt normal. Sometime before his son's death, for sure.

Oh, well. What had to be done had to be done. What was that saying he'd heard a few times, usually from his friends at the bar?

"It isn't paranoia when they're really out to get you," Fred said aloud to the night's growing breeze.

He chuckled nervously as he shambled toward the Little house.

Toward the child inside.

The first really bad nightmare came just a couple days after the Santa fiasco at the mall. But even that had been only a start of the surreal dreamscape which had become Fred Dawson's dark reality. Oh, the things Fred saw when he lay down to sleep at night. And his growing habit of driving out to the old Heller place more and more frequently didn't help matters. He'd drive out there to the ruins against his better judgment, and he would just sit for hours in his truck, sipping at a can of Milwaukee's Best, watching the breeze stir up the ashes, listening to the weeds whisper his name. Sometimes he would sit there well past sundown, thinking about the things that lurked out there. Wondering what had killed his son.

Hallucinations, that quack Dr. Whitman would've called the things Fred saw not only when he slept but also in broad daylight. *You need to quit drinking, Mr. Dawson*, that holier-than-thou sonofabitch said the last time Fred kept one of his appointments, *before it kills you once and for all. Remind me sometime, I'll take you down to the County Morgue, show you what your liver's gonna look like one day. Heck, what it probably looks like now.*

Fuck that self-righteous prick. Dr. Whitman didn't know what it was like to lose a son. He didn't know what it was like to feel...*things* all around you, every second of the day. To hear them hissing in your ear, crawling across your skin, telling you what to do. You couldn't understand their arcane language, though you knew what they wanted all the same.

Fred couldn't forget the things Mr. Moloch had showed him even if he tried. The visions he displayed before Fred's terrified, bloodshot eyes as he peeled back that filthy curtain of beard and the darkness came out to play. Fred didn't like to think about that, though he couldn't deny the *other* things he had seen in there. Inside the gray man's beard, there also lived a world of *good*. Beautiful things, miraculous things man was not meant to see, but only because God was so fucking selfish He wanted to keep all those secrets to Himself. How fair was that? So much more in there, so much goodness beyond this hateful world, beyond that awful darkness. It was breathtaking.

Once, Fred even caught a glimpse of Billy in there. Precious Billy, waiting. Waiting for Daddy to save him.

"Please help me, Daddy," Billy had said as Fred stared into the swirling eternity of the old man's matted beard. Fred had known right then, recognized the opportunity clearer than anything he had ever seen in his life, that this Moloch dude had given him one last chance to make right again everything he had fucked up.

First things first, though.

Moloch wanted the little girl.

Fred licked his lips. God, how he needed another fuckin' beer. Shot of booze. Something. He couldn't function without it.

But he had to go on, he knew.

It was his destiny.

To take the child.

Tonight.

Now, here she was. Through the window. Sleeping. Such a precious little angel. Golden curls spread out on her pillow, tiny nightgown with the puppy-dog paw-prints all over it hitched up above her ass so Fred could see a hint of soft pink panties.

This wasn't right. It wasn't.

Fred Dawson swallowed loudly in the night, ignored his conscience as best he could. He had no choice in the matter, goddammit. This had to be done. Mr. Moloch commanded it.

He stared at the moon for several long minutes before opening the little girl's window.

Wouldn't be long now.

Soon, Moloch would have the brat. He could take her away, to the Land of Tears or wherever the hell he said he was from...

And then, even if Billy did not come back to him, maybe that old bastard would get out of his head once and for all.

CHAPTER 37

David parked the 4Runner alongside the curb, flinched when Joel appeared beside him in the Mustang before the vehicle had rolled to a complete stop.

"Thanks for coming, man," Joel said through the open passenger side window. "I'm sorry to run off like this, after I promised I'd watch Becca for you."

David shook his head as he climbed out of the 4Runner. "It's not a problem at all. You have a job to do."

"Mommy and Christopher are doing well?"

"They're doing great. Now get to work. I'll take it from here."

"Thanks, David. I'll talk to you guys later, okay?"

David threw up one hand as he headed across the lawn toward home.

Joel took off with a short, sharp squeal of tires.

At first, David thought Becca might have merely gotten up in the middle of the night to use the bathroom.

But then he saw the open window.

And he heard his daughter's scream.

"Becca...?"

She had only been alone for a minute or so at the very most, hadn't she?

He turned on the light.

"Jesus...Becca!"

She was gone.

His little girl was gone.

He ran to the open window.

His breath caught in his throat when he saw the scene in his back yard.

"*Becca!*"

CHAPTER 38

Joel turned down the Mustang's radio as he pulled off of Pellham Road and onto the property where Heller Home once stood. Instantly his senses were assaulted by the sights and sounds of an accident across the meadow: swirling emergency lights, the smell of burnt rubber, the shouts of bustling police and rescue squad personnel. In the foreground, all about the scorched perimeter of Heller Home, the dozens of white crosses seemed to triple in number, their gaunt black shadows stretching across the meadow beneath the frantic emergency strobes. This despite the fact that most of them had been destroyed in the accident, and now those former rows of crosses looked like crooked, gapped teeth against the thick black night behind them.

Nothing could have prepared Joel for the hot rush of terror that shot through his body like a shock of electricity as his eyes fell upon the car in the heart of the chaos.

"Oh, God," he cried, throwing open the Mustang's door. "No!"

It was his lover's Dodge Charger, out there in the meadow. Black and maroon, so sleek and shark-like when it had prowled Morganville's streets, now crumpled against that oak tree like some cheap plastic toy fallen prey to a spoiled toddler's tantrum.

Nonononono. This couldn't be. This wasn't right.

Michael. Out there. Lying half in and half out of the Charger. Joel took it all in, unable to believe his eyes. His knees grew weak.

Jesus. So much blood. All over him. Michael looked like he'd taken a *bath* in the stuff. Even from where he stood, still a hundred feet or so from the scene, Joel could see the blood splashed everywhere. On the interior of Michael's car. In the weeds. A grisly swath of it led away from the car and off into the woods like a trail left by some monstrous crimson snail.

"Michael! Michael...*no!*"

In the state of mind he was in, Joel did not consider for even a second how the other men on the scene might view his reaction. He did not care, at the moment, whether Sheriff Guice and his deputies knew of his love for the man who lay in the Charger. He had never been sure if they were aware of his "alternative lifestyle", but none of that mattered now as he ran toward the men he loved, his eyes burning with salty tears. He wanted to hold Michael, to know his boyfriend was okay despite the ragged red-black hole that gaped open in his groin.

"Jesus...God...what happened?" Joel cried.

Sheriff Guice and Deputy Keenan turned toward him as Joel burst through the weeds.

"Joel," Guice said. "Hey—"

"Oh, G-God...what happened to him?"

"You knew this guy?" Guice asked, moving toward Joel.

"I can't handle this right now," Joel wept. "I can't..."

Joel fell to his knees then, could do nothing else but collapse onto Michael's corpse even as Guice and Keenan tried to pull him off. He held Michael, ignoring the steady dripping which came from his boyfriend's body as he held it close, ignoring the cloying copper-smell of freshly-spilled blood which seemed to coat not only his nostrils but the inside of his mouth as well. He raised his head toward the heavens, sobbing uncontrollably.

"Here, here," said Sheriff Guice.

"I loved him," Joel said, tears streaming down his face. "Oh, God, Michael, I'm so sorry..."

"Joel?" Deputy Keenan called to him.

"Leave him alone," Joel said. He kissed Michael's still-warm forehead, started rocking the corpse in his arms. "Oh, God, Michael. What happened to you, *why*...?"

Guice and Keenan stared at one another, until finally Guice looked away. Understanding now. It all made sense.

"Oh," Keenan grunted. "I get it."

"Joel, come on," said the sheriff, but for several minutes his gentle reassurances and comforting touches were ignored.

Joel just kept kissing the dead man's head, oblivious to everything else around him.

CHAPTER 39

"Hey!" David shouted at the man in the filthy Santa suit. He was running through George Heatherly's yard with the little girl tucked under one arm. Becca fought him all the way, kicking and punching and screaming, but the man did not seem fazed by her struggling.

"Wait!" David yelled, struggling to climb onto the windowsill. "Stop!"

"Daddy!" Becca reached out with one free arm toward her father. "Daddy, *help!*"

"Motherfucker! What are you—" David leapt through the window and to the ground.

He sprinted through the light copse of trees that separated his yard from the ex-Marine's. Santa Claus had one hell of a head start on him, but Becca's struggles were slowing him down.

"Stop it!" David heard the man say to Becca as she fought to worm her way out of his grip. "Stay still, you little shit!"

David growled with fury, lunging after the man. His movements felt dream-like, as if he were stuck in slow motion while the man before him continued on at reality's pace.

"Put me *down!*" Becca cried. "*Daddy!*"

"Stop!" David shouted.

"Ow!" The man in the Santa suit yelped, and David's heart stuttered. Becca must have bitten him.

That's my baby. Do it again!

And then it was over as quickly as it had begun.

David slid to a stop in the dewy grass as a shape suddenly came at them. Before he even knew what was happening, the tall black figure brought a bottle down hard as it could atop the kidnapper's head. Looked like a big empty liquor bottle, David thought, though he couldn't tell for sure in the darkness. The bottle did not break, just made a hollow *clunk* sound atop Santa's skull, then went twirling away in a sparkle of moonlight to land in the grass.

Santa crumpled to the ground and Becca tumbled out of his arms into the grass.

"You okay, honey?" George Heatherly asked Becca.

The little girl didn't answer. She ran for her father, fell into his arms, and David collapsed to his knees as he embraced her.

"Oh, baby, baby," he whispered, showering his daughter with kisses. "Are you okay, baby? He didn't hurt you, did he?"

Becca shook her head, whimpered into the crook of David's shoulder.

David watched his next-door neighbor walk toward them. The old man wore a dirty white T-shirt—HOOF ARTED? read its logo—and tight cut-off blue-jean shorts beneath his maroon bathrobe. His legs were even paler than Becca's in the night.

George offered David a reassuring smile as he closed the distance between them. David wanted to smile back, but did not have it in him. He held Becca tighter than ever, afraid to ever let her go.

"What the hell was *that?*" David said, watching the shape of the fallen man a few feet away. As if Santa might jump back up and tear Becca from his arms any second.

George Heatherly gave a barely noticeable shrug, glanced over his shoulder at the dark shape in the middle of his property. It wasn't moving. "Couldn't sleep. Thought I heard something. There he was, outside your house, snooping around."

"Daddy...what's wrong with Santa Claus?" Becca wept, her tears dampening David's shirt. "Why's he turned so mean?"

David didn't know what to say.

"Kate, we have a problem," David said as soon as she picked up the phone. He stood in the center of their kitchen, pacing back and forth while George brewed a pot of coffee nearby.

"Looks like it's gonna be a while till I get back to the hospital, honey."

"What's the matter?" Kate's voice was instantly worried. "Is Becca okay?"

"Becca's fine," David said. "I started not to call you, because I didn't want you to freak out. But I'm going to be a while."

"Oh my God, David. What's happened?"

"First of all," David said, "how's the baby?"

"He's fine. Sleeping. David, please tell me what's going on."

David told her what had happened, trying to keep his voice calm as the memories of the last few minutes came rushing back to him, trying his best to downplay the situation as he relayed the events to his wife. Still, he knew how she would react.

"Oh, God!" Kate cried. "Who is he? What did he want with her? Oh, my poor baby!"

"Everything's going to be fine, sweetheart," David said.

"Where is she? Where's my baby? I want to talk to her."

"Becca's okay," David said. "You know how kids are. So resilient." He smiled uneasily at Heatherly, but George's back was to him. The ex-Marine was staring out the window over the kitchen sink, nervously tapping his knuckles upon the countertop. "She's asleep, on the couch. You'd think nothing even happened."

"Oh, God, David," Kate cried. "Please don't let her out of your sight. That's just *awful*. The poor thing..."

"I won't," David said. "I can see her right now." He glanced down the hall, toward the living room, where Becca slept on the sofa beneath the soft glow of a nearby lamp.

"Where was Joel?" Kate said. "I thought he was watching Becca!"

"He was," David said. "We met in the driveway. This guy must have sneaked into the window during the minute or so we were outside talking."

"You mean he left her *alone?*"

"It wasn't like that, Kate. He didn't do anything wrong."

"Oh, God, my baby...are you sure she's okay, David? Please tell me the truth."

"She's fine, hon, I promise. She was a bit shaken up by the whole thing, but she's sleeping now. She's going to be okay. You just need to take care of yourself and Christopher. You don't need this. I'm here. Becca is fine. Mr. Heatherly—"

"George," the ex-Marine said, and David flinched. He hadn't realized his neighbor had been paying attention to their conversation.

"George has promised to hang around until the sheriff arrives."

The coffeemaker at last stopped, and George poured steaming mugs of java for them both.

"Thanks," David whispered, tilting the phone away from his mouth.

In David's ear, Kate cried, "I can't believe someone would...oh, my poor Becca—"

"I know. But it's gonna be okay. The man who tried to take her... believe me, he's gonna get what's coming to him."

"They caught him already?" Kate asked, and David could hear her shifting over the phone, changing positions in her hospital bed. "Please tell me they caught him."

"We did. We have him."

"You do?"

"In the bathroom. We got that sonofabitch."

Considering the situation, Kate did not scold him for his profanity.

"David, he's in the...in our bathroom?"

"Tied up with duct-tape. He's not going anywhere."

"Oh, my God," Kate said, for what must have been the millionth time.

"It's the guy from the mall, Kate. Santa Claus." David tried his damnedest to keep that *I-told-you-so* tone out of his voice.

Kate could do nothing but stammer into her end of the phone, confused. "But, no...that can't be. I mean...*why*, David? What does he want with Becca?"

"I don't know. But I intend to find out."

"David...please don't do anything stupid."

"I won't," he assured her, though he didn't sound very confident.

At the sound of several pained grunts echoing through the lavatory in the next room, David told Kate he had to go. She protested, but he told her he loved her, promised to call her later with any new developments, and with a final goodbye and a "kiss little Christopher for me" he hung up the phone.

"Let's do this." George headed down the hallway before David had set the phone down.

Both of their cups of coffee remained untouched for now.

David followed the ex-Marine toward the bathroom, his heart thudding almost painfully in his chest.

CHAPTER 40

Sheriff Guice and Deputy Keenan were finally able to calm Joel. Tears streaked Rohrig's tan face but at last his sobs had softened into quiet whimpers in the back of Keenan's patrol car as the deputy drove him back toward town. Sheriff Guice stayed behind at the scene of the accident, calling in a fellow from Plymill & Sons Funeral Home to take care of Michael's body. Meanwhile, it was up to Keenan to respond to the call at Rohrig's brother-in-law's place, something about an attempted kidnapping.

Deputy Keenan opted not to utilize the patrol car's siren, though he did engage the vehicle's swirling lights as he approached Honeysuckle Lane. They washed across the houses along Morganville's dark streets, changing their colors from red to blue then back again as Keenan cruised by.

"I'm sorry you had to see that," the deputy said to Joel as they headed down Pellham Road toward town. "We never knew..."

Joel's only reply was a soft sniffle from the backseat.

"It's hard, I know," Keenan said. He glanced in the rearview mirror, saw the younger man's swollen red eyes staring back at him. "I know it sounds like so much bullshit, but it's true what they say. Time does heal all wounds."

"First Michael, now Becca," Joel moaned. "This is all too much to handle."

"I know," Keenan said.

Only the gentle rumbling of the vehicle's engine and the rhythmic hum of its tires on the asphalt below filled the silence between the two men for the next few minutes.

Finally though, Deputy Keenan said, so matter-of-factly that Joel thought at first he might have drifted off there in the backseat of the patrol car and dreamed it altogether: "In all honesty, though, I just can't relate. Seeing how I've never sucked a dick before. Or let another man ream my ass."

Joel's breath caught in his throat.

"Excuse me?"

Surely he had misunderstood. Joel stared at Deputy Keenan's broad back, at the fiery orange sprigs of hair sticking out from beneath his Smokey-bear hat. He'd always liked Hank Keenan, had always thought the deputy was a good man. But now this...

Keenan took a right onto Honeysuckle Lane, said nothing else.

No way, Joel thought. He had to have misunderstood the deputy's words. He could think of no other explanation.

"Why did you do it?" David asked as they stood over the man in the filthy Santa suit. His costume stank of mildew, and was more a red-gray now than its original bright crimson. Looked like he'd worn the damn thing for the last six months. Smelled like he'd shit himself in it several times as well.

He was sprawled beneath them, in the bathtub.

"Hold on," George said. He ripped the piece of duct tape off the man's mouth. The man hissed through his teeth as some of his moustache came off with it. "Now."

"Fuck you," said the false Santa. They had already removed his thick white wig and beard and his elfin hat to expose the man beneath: late thirties, greasy black hair speckled with flakes of dandruff, thick stubble at his jawline and all the way down his double chins. A thin rivulet of blood trickled from the nasty red welt just below his hairline, and his bloodshot eyes twitched back and forth in futile efforts to focus on his captors. "I don't have to tell you nothing."

"That's fine," Heatherly said. "You can tell the sheriff."

David said, "You're going away for a long time, asshole."

"Suck my dick," said Santa Claus.

It took every bit of willpower David had not to punch the man. His right fist clenched so tightly that he would later see the blood-red crescents left by his fingernails in his palms and he would forget how those little cuts got there, but he was able to refrain from doing anything stupid. Just barely.

"You some kinda fucking sicko?" said George Heatherly. "Maybe you get off on touching little girls?"

Santa said nothing, just stared at the men standing over him. Sweat ran down his forehead and across his nose. He bared his teeth at George, teeth that were yellowed and speckled with crumbs from his last meal.

"Come here, you piece of shit," George said. He leaned over the man, reached into Santa's pocket, searching for something. The man rocked back and forth, fighting him, but his movements did little to deter George's search.

"Here we go." George pulled out the man's wallet.

"Give that back!"

"Shut up." Heatherly rifled through the man's wallet, pulled out the man's driver's license and held it up toward the light.

"Frederick Leonard Dawson."

"What were you trying to do with my little girl, you bastard?" David demanded to know.

"I ain't no kiddie fucker," Dawson finally explained, his voice hoarse. "I did it 'cause I had to."

"Had to." David shook his head, looked at George. "What the fuck is that supposed to mean?"

George Heatherly did not have to *try* to be intimidating. Here was a man for whom such a thing came naturally. A guy who didn't take shit from anybody, never had. David was glad to have the old man on his side.

"Maybe we'll tell the sheriff we *had to* stomp the living hell out of you," George told the man in the tub. "Didn't have no choice."

"Fuck you. I don't have to tell you nothin'. You're gonna see, though. Soon." The man in the Santa costume nodded vigorously, as best he could within his tight, sticky bonds. "Oh, yeah. You're gonna see."

"Hm," said George, unimpressed.

"You wouldn't understand anyway. This is all so much bigger than you two fucks."

"Why don't you try us?" George said, and his calm tone mocked the man's incoherent rambling. He glanced toward David, his eyebrows raised. David shook his head, gave a barely-perceptible shrug. "We're trying to understand, believe me. We're also trying not to beat the living shit out of you right here, right now, but then that's just us. We like to think we're good upstanding citizens."

"He's gonna kill you all, you know," Dawson said, and his voice was unbelievably calm for a man who had obviously lost his mind long ago. "Every last one of you."

"And who the hell is 'he?'" David asked.

"Tell whoever *he* is to bring it on," said George.

"You're all gonna die, for getting in his way. Slowly. I can promise you that."

"Who's 'he?'" David asked again.

"He's older than God," Dawson insisted. Where his voice was calm before, as his lunatic preaching grew more and more bizarre, his tone grew louder. Spittle flew from his lips now as he ranted. His sour breath wafted up to assault his captors' nostrils, and the smell of alcohol that seemed to ooze from his every pore filled the air stronger than ever. "He's more powerful than anything you've ever seen! He's gonna bring my son back...he's gonna make everything all right again. Because he can. Because he can do anything. The master is growing more powerful every day. And he's gonna make you cocksuckers wish you were never fuckin' born."

"Wait a minute," said Heatherly. "Your son?"

"My boy." Tears welled up in the man's eyes. He sniffled loudly. "Billy."

"Ah, shit." It had already hit George. He understood now. He understood everything. "Billy Dawson..."

"Oh, hell," said David. This explained everything. David felt, for at least a second or two, a knot of pity deep in his stomach for the man who lay before them. No wonder the guy had lost his frigging mind—David figured he would do the same, if something ever happened to Becca. Or baby Christopher, who was only a couple hours old. He'd go stark raving mad, he was sure of it.

"What's with the Santa getup, anyway?" George asked the man. "Christmas was over a month ago, freak."

"He's gonna make you pay," was Dawson's only reply, and now the smile upon his pale, sweaty face sent chills down David Little's spine. That awful yellow smile seemed to belong not to Fred Dawson at all, but to something dark hidden deep inside of him.

"You're gonna wish you never fucked with Moloch," Dawson growled.

"I think the sheriff's here," George said above the sound of a car pulling up outside. He turned to leave the room, but then stopped as David squatted again, leaned down before his prisoner so their faces were mere inches away from one another.

"What did you say?" David asked the man. His eyes grew impossibly wide, almost as wild as those of the man in the Santa Claus suit. George touched his shoulder, but David did not seem to notice the gesture. "What the fuck did you just say?"

"Mr. Moloch's gonna kill every last one of you motherfuckers," Dawson said, still smiling that terrible smile. "But he'll reward me. In the end. You'll see."

"Gimme a break," George Heatherly said. "Fuckin' drunk. David, this guy doesn't even know where he's fuckin' *at*."

David's expression, however, seemed to hint that there might be more to this than they first thought. He looked ill now.

"*Moloch*," David said. He grabbed the man's collar, shook him. "Where did you hear that word?"

"You're not even worthy to say his name!" Fred Dawson spat, rolling about in the empty tub. "He'll punish you for that! He will punish you for that! Oh, motherfucker, you are going to *burn*."

"Shut the fuck up, will you?" George Heatherly said, before punching the man in the nose.

Fred Dawson's nose gushed thick, dark blood. George stepped back and grimaced at the sight of the man's fluids on his tattooed knuckles. He wiped his hands on his blue-jean shorts.

"What's with this fuckin' psycho?" the old man asked.

David's only reply: "Moloch."

David's knees were weak and he was dizzy as that name buzzed through his head like a swarm of angry hornets. What the hell was going on around here? What kind of screwed-up town had Kate dragged their family into?

And why did that name—Moloch—*keep popping up every time he turned around?*

On the other side of the house, someone knocked urgently and a muffled voice called out from behind the front door: "David? Are you there? It's Joel. Open the door, man!"

CHAPTER 41

Joel shot a nervous glance toward the big redheaded deputy sheriff standing beside him as soon as David opened the door.

"David, this is, um, Deputy Keenan," he said.

David couldn't help but notice how Joel seemed obviously bothered by something as he introduced the man without making eye-contact with the deputy.

"Glad to meet you, Deputy," David said.

The deputy nodded, shook David's hand, but smiling seemed to be a habit this man had not been born with. At least as far as David could tell.

"And this is..." Joel trailed off. "I'm sorry...?"

George stuck out his hand. "George. George Heatherly."

Keenan quickly shook George's hand, and then he got down to business.

"What seems to be the problem, Mr. Little?" the deputy asked, stepping into the foyer of the house. He glanced around the interior of the Little home as he came in. His no-nonsense expression seemed chiseled from stone. "I got a call about an attempted kidnapping?"

David told Deputy Keenan about the night's events. If it hadn't been for George Heatherly, he explained, that sick sonofabitch might have Becca even now.

"You're new in town, aren't you, Mr. Little?" the deputy asked.

"Um, that's right," David said, not understanding what that had to do with anything. He led the other men through the house, down the hallway toward the bathroom. "We just moved to Morganville a couple months ago, from New York."

Change jingled in the deputy's pockets and his shiny gun-belt made low squeaking noises as he walked. When they passed Becca, who still slept soundly on the sofa, Keenan glanced down at the child but did not stop.

"Poor little angel, I can't begin to imagine how terrified you were," Joel said, taking a second to lean down and kiss his niece on the cheek, but then he followed the other men through the house without another word.

"Here's the crazy bastard," George said, gesturing for Deputy Keenan to enter the bathroom ahead of them.

Keenan said nothing. He entered the bathroom.

And closed the door behind him.

George stared at David, and both men frowned. *Why did he close the door?*

"I'm so sorry, David," Joel whispered, biting at his fingernails. "I feel like if I hadn't been in such a hurry to answer that call..."

"It's not your fault, Joel," David replied.

"But if I had waited in the house until you got here..."

"Stop, Joel. I told you, it's not your fault."

"I couldn't live with myself if anything happened to Becca."

George Heatherly knocked twice on the bathroom door. "Uh, Deputy? Everything okay in there?"

"I guess you haven't heard yet, with everything else going on," Joel whispered, standing close to David in the hallway.

"What?"

"There was an accident. Michael's...Michael's dead." Joel's voice grew moist as he spoke, but he fought back the tears. He sniffled once, feeling as though he had cried all he could cry tonight.

"No," David said. "I hadn't heard." He turned to Joel, and Joel was surprised to see genuine sincerity in his brother-in-law's face as he said, "Damn, Joel, I'm sorry to hear that. When did it happen?"

"Several hours ago."

"Jesus. Are you okay?"

"I think so. For now."

"Does Kate know?" David asked.

"Not yet. I should call her."

"I'm sure she'd want to know."

"Do you mind—"

David gestured toward the kitchen, where he had left the cordless phone earlier. "Help yourself. She's in Room 311."

Joel nodded and moved through the hallway past George Heatherly, giving the older man a polite nod as he did so.

"Everything okay?" George asked David.

"I don't know anymore," David replied, his face pained.

"Who is Michael?" the old man whispered.

David cleared his throat. "Joel's, er, boyfriend."

"Ah." George seemed unfazed. He glanced toward the kitchen, but then back to the bathroom door before them.

"Shit, man," David said. "Do you ever feel as if the whole fucking world is coming apart around you?"

"Too bad we haven't had the chance to chat under different circumstances," George said, with a dry little laugh. "Remind me, this is all over, I'll spring for a couple cases of Michelob. We'll get shit-faced one night."

"Sounds like a plan."

Neither man said anything for a few long minutes.

"Jesus Christ," George said, after Deputy Keenan still had not exited the bathroom seven or eight minutes later. "What's he doing in there, givin' the guy a bath?"

He knocked on the door several times fast. "Deputy? Everything okay in there?"

In the bathroom, they heard a gentle sighing noise. Not unlike the sound of someone quietly reaching orgasm. Whether the sound came from the man in the bathtub or the deputy, neither George nor David could tell. They stared at one another, bewildered.

And then, at last, the bathroom door opened.

Deputy Keenan came out, his face a bright red mask of anger. His gun was drawn.

"Deputy—" George said with a start.

"Is something wrong?" David said.

"Damn right it is," said the burly deputy. "Where do you two get off?"

"I don't understand," said George.

"You got some nerve picking on a man who just lost his son."

"I don't understand," said David. "What do you mean?"

"Fred Dawson's got problems," the deputy said, lowering his voice a bit. "I'll give you that." He glared at David, and David had no choice but to look away beneath his furious glare. "But you would too, if your kid just died. Jesus. What's your fucking problem?"

"What the hell are you talking about?" George asked.

"Shut your mouth," Keenan snarled, pointing a fat finger in the old man's face. "You listen to me. Fred Dawson lost his only son less than a month ago. He drinks too much, yes. And maybe sometimes the guy tends to run off at the mouth a little. But that doesn't give you the right to lay your filthy hands on him." He stared at David, his nostrils flaring with anger. "This may be the way they do things in New York City, buddy, but we don't stand for vigilantes in Morganville."

"Vigilantes? What are you—"

Deputy Keenan turned then, allowing the men to see what lay behind him in the bathtub. George and David both gasped, shaking their heads as their eyes fell upon the impossible scene in there.

"No fuckin' way," said George.

David's jaw dropped. "That can't be."

Fred Dawson still lay in David's bathtub, but he looked quite different from the last time they had seen him. Now Dawson looked as if someone had battered him within an inch of his life. He was unconscious, his face cracked and bloody, covered with ugly purple bruises and thick pink welts. One of his eyes was swollen shut, and a thick gash hung open in his forehead as if someone had sliced him there with a knife. He only vaguely resembled the man they had captured earlier. Thick spatters of dark blood speckled the porcelain all around him.

"That can't be," David said. George's single punch to Dawson's nose, he knew, had certainly not been responsible for *that*.

"Turn around," Deputy Keenan told them. "Against the wall."

"What the hell are you—"

In one swift movement, Keenan twisted George's arm behind him, slammed the old man against the wall. George hissed through his teeth, but did not fight him.

"What the hell is going on?" David cried.

"You're both under arrest. You too, against the wall. Now."

"For *what?*" David said.

"Assault and battery," said the deputy. "Now shut up."

Keenan reached behind his back then, brought out two sets of handcuffs.

"This is bullshit!" David spat. "He wasn't like that when we left him!"

"Shut the fuck up!" Keenan screamed in David's ear. He brought up the gun, and David could feel the hard tip of its barrel at the nape of his neck. Its touch was strangely warm, like something alive. "I guess you expect me to believe he did that to himself."

"Okay, okay," David said. "Easy..."

"You both have the right to remain silent. *Moloch.* Anything you say can and will be used against you in a court of law. You have the right to an attorney. If you cannot afford an attorney, one will be appointed for you. *Mohh-loch.* Do you understand your rights as I have explained them to you?"

"Oh, my God," David said. "OhmyGodohmyGod."

Joel stood in the kitchen doorway, watching with wide eyes. The cordless phone was in his hands.

"What's going on?" he shouted. "What did you do, David?"

David could faintly hear Kate's voice on the phone, tinny and distant: "David? Who's there? Joel? What's going on?"

"Please, Joel, tell her what's happening," David shouted over his shoulder as Deputy Keenan led him and George down the hall, toward the front door. He glanced at Becca on the couch. She stirred as they passed, but did not wake. "And watch Becca for me. Please!"

"I will, David. Don't worry. We'll get you out of this."

"This is horseshit!" George Heatherly shouted once they were out the front door.

Keenan shoved him, and the old man nearly fell.

"Get in the fucking car," said the deputy. "Now."

They stumbled across the yard beneath his prodding, and when they reached the patrol car Keenan pushed first George's head down and then David's, forcing them roughly into the backseat.

"*Moloch*," said the deputy then, one last time, before slamming the door in David's face.

"Fuck!" David shouted, struggling to no avail within the cuffs at his wrists. He kicked the seat in front of him. *"Fuck!"*

Deputy Keenan slammed his door. But he did not pull away from the curb just yet.

Before the patrol car took off, he turned toward the men in the backseat, behind the steel cage.

His eyes seemed to glisten. He smiled at them.

CHAPTER 42

The patrol car cruised into the town common like a sleek white beast stalking the night. No siren, no lights. Just the steady purr of tires upon asphalt.

David noticed after a few minutes that the fucker hadn't even turned on his headlights. As if he could see in the dark and didn't need them.

The clock on the dashboard read 4:44. Almost dawn. David shook his head, gnashed his teeth, wondered when he would ever get back to Kate and little Christopher.

"So I'm over at Martha Simms' place earlier tonight, right?" George Heatherly said suddenly, but under his breath, so low only David could hear him. His tone was conspiratorial, but tinged with fear. "Before all this shit happened."

David whispered, "Go on."

"She's always loved my broccoli casserole, so I fixed her up a batch. Figured it was the least I could do since I haven't spoken with her since Randall's funeral."

David nodded, wondered where George was going with this.

"So I knock on the door. Several times. But no one answers. I know she's home, 'cause the Cadillac's out front."

David listened intently as his friend spoke, but he had a bad feeling about where this story was going. He didn't know *how* he knew, it just seemed reasonable that George's story would not have a happy ending after everything else that had happened tonight.

"I knock a few more times. She never comes to the door. I call out her name. Nothing."

"What are you two talking about back there?" Deputy Keenan barked, staring at them in the rearview mirror.

"Nothing," said David.

"He doesn't like secrets," Keenan insisted.

George never missed a beat: "Tell 'him' I said 'bite me.'"

David couldn't help it. He laughed at that, in spite of everything he had been through. It felt good. Just to laugh.

"Keep runnin' that mouth, old-timer," growled the deputy. "*Moloch.*"

"So what happened with Simms' widow?" David asked softly, distracting Heatherly's attention from pissing off Deputy Keenan any more than he already had. He winced, shifted in his seat. The cuffs on his wrists were starting to chafe him.

"I hear something through the door," George continued. "Swear to God, it sounds like somebody dying. Moans and groans, shit like that. Either that, or somebody fucking their brains out."

"That's weird. Mrs. Simms?"

"Yeah. I try the door. It's unlocked, so I go in. Not something I'd normally do, of course, but my spider sense was tinglin'."

George leaned over closer to David as he went on, his voice going lower.

"Martha's sitting in the living room, right? Her back's to me. She doesn't answer me when I say her name, just keeps moaning and groaning like somebody's throwin' some major dick her way. I walk around her, and you'll never guess what she's doing."

David shook his head.

"She's got her skirt pulled up, and she's masturbating like crazy. To a picture of her husband."

"How pitiful," David said.

"To hell with 'pitiful.' It was fucking creepy, what it was."

"She must really miss him."

"I'm sure. But you haven't heard the least of it. This photo of the fire chief, it's their wedding picture. She's taken a Magic Marker to it. Scribbled all over it—you know, like kids draw devil-horns and missing teeth on a picture of somebody they don't like?"

"Right."

"Except Martha's drawn this long black beard all over Randall's face, this stringy thing that goes all the way down to the bottom of the picture, then over the bottom of the frame, too. Where that stopped, she even kept drawing that beard all the way across the carpet, right up to her crotch."

David's stomach churned. "What's that all about?"

"I don't know," George said. "There's not a whole helluva lot that scares me, man, but that was the most bizarre fucking thing I've ever seen. I left without saying another word, and I don't think she ever knew

I was even there."

Several minutes later, the patrol car stopped again.

George and David peered out the window and were surprised to find that Keenan had pulled the car alongside the curb in front of Morganville First Baptist.

The interchangeable black letters on the sign out front pronounced the place was CLOSED.

David stared at that, his mouth hanging open.

"What are we doing here?" George said, and even he was not quite sure if his question was directed toward David, Deputy Keenan or no one in particular.

Deputy Keenan said nothing. He just sat there in the front seat, staring at the church.

He let out a little sigh.

At least five minutes passed, and Deputy Keenan continued to sit there. Staring at the church.

"What's going on?" David said.

"*Moloch.*"

David Little and George Heatherly stared at one another, bewildered.

"Moloch," Keenan said again, and this time it was a strained sort of sound. As if he might start crying any moment. He continued to stare at the church, almost longingly, and now seemed completely unaware of the two men in his custody.

Finally, he started up the car. Headed once more toward the station, as if nothing had happened.

"Since when is a church *closed?*" George whispered. More than ever, David thought the retired Marine's pale flesh appeared ghost-like beneath the blanket of night all around them. The tattoos on his forearms resembled dark scabs.

David shuddered as the church grew small behind them.

CHAPTER 43

Keenan made yet another stop on their way to the station, this time in front of a house at the corner of Cangro and Tenth Street.

David glanced over at George. The old man shrugged.

The house Keenan parked the car in front of was small—one-story, white brick. The soft blue glow of a television set burned in one window. Otherwise, the house was dark. A single car was parked in the blacktopped driveway, a Ford Taurus. PROUD PARENT OF AN HONOR-ROLL STUDENT boasted one of its bumper stickers; the other: D.A.R.E. TO KEEP KIDS OFF DRUGS. Against one side of the house sat a fancy Charbroil grill; nearby, a child's bicycle lay abandoned in the front yard like lazy metal dogs. Beneath the patrol car's headlights, the bicycle's red and white reflectors seemed to wink at the men in the backseat as they stared at the place, perplexed.

Deputy Keenan turned to George and David, said in a low monotone, "I'll be back. This will only take a minute."

His door opened.

"Take your time," George Heatherly replied. "We'll wait right here."

Deputy Keenan reached beneath the dash then, and brought up the largest shotgun David had ever seen. He climbed from the patrol car, his face expressionless.

A thin rivulet of sweat tickled its way down David's left temple as he watched Keenan walk stiffly around the front of the patrol car.

Across the lawn.

Toward the house.

He ratcheted the pump-action as he stepped onto the porch.

"I don't like this, David," said George. "I don't like this at all."

The two men watched the house, saying nothing for the next few seconds. George swallowed, and the sound was very loud in the quiet confines of the patrol car.

The front door was unlocked. Keenan stepped inside the house. He was nowhere to be seen now.

David and George both jumped when they heard a shotgun blast boom in the night. From where they sat, they could see the muzzle flash of the weapon, a split-second strobe-effect through the window as if someone had turned the lights on and then back off again just as quickly.

"Jesus Christ," said George. "Jesus H. Christ."

"He killed them. Oh, my God, George..."

Less than a minute later, two more gunshots rang out in the night. David was quite sure he could feel the vibrations of those reports in his ass, in the seat beneath him. He stared off into space, looking at nothing in particular. This had to be a nightmare. It couldn't be happening.

"David," George said, and David's attention shot back to the old man. George nodded toward the front of the patrol car. "Look."

David gasped.

He barely even noticed that Deputy Keenan had come out of the house now and was walking zombie-like back to the patrol car, when he saw the name on that mailbox at the curb.

The name of the family who lived here. The name of the family Hank Keenan had just slaughtered in cold blood, in the name of someone—or something—called Moloch.

In stylish calligraphic letters, the word was underlined by a painting of a single thorny rose: KEENAN.

CHAPTER 44

"But we didn't *do* anything!" David shouted at the man behind the desk. "That motherfucker tried to kidnap my daughter!"

"Watch your mouth, sir," said the deputy who had fingerprinted them and filed the report at Keenan's request. He was a skinny middle-aged man with salt-and-pepper hair and a face stippled with faint acne scars. His fingers were permanently stained blotter-ink-black and nicotine-yellow. His gold nametag read HARWOOD. "I'm a church-goin' man, don't appreciate profanity."

"This is such bullshit."

"Sir—"

"Look," said George Heatherly. He tilted his head toward Deputy Keenan, who had just walked out of Sheriff Guice's office, passed them without a word, and headed in the back where the cells were located. Keenan seemed to exist in his own little world now, as if after bringing them in he had become oblivious to their presence altogether. "You're arresting the wrong men here. Do you understand what we're trying to tell you? That psycho just killed his whole family."

"And how do you know that, sir?" asked Deputy Harwood.

"We were there."

"You saw this with your own eyes?"

"We heard it," David said, and George explained, "We saw the muzzle flashes through the window."

Harwood stared at them, and it was obvious from the expression on the man's face that he believed their story about as much as he bought their claim of having nothing to do with this assault-and-battery charge on which Hank had hauled them in.

"We'll send a man out there," Harwood said once Deputy Keenan was out of earshot. "But let me tell you something. Hank is one of the Department's best. He's a respected man in this town. A member of the Fire Department, president of Morgan County's Dads Against Domestic Violence chapter. Not to mention a lifelong friend of the sheriff. If this is some kinda sick joke, you better believe you two are gonna regret it."

"It's not a joke," said David.

"He killed them," said George.

"Fine." Harwood came around the counter. "Now come with me."

"I wanna talk to Sheriff Guice," George demanded. "He'll listen to what we have to say."

"In due time. Walk."

The jail stank of stale piss and sweat. Attached to the rear wing of the station, there were only eight cells in the place, four on each side of the corridor. The walls were an ugly lime green. Each cell held a single lidless toilet and a dirty cot. At present, the facility was empty of prisoners, save for David and George. Their footsteps echoed through the corridor like the ghosts of past inmates tapping out bored rhythms on the jailhouse walls.

"I can't believe this is happening," David groaned.

"We'll make it," George said. "Hang in there."

Deputy Harwood ushered them into a cell together, locking the heavy iron door behind them. When it clanged shut, the resulting sound seemed so harsh, so final, it brought tears to David's eyes.

"We get a phone call, right?" David asked as the deputy removed their cuffs through the cell bars.

"Sit tight," Harwood replied. "We'll get to that soon."

David shook his head, gazed at his surroundings. He tried to breathe through his mouth as the stench of the jailhouse assaulted him like a heavy fog. He rubbed at his wrists, wincing, but it felt good to have his hands free at last.

"This sucks."

"What time does the maid drop by?" George asked Harwood as the deputy turned to leave.

"Funny," Harwood said. But then the deputy stopped in his tracks as soon as the word was out of his mouth. He looked toward the rear of the jail, to the end of the corridor between the cells.

"Hank?"

All three men had seen Keenan walk back this way, when David and George were being booked, but now he was nowhere to be seen.

"Where'd you go, man?"

David joined George at the bars now, holding onto the cold steel as he tried to peer out toward the rear of the jail. He had already begun to feel like an old pro at this. All he needed was a mirror to hold through the bars, and the image would be complete. He sighed.

Harwood left his prisoners standing there and headed down the corridor at an urgent trot.

"Hank?"

George and David glanced at one another, puzzled.

Harwood's jaw dropped.

The heavy steel door at the back of the jailhouse stood open. But the only way to unlock that door—from either side—was with a succession of keys on a heavy iron ring that stayed beneath the desk out front. And then there were the multiple deadbolts to get past.

"What the...?" Harwood began, but his voice trailed off.

Birds chirped in the back alley behind the jail. A hint of early-morning sunlight washed across the steps. Somewhere in the distance the *beep-beep-beep* of a reversing garbage truck wafted in with the breeze like a muted, insufficient alarm indicating that the back door had been breached.

But no Hank Keenan.

Just that heavy metal door, standing wide open.

And the khaki puddle of Keenan's uniform, lying there abandoned in the threshold.

HE'S COMING had been scratched into the wall above the cell's toilet in long, narrow letters. Below that, in pencil: EAT SHIT, followed by a crude drawing of what looked like a mutated anus with teeth.

David sighed, looked away from the scrawled memos left by prisoners before him. He tilted his head to one side, and his neck made a popping noise. He stretched. Groaned. Rubbed some more at his raw, red wrists.

"What the hell are we supposed to do now?"

"This whole goddamn town's going to hell in a hand basket," George said.

"No kidding," David said. "It's like everybody's lost their fucking mind."

George cleared his throat, walked away from the bars and sat on the dirty cot against the wall. The thing squeaked like something slowly dying beneath his weight.

The old man sighed, rubbed at his temples. He stared at David for a long minute or two, as if debating whether or not he should say whatever he was about to say.

"I don't think I have to tell you that Morganville hasn't been the same since the night Heller Home burned down," the retired Marine finally said.

"I figured as much," David replied.

"I don't mean what you think I mean, David. There's a lot more to it."

"Like what?"

"I'm gonna ask you a question. You may think I'm crazy, and that's fine. All I ask is, don't insult me by laughing in my face."

David glanced down at the dirty cement floor before plopping down there, his back against the wall. "Far be it from me to insult an ex-Marine."

George didn't laugh. His mind seemed preoccupied with much darker thoughts.

David said, "So? Shoot."

"Do you believe in demons?"

David blinked several times fast.

"I'm serious," said George. "You know, like in the Bible, principalities, powers of darkness. Shit like that."

David said, "I don't read the Bible much."

"Humor me, then."

"Okay," David said. "No. I don't think I do. Believe in demons."

"Why not?"

David shrugged. "I'm not even one hundred percent sure I believe in God, George. Much less devils and demons."

"Fair enough."

"I do believe in evil," David said. "But not Evil with a capital 'E.' I think it exists, but in the heart of man. I don't believe there are invisible forces out there, things with horns and forked tongues, things that can possess us like something out of *The Exorcist*." David gave a nervous little laugh at that, but otherwise went on without pausing. "I believe it's in here." He jabbed a thumb into his own chest. "Inherent. The 'heart of darkness' and all that."

George Heatherly's eyebrows rose. He nodded slowly, seemed to be in deep thought for the next few seconds.

"Good," he said finally. "Because I don't think I believe in demons either."

David almost laughed. George Heatherly was one in a million, no doubt about that. "Then why did you ask?"

George sounded very tired, as if he could lie down to sleep right there on that dirty cot and sleep forever. "I don't know. I'm just an old

175

fool, I guess, growin' senile before my time."

"What are you getting at, George?" David said.

"Shit, man...I don't know why I even brought it up. There just seems to be so much about this town that I don't understand anymore."

"Like what?"

"I used to think I knew this place. It was home. I was born and raised in Morganville, lived here all my life except for my stint in the Corps. My kids grew up, moved away. My daughter, Janie, when she got married, her and her husband wanted me to come with 'em, out to California. I *love* California, David—spent several years there when I was with the Corps—but I never *wanted* to live anywhere else but here. In Morganville. At least, I could say that at one time. But these days, I find myself thinking about leaving more and more. I don't like it here. Haven't for quite a while."

"Since Heller Home burned down," said David.

"That was the start of it all, yes."

"Now I'm going to ask *you* a question," David said.

"Knock yourself out."

David took a deep breath, said, "What do you know about this... Moloch?"

George stared at him, his expression tight.

"You've heard that word before, haven't you, George?"

George just kept staring at him, his old-man eyes so sad and oddly yellow.

"What does it mean?" David said. "Is it a name? Who is he? *What* is he?"

George still said nothing.

"He did something to that man back there, at my house, didn't he?" David asked. "Whatever this Moloch is, he did something to that deputy."

George bit his lower lip, bowed his head. "You think the guy was... possessed, somehow?"

"Jesus Christ, that sounds so crazy," David said. "We told one another, not two minutes ago, that we didn't believe in shit like that."

"Yes," George said. "We did."

"But there's something going on."

"Yes."

"And as desperately as I try to deny it, I don't think it's anything that has a logical, scientific explanation."

"I think you're right."

"Fuck, man, what the hell are we saying?" David said. "We sound like we're stuck in a bad horror movie."

David winced as his foot began to fall asleep. He stood, never taking his eyes off his friend.

"Talk to me, George. This Moloch I keep hearing about—who is he?"

Finally the retired Marine looked up and David nearly gasped when he saw the shiny tear that rolled down the old man's wrinkled cheek.

"You want to know who he is?" George asked. "I'll tell you what I know. Which ain't a whole helluva lot. Not that it matters anyway, though. 'Cause it's not gonna do us a damn bit of good..."

CHAPTER 45

Sheriff Guice stopped at the house on the corner of Cangro Boulevard and Tenth Street and quickly exited his patrol car. He didn't expect to find anything, it was his job to check it out anyway.

Damn, what a night. First the accident out at the old Heller Home property, the casualty that turned out to be Joel Rohrig's gay lover, then the thing at that new family's house. He'd been forced to give the attempted kidnapping call to Hank. And now this, something about Hank's family being murdered in the middle of the night?

And supposedly at the hands of Keenan himself?

Impossible. Surely he had misunderstood Al Harwood on the patrol car's squawking radio.

Couldn't be.

Still, he had to check it out.

Guice saw nothing out of the ordinary yet. The property was dark, quiet. The eerie blue glow of a television set was visible through the bay window at the front of the home. Someone was up. Probably Marjorie, Sam assumed, getting ready for her job at the Bonworth factory over in Hendersonville.

Guice cleared his throat, took the steps onto Keenan's porch in two big strides, and wondered what he would say to Hank's wife when she opened the door. He sure as hell didn't want to scare her. And God knew the sheriff standing on your doorstep at five o'clock in the morning qualified as one of those "no-way-it-can-be-good-news" moments.

Guice flinched as the door swung inward beneath his knock.

Ah, shit.

The tinny sound of canned sitcom laughter on the television filled his ears. Otherwise, the house was silent.

Guice unholstered his .357, swallowed, and stepped through the threshold as quietly as possible, his heart pounding in his chest.

He crossed himself as he stepped through the foyer of the Keenan home. His mouth was dry, coated with the metallic taste of his own fear.

No, not fear, he realized. Not *only* fear.

The unmistakable odor of blood. Lots of it.

He turned the corner into the Keenans' living room, and found he was correct.

CHAPTER 46

George told David about Moloch, what little he knew about that word, anyway, which for the most part consisted of news reports and town rumors detailing Bobby Briggs' fascination with variations on that word. How he had scribbled it on his arms during his trial.

"Is this all because of him?" David asked.

"I think so. For the most part."

"What was the little fucker into? Satanism? Devil worship?"

"Your guess is as good as mine, David."

David sighed, shook his head. "Jesus Christ. This gets weirder and weirder all the time. What do you think he is, George? I mean, what do you *really* think Moloch is?"

"I don't know what he is," George replied, "I don't know where he came from, or why he's here in Morganville, but I damn well believe he's real."

"Is he...a demon?"

"I didn't say that." George bit at his lower lip. "Hell, I don't know, David. You and I both agreed that we don't believe in such silliness. But everything that's happened in this town...it makes me question everything I've ever believed. *Something* is out there...*something* is responsible for the deaths. All the craziness. I just don't know what."

"Do you think we can stop him? Because I'll help you, whatever you need."

"You want to be a hero, do you, David?"

"No, but..."

"Well, our first step is to get the hell out of here. There ain't a damn thing we can do in this dump. Let's get home—then, we'll see what happens."

Ten minutes later, Sheriff Guice arrived at the station. He was short of breath, his forehead stippled with droplets of sweat.

"He killed them, Frank." His eyes were wide and wild. "Jesus God... he killed them all."

"Sir?"

"They were telling the truth. Hank killed his whole family. With a shotgun."

"Oh, Lord, no."

"I want an APB out on Hank. And I want it yesterday."

"Yes, sir."

"And let those two out."

"Sir?" Al Harwood said again, as if it was the only word he knew.

"You heard me. Let those two gentlemen out. Now. I need them. I need Little's brother-in-law. We've got three bodies back at Hank Keenan's house, and two of them are children."

"Dear God," said Deputy Harwood, and his face went as white as the top of his desk.

"I need you to fill me in on everything that happened tonight," said Sheriff Guice as he slid into the front seat of his patrol car.

David and George got in the back, slammed their doors.

"What good would it do?" David said. "Everyone thinks *we're* the criminals here."

"I don't," said Guice. "I believe you. I saw the evidence myself."

When neither David nor George said anything for several minutes, the sheriff said, "Look, I saw a man earlier tonight who looked like his cock had been *chewed off*, for Chrissake. Not to mention the bodies of my best friend's family, dead at the hands of my best friend. There's very little you could say that I *wouldn't* believe right now."

David's stomach churned. He looked ill. He glanced toward George, and the old Marine's expression mirrored his own.

"I'm all ears," Guice said.

"Okay." David cleared his throat and proceeded to explain to Sheriff Guice everything that had happened since he first received Joel's call— six hours ago, *had it really been that long?*—at the hospital. He told him all about Fred Dawson, and how they had subdued him until the deputy arrived, and how Keenan had treated them after closing the door and spending several minutes alone with the man in the Santa Claus suit. David held nothing back. Perhaps, he thought, Sheriff Sam Guice might turn out to be their only hope through this whole mess. God knew they needed someone who might believe their insane story, who would listen without committing them to the sanitarium in Fleetwood before they were halfway finished.

"I see," Sheriff Guice said several times, but for the most part he allowed David to speak without interruption. He kept his eyes on the road as he drove out of Morganville's business district, only glancing in the rearview mirror every couple of minutes to assure David that he was listening.

"And then he took off," David concluded. "We don't even know if someone's picked up the man in my bathtub yet."

"Keenan never called for backup," Guice said.

"Jesus," said David. "My daughter's in the house with him."

At that, Sheriff Guice accelerated, zooming by the houses of Morganville that were just now beginning to show signs of life beneath the rising sun. So many families, waking to begin their day, oblivious to David and George's dilemma.

"What's the deal with the church?" Sheriff Guice asked. "You said he just stopped, stared at it?"

"Yeah," David replied. "For like ten minutes. It was...damn creepy, is what it was."

Guice nodded, but his expression betrayed nothing as he drove on.

"Did you know the church is closed?" George asked.

Guice glanced at the older man in the rearview mirror, nodded. "Been meaning to check that out. Rumor is Reverend Rhodes has skipped town."

A chill shot down David's spine as they passed the church. Somehow he knew, though he did not know *how* he knew, that Rhodes had not "skipped town." No, the truth was much more sinister than that.

"Honeysuckle Lane, right?" Guice glanced back at David.

"We're in the cul-de-sac."

"My God, I've known Hank Keenan my whole life," mumbled the sheriff after several more minutes of awkward silence. He seemed to speak more to himself, however, than the two men in the car with him. "We graduated together, me and Marjorie. Class of '81. They used to come over for cookouts in the summer. The guy was Nathan's godfather, for Chrissake..."

Guice made a little choking sound in the back of his throat.

"Nathan?"

"My son," explained the sheriff. "He used to call him 'Uncle Hank,' loved that man like he was blood. How am I supposed to tell a ten-year-old his Uncle Hank just blew away his whole fucking family?"

David hadn't a clue what caused him to ask it, but it was out of his mouth before he even realized he'd said it: "Sheriff, do you know anything about this...*Moloch?*"

"What's that?" Guice said.

"Moloch."

"Never heard of it."

"There was the thing at the Briggs trial," George said, jogging the sheriff's memory. "Remember?"

"Oh, right," Sheriff Guice said. "That gibberish he wrote on his hands. Kid was so whacked out on drugs I don't think he even knew what he was on trial for."

"We think there was more to it than that," George said, glancing at David.

David nodded, as if to say: *Go ahead, tell him.*

And George would have done exactly that, but now they were pulling up in front of David's house, so it would have to wait.

Sheriff Guice entered the Littles' house with his gun drawn, and walked as stealthily as his bulk would allow toward the bathroom. Joel sat on the sofa, asking questions with his eyes, but David and George both shook their heads, indicating that he should remain quiet.

Becca was awake now. She sat on the floor, playing with her dolls. But the little girl ruined whatever element of surprise the sheriff had the instant she saw her father. She ran for him, squealing, "Daddy!" and jumped into his arms.

Sheriff Guice winced, shot a glance toward David as he eased toward the bathroom with his back against the wall. He swung into the room, gun extended outward.

"Can we go see Mommy now?" Becca asked.

David placed one finger in front of his lips, shushed her.

"He's gone," said Sheriff Guice from the hallway. "Shit."

"Keenan came back," Joel said. He looked at David. "About thirty minutes after you left. He took the man in the tub with him."

"You let the crazy bastard back in the house?" George asked.

"I didn't know what to do! Somebody knocked, I asked who it was, and he said 'Sheriff's Department.' So I opened the door. Guy didn't have a stitch on. It was the weirdest damn thing."

Sheriff Guice stared at him. David and George both gave the sheriff a look that seemed to say *we told you so.*

Guice covered his mouth with one trembling hand.

"He was naked, Daddy," Becca giggled.

David held his daughter tighter than ever, smoothed down her dirty blond hair. "Shh, baby. Shh."

"Joel," Sheriff Guice said, "I know this is a bad time, and you've got a lot going on right now, but I need you over at Keenan's place. 17 Cangro Boulevard. Multiple homicide."

"Oh, no," said Joel. "What happened?"

"There's no time for that now. Just get over there, please. A couple of my men are already on the scene, but I'll need you to do your thing."

Joel felt so tired, as if he might drop any moment. The bags under his eyes resembled smudges of soot and ash, like some sort of bizarre tribal paint. He sighed. "I'm on it, Sheriff."

"He was naked, Daddy," Becca whispered again, into her father's ear. Another giggle. To David, at that particular moment—despite the circumstances—it was the sweetest sound in the world.

CHAPTER 47

From the *Morganville Daily Register*, Jan. 5:

LOCAL FAMILY MURDERED
Suspect "On the Run," Says Sheriff

Authorities are searching for the lead suspect in a triple homicide that occurred this past week-end.

Early Sunday morning, Marjorie Keenan, 38, and her two children, Nathaniel, 10, and Nora, 4, were found dead in their home, the victims of multiple gunshot wounds.

The lone suspect in the case is Henry "Hank" Keenan, 37, of 17 Cangro Boulevard. Henry Keenan is the husband and father to the victims.

"It's tragic, and hard to believe that a father could do such a thing," said Sheriff Sam Guice. "However, at this time I have no option but to believe that Mr. Keenan is responsible for the deaths of his family."

Henry Keenan is a senior deputy of the Morganville Sheriff's Department, a volunteer member of the Morganville Fire Department, as well as president of the local chapter of Dads Against Domestic Violence. He has not been seen since the night of the murders.

The Morgan County Sheriff's Department welcomes any information leading to the suspect's arrest. Anonymity is guaranteed, says Guice, and he urges anyone with knowledge of Keenan's whereabouts to call 555-6795.

CHAPTER 48

Inside the dark walls of Morganville's First Baptist Church, Reverend Darryl Rhodes wept. It seemed that was all he ever did these days, cry. His eyes were red and raw, shot through with wormy veins, and when he rubbed at them he wailed in agony.

Alas, his tears were born not in remembrance of a past life that he would never know again, a life that seemed like little more than some foggy, half-remembered dream now...

These were tears of awe. And wonder.

Reverend Rhodes had been instructed to build.

Exactly *what* he was to build, he did not know. Yet.

Rhodes only knew that Moloch had commanded it.

And so it would be done.

The others were here now.

Together, they obeyed. Together, they began to build.

CHAPTER 49

Two days after her husband and George Heatherly were released from jail and subsequently cleared of all charges against them, Kate Little returned home from Cecil R. Purdy hospital.

David and Kate didn't talk about what happened, at least not where their daughter could hear. David explained to Becca the morning after their arrest that he had done nothing wrong, that he had been hauled off to jail because of someone else's mistake, and for the most part his daughter seemed to buy it.

Despite their ordeal the night Christopher was born, David and Kate could not stop smiling every time they looked at their new son. David still felt more than a little edgy since that night, always sensing he should be on the lookout for a psycho in a Santa suit, and he had lost quite a bit of sleep over it, but now he pushed all of that to the back of his mind as they headed home. He felt as if God had given him the responsibility of chauffeuring an angel as he drove his family home, as if everyone in town knew the 4Runner carried royalty through Morganville's streets. Temporarily, at least, David was able to forget everything that had happened the past few days. His worries were gone, all thoughts of darkness and—how silly it sounded now, in the bright light of a new day—*demons* disappeared every time he gazed upon his beautiful family in the 4Runner's rearview mirror.

Meanwhile, Becca fell into what David called "big sister mode" with a dedication like nothing he or Kate had ever seen from their daughter. All the way home from the hospital, she could not keep her hands off baby Christopher, a constant murmur filling the back seat as she whispered into her little brother's ear, her eyes wide with wonder as she kissed him on his fat cheeks or played with his tiny fingers or bent over his car-seat to squeeze him so tightly that Kate had to warn her to be careful.

Halfway on their trip home from the hospital, David slowed the car, and Becca saw her Daddy's brow furrow in the rearview mirror. Like it did when he was concentrating on one of his paintings or thinking hard over the monthly bills at his desk, when he would tell her *not-now-honey-Daddy's-busy.* She sat up, stared through the windshield, but saw nothing out of the ordinary.

The 4Runner slowed.

Kate glanced at David. "What is it?"

"That is so strange," said David.

He brought the vehicle to a stop alongside the curb, ignoring a honk behind him as he did so. He waved whoever it was to go around them.

"Go back to New York!" a youthful voice yelled from a passing yellow Camaro, but neither Kate nor David paid it any mind. David barely even noticed the middle finger sticking out the window in his peripheral vision.

His attention was elsewhere.

The sign on the front door of the First Baptist Church of Morganville revealed it was CLOSED FOR RENOVATIONS, and the message was repeated on the large sign visible from the highway, the one with the interchangeable letters. UNTIL FURTHER NOTICE, added the latter in a smaller font. The church was dark, and the weeds about the property looked to have been ignored for quite some time. A pall of neglect hung over the place like a black cloud.

"Closed?" Kate said. "Since when does a church *close?*"

"Right," said David.

Baby Christopher released a low, bubbly fart from his car-seat then, as if adding his own proverbial two cents to the conversation. Becca said "ewwww," held her nose and giggled like it was the funniest thing she'd ever heard.

David pulled into traffic again and headed toward home, new questions forming in his mind every second.

CHAPTER 50

Michael Morris's funeral came and went, and attending the services proved to be one of the hardest things Kate Little had ever done. She held Joel, attempted to console him, but knew there was nothing she could do except be there for him when he needed her most. By the end of the day, her collar was soaking wet from her brother's constant tears, her shoulders and forearms sore from holding him up every time he seemed as if he might collapse upon Michael's grave.

David embraced Joel at the end of the services, told him how very sorry he was for his loss. He assured Joel that he would help him get through this in any way possible, and if there was anything he needed, *ever*, Joel should not hesitate to let him know.

Kate mentioned to David on the way home that she was afraid her little brother might not make it through this, and that scared her more than anything else in the world.

CHAPTER 51

Sheriff Guice pulled into the parking lot of Morganville First Baptist expecting to find nothing, and that was exactly what he got.

For the past ten days, no one had heard anything from Reverend Darryl Rhodes and several members of his congregation were becoming worried. There had been no Sunday services here for the past three weeks. Mavis Ledbetter had been receiving more and more calls regarding the reverend's sudden disappearance and the subsequent closing of his church, and Guice knew he needed to set aside everything else on his agenda in order to deal with this situation.

He exited his patrol car, walked across the parking lot and climbed the steps to the front doors of the church. A stray candy-bar wrapper blew across the concrete in front of him, and Guice thought the sound it made as it flipped and scraped across the mottled stone seemed strangely snake-like. He shivered, unsure if he did so because of the day's cool breeze or the imagery such a thought brought to mind.

The wooden sign nailed at eye-level upon the doors read CLOSED FOR RENOVATIONS, but the explanation ended there. Using black spray-paint, someone had written across that: GO AWAY.

Guice knocked. "Reverend Rhodes? Hello? It's Sheriff Guice. You in there?"

Guice placed his ear to the door, held his breath, and listened for any signs of life inside the church.

Nothing.

He knocked again.

Nothing. Only the hollow sound of his own loud rapping, echoing through the church's empty halls like the building's own off-rhythm heartbeat.

Perhaps that was the weirdest thing of all. The silence. If the church had indeed closed for the purpose of some sort of remodeling, Sam thought, shouldn't he hear the buzz of saws inside, the heavy pounding of hammers against nails? Perhaps the muffled shouts of a stressed-out Reverend Rhodes as he supervised the project?

But the sheriff heard nothing. Not the slightest creak, the faintest footstep. It was as if the church had been closed for years. As if the building had never been occupied at all.

"Reverend? Hello? I need to talk to you. Folks are worried."

Guice frowned, descended the steps, and walked through the high grass that had usurped the property for the past few weeks. The weeds swished against his legs like the thin green fingers of children desperate for his attention as he ventured toward the rear of the building.

He tried peering through the stained-glass windows for any sight of Reverend Rhodes. For anybody. The sad face of Jesus looked down upon the sheriff as he cupped his hands around his eyes to squint through the pool of hot-pink blood at the base of the Savior's cross.

He couldn't see a damned thing.

Guice stood with his hands on his hips as he surveyed the overgrown property.

What the hell was he supposed to do? Technically, Darryl Rhodes owned the church. His father, a good friend of old Sam Guice, Sr., had set it up years ago, building the place from the ground up with the help of several dedicated relatives. Theodore Rhodes had been a loyal man of God, had put everything he owned into opening up his own place of worship when he grew disillusioned with other churches in Morgan County, and what he saw as their all-too-materialistic doctrines. It had been quite the successful venture, this new church, and Darryl Rhodes had continued to expand upon his father's dream long after the old pastor left this world to claim his reward in Heaven.

When all was said and done, Darryl Rhodes did not owe anyone a thing. He was entitled to close up shop, if that was what he wanted to do. Doing so left many loyal Morganville churchgoers confused and perhaps a little lost, of course, but *legally* the man owed them nothing. His only debt was spiritual, Guice supposed.

Still...

The sheriff could not deny the feeling that nagged at the back of his brain like a needle pushing its way through his skull. The sense that something was *not right* here.

He knew he would be forced to get a search warrant before he could enter the church. And what would he tell Judge Kramer?

I have a hunch, *your honor. A bad feeling about this.*

Sure. That would work. Hateful old Vince Kramer would laugh Guice out of his friggin' office, he tried some shit like that.

What it all came down to was, Guice wasn't sure. And there were a million other things he had to deal with. More important things to worry about than a pastor who had probably just skipped town with some young mistress, taking the last couple months of his devoted congregation's offerings with him to blow in Maui or Key West.

Yes, he had more important things to worry about than this.

Matters like the hunt for Hank Keenan, who was still on the loose.

For now, Reverend Rhodes and his church would have to wait.

Guice sighed, turned to leave.

"Is there something I can help you with, Sheriff?" said a voice behind him.

Guice's heart skipped a beat. He pivoted, his hand going to the holster on his belt.

At the corner of the church, Reverend Darryl Rhodes stood half-in and half-out of the threshold of his parsonage. A sick-looking rosebush hid his legs from Guice's view, and the spidery brown vines that climbed the walls of the rectory almost seemed to be a part of the man's body from this angle.

"Are you looking for something?" Rhodes asked. His expression was stern, curious but not quite angry. "I assumed so, the way you were lurking around out here."

The preacher appeared as if he had not taken a bath in months. He wore a gray suit, complete with a red tie and fancy black shoes, but his hands and portions of the suit were smudged with filth. His hair stuck up in greasy spikes. His glasses were covered with a thick layer of dust. Gray stubble lined his jaw like another layer of grime beneath his crooked mouth.

Even from where he stood, Guice could smell the man. Damned if the reverend didn't smell like soot and ash, like something *burning*.

Guice said, "Actually, I, um, I was looking for you, Reverend."

Rhodes said nothing. His stern expression did not change.

Guice looked down at the ground. He suddenly felt awkward as hell and wished he had not come here at all. Let the frigging church rot, for all he cared. Same for Darryl Rhodes.

"There are a lot of people in town, members of your church who haven't seen you in weeks. They're concerned. It's not every day a church closes its doors with no explanation. I just wanted to make sure everything was okay."

"Well," Rhodes said, "as you can see, everything is...okay. I am fine, and it is no one's business but my own that I have chosen to close up this 'House of God.'"

The sheriff frowned. Damned if that last bit hadn't sounded... *sarcastic.* As if the reverend would rather spit the words from his mouth than speak them in that cold, calm way of his. As if those very words— *House of God*—were profane.

"I don't expect you to understand," Rhodes said.

The two men stared at one another for a moment, not speaking. A few feet to Sheriff Guice's left something slithered through the high weeds. Something alive. Guice flinched, took several steps back, in the direction of his patrol car.

"Is there anything else that I can do for you, Sheriff?"

"N-no," Guice stammered. "I don't suppose there is."

"Well then, I have much to do. I must bid you good day."

"Yeah. Okay. You take care, Reverend." Guice took several more steps backward, turned and started to walk back toward his car. He could feel the pastor's creepy eyes burning into the back of his head, knew that the man was watching his every step.

What the hell was wrong with him? Why did that man in the Coke-bottle glasses, with the bushy gray eyebrows, a meek little man whom Sheriff Guice would otherwise find anything *but* intimidating any other day...why in the hell did he make Guice feel as if he were some disobedient child being scolded by an angry schoolmarm?

He didn't know. But he felt it all the same. The guy gave him the fucking *creeps.* Though the day was warm, Sheriff Guice could not deny the ice finger that had trailed down his back each time the supposed man of God had spoken.

Guice shook his head, cursed himself.

He stopped in his tracks and turned back toward the church one last time.

Reverend Rhodes was still standing in the doorway of the parsonage, watching him. The breeze lapped at his greasy hair, forcing it to sway and bob like the living weeds at his feet.

"Actually," Guice said, "there is one more thing you can do for me, Reverend."

Rhodes's eyebrows rose, but he said nothing.

"I don't suppose you've seen my deputy around here, have you?" Guice asked, finding it very hard to meet the preacher's bloodshot gaze. He forced himself to stare into Rhodes's eyes, however, as uncomfortable as such a thing made him, because usually this was the most surefire way to recognize a lie. "Hank Keenan? I've been looking for him."

"No," Reverend Rhodes said. He blinked behind his dusty lenses, and Guice was quite sure this was the first time he had done so the entire time they had spoken. "I haven't."

"He's wanted for questioning," Guice said.

"Is that so?"

"Yeah. I, uh, guess you heard what happened."

"No," Rhodes said, "I didn't."

The pastor brought one hand up then—a hand that trembled slightly, Guice couldn't help but notice—and picked something out from between his thinning strands of dark gray hair. He broke eye-contact with Sheriff Guice only long enough to look at it, whatever he had pulled from his scalp, before popping the wriggling object into his mouth. He swallowed it.

Guice turned and headed quickly back to his patrol car, practically leaping into it, beads of cold sweat breaking out on his forehead. He started it up, and pulled away from the curb. He continued to feel the preacher's blank stare burning into the back of his head as he sped down Shorewood Avenue.

Dammit, he could feel it. Beyond a doubt.

As surely as he knew his own name, Sheriff Sam Guice knew that Reverend Rhodes had lied to him.

Rhodes *was* aware of what had happened, of Hank Keenan's horrible crime against his family.

He knew, too, where Hank was hiding. He just wasn't telling.

"Any word yet, Mavis?" Guice asked as he came through the door of the station.

"Sorry, Sam. Nothing."

"Shit."

"Where do you think he is?" Mavis asked. "Do you think Hank's even alive?"

"I don't know about that," Guice said. "But tell me something, Mavis, how in the hell can a man everyone knows, a man who is such a recognizable face in this community, just disappear and no one has a clue where he is?"

"Good question," Mavis said, but she offered no answer for now.

Guice shook his head, went to the coffee machine in the corner of the station house and poured himself a cup.

"I wouldn't—" Mavis began.

He took a sip.

Spat it back out, into the cup.

"This tastes like shit."

"Doesn't it always?" Mavis laughed.

"I'll never learn."

Guice tossed the cup in the wastebasket beside Mavis' desk. "What are you drinking?"

She showed him the contents of her cup. "Mello-Yello. Want some?" She reached into her desk drawer, pulled out the half-empty bottle.

"No." Guice sounded ill and tired of the small talk, as he sat on a corner of her desk that was free of clutter. He slid aside her TAKE A NUMBER gag (the novelty thing with the hand grenade and the numbers attached to its ring), asked, "You got anything for me this morning?"

"As a matter of fact, I do." Mavis glanced down at one of the many loose scraps of paper and various Post-It notes scattered about her desk in a rainbow-colored blizzard and immediately found what she was looking for. "Here. You got a call about an hour ago. Simon Short, from the paper."

"What'd Short want?"

"He was up at the sanitarium, in Fleetwood. Said he'd just finished talking to a...Dr. Corriher, I believe it was."

"And why does this concern me, Mavis?"

"He said to leave you a message, thought you might like to know..."

Mavis paused for a second, as if to build suspense. Took a deep breath. She always did shit like that. Guice made an impatient circular motion with one hand, urging her to continue.

"Bobby Briggs is dead, Sheriff. He killed himself this morning."

If he hadn't known better, Guice would have thought it was all one big, sick joke. He pressed Mavis for details, deciding there was no pertinent reason he should call Short back for now, and she gladly filled him in on the sordid details. Guice blanched as she did so, as he discovered how Bobby Briggs had taken his own life.

Evidently, the doctors had started allowing Briggs to venture outside once a day, to wander about the grounds as a reward for his general good behavior and cooperation the first few months of his stay at the sanitarium. All had been fine until this morning. Shortly after breakfast, Briggs had sneaked into an old groundskeeper's shed, a small building on the edge of the property that someone had neglected to padlock.

Inside the shed, Bobby Briggs found a full jug of gasoline sitting atop the asylum's new John Deere mower.

He doused himself with its contents and wandered back outside.

"My gift to thee, my gift to thee," he kept saying over and over, according to eyewitnesses at the scene.

"For Moloch!" the boy supposedly screamed, right before he did it.

Somewhere, earlier, he had found a lighter. Probably from some absentminded intern who had left the thing lying around after his or her smoke break.

There, in the sun-dappled courtyard of the Fleetwood sanitarium, as birds chirped merrily and patients laughed and sang and cried and did what patients at insane asylums do, Bobby Briggs lit himself on fire.

And burned.

And burned.

He laughed as he died, or so the witnesses said, laughed as if his agony was nothing short of ecstasy, as if his act of self-immolation was the greatest thing he had ever done in his short life.

Guice sat before his desk and rubbed at his temples. For the past several days, he seemed plagued with a permanent headache. And not your everyday headache, either—this thing felt like knives jabbing into his skull. Even the Excedrin Migraine pills he'd been taking weren't doing a damn thing for his headaches, and those usually worked like gangbusters.

Guice hit his phone's speakerphone button, followed by Mavis's extension. "Mavis."

"Yeah? Whatcha need, Sheriff?"

"Hold my calls, will you? I've got some things I need to catch up on."

"Will do."

"Thanks."

Sam hung up, swiveled around in his chair to look out his window. A panorama of small-town life stretched out before him—across Lincoln Street was the new AutoZone, beside that Lauren's Bicycle Shop and old Dean Schweitzer's bookstore. In the distance Sam could see Frank's Grocery, the store's vast parking lot already filling up with early shoppers. Beside that sat the new Arby's, its big orange cowboy hat like a beacon for the hungry.

There had been a time when Sam Guice could look out this window and feel as if his job as Sheriff of Morgan County *meant* something. A sworn protector, he had sometimes looked at himself as a proud marshall of the old West; with his shiny badge he viewed Morganville as *his* town, and woe unto those varmints who chose to muddy the place up. But it no longer felt as innocent as all that. Not these days. Sam couldn't remember the last time Morganville seemed innocent at all.

Guice stood, went to his file cabinet in the corner and opened it. He thumbed through the various files, found a thick brown folder marked BRIGGS. He pulled it out and returned to his desk.

He spread the file out before him. Inside this particular folder lay everything relating to the Bobby Briggs case that the State Bureau of Investigation had allowed him to keep after it stuck its nose into the investigation. Which wasn't much at all, really. Several sheets of paper, a couple books, some photographs.

Here was a copy of something called *The Anarchist's Cookbook*, which—as far as Guice could tell—had been written for the sole purpose of serving as a sort of training manual for aspiring terrorists. Guice had thumbed through the thin black book several times after he arrested Bobby Briggs, but had never read any of it thoroughly. It seemed to offer little more than recipes for making homemade LSD and marijuana brownies, how to hack into other folks' bank accounts, a couple illustrations on how to make pipe bombs, that sort of thing. Exactly the type of book that should never fall into the public's hands, Guice believed, especially the hands of a minor. Sheriff Guice was all for free speech, but you had to draw the line somewhere.

Also in the folder was a picture of Bobby Briggs. Not a bad-looking kid by any stretch of the imagination, though you could see that *look* in his eyes. The kid had thin brown hair cut just shy of his shoulders, a grin exposing clean but crooked teeth. In the picture, he wore all black, what looked like a rock 'n' roll T-shirt with a bunch of skulls on it. The kid sported the peach-fuzz beginnings of a goatee. Small gold hoop in his left ear.

Guice shook his head, wondered where things went wrong. Was it the parenting? Should the parents be held accountable when their offspring commit a violent crime? Where was the leadership, the induction of morals into children from a young age?

Was there even a definite answer to that question?

Guice wasn't sure.

Also in Briggs' file lay another, smaller book than the first. Something called—Sam could barely pronounce it—the *Necronomicon*. Looked like some kind of devil shit, though he couldn't be sure. It too had been confiscated at the time of Bobby's arrest, one of many such books found in the arsonist's bedroom. It may have been nothing more than a trashy horror novel, for all Guice knew. The thing's pages were yellowed and dog-eared, as if it had been read many times over.

Inside the first page of that book was a photograph Guice had taken on the day of Bobby Briggs' arrest, in the teenager's bedroom. A close-up snapshot of the stack of books that had lain on the punk's desk, lined up so their black and purple and blood red spines were visible to those gathering evidence on the scene. Briggs' bizarre library had consisted of books with names like *Ritual Magick, Magick in Theory and Practice*, and *Ceremonial Magic*. Something called *777 and Other Qabalistic Writings of Aleister Crowley*. All of their titles were illustrated in swirling, archaic fonts, as if to insinuate that the knowledge within originated from sources esoteric and arcane.

Guice laid the photograph aside and reached for the loose pieces of spiral notebook paper within the folder. There had been rumors, during the investigation and subsequent trial, that Briggs had dabbled in devil worship, black magic stuff, but Guice had never placed much stock in that despite the evidence at hand. To Sheriff Sam Guice, Bobby Briggs had always seemed like nothing more than a very troubled young man who needed not only parental guidance, but a couple drug tests as well. Perhaps a good hard spanking to boot. Sam thought briefly of his own son, Nathaniel, and how he would not hesitate to bend the boy over his knee when Nathan got out of line. That would have solved Bobby Briggs' problems a long time ago.

Guice pulled one page from the stack. His lips moved as he read to himself the words that took up the entire sheet of paper. Briggs had obviously been whacked out of his mind when he wrote this junk:

people think they got it all figired out.

they think its all about good and EVIL, god and the devil.

but 1 day there gonna realise its all so much bigger than that.

Theres something comin down, man.

And one day this whole fuckin world's gonna go up in flames.

I want to be by HIS side to see that.

Blessed be

MOLOCH
cheif of Hells army, prince of the land of tears

Guice shook his head again. Lunatic ramblings, all of it. Still, he could not deny the chill that ran down his spine as he skimmed the page, as he stared at the scrawlings at the bottom of that page and on the papers following. Strange drawings, undoubtedly designed to portray ancient runes and religious markings.

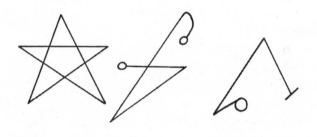

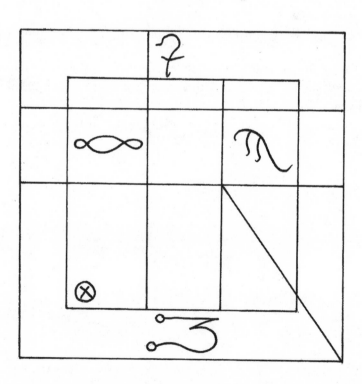

He removed his hat, ran his hands through his hair, and wondered just who the hell this "Moloch" was, why that name kept popping up.

Some kind of rock star or something?

Guice doubted it. Though he wouldn't have been too surprised. Kids sure did listen to some weird shit these days. He thought he might check that out, do some research a little later at Play It Again Records out on Worthington Boulevard. Maybe he could get some answers there.

Or maybe not. Probably not. He knew he was grasping at straws.

Guice sighed for what must have been the millionth time today, and called Mavis again on the speakerphone.

"Yeah, Sheriff?"

"How about throwing that pond water out, fix a new pot of coffee. Would you do that for me?"

"I suppose I could. Everything okay?"

"I don't know anymore, Mavis." He paused, then asked on a whim, "You know anything about this 'Moloch'?"

"What's that?"

"I don't know. I was asking you."

"Sorry," Mavis said. "Doesn't ring a bell."

"Great."

"Anything else?"

"Just get me that coffee, would ya? And put a rush on it, Mavis. I need it."

He hung up, and though their connection was severed, he could hear the old woman in the other room, through his closed door: "Mr. Grumpy."

Normally he would have laughed at that. But not today.

Not today.

CHAPTER 52

Joel called while Kate was fixing breakfast.

"Kate," David shouted from the living room. "It's for you."

Kate reached atop the refrigerator and turned down the radio. Her gospel music faded to a dull murmur, and the volume knob was now covered with a white blotch of pancake batter.

"Could you bring me the phone, please?" Kate said. "I'm making the pancakes."

She waited. "David?"

Finally, when he hadn't brought her the cordless phone after a minute or so, she walked into the den.

David was kicked back in his favorite armchair, watching some PBS Special on the mating habits of the duckbilled platypus. Becca sat nearby, reading a *Blue's Clues* book.

"Nevermind," she said with a scowl. "I'll get it. I'm not doing anything at the moment."

David didn't look up at her, just handed her the phone. "It's Joel."

Kate exhaled loudly, wiped her sticky hands on her apron before taking the phone back into the kitchen with her. Christopher stared up at her from his bassinet on the table and Kate smiled at him.

"Hi, Joel."

"Hey, sis."

"It's about time you called, little brother," Kate said. "I've been worried sick about you."

"Sorry. I've been busy."

"I tried to call several times," Kate said, "But you're never home."

"I've tried to throw myself into my work," Joel said. "I can't stand being in that house anymore. It's so...empty, ya know? So many memories."

Kate realized that her brother sounded like he'd been crying.

"That's probably a good idea. Staying busy, I mean." She placed the phone between her neck and shoulder, held it there as she went back to making breakfast. "You need to do that, so you can try and move on."

"It's been tough, sis. I miss him *so bad.*"

"I can imagine. But you know if there's anything you need, Joel, do not hesitate to ask—"

"Sis," Joel said. "Would you do me a favor?"

"Anything."

"Well, I know you have a lot going on right now," Joel said. "With the baby and all. But...is there any way I could talk you into going out to Heller Home with me?"

Kate said nothing for a few seconds. She stopped mixing the pancake batter and listened to the silence on the line between them. The line crackled and popped almost like a living thing.

"Whatever would you want to go out there for?"

"It's not that I want to," Joel said. "I *need* to."

"Do you really think that's wise?"

"I do. I need to see it again. Where it happened."

"Why don't we visit him up at Brookside Hills instead?"

"I have. Every day. It's not the same."

"I'll spring for the flowers. David can watch Becca and Christopher. It's not a problem."

"It's *not the same,*" Joel said again.

"How's that?"

"I don't know. But it's like...he's not there. Like when I visit him at the cemetery I'm just talking to this cold gray stone. It doesn't mean a damn thing."

"Oh, Joel...honey..."

"I feel like he's...as if his *soul* is still stuck out there at Heller Home. Shit, Kate, I know it sounds crazy, but I don't know how to explain it better than that." When Kate said nothing for the next few seconds, he went on: "I need to do this, Kate. I *will* do this, whether you go with me or not. But please...I need you."

"You know I'm here for you, Joel. I just don't understand—"

"Will you go with me, then? *Please?*"

"We're not supposed to be messing around out there, I don't think," Kate said.

"It's okay. Even if we do get caught, what's Sheriff Guice gonna do? Lock me up? I hardly think he can afford to do that."

"You have a point."

"Please, sis..."

"Um, sure. I guess I could go with you," Kate finally relented. "When?"

"Now. Please."

"How about after breakfast? I'm making pancakes."

"Fine. I'll pick you up. Around nine?"

"That'll work," she said. "Hey, Joel, why don't you come eat breakfast with us? You know you're more than welcome."

"I'll be there at nine," Joel said, as if he hadn't even heard her.

He hung up.

The day was cool and more than a little foggy. After breakfast, Kate tied her hair back in a ponytail, grabbed a light jacket and her pocketbook for the drive.

"Are you sure you don't mind watching the kids?" she asked David before she heard the rumble of Joel's Mustang outside.

"No problem," David said. "I need to work on that new painting, but it can wait 'til this evening."

"I won't be long. An hour or so at the most. Christopher's taking a nap. He should be fine."

"Take your time."

"Becca, you be good," Kate said to her daughter. Becca had propped Lucky the bunny beside her on the couch, and was reading to him as if she were a parent reading her child a bedtime story.

David smiled up at his wife from his armchair, but his smile quickly disappeared as he watched her leave.

The weeds about the old Heller Home property seemed unnaturally still, like yellow-brown spikes guarding the land from unwelcome intruders. Joel's Mustang pulled off Pellham Road and came to a smooth stop on the shoulder. In the distance, a whippoorwill's high-pitched song greeted Kate and her brother as they exited the Mustang. The sound seemed far too lively, too merry, for the melancholy scene before them.

"I still don't understand why you want to do this," Kate said.

"Just humor me, will you."

"I'm sorry."

"Don't be." He walked to the back of the car, opened the trunk and reached inside. "I appreciate your coming with me, sis."

"What's that?" Kate asked, as her brother pulled something out of the trunk.

It was a massive wreath of flowers, REST IN PEACE printed in red across the plastic white cross spanning its width.

"Oh." Kate offered her brother a sympathetic smile, but then her gaze quickly averted from him. She stared down at her feet. She didn't want to see his eyes. Such sad, sad eyes.

Joel hefted the flower arrangement in one hand, came around the front of the Mustang to hook his other arm in hers.

They said nothing as they headed through the meadow, past the craggy black ruins of Heller Home, toward where Michael's crash had occurred several weeks earlier. The ground was still scuffed, the Charger's treadmarks still visible in the dirt like the tracks of some ferocious animal that had been dragged there to die. Pieces of glass glistened like diamonds in their path as they approached the large oak tree that had stopped Michael's car so suddenly. Its base was ruined, pieces of it hanging off as if from some giant, half-peeled banana.

Joel sat the wreath upon the ground a dozen feet or so from the site of his lover's accident. He knelt there for a few seconds, his lips moving silently. He stood again and looked off toward Pellham Road, at the other side of the woods bordering the meadow, at what used to be Heller Home. Everywhere but at that blackened tree. In the day's fog, the ruins of the old children's hospital resembled the bottom jaw of some crooked, rotten mouth.

"God, this is tough," Joel said.

"I'm sure it is."

"You know," Joel said, "I realized after Michael died that I didn't tell him I loved him as much as I should have."

"Oh, Joel..."

"I know it sounds crazy, but there's this weird part of me that thinks...if I'd told him just *one more time* how much he meant to me...this never would have happened. He'd be here, now."

"I'm so sorry," Kate said, feeling useless as she stood by him and watched his eyes grow moist. "You loved him very much, didn't you?"

"He was my soul-mate."

Joel stared off toward Pellham Road again, and a light breeze lapped at his hair like the hands of a phantom lover. He licked his dry, chapped lips.

He turned back toward Kate. "Did I tell you we fought that night?"

"No."

"We did. I'll never forgive myself for not staying there with him. For at least trying to make it right before I had to answer that call. If I had known that was the last time I would see him..."

"You couldn't help it," Kate said.

"No. But I think I should have realized a long time ago that Michael was more important than my career. I didn't. And now he's gone. I'll always have to live with that."

A single tear trickled down Joel's cheek, catching in the five o'clock shadow at his jawline.

"Oh, honey." Kate reached up and wiped the tear away. "I'm sure he was very proud of you. He loved you so much. And you loved him." She peered heavenward. "He's looking down on you right now, Joel, and he knows that."

Joel followed her gaze.

"Why don't you tell him?" Kate said softly.

Joel glanced briefly at his sister, then to the sky again.

"Right now. Tell him. What's stopping you?"

"Yeah," Joel said. Another loud sniffle. "Maybe I should."

"I'll leave you alone, if you'd like," Kate said. "I can wait in the car. I don't like it out here anyway. It's creepy."

"No." Joel grabbed her hand. "Don't go. I want you here."

"Go ahead, then."

Another tear trailed down his cheek. He glanced at her again, and she nodded at him to do it. Say what he had to say. Michael was listening.

"I loved you, Michael," Joel said. He removed his glasses and wiped the dampness from his eyes with the back of one hand. "I always will. I wish we could have gotten married, spent the rest of our lives together. I'm sorry that I always had to work, that you felt I wasn't there for you. But I was. I loved you more than anything. And I'll never, ever, forget you."

He looked at Kate again when he was done, as if for her approval. She smiled sadly. He looked so tired, as if his heartfelt monologue had drained him. Despite the morning chill, a thin film of sweat glistened upon his tan forehead.

"I love you, Michael. I don't know if God approved of what we had or not...but it felt right. And I think that's all that mattered."

He squeezed Kate's hand so tightly she hissed through her teeth. But she said nothing.

"Oh, God—do you feel that, Kate?"

"What?"

"Come on. Let's go."

They took several steps back toward the car, leaving the accident scene behind them, and then Kate did feel it. A sudden rash of frigid chills splashed down her spine like ice water. She *did* feel something, something tangible in the air, but she couldn't quite identify what it was.

It almost seemed as if they were no longer alone. Kate had read about that sort of feeling before, but she had never felt it herself. The feeling of being *watched*.

More chills ran down her spine as they passed the ruins of Heller Home and drew closer to the Mustang.

"I do feel it," she said.

"Come on," Joel said, his voice cracking. She could see it in his eyes now—the sadness was gone. It had been replaced by *fear*.

The Heller Home property had been quiet the whole time, only the sound of that lone whippoorwill in the woods giving any semblance of life to the meadow, but now the quiet was different. Kate sensed a *presence* in the quiet itself, a silence about the area that now seemed like some living vacuum, so deafeningly silent where only minutes ago the breeze had played with the weeds and their voices had echoed through the valley. Not anymore. Now, even the sounds of their footsteps through the dead grass, crunching on the gravel as they made their way past Heller Home and ever closer to the Mustang, everything seemed swallowed up by that sentient quiet.

"Do you hear that?" Kate whispered.

"I don't hear anything," Joel whispered back.

"Exactly."

Kate's body broke out in goosebumps. She looked down at Joel's arm, hooked into her own, and saw that his flesh was also stippled with fear. He was practically carrying her now, and their walk toward the Mustang had quickened into not quite a run but a steady, urgent trot. As if their lives depended on reaching that car.

"Joel, I'm scared."

Joel's keys were already in his hand. "Go. Go."

"It feels like we're not alone anymore, doesn't it?"

"Yes. It does. Get in the car."

They began to run now, faster and faster, still holding on to one another's hands, and the distance to the Mustang seemed to grow greater with every step they took. To their left, several feet away, something metal rattled and clanged in the soot and ash that was once Heller Home.

"Oh, God," Joel said, and despite her better judgment Kate looked toward the noise as she ran.

It was the bumper from Michael's Charger. In the growing breeze, the battered hunk of metal scraped against a mound of broken concrete blocks and jagged two-by-fours with an intermittent, high-pitched squeak. The sound resembled an old man's rasping cackle.

"Don't look, Joel," she said. "Just keep going!"

They ran.

And at last reached the Mustang.

Joel fumbled with the keys. His hands shook like those of a man three times his age as he started up the Mustang, put it into gear, and took off. Gravel sprayed behind the car as it shot back onto Pellham Road, rattling against the undercarriage like pieces of Heller Home screaming for them to stay.

Joel and Kate both glanced back, one last time.

Joel gasped. Kate's heart skipped a beat.

Damned if it didn't look like a *man*, out there in the center of it all.

They both shivered despite the heat inside Joel's Mustang, but neither sibling spoke of what they saw.

A man with a long gray beard, watching them leave.

A man surrounded by what looked like giant, hovering bees...with the faces of sad, haunted children.

CHAPTER 53

Father Jacob Rehm woke to a distant rapping sound. At first he could not differentiate between the thudding of his own pulse and that pounding noise, as his mind was still murky with sleep.

But then he realized someone was knocking at the door. Down in the church.

Rehm rubbed at his eyes, sat up. Yawned.

He glanced at the clock on his nightstand and frowned.

He hadn't been in bed as long as he'd thought. Must have just drifted off. He had only turned in a few minutes after ten p.m. Now it was just eleven o' clock. But who in heaven could be visiting at this hour?

No problem, he figured. If someone had come to make a confession, Father Rehm saw nothing wrong with politely turning them away, asking them to come again tomorrow between the hours of eight a.m. and six p.m., like the sign outside made clear. However, if some truly troubled soul awaited him, someone who was truly lost and needed to speak with a clergyman who might show him or her the way, Rehm knew he had no choice but to let the person in. No matter the time of day.

He grunted, rose from the bed, retrieved his collar from its place on the nightstand and wrapped it around his neck. It would have to suffice—with his black silk pajamas the image was as complete as it could ever be at such an inconvenient hour.

He yawned again, walked from the rectory and into the chancel.

At the front door of the Morgan County Church of the Immaculate Conception, someone kept knocking. Loudly. Urgently.

"Just a moment, please," Father Rehm called out, to no avail. He walked through the nave, ignoring the eerie stares of the various saints depicted in the stained glass windows on every side of him.

Whoever was at the door kept knocking.

"One moment!"

Father Rehm made his way to the front door with little effort. The building was dark, all but pitch-black at this hour, but he knew his church like the back of his hand.

He unlocked the door, swung it wide. "May I help you?"

Three men stood on the church's front steps. Behind them, a battered Chevy pickup truck was pulled onto the patio, straddling the first few steps. Its tailgate hung open like a rusty metal mouth waiting to be fed.

Father Rehm recognized two of the men. His jaw dropped, and he gave a little gasp.

"Reverend Rhodes? Deputy Keenan? What are you doing here? It's quite late for visitors, I would think—"

Rhodes and Keenan were both unwashed and unshaven. They were also completely naked.

"What are you...why are you..."

Rehm could think of nothing to say but the obvious as the men took several steps toward him. "You're *naked*..."

Hank Keenan nodded, smiling at Father Rehm in a way that sent chills down the priest's spine.

"What do you want?"

Perhaps even stranger than the fact that these men were naked—if anything *could* have been more bizarre than that—was the fact that they were accompanied by a man in a filthy Santa Claus suit. Even from where he stood, several yards away, Rehm could smell the man. He reeked of urine and feces. His false white beard was long and filthy, speckled here and there with crumbs of his last meal.

"*Moloch*," said the man in the Santa Claus costume.

"Is there something I can *do* for you gentlemen?" asked Father Rehm. He tried his damnedest as he spoke to them to ignore the fact that the men's bare privates pointed stiffly at him in the moonlight. "I, uh...think the authorities have been looking for you, Hank."

The man in the Santa costume stepped forward.

"We've come for your metal, Father," he said. His head jerked to the left several times fast, a nervous tic, and his bizarre statement was punctuated by a hoarse little giggle. "We need more metal. We don't have enough, and we need all we can get."

"My...metal?"

"Your metal," said Reverend Rhodes. "We need it."

"I don't understand..."

"*Moloch* needs it," said Hank Keenan. Father Rehm no longer recognized the man who had once attended mass every Sunday with his late wife and children, the man who had done so much for not only the church but for Morganville in general.

Something *else* stood before him now.

The men's eyes seemed to glow in the moonlight.

They came closer.

"What do you want? I don't understand. Please..."

"*Moloch.*" All three of them said it together now.

"What—"

"The metal, please, Father," said Reverend Rhodes. "We need your brass, your copper, your silver, your gold. All of your metal."

"We need the metal," said the man in the Santa suit.

Rehm's head shook back and forth. His mouth hung open. He did not know what to say, what to do. He felt frozen where he stood.

He glanced back, just for a second, at the huge silver crucifix that hung above his pulpit area.

"We need your metal."

And then they were upon him. Punching, ripping, tearing...

Father Jacob Rehm screamed. The sound echoed throughout his church like a thousand angels screaming along with him.

One hour later, at Rudy's Junkyard just outside of Morgan County, the process was repeated.

Word for word.

As if the men in Fred Dawson's Chevy pickup followed to the letter some unholy script.

"We need your metal. All of it. We need your metal."

Again, at the St. Paul Lutheran church, out on Henderson Lane.

"We need your metal. Give us all of your metal."

Soon, they would have enough.

And Moloch would be pleased.

CHAPTER 54

The others had gone on, to continue their work at the church.

Now Hank Keenan was alone.

The former deputy grinned, his teeth very white in the moonlight despite the fact that he had not brushed them for several weeks. He slid beneath Sheriff Sam Guice's patrol car. The driveway gravel scratched at his bare ass, even drawing blood in some places, but Keenan never noticed.

Somewhere in the distance a dog barked, as if trying to warn the sheriff to Keenan's scheme.

Hank was not concerned with the animal. He knew that Guice was fast asleep inside his home. He had made sure before going about his plan. He had seen his old friend through the window, snoring in his armchair before an old *Three's Company* rerun, still clad in his wrinkled khaki uniform, a bottle of O'Doul's in one hand.

It had sickened Hank to see the sheriff in there. Living his mundane life. Serving nothing, oblivious to the rewards the master would bestow upon the faithful. Just another leech, drudging through life with no direction. Another empty soul.

Though Moloch might not approve, Hank had also taken a couple minutes to sneak around the rear of the house to ogle Sarah Guice in her bed. The sheriff's wife had been wearing a sexy negligee, not quite see-through but enough to fuel Hank's imagination. When this was all done, and the master's plan was complete, Hank suspected he might take a few minutes to fuck her.

Later.

For now, though, Hank knew that he had other things to think about. His god was growing impatient, and Hank knew what he had to do.

Positioned perfectly where he was supposed to be, Hank squinted and read the teenager's lazy scrawl on the crumpled piece of notebook paper before him. He had taken it from Guice's office, from the Briggs file the night he arrested pesky old George Heatherly and that Little prick from New York. Somehow he had known he would need it. Somehow he had suspected, even then, what Moloch commanded of him.

Hank followed the instructions carefully. His tools for tonight: a pair of wire-cutters, a coil of copper wiring, and an aluminum box approximately twice the size of a cigarette pack.

He breathed heavily as he worked, whispering dark, unintelligible words that—even if someone else had been there to listen—only he could understand.

He, and his god.

Hank compared his work to the hastily-sketched diagram one last time before sliding from beneath the patrol car as quietly as possible.

"Moloch," he said to the darkness. "Blessed be."

And then he disappeared into the night.

The whole process had taken less than ten minutes.

CHAPTER 55

At approximately four forty-five a.m. on the morning of January 7, Sheriff Guice awoke to a frantic screaming in his ear. A high-pitched, electronic shriek that sounded like someone being killed right there in the room with him.

"What the—"

Guice sat up with a start. He stared at the TV dumbly for several seconds, taking a moment to fully awaken. On the screen, a plethora of falsely-perfect smiles explained to him how, by ordering this collection of hot new videos, he could learn how to be his own boss and become a multi-millionaire in less than a year.

Guice licked his lips, tried to wash away the taste of sleep that had accumulated inside his mouth like a cottony film.

And then he realized where that screaming had come from.

It wasn't someone being killed. It was the phone.

Thank God for small favors.

Guice squinted, his eyes still only partially adjusted to the darkness of his living room. He found the phone on the lampstand next to him, picked it up. It trilled again as he brought it to his ear. He winced, pushed the TALK button.

"Guice speaking."

"Sheriff, it's Al."

"Harwood?" Guice scratched at his balls, the rest of his body starting to awaken now while his brain took its own sweet time. "What's going on? Something wrong?"

"Sheriff, we've got a problem. A big problem."

"Give it to me," Guice said.

"We've received reports of three more bodies being found."

"You gotta be kidding me."

"Sure ain't. They were found in three different places."

"Shit." Guice stood, wide-awake now. He glanced down at his wrinkled uniform, decided it would have to do for now. He grabbed his hat from atop the television, checked his gun.

"Who were they, Al? What happened?"

"Father Jacob Rehm," Harwood said on his end of the line. "You know him, right?"

"Sure do." As a matter of fact, Sheriff Guice attended Rehm's church on a semi-regular basis. "Aww, hell, Al. What happened to the priest?"

"Stu Bannerman found him a few minutes ago. Stu was on his paper route, found Rehm sprawled on the steps of his church. Said he looked like he'd been beaten to death."

"Who else?"

"Janet Nordhaus. At the Lutheran church on Laswell and Fifth. Same M.O. Looked like she'd been beaten to death."

"Jesus Christ," Guice said. "It takes a sorry sumbitch to do something like that to a couple of preachers."

"That's not all. I also received an anonymous call not ten minutes ago from a fellow reporting a possible homicide out at Rudy's junkyard."

"Rudy Reznor?"

"That's him."

"What the hell happened to him?"

"Beaten to death, like the others."

Neither man said anything for the next minute or so. Unbridled fear filled the gap in their conversation.

"Don't move a muscle, Al," Guice finally said. "You hold down the fort at the station. I'll check this out right away."

Guice hung up then, grabbed his keys, and ran for his patrol car.

He closed the door and strapped on his seatbelt. Stuck the keys in the ignition. Adjusted the rearview mirror to his liking.

He prepared to start the car.

But then stopped. He reached to the glove compartment and pulled out his cellular phone.

He dialed Joel Rohrig's number.

When no one answered after nine or ten rings, Guice hung up. Then he dialed the number again.

Finally, someone picked up on the other end.

"Hello," said a voice thick with sleep.

"Joel. Sheriff Guice here."

"Yeah?" Joel said, unimpressed. "What do you need, Sheriff?"

"We've got a report of three bodies at three separate locations. How fast do you think you could make it down to the Catholic church?"

"I don't know. I don't...I don't think I can, to be honest with you."

"The Church of the Immaculate Conception," Guice explained, preparing again to start the car. "Can you meet me there in ten minutes?"

"I don't think so, Sheriff," Joel said. "I'm sorry."

Guice frowned. "Come again?"

"I've been thinking a lot about this lately, Sheriff. And I...I'm sorry to say...I don't think I can do this anymore."

"What do you mean?"

"I'm sorry." A slight pause, and then: "I quit."

"Joel, what the hell—"

Guice realized he was talking to a dial tone. He shook his head, wondered what the hell he was supposed to do now.

Still shaking his head, the sheriff turned the key in the ignition.

CHAPTER 56

The explosion was felt, if not heard, for miles around. Shrapnel from Sheriff Guice's patrol car flew for many blocks.

In the parking lot of Frank's Grocery, a bagboy named Shannon Flick later found the sheriff's left boot.

In Brookside Hills, one month after the explosion, cemetery caretaker Pete Gosnell would find the sheriff's partially-melted badge, which—coincidentally enough—had landed like a silver flower left by some unseen mourner atop the grave of Guice's old friend and former Morgan County Fire Chief Randall Simms.

In the house of one Ken and Susan Lockley, one mile from the disaster, a thump was heard several seconds after the explosion. It sounded like someone walking around up there. Ken said he'd check it out. When he did, Lockley found atop his roof, mixed in with the leaves and bird droppings in his gutter, the sheriff's charred right arm.

The rest of Sheriff Sam Guice was never found. Mr. and Mrs. Plymill, at the funeral home, would eventually prepare an empty coffin for burial in Brookside Hills.

Empty, save for that single arm and one scuffed boot.

Across town, in the dark halls of Morganville's First Baptist Church, three men smiled.

They stopped in their building long enough to tilt their heads toward the heavens, and together they sang a dark, unholy song, words not spoken for centuries.

Moloch watched the gathering from his place in Hell, and he said that it was good.

PART
3

"I loved him. With all my heart.
  I wish I could take it back.
  God forgive me...I never meant to hurt my baby."

—Excerpt from an interview with the accused, Morgan County
Sheriff's Department

CHAPTER 57

David woke to a distant rumbling from a dream he could not quite remember—something about fire and ash, thousands of people screaming in a bizarre mixture of unbearable agony and unimaginable ecstasy—and realized he had fallen asleep on the sofa.

He yawned, stretched again and looked at the clock on the VCR. It was just a few minutes before five in the morning.

He made his way through the house, wondering what had awakened him so abruptly.

He stumbled groggily into the kitchen and opened the refrigerator. Thought about a beer, but it was far too early for that. He twisted a can of Mountain Dew from the six-pack at the bottom of the fridge, popped the top, took a couple sips before dropping the can into a nearby wastebasket.

He headed back down the hallway, scratching his balls through his sweatpants as he went. He took a moment to check in on Becca, then Kate and little Christopher. Christopher was sleeping on the bed beside Kate. The baby looked so much like one of Becca's dolls lying there in the moonlight that David did a double-take at first, but then he realized Christopher must have woke up crying in the middle of the night, and Kate had taken him out of the cradle to sleep with her.

Briefly, David wondered what they were going to do about a nursery for the baby. He sure as hell didn't wish to give up his studio. But he knew Christopher couldn't sleep in a cradle beside their bed forever. One day the baby would need his own room.

He shrugged, figured they would cross that bridge when they came to it.

And then he stopped before his studio door. He frowned when he noticed a thin sliver of bright white light beneath the closed door.

Had someone been in there?

David froze.

Was someone in there *now?*

Kate rarely, if ever, had any reason to venture into his studio. And Becca knew Daddy's workshop was off-limits.

So why was the light on?

Perhaps that was what had awakened him, the sound of an intruder. David's breath caught in his throat.

Moving as quietly as he could, David tiptoed back through the house, looking around for something—anything—he might use as a weapon.

He remembered using a hammer in the kitchen the day before, to put up a shelf Kate had been nagging him about since they first moved in.

David crept through the house, breathing through his nose the whole time so as to make as little noise as possible. He went into the kitchen, where he retrieved the hammer from atop the refrigerator.

Makeshift weapon in hand, he sneaked back toward his studio. As he went, he could smell his own body odor, the strong aroma of fear wet beneath his armpits, trickling down his forehead and cheeks.

David stood outside his studio for several minutes, deciding on a plan of action. That sliver of light beneath the door seemed to mock him. He stared at it, his heart thudding in his chest. He could see no flickering shadows within that thin glow, nothing to suggest movement in the room, but he swallowed nervously.

He reached for the doorknob.

Held it for what felt like forever.

He hefted the hammer above his head, ready to take the offensive. His flesh felt hot, seemed to burn with the drug-like rush of adrenaline flowing through his veins.

He turned the knob, threw open the door, and stormed into the room.

CHAPTER 58

Even as it happened, George Heatherly knew it was only a nightmare. But that did not stop the dream from clutching his soul in its terrible grip, from breaking him out in a stinking film of cold sweat like nothing he had ever experienced.

Wakeupwakeupwakeup, he told himself. *Please, God, let me wake up* now!

He dreamed of a man with a very long beard. An ancient man, older than anything George Heatherly had ever seen before.

He thrashed about in his bed as the thing came to him.

"No," he moaned. "Please...no..."

"Don't fuck with me, *worm,*" rasped the demon in his dream. "*I will eat your soul.*"

The man's fingers were unnaturally long, like the legs of some monstrous spider. His fingernails were ghastly, curved things caked with dirt and dried blood. His belly was distended, his ribcage jutting from beneath his mottled gray flesh like knives carved from bone. A constant halo of shiny green shit-flies buzzed about his head, flew in and out of his mouth and nostrils as if they were a part of him. Oozing black sores covered the ancient thing's body from head to toe.

The creature took George Heatherly's uncircumcised penis between its mottled gray hands, held it like some connoisseur of exotic foods savoring a piece of rare meat. It licked its cracked and blackened lips as it stared at George's cock, as it promised George that he would surely die if he fucked with mighty Moloch. The creature pulled and stretched at George's foreskin, like a child playing with putty but not quite knowing what to make with it.

George could not move, was helpless to stop what was happening here, as the thing leaned forward, crooked yellow teeth bared.

It bit down.

George woke up screaming..

"Oh, God," he said, "Oh, God..."

The creature's stench still lingered in the room, the smell of soot and ash. The unmistakable smell of something *burning.*

George rose from bed, trembling and sweaty, not even bothering to pull on any clothes over his sweat-soaked underwear. He headed for the phone.

Middle of the night or not, he planned to call David Little.

Little was the one man who seemed willing to listen with an open mind to these insane thoughts he'd been thinking lately.

Heatherly's hands shook as he dialed, so badly that at first he dialed a wrong number. He offered no apology to the sleepy voice on the other end of the line, just hung up and tried dialing David's number again.

His heart pounded in his chest, so violently that George wondered for those next few minutes if he might be having a heart attack. He winced, held a fist to his sternum as he waited for his neighbor to pick up.

CHAPTER 59

David exhaled loudly. The room was empty.

Well, not quite empty. Someone *had* been in his studio.

Only a single item, however, was out of place in the brightly-lit room.

"What the hell?" David set the hammer on his desk in the far corner of the room, walked to the bookshelf along the opposite wall.

A paperback book lay on the hardwood floor. Open, but facedown.

David picked it up, smoothed out several bent pages. Closed it, turned it over.

It was Andrew Holland's *The Feasting*.

David's eyes grew wide and his mouth hung open as he turned the book over. He stared at the back, at the last line of the cover copy.

"What the fuck?" he whispered.

Goosebumps stippled his forearms. A chill ran down his spine.

There was a *hole* in the back of the book.

The word "Moloch" had been meticulously cut from the synopsis detailing the novel's contents, as if someone had taken a razor and carefully removed it from the thin black paperboard. David could see the yellowed final page of the novel through that perfect square hole where the word had been, THE END staring back at him in bold black type.

He stood there staring at that hole in the back cover of Andrew Holland's book for what seemed like forever as his heart thudded in his chest. Still, he did not feel true fear. Not yet. Only a dizzy sort of confusion over the whole matter. He didn't understand: How? Why? *Who?* And perhaps that scared him most of all. He thumbed through the book, not sure what he was looking for but sensing there was more to be discovered. The pages blurred before him, and their movements beneath his fingers sent a cool breeze across his face.

David's heart began to beat faster than ever. His knees felt weak. Bile rose in the back of his throat, but he swallowed it back.

He rifled through several more pages, and his suspicions were confirmed. As much as he did not want them to be true, he could not deny the evidence right there in front of his face.

Throughout that 340-page novel, every appearance of the antagonist's name—Moloch—had been removed.

Razored out in perfect rectangles.

David jumped when the phone suddenly rang in the living room. He dropped the book, and his head jerked toward the door.

"Swear to God, I feel like an old fool," the voice said when David picked up the phone. "I know it's early, but...do you think you could come over here for a minute?"

"George?"

The ex-Marine's voice cracked on every other word. "I need you to come over here. I need to talk to you. Please."

"Are you okay?" David asked him.

"No, I'm not. Not at all. I can't handle this alone anymore, David. There's some stuff I think you'll wanna know. A lot we need to talk about."

"I'll be right over," David said, and as he thought of that book again—about all those missing *Molochs*—his own voice cracked as well.

CHAPTER 60

George greeted him at the door with a handshake. The old man wore only a pair of black knee-high socks and maroon boxers—the swirling mass of tattoos all about his otherwise pale torso resembled harsh, ugly battle scars—but the retired Marine seemed oblivious to his own near-nakedness. He ushered David inside like a man on the run from something, glancing nervously outside before closing the door behind them.

"Come in, David. Have a seat."

"Thanks," David said, his expression solemn. "What's this about, George? You look like you've seen a ghost."

"I can handle *ghosts*, David." A nervous snicker. "Just sit. There's a lot we need to talk about."

"What exactly are we—"

"Moloch," George said.

"I see."

David sat.

David said nothing as he watched the ex-Marine pace back and forth across the room like a man gone mad. George looked like he was going to have a heart attack if he didn't slow down, breathe easy.

"I knew there was something going on, David, but I didn't want to admit it. I've been putting this off all along, and now people have died because of it. Good people. And folks have changed. I can't just sit by and ignore it any longer."

"Changed?" David said. "What do you mean?"

"Have you ever seen that movie *Invasion of the Body Snatchers?*"

"Sure. Good flick."

"I guess," George said. "My point is, this town is starting to feel like that, David. Like people have been taken *over* by something. I feel like the crazy Kevin McCarthy character who knows what's going on, but everyone thinks he's lost his frigging mind. You know what I mean? But I haven't, David. I haven't lost my mind. People in this town aren't themselves anymore. I mean, they look the same. But they're different. Something's inside them. But instead of outer-space fuckers, they've been infected by something from Hell. Something evil. A demon, I guess. Goddamn."

George stopped just long enough to take a deep breath.

"First things first, I need to fill you in on what we're dealing with. At least, what I *think* we're dealing with. That's one of the first things I learned in the Corps. You've got to know your enemy before you can defeat him. Of course, I may just be some senile old man, David. You'll probably think so after I tell you what I think about all this. But please, will you just hear me out?"

"Sure," David said. "That's why I'm here." He shifted uncomfortably on the sofa, fidgeting beneath the old man's agitated gaze. "Explain to me what's going on, George. Please."

The grandfather clock ticked quietly away in its corner, like some ominous soundtrack to George's story, as the ex-Marine first told David about his nightmares.

"That's awful," David said when he was finished. He shuddered.

"'Awful' ain't the word for it," said George. "It was so fucking real..."

George turned to leave the room.

"Where are you going?" David asked.

"Wait here. I want to show you something."

David sighed, ran one hand through his unwashed hair.

George came back into his living room a couple minutes later, a stack of books in his hands. Most of them looked heavy enough to use as doorstops. Some were thick tomes that might have been centuries old, though just as many were protected by shiny dust-jackets as if they had been published yesterday. Perched atop the old man's nose was a pair of plastic-rimmed reading glasses. A cigarette burned between his lips.

"I didn't know you were a smoker," David said.

"I'm not," George replied. "At least, I haven't been for the past thirty years."

David watched the old man with an expression somewhere between bewilderment and an odd sort of pity as George dropped the pile onto the table between them. "Books?"

George took a long drag on his cigarette, placed it in the ashtray atop the coffee table. "Hear me out, David. I need you to believe me when

I say that I didn't jump into this without thinking about it first. I've studied up on what I'm about to tell you, so I would know exactly what I was going to say. Admittedly, I'm still not quite sure. All I know is, it doesn't matter how crazy this is all gonna sound because it's true. *He* doesn't care if you believe in him or not. He exists either way."

David ran his hands through his hair again, grimaced. "You're talking about Moloch."

"Right."

"Just spit it out, George. Nothing you say is going to shock me, I don't think. Not at this point."

"Just wait," said George.

George spread the books out before them on the table, but he didn't join David on the sofa. Instead, he knelt before the coffee table, took another long drag off his cigarette.

"*A Study in Demons? Black Magick in Modern Society?*" David read off several of the titles. "Where did you get this shit?"

"Public library," George replied in a dismissive tone that seemed to say: *That's not important right now.*

David shook his head, waited for George to begin.

"Now," said the old man. "We both agreed that we don't believe in demons. I'm aware of that. But they exist, David. They're as real as you and me, I think. And there's one living here. In Morganville."

"Moloch," David said.

George picked up his cigarette from the ashtray again, stuck the thing between his wrinkled lips, and let it dangle there while he read aloud from a hefty black-bound tome titled *The Encyclopedia of Demonology.*

"'Moloch was a divinity worshipped in the land of Canaan before the birth of Christ,'" George read, his voice grave. "'This pronunciation, Moloch, represents the Hebrew version of the god, though he has also been referred to in ancient texts as *Melech,* or 'king,' *Maluk,* 'ruler,' and *Malik.'*

"'The worship of Moloch among the early Jews subsisted mostly in the form of child sacrifice. Outside Jerusalem, in the valley of Geennom, existed a place called *Tophet*—loosely translated, 'a place of abomination'. Here, worshippers of Moloch committed their atrocities in a temple erected by Solomon, who has hence been regarded as the monarch who introduced the cult into 'God's Land.'

"'Said atrocities included—though were not limited to—parents offering their children to the fires in Moloch's temple. The temple was constructed from solid gold and/or other precious metals, was approximately the size of a small modern gazebo, and was molded to resemble Moloch himself. Moloch was portrayed as a massive bull with a humanoid body—note the similarity to the Minotaur in Greek mythology—and his sacrificial altar was built with the god's hands outstretched, palms up. Here, within Moloch's palms, worshippers would lay their children. Inside the hollow body of the altar itself they would stoke a roaring fire, and once the metal of the altar grew hot the child would burn to death.'"

"Jesus, that's awful," David said. "People really did that?"

George took a deep drag off his cigarette, read on: "'Moloch is also visible in classic literature, the name of the fallen angel in John Milton's *Paradise Lost* who urges his fellow demons to implement a new war against Heaven. In Milton's manuscript, Moloch's ultimate goal is to build a place in Hell called *Pandemonium*—or 'The Palace of All Demons'—a sort of anti-paradise he believes will rival Heaven.

"'Moloch's role in Hell, according to ancient theology and demonology, is the Chief of Satan's army. He has also been called the 'Prince of the Land of Tears.'"

George closed the book, reading the last few lines without the words before him, as if he had read over the text so many times in the last few weeks he had memorized great chunks of the dark knowledge contained therein and would never forget it: "'Many ancient gods, in Qabbalistic rituals, are paired with a specific number as well as a specific month of the Roman calendar. Moloch's number is sixty. His month is December. His colors—like those of the original fallen angel, Lucifer—are red and violet.'"

David stared at George for several long seconds after the old man finished.

"This all started in December," he said at last, his voice no louder than a whisper.

"Right," said George. "I thought you might catch that."

"Do you think it means anything?"

George licked his dry lips, said, "If you had asked me that six months ago, I would have said hell, no. I would have called you a fool, and chalked it up to coincidence. Now...I'm pretty sure I do believe it. That there is relevance there. Very much so."

"Do you think there's any significance to the number sixty?" David asked.

"Think about it."

David thought about it for several seconds, but came up with nothing.

"Sixty children died in The Great Fire," George said. "At Heller Home."

"Jesus. You're right."

George nodded. "That's not all," he said. "Have you noticed the church? Morganville First Baptist?"

"It's closed."

"Besides that. Someone's painted it, David."

"Don't tell me—"

"Red. And violet."

"Goddamn." David hung his head for a second, then looked back up at the old man. "It all seems like too much to be simple coincidence, doesn't it?"

"It does."

"Do you think The Great Fire...do you think it somehow...brought Moloch here?"

George nodded slowly as he finished off his cigarette, then snubbed it out in the ashtray. "I think maybe it did. I think that Bobby Briggs kid was involved in some fucked-up shit. I don't know what—black magic, devil worship, fucking New Age Shirley McLaine claptrap—it doesn't really matter, does it? All I know is, when Briggs burned down Heller Home, and sixty people died in that fire...it somehow brought Moloch here. Did the boy specifically plan for that to happen? I don't know. Probably. But how did he know exactly sixty people would die? Maybe he didn't. Damned if I know. All I do know is, this *Moloch* is growing stronger every day. And that scares the living hell out of me."

David stared at the books on the table, then finally looked back up at his friend. "There's this saying I heard one time. Sherlock Holmes said it, I believe—"

George nodded, knew where David was going. They said it together: "'When you have eliminated the impossible, whatever remains—however improbable—must be the truth.'"

The grandfather clock in the corner ticked on as the men sat silent for several minutes, contemplating that.

"Scary, huh?" George said.

George looked so, so old in that moment, David thought, and he quickly looked away from his neighbor.

"This is insane," David said. He reached down, began thumbing through a book called *Dark Gods: A Guide to Ancient Religions and Arcane Cultures*. He turned it to the index, looked up "Moloch," then flipped to the page to which he was referred. It was a reproduction of an old woodcarving, a faded picture depicting the bull-god's altar, his golden arms outstretched to hold a screaming baby. Inside his hollow stomach, a fire blazed...

Were such things still happening *today?* David wondered.

Impossible.

"What do we do?" David asked his neighbor. "You're the old leatherneck, George. Tell me what we have to do to fight this thing."

George pondered the question for a minute or more. "I'm afraid it's not that easy, David. I've fought Japs, I've fought Germans. They bleed. They die. Don't need much more than an M-14 to make that happen. Something outta Hell, I don't think it's gonna be so easy to kill."

"Good point," David said.

"I think the best thing we can do is wait," George said. "For now. Wait and watch. Watch everybody. I think there are very few people left in this town we can trust. I think they're all under his influence, in some way or another, and we have to know what we're getting ourselves into, first and foremost."

David bit his lip, tried to hide his fear.

"What's the matter?" George asked.

David's head hung low. "I think..."

"Spit it out, David."

"What I'm about to tell you doesn't leave this room," David said.

George laid one hand over his heart. "You have my word."

"I'm scared, George. I'm starting to think...there might be something wrong with my wife."

"Oh, no." George stood up quickly, came around to sit on the sofa beside David. "Why do you say that?"

"I don't know. She's just...she's been acting strange. Ever since she went out to the old Heller Home property with her brother."

"Aw, shit, man," George said. "When did she go out there?"

"A few days ago."

"Why?"

"That's where Joel's boyfriend died. Remember, the wreck that night?"

"Damn. And Kate went with him?"

"Yes."

"You said she's been acting strange. How so?"

"It's nothing major. Little things. Sometimes it's just...a *feeling*. I can't quite put my finger on it."

"What about your brother-in-law? Has he acted any differently?"

"No, not really. I can't say. I haven't seen much of him since Michael died."

"I see," George said. He stared up at the ceiling, in deep thought.

"I found something tonight, George," he said. "Just before you called.

Something I think Kate might have done."

George stared at him, let David tell his story. When the younger man finished, George said, "You think Kate did it? Cut through the book like that? Removed all the...*Moloch*s?"

"I certainly don't think it was Becca," David said. "Do you?"

"Doubtful. But there's no way to be sure. You'll have to watch both of them."

David's heart grew heavy. He hung his head, buried his face in his hands. "Why did I ever agree to come here? My whole fucking life feels like it's been turned upside-down. I hate this goddamn town!"

George nodded, patted his friend on the back, but said nothing.

"Here's something I don't understand," David said a few minutes later, after regaining his composure. He stared at his neighbor, his eyes moist. "Explain something to me."

"Shoot."

"My wife has been a die-hard Christian all of her life," David said. "Sometimes to a fault, if you want to know the truth. She believes in Jesus, that He died on the cross for her sins, all that stuff. And I do mean she *devoutly* believes it. Her father was a Baptist minister. So tell me, George, if she's 'under the influence,' as you say, how is that *possible?*"

"Good question," George replied. "And to be perfectly honest with you, I don't have a definite answer. I don't think there is one."

"I can't imagine Kate would—"

"If you want to know what I *think*, however," George went on, "And mind you, this is just a theory...I believe, if Kate really is 'infected'—for lack of a better term—her religion somehow enabled it. It made her more...*susceptible*, if you will, to Moloch's power. It left the door open, so to speak."

"I don't get it," David said.

"Let me put it this way," George explained. "I think that someone who believes so strongly in the good...must also believe in the *bad*. No light without dark, that sort of thing. And if that's the case, the person in question damn well better be secure-as-fuck in his or her beliefs. Otherwise they're fair game. For both sides of the battle."

"I hope you're wrong. Jesus Christ, I hope you're wrong."

"Do you believe in God, David?" George asked.

"Why?"

"Just curious."

"I don't know. I'll believe in Him when I see Him one day, I guess."

"Hm."

"Why?" David asked. "Does it matter?"

"Maybe. We need all the help we can get, don't you think?"

"Yeah, but if you're right about Kate—"

"Exactly. Which is why I said 'maybe.'"

David just stared at him.

"I'm no expert in this stuff, David. I'm learning as I go, just like you."

"Do you believe in God?" David asked.

"Yeah," George said. "I do. But I don't allow that belief to control my life. I think there's a fine line between faith and fanaticism. And once you cross that line, religion can be a dangerous thing."

David stared at the floor, nodded but said nothing. He thought of his wife, and what might be happening to her.

"Take Reverend Rhodes, for instance," George said. "He's a man of God—or used to be, I should say—and I think he's tied up in this shit worse than anyone else."

"How?"

"Remember the way Keenan just stopped and stared at the place that night? Like he'd seen God in the flesh or something?"

"Yeah," David said. "Fucking creepy."

"There's got to be something to that."

"You think Moloch's using the church as his...*headquarters?*"

"Possibly," George said. "I told you, David, I did plenty of research before I called you over here. I drive around in the middle of the night sometimes. I see things. Because of the dreams, I find it harder and harder to get a good night's sleep anymore. Sometimes I'll hop in the Ranger, take a ride around town in the wee hours of the morning. You'd be surprised, some of the things I've witnessed."

"Like what?" David asked, his face pale.

"People going in and out of the church at all hours of the night. Sneaking around. Out of Rudy's Junkyard too, on Sourtree Road next county over. Like there's anything to see out there. One of them, swear to God, was that Dawson fellow who tried to snatch your daughter. Still had on that fuckin' Santa suit, too. How weird is that? I saw one couple, just last night, fuckin' on the front steps of the church. Damned if one of them didn't look like Gerda Greenhorn."

"So?"

"Gerda Greenhorn's ninety-nine years old."

"You're kidding."

"I know what I saw," George said. "And just so you know, it was the good reverend I saw Ms. Greenhorn ridin' like a Harley on a bad piece of road."

They sat there for several more minutes without saying anything.

Finally, though, both men jerked to attention as the grandfather clock in the corner bonged loudly, announcing it was six in the morning.

"I should go," David said, standing, "try and get some sleep before the kids are up and running for the day."

"Sounds good," George said. "I'd like to do that myself, but I know it ain't gonna happen. Probably do a little work around the yard, catch a few Zs after lunch. Helps the nightmares, sleeping in the middle of the day like that." As an afterthought, George added, "Sometimes."

David nodded, offered the old man a nervous smile before turning and heading for the door.

"Watch your wife, David. Don't let your guard down."

"I won't."

"I'm sorry I have to say that."

David cleared his throat. "So...what now, George?"

"I'm gonna continue to ride by the church every so often until we can come up with a definite plan of action," George said. "Sit tight, cover your ass, and I'll let you know when I can come up with something tangible."

"Gotcha," David said.

"So you're not ready to have me committed now?"

"No," David said. "Anything but."

And then David left, leaving George standing in the doorway. Heatherly's face was a wrinkled mask of worry as he watched his neighbor go. The old man wondered if he had just alienated his only friend in the world.

CHAPTER 61

David watched from his place at the kitchen table as Kate slid a fried egg out of the pan and onto Becca's plate. Outside the window above the sink, a bird chirped merrily. David contemplated walking outside to strangle the thing, the mood he was in.

"Yummy," Kate said. "Looks good, doesn't it, baby?"

"You're the greatest cook in the world, Mommy!" Becca exclaimed.

"Well, I don't know about that."

"Can I have some more bacon?"

"Finish what's on your plate. After that, you can have all you want."

Across the table, little Christopher stared at his father from his vibrating bassinet. David rubbed at his tired eyes, groaned beneath the pain of a dawning headache, but stuck out his tongue, made a face at his son. The baby smiled, or at least seemed to, waving his tiny hands at David as if he understood such a gesture. David laughed tiredly, turned back toward Kate.

He'd been watching his wife's every move all morning, ever since she got up and came into the living room where he sat—wide awake, thinking—before a television that had been busy with static snow for hours.

"Thanks, Mommy," Becca said, pouring herself a glass of orange juice. Done with that, she picked up her plate from the table and headed toward the hallway. "I'm going to watch *Fairly OddParents.*"

"No, you're not," David said from the table. "Pull up a chair."

Kate turned, looked at her husband, but said nothing. Becca eyed him with a look of exaggerated confusion.

"But, Daddy—"

"Sit."

"You always let me watch cartoons while I eat."

"Not anymore," David said. "New rule. The family eats together, at the table. No one is dismissed until we've all finished eating."

"Daddy—"

"Sit. Now."

Becca pulled up a chair next to her little brother, pooched out her lower lip. "I wanna watch TV."

"Don't pout," David said. "You know I hate that."

"Grumpy this morning?" Kate asked as she set David's plate down in front of him. She took a seat at the table beside baby Christopher, across from Becca.

David said, "I think we need to start spending more time together as a family, that's all."

"Wake up on the wrong side of the bed?"

"Nope." David took a sip of his orange juice. "This is what the table's for. We've barely lived here a month, and have you seen the carpet in there? It's ruined."

"Jeez," said Kate. "Oscar the Grouch."

Becca giggled. "Daddy's Oscar the Grouch. But you're not green, Daddy!"

"Blagggh," Christopher added his own two cents from his bassinet.

"Something's on your mind, hon," Kate said to her husband. "What is it?"

Bacon crunched loudly between David's teeth. Kate had never known how to make bacon without burning it. He smirked, took another sip of orange juice to wash it down. He wasn't sure why, but her saccharine tone and use of the word "hon" made his stomach churn. He thought of his conversation with George the night before, and suddenly he wasn't hungry anymore.

He propped his elbows up on the table, stared at his wife and daughter sternly. "I need to know who's been messing around in my studio."

Becca was trying to hold Christopher's bottle up for him as he fed and didn't even hear the question. Kate just stared at her husband, confused. The baby drooled milky spit down his chin, onto his bib. Becca giggled.

"Pay attention, Becca," David said. "Playing in Daddy's studio is a no-no. You know that. That's *not* a new rule."

Becca laid Christopher's bottle down beside him in bassinet, looked at her father with wide, innocent eyes. "I don't play in there, Daddy," she said. "I know I'm not supposed to."

"You haven't been in there at all?" David asked, pointing his fork at her. "Specifically, I want to know if you were messing around in there yesterday. Last night."

"No. Really, Daddy. I haven't been in there. Cross my heart and hope to die."

"Becca—"

"For God's sake, David," Kate said. "She told you she hadn't been in there. What's wrong with you?"

David glared at his wife, and she glared back. Her eyebrows rose, as if challenging him.

"She told you she hasn't been in your studio," Kate said. "So stop interrogating her."

"I wasn't interrogating her." David stared down at his plate, started picking at his food.

"What's the big deal, anyway?" Kate asked. "Is something missing?"

David took a deep breath, exhaled loudly. Slowly, as if talking to a child, he explained, "The 'big deal' is, someone was messing around in my studio. Everybody knows that room is off-limits. Last night someone took a book off of my bookshelf and cut it up. One of the first covers I ever painted, and the book is ruined now."

"That's weird," Kate said.

"Yeah," David agreed. "Very weird. The damn thing didn't just fly off the shelf by itself. It sure as hell didn't cut *itself* up. So who did it?"

Kate said nothing. But David couldn't help but notice how she would not meet his eyes.

"Moloch," David whispered suddenly. He wanted to gauge his wife's reaction. See if she acted any differently when he said that word, or if she recognized it. Crazy, but worth a shot.

He said it again, under his breath: "Moloch."

"I haven't stepped foot in that room since we moved in," Kate said. "You know that."

She slid her plate aside then, stood, and removed Christopher from his bassinet. The baby started whining softly. With her one free hand, Kate picked up her plate again and turned to leave the kitchen.

"Come on, Becca. We're eating in the living room."

David clenched his fists, scowled at his wife, but said nothing.

CHAPTER 62

"Christopher and I are going to take a bath," Kate said. "Will you keep an eye on the lasagna?"

David looked up from the Elmore Leonard novel he was reading and nodded. Clad in a soft pink bathrobe, Kate stood in the hallway connecting the living room to the kitchen. Baby Christopher, barely two weeks old, squirmed in her arms, staring at David with eyes like two pools of clear ocean water. The smell of lasagna, David's favorite dish, drifted in from the kitchen. He inhaled deeply, savoring the aroma.

"Sure," David said. "If I can keep from scarfing it down while you're in there."

"Don't let it stay in the oven too long. It only needs another ten minutes or so."

"Gotcha. And make sure you don't stay in the bath too long."

"Why's that?"

"Because I don't fancy being married to a walking prune."

Kate smiled, shook her head. She moved on toward the bathroom, baby Christopher in her arms, and within minutes David heard the sound of water running in the bathtub.

He closed his book, placed it on the arm of his recliner, and sat back, his hands behind his head. Becca sat on the floor in front of him, watching *Tom and Jerry* on TV.

David closed his eyes, smiled. Wondered how a levelheaded fellow like himself could have ever allowed George Heatherly's delusions to infect him.

It was crazy. Too crazy.

He sighed.

Maybe things would end up okay after all.

Kate tested the water with her toe, hissed through her teeth. She rocked little Christopher gently upon her shoulder as she leaned over to add some cold water to what was already in the tub. She eased the lid of the toilet down and sat. Bounced Christopher up and down on her knee while she waited, holding him by the arms.

"My little sweetheart. You like to ride the horsey?"

Christopher smiled up at her.

"Mommy wouldn't want to burn her baby," she told him. "We have to wait a minute, let the water cool down. Okay?"

She hugged him to her chest, tenderly kissed his forehead.

"You look just like your daddy, you know that?"

Christopher smiled at her, wider than ever, as if he understood and was indeed proud of this fact.

"That's a very good thing, you know. Your father's one handsome devil."

Christopher seemed to purr.

"If a bit moody at times."

The baby seemed to nod. Agreeing with that.

"Let's try the water now," Kate said. She eased the baby back up to her shoulder, stuck her foot into the tub once again. A little warm, but she supposed it would be okay. With Christopher nestled in the crook of one arm, she allowed her bathrobe to slip off her shoulder.

She eased into the tub, wincing as the warm water lapped at her sore vagina, against the stitches from her episiotomy.

"Ouch."

She propped Christopher up between her legs, holding his stubby arms so he would not go under. With one hand, she slid the shower curtain halfway closed.

"Splish-splash, we were takin' a bath," Kate sang, giggling when the baby stared at her as if she had gone mad.

And then she heard the whisper, in the room with her. On the other side of the shower curtain.

"Kate..."

She sat up with a start, the water splashing around her. Christopher bobbed up and down like a fleshy buoy against her legs.

"David?"

She pulled back the curtain.

And she saw the thing called Moloch, in the mirror above the sink.

David sprang from his chair at the sound of Kate's muffled shriek in the bathroom.

"What the hell?"

"Mommy?" Becca looked up at David. She looked as if she might start crying.

"It's okay, baby. Watch your cartoons." David ran to the bathroom. "Kate?"

He tried to enter, but the door was locked.

"Kate, what's the matter? Unlock the door."

He heard nothing from the other side of the door now. Only the gentle sloshing of water.

"Kate? Open the door!"

A mottled visage leered at her from the mirror. It was the most grotesque thing Kate had ever seen.

The demon's beard was matted and crawling with vermin. Flies swarmed about his huge, misshapen head like a halo of pestilence. The creature's eyes were black as coal, yet at the same time they seemed to glow with an otherworldly light. His nose was long, sharp, and bird-like, his teeth crooked and stained with something that looked like mossy green fungus.

He smiled at her, told her his name.

"Moloch..."

His voice seemed to come from everywhere and nowhere at once. From all around Kate, from beneath the house, from the toilet and from the drain in the sink. It filled her head and seemed to echo in her bones.

Her ears rang, her temples throbbed.

Kate could not move as she sat there in the tub, staring at the man in the mirror. She felt frozen, barely even aware of little Christopher slipping into the water between her legs. Her arms and legs refused to obey the commands given by her brain to *get out of here, now!*

"Kate Little," said the man in the mirror.

He stuck his tongue out at her. Waggled it like some fat black worm trying to push its way out from between the burrow of his cracked gray lips. His grin seemed so perverse...so *wrong.* Flames danced in the mirror behind him now, flames that grew so bright Kate could not look directly into them.

She stared into Moloch's eyes instead, letting out a soft little moan.

She barely even heard David in the background, pounding at the door. His frantic knocks were little more than distant echoes of her own thudding heartbeat, and his voice was distorted, muffled, as if it came to her through water: "Kate, open the door! Open the door!"

"Who...are you?" Kate said to the man in the mirror, and a single salty tear trailed down her cheek.

He was the most beautiful thing she had ever seen.

"Kate!" David shouted again.

Still nothing, from behind the other side of the bathroom door.

"Godammit, Kate, open the door! I heard a scream! Is the baby okay?"

Nothing.

He kicked at the door, but only succeeded in stubbing his own bare toes.

"Shit!"

He glanced toward Becca, who stood in the middle of the living room, sucking at her thumb.

"Daddy, I'm scared."

"It's okay, baby. Watch your cartoons. Daddy's got everything under control."

Becca sat cross-legged on the carpet, but continued to stare at her father, tears glistening in the corners of her eyes.

"Kate!" David shouted again.

He turned and rammed his right shoulder into the door. He heard the wood crack, but only slightly. He gnashed his teeth, rammed it again. Again.

"Kate!"

Once more, he slammed into the door.

Finally, it crashed inward beneath his weight.

"Kate, what's the mat—"

David gasped as he stumbled into the bathroom.

And saw his wife and son.

CHAPTER 63

Kate blinked several times fast as David barged into the bathroom, but she did not turn to her husband. She just kept staring toward the mirror.

One hand cupped her left breast. Her nipples were hard, harder than David thought he had ever seen them before. Her other hand lay in the patch of hair at her crotch, a single finger extended inside. Her vagina was wet not only with bathwater but also, David recognized, the glistening juices of arousal. She moaned softly before looking up at her husband. A tear ran down her cheek, clung for a second to her jawline, then dripped into the soapy bathwater.

"Kate, are you okay?" David asked. He glanced toward the mirror, where she stared so longingly.

"Kate?"

David took a couple more steps forward, into the bathroom.

"Oh, my God, Kate—*the baby!*"

In her strange trance-like state, Kate had allowed little Christopher to slide away from her in the tub. The infant's butt squealed against the porcelain, as he slowly slid under...and then went sloshing down into the water.

Kate blinked several more times, looked first at David—*through* him—and then down at the baby.

She seemed to stare right through the child, not really seeing him at all.

"Christopher!" David cried, running to the tub. He leaned down, grabbed the baby's arms and pulled him from the water.

Kate watched, still seemingly unaware of where she was and what was going on.

David frowned at her as he pulled the baby from the tub, and Christopher began to bawl.

"What the hell were you *doing*, Kate?"

"I...I don't know..."

David grabbed a towel from the narrow closet behind the tub and wrapped it around the baby. He held Christopher to his chest until his wailing finally stopped. The baby coughed several times, tiny high-pitched chuffing noises, but otherwise seemed uninjured.

David glared at Kate. "You almost let him *drown*, dammit."

Kate shook her head slowly and met his eyes at last. She licked her lips as she stared up at him.

"I..."

"Kate, what's with you?"

"Have you checked the lasagna, David?" she asked. "You didn't let it burn, did you?"

"*What?*" David's mouth hung open.

"I hope you've been checking the lasagna...'cause I thought I smelled something burning."

"Jesus, woman!" With Christopher still on his shoulder, David left the bathroom, shaking his head furiously as he went. "Fuck the lasagna!"

"Language," Kate said behind him, groggily, but David did not hear her.

CHAPTER 64

The phone rang shortly after eight-thirty p.m. the following evening. David sat there staring at the *All in the Family* rerun on the television before him—watching it but not really *seeing* it.

"David, can you get that?" Kate called from the bathroom. "I'm trying to give Christopher a bath."

"Hopefully you can do it without drowning the kid this time," he said.

"What was that?"

"Nothing."

The phone continued to ring.

"The phone!" Kate shouted. "Please?"

"Okay, okay."

David stood, walked down the hall to the kitchen and answered the phone. "What."

"David, it's George. How you doin', man?"

"Not so good."

"Why do you say that?"

"I hate my life. I hate this goddamn town. I think my wife's losing her fucking mind. Everything okay on your end?"

"I'm old and I got hemorrhoids. Life's a bitch."

David didn't laugh. "And then some."

After several more seconds of awkward silence on the line between them, David said, "Did you need something, George?"

"Oh, yeah," said the ex-Marine. "I was wondering if you'd heard the news."

"News? What news?"

"Shit. You haven't heard."

"I guess not," David said. "I don't read the paper anymore. Nothing but bad news, anyway."

"Sheriff Guice is dead," said George.

"Fuck. No. What happened?"

"His patrol car exploded. With him in it."

"Jesus..."

"Supposedly they found three more bodies as well. The priest, at the Catholic church. Pastor Nordhaus, at the Lutheran. Guy who owns the local junkyard."

"My God. This place is a walking morgue."

Neither man said anything for several long seconds.

Finally, George said, "I'll letcha go, David. I just thought you would want to know."

"Do you think all of this has something to do with..."

"Yeah," George said. "I do think there's some connection with what we were talking about last night. No doubt about it." George cleared his throat. "I gotta run, David. Let's get together for that beer soon, okay?"

"Sounds good."

"Watch your back."

"Will do. You, too."

David walked back into the kitchen and hung up the phone. He walked quietly down the hall, stood for a minute or two outside the splintered bathroom door, listening to the sound of running water in the bathtub. Listened to the sound of Kate laughing and playing with Christopher as if everything was fine.

As if she wasn't changing. As if Moloch hadn't crawled inside her mind.

David grimaced, forced that thought from his mind as he turned from the bathroom door, shoulders slumped, and headed back to the living room.

CHAPTER 65

The hardest part of all was the unreality of living his life without Michael. On those lonely nights when he sat in the darkness, feeling as if he were drowning in his grief, Joel often expected the phone to ring. It would be Michael calling, on his way home from work, and over the rumble of the Charger's engine he would ask if Joel wanted him to pick up some dinner. Every second of the day, Joel expected Michael to walk through the front door, to shout out his customary "Honey, I'm home".

That was undoubtedly the hardest part. The surreal feeling that nothing had changed, nothing at all...that Michael was gone, but he couldn't really be *gone*. Not *forever*. Surely he had just stepped out for a moment. For a few days, even. They had been fighting, after all, the last time they had spoken.

But no...reality was so much crueler.

If he hadn't seen his boyfriend's coffin slowly lowered into the earth, if he hadn't thrown that first handful of dirt into his lover's grave, Joel would have been unable to believe that Michael Morris was truly *dead*.

That he was never coming back.

Three days had passed since he had told his soul-mate goodbye, and still it all felt like some sick fucking joke.

Shortly after nine p.m., Joel got drunk. Not just drunk, but—as he and his buddies used to say back in college—"positively obliterated." Joel might have been disappointed in himself had circumstances been different, as he had never been the type to turn toward drugs and alcohol to ease his problems. People who did that earned no sympathy from Joel, as he had witnessed all too often the tragic consequences of such behavior. He had assisted in numerous autopsies—more than he could count—during the last few years, postmortem examinations upon the bodies of folks whose lives were cut short due to drug overdose, cirrhosis of the liver, and of course accidents caused by drunk drivers.

He didn't want to be one of them. Joel didn't want to be a statistic.

Tonight, however, he was in mourning.

Tonight he was grieving the loss of his lover. His best friend.

More so, Joel told himself, this was a celebration of Michael's memory. Of the short time they had spent together.

Tonight, Joel figured, he had every right to numb his pain.

He deserved this.

He planned on getting "positively obliterated," and it was nobody's fucking business.

The water was hot. Almost scalding hot. It turned his flesh bright pink.

Joel didn't care.

Like passing through the fire. The phrase leapt into his mind as he made himself comfortable. Joel frowned, wondered where the hell *that* had come from, but then he shrugged. It didn't matter. Nothing fucking mattered anymore, except Michael's precious memory.

"I love you, Michael," Joel wept, his voice echoing off the walls and floor of the small bathroom. "God, I miss you."

He sank deeper into the bubbles filling the tub, letting them swallow him up to his chin. He sighed loudly. On all sides of him, the candles he had placed about the room cast their flickering light. The shadows of the toilet, the sink and Joel himself twitched and danced in that melancholy orange glow.

Joel sighed again, took a long pull off the bottle of merlot on the edge of the tub. He planned to drain the whole damn thing if he didn't pass out first.

"To you, Michael," he slurred.

Again, he tipped the bottle back, letting the wine burn down his throat.

His senses began to dull, and an odd, droning *hummm* filled the room.

And the smell of something...burning.

Joel's heart skipped a beat when Michael rose up from beneath the bubbles on the opposite end of the tub, rose up as if he had been hiding beneath the water the whole time.

Joel let out a soft gasp.

Strangely enough, he found he wasn't too surprised.

It was impossible, yes. But he was drunk.

And their love *was* eternal.

He smiled, felt an odd sense of peace like nothing he had ever felt before, as his dead lover stared at him, and he stared back.

Michael's body glistened in the candlelight. His beautiful brown eyes reflected the flames, as if a fire burned deep inside his skull.

"Hello, Michael," Joel said.

"Hello, Joel."

Something about the whole thing felt...*not quite right*...like some odd, half-remembered fever dream that was not entirely good *or* bad...yet Joel couldn't figure out what it was through the fog of bliss which numbed his brain.

This was too good to be true, he knew. *Impossible.*

"Come here, lover," Michael said.

The water sloshed around in the tub, bubbles engulfing their naked bodies, as Joel fell into his lover's arms.

"Together again," Michael said.

Joel shuddered with delight. His heart raced. He could barely breathe.

"My Michael," he gasped. "My sweet Michael, I can't believe you're really here..."

"Believe," said Michael, and throughout the room the candlelight danced as he spoke.

The water was hot. But the room grew colder each time Michael opened his mouth.

Joel shivered.

And tried not to notice.

Their embrace was not sexual. They held one another, there in the tub, for what felt like many hours. And perhaps hours did pass. Time lost all meaning to Joel, as he lay there in the tub, flesh tingling, his lost loved one at last returned to him. *Reality* no longer felt like anything more than a nightmarish, nonsensical word...

This couldn't be happening. But it was.

Michael was back, and Joel couldn't have been happier.

The tears that streamed down Joel's face now were tears of overwhelming joy. No more sadness. No more loneliness. His prayers had been answered...

Michael was alive. Not dead, but gloriously, impossibly, miraculously *alive!*

"Oh, Michael," Joel cried without restraint now, holding his boyfriend tighter than ever lest he leave him again.

Joel blinked several times fast as it dawned upon him...the only thing about dear Michael that didn't quite match up was that *beard.*

Even as he ran his trembling fingers through his lover's stiff wet hair...as he began to laugh and cry at the same time, delirious with gratitude toward Michael for returning home as well as the merciful Lord who allowed it...Joel found himself trying to remember...through the haze of wine and bliss that numbed every part of him now...when was the last time Michael had worn a beard?

Had he *ever* worn a beard?

A few minutes later, Joel realized there was something strange about his lover's *voice* too; at the same moment Michael reached beneath the suds to grasp him in one hand.

"Come with me," Michael said, squeezing gently, one thumb rubbing back and forth against the tip of Joel's penis.

"Where...where do you want to go?" Joel asked, with a nervous swallow.

"Nowhere, everywhere," Michael replied.

"I don't...understand," Joel said, groggily.

"To the Land of Tears."

"Michael..."

"Anywhere I want. Just say you will come with me, lover."

"Yes," Joel moaned. "I'll come with you. God, yes!"

"Gooooood..."

And now Joel realized what was wrong with Michael's voice.

It didn't sound like a *voice* at all.

It was a sound closer to crackling leaves. Burning brush. A sound not unlike ravenous flames, consuming everything in their path...

"Michael?"

"Shhhhhh," his lover replied.

And then he took Joel beneath the water.

Together they sank, into the abyss of the bottomless tub.

Joel did not fight it.

Even as his soul was consumed by an overwhelming sense of severe sadness, of heartrending regret, Joel allowed his lover to take him.

He went willingly, into the steaming depths, with the thing that looked like Michael.

Down into the water. Into that all-embracing beard.

It filled his mouth. His nostrils. His every orifice...

But Joel did not care.

He did not scream.

Anything to be with Michael again.

Forever.

CHAPTER 66

"Nonononononono," Kate cried. "This can't be happening! It's got to be a mistake, David...it can't be, oh, God, it can't be..."

She fell into David's arms and he nearly collapsed beneath her weight. He dropped his paintbrush, leaving a mark resembling a long red exclamation point on the hardwood floor of his studio, and held her tighter than he had ever held her before.

The clock on the wall above his desk displayed 10:47 P.M.

Neither Kate nor David had spoken to one another very much in the days following Kate's bizarre blackout; for the most part David had just stayed away from his wife. He threw himself into his work, painting two new dustjackets for which he had been contracted but didn't owe to his client for another six months...if only so he wouldn't have to venture out of his studio and face *her*.

David felt as if he no longer knew his wife. As if Kate had disappeared, and in her place lived an enigma who might turn on him at any moment. Every time he looked at her, he saw not Kate but a stranger. In her eyes lived a soul no longer devoted to the teachings of Jesus Christ, but now an ancient, bloodthirsty entity whom David was not entirely sure that he even believed in.

Hell, maybe he was going crazy, too. How ridiculous it all sounded. This was *Kate* he was thinking such thoughts about. *Kate*, for God's sake! Once again, David found himself thinking that perhaps Heatherly's insanity was contagious, and now he was infected too.

"What, honey? What is it? What's wrong?" David said as his wife bawled into the crook of his neck.

She trembled in his grasp, her shoulders hitching violently. "Joel's dead."

David's jaw dropped. "*What?* Oh, no...what happened?"

"He drowned," Kate explained as best she could through her tears. "In his...in the tub. Supposedly he'd been drinking, and he...he drowned."

"Oh, my God!"

"I wasn't there for him, David. I wasn't there for him, when I should have been, and now...now he's gone."

"Neither was I," David said. "I should have been. God, Kate, I'm sorry."

She stared up at him, her makeup streaked down her cheeks.

"Shh," he said, easing her head back onto his shoulder.

"You never did like him, did you?" Kate asked.

David didn't know what to say to that. At first, he thought he might have misunderstood her. "What? Of course I did. I'll miss him, Kate. You know that."

"No, you won't," Kate cried. His arms dropped from around her as she took a step back and glared at him. "You never liked him. Because he was gay. You're probably *happy* that he's dead. You wish it had happened sooner."

David stared back at her, incredulous. "I can't believe you would say such a thing."

"It's true, isn't it?"

"It most certainly is not."

"You thought he was just a silly faggot. You didn't even want to touch him when he tried to shake your hand."

"Kate, that's not fair..."

"It's true though, isn't it?"

"Kate, come on, you're just upset. Please, don't do this."

"He was just a cock-sucking homo to you, wasn't he? A jizz-hungry queer."

"Kate?" David's eyes felt wide as golf balls. His mouth hung open. "What the fuck?"

"You're heartless, David," she wailed. "You make me sick."

She ran from the room.

David ran after her. "Kate, wait! What's wrong with you?"

She ran through the house to their bedroom and slammed the door in his face.

"Kate, open the door."

He heard nothing behind that door but Christopher, crying.

Great. They woke up the baby.

"Kate, please...you know I cared for Joel. Why are you acting like this? What's gotten into you?"

He knocked on the door. Waited.

"Kate?"

Nothing.

"I can't believe how you've turned this around," he said to the doorjamb. "What the hell did *I* do?"

She still did not answer.

"Kate! Open the goddamn door!"

"Bigot!" she screamed at him through the door. "Homophobe!"

Christopher was shrieking now. David wanted to get through, hold the baby—he sure as hell trusted Kate less and less to do the job these days—but he knew this door was too thick. He couldn't break through it if he tried.

"Open the door, Kate! Now!

"Go away!"

David stood there for another couple of minutes, his fists two tight white balls and his eyes wide and bloodshot from stress and lack of sleep.

"What is your fucking *problem?*" he shouted at his wife through the door, and he struck it once with the heel of his hand before turning to walk back down the hall.

"Daddy?" Becca called out as he passed her bedroom. "Daddy, what's wrong? Why are you and Mommy fighting?"

She started crying in the darkness, and David entered her bedroom.

"Shit," he said, beneath his breath.

Fucking wonderful.

Chapter 67

Tomorrow was the day of Joel's funeral. David dreaded that event worse than he had ever dreaded anything in his life.

In an attempt to get his mind off of the whole thing, he had been working all day in his studio. Nothing seemed to turn out right, however, and at one point he threw his brush across the room, called himself a "talentless fuck."

He decided to wash up, relax in front of the television for a while, and maybe afterward he would have that talk with Kate he had been putting off for the past few days. They really needed to discuss some things, and procrastinating on the matter surely would not make the situation any better. Perhaps it was a tad coldhearted of him to do it today, David knew, but with her brother's funeral coming up, he thought Kate's vulnerable state might enable him to get some real answers.

He headed into the living room after washing up and changing into his pajamas, started to sit down in his favorite armchair.

But then he stopped.

He frowned, annoyed, as he noticed the Bible sitting on Kate's chair on the other side of the sofa. It was a fat white volume, expensive, a copy with their names monogrammed on the cover in gold. Kate's father had given it to them on their wedding day. Normally they kept the book on the bottom shelf of the knick-knack cabinet across the room, but Kate must have been reading it earlier and hadn't put it back where it was supposed to go.

"And she nags me about not putting shit back where it belongs," he mumbled. He picked up the Bible, preparing to return it to its rightful place.

As he walked across the room with it, though, a tiny slip of paper fell from the thick white book, drifting down to the floor like a pale, miniature leaf.

David bent, pinched the tiny piece of paper between his thumb and forefinger, and brought it up out of the thick carpet. Its backside was sticky, shiny with a smear of some glue-like substance.

His jaw dropped.

Six letters were printed on that small piece of paper:

MOLOCH

David's knees grew weak. He stared at the all-too-familiar word for what felt like hours.

Finally, he staggered across the room and plopped down on the sofa. The cushions made a soft wheezing noise beneath him. He opened the Bible before him on the coffee table, his hands trembling like those of his late grandfather, who had suffered from Parkinson's disease in the latter years of his life. He started flipping through it, stopping every few pages to stare at the text before him.

He felt as if he might puke.

Those tiny slips of paper were everywhere he looked.

"Oh, Jesus," he whispered, as he skimmed over several random passages throughout the Bible:

But I know that, even now, whatsoever thou wilt ask of **MOLOCH**, **Moloch** will give thee.

MOLOCH said unto him, 'It is written again, Thou shalt not tempt the Lord thy **Moloch**.'

And **Moloch** went about all Galilee, teaching in their synagogues, and preaching the gospel of the kingdom, and healing all manner of sickness and all manner of disease among the people.

David swallowed loudly. He turned more pages, reading on as his guts roiled and the bitter taste of his own fear coated his tongue like something electric:

But **Moloch** said, 'Suffer the little children, and forbid them not, to come unto me, for of such is the kingdom of Heaven.'

And he said unto them, 'I must preach the kingdom of **Moloch** to other cities also, for therefore am I sent.'

David turned to the front of the Bible again, to its very first line. He knew what he would find, and it sickened him, but he turned there anyway. Goosebumps stippled his forearms, as if his entire body had been submerged into a pool of ice water, as he read that opening line in the Book of Genesis:

In the beginning, **MOLOCH** created the heaven and the earth.

From cover to cover there were few exceptions. Throughout the Bible, wherever David looked, every appearance of the word "God" or "Jesus" had been replaced with that terrible name: Moloch. Someone— *Kate?*—had carefully pasted those tiny snips of paper removed earlier from Andrew Holland's *The Feasting* over God's name, blocking it out completely.

MOLOCH

Hundreds of times. Perhaps thousands.

The task—all that meticulous cutting and pasting—must have taken *hours*.

It was pure sacrilege. David knew it, recognized it as such despite the fact that he had never been a particularly religious man and did not think such things bothered him.

The dedication it must have taken, the sick obsession...

David threw the heavy Bible across the room, and ran for George Heatherly's house, not even stopping to close the door behind him.

CHAPTER 68

He couldn't even remember returning to the sofa. He must have fallen asleep instantly.

For another minute or so David tried to remember what day it was. And then he recognized his surroundings. He wasn't home. This was George's house. They had talked until well after midnight, drank one too many beers, and David realized he must have passed out on the old man's sofa. He cursed himself now, thinking how selfish he had been to run off and leave his children in that house, in that house with *her*...

Fucking stupid!

"George?" he called out.

The only reply was the buzz-saw rhythm of Heatherly's loud snore coming from the master bedroom a few yards away.

David stood. He considered leaving his friend a note, but knew that George would figure out he had awakened in the middle of the night and returned to his own house. They could talk more in the morning. *After* David and his wife had a long discussion about certain things.

He left, quietly closing the door behind him. George's harsh snore faded to little more than a muffled basso drone in the night as David made his way through the ex-Marine's yard and back toward his own home. He wondered what he was going to say to Kate, how he would confront her with the topic of the Bible he'd found the previous night.

As soon as David walked through the front door, though, those thoughts disappeared. He frowned, stood motionless in the foyer for several minutes.

From somewhere in the house, he heard a noise. Like furniture scraping against the floor. Someone moving about. A muffled thump. A sigh.

The latter sent a chill down his spine.

"Kate?" he called out, though his voice was little more than a whisper. He looked at the clock on the VCR. It read 3:13.

More noise, from somewhere in the house. A baby, crying softly.

David exhaled, relieved. Christopher must have woken up hungry. David headed down the hallway. If he could hear the baby, that meant Kate had unlocked their bedroom door in the middle of the night and opened it. Maybe he would catch her awake, feeding Christopher. Maybe they could talk things over *now*.

A fat square of bluish moonlight from the window above the kitchen sink illuminated his path down the hallway. He froze outside their bedroom door.

He titled his head to one side, frowning.

Damned if it didn't sound like...*eating* noises, in there. Coming from the bedroom. Licking and slurping noises. *Wet* noises.

David leaned against the wall, poked his head into the doorway.

Too dark. His eyes were still adjusting to the blackness of the house, and the curtains were drawn tight over the big bay window on his side of the room. He could just make out the shape of Kate's dresser in the corner, the laundry hamper squatting beside it like some box-shaped dwarf standing statue-still in the night.

Slowly, he entered the room. Stood there in the threshold.

Those licking, smacking, slurping sounds grew louder.

"Kate?"

Ah. He realized the origin of those sounds now. Kate was breastfeeding Christopher, that was all.

Damn, but it was loud. Poor thing must have been starving.

David's voice cracked as he called out: "Kate...is everything okay?"

"Shhhhhh," said someone—*Kate?*—from the darkness.

A low belch. *The baby?*

"Kate?"

Still, those sloppy *eating* sounds continued.

David could see them now, in the night—mother and child. Kate sat in the middle of the bed, one large dark shape holding another, smaller black shape.

"Kate, I'm glad you're awake. We need to talk about some things."

She said nothing.

David frowned, reached behind himself and felt for the light switch on the wall.

He found it. Turned it on.

And his breath caught in his throat. He could not move for those first few seconds, could not speak. His heart skipped a beat or three. A sharp pain ran through the center of his chest.

"Oh, Jesus," David gasped when his lungs started working again.

David suddenly felt, as he stared at the scene before him upon the bed, as if his mind had slipped completely off the brink of sanity, and now he was falling deeper and deeper into oblivion.

"Kate...what...*how*...?"

Kate and a baby were indeed sitting there on the bed.

But the baby wasn't Christopher.

She sat cross-legged, with the infant propped up in her lap like some gray-skinned doll. It sucked urgently at her left nipple, and a thin trickle of dark blood trailed from her areola all the way down to her thick thatch of pubic hair. The baby made soft purring sounds as it fed, but every few seconds David was quite sure he heard a sound that could only be the pleasured grunt of a grown man. It was deep, hoarse. An... *orgasmic* sound. David grimaced.

"What's the matter, David?" Kate whispered, and her voice seemed oddly seductive, a sexy bedroom hiss that normally would have turned him on. "He must be fed. A growing boy must always be fed."

"Agh, God," David wheezed. His head swam as he stared at the scene before him. His vision blurred. "Kate...what *is* this?"

She smiled up at him, as if proud of what was transpiring.

And then the baby turned to look at him, too.

The bottom half of the child's face was covered with a thick, filthy gray beard. It trailed over his shoulders, across the bed, under Kate's ass, and back over her shoulder, where it lay atop her right breast like some hairy tendril.

It covered the bed, like a heavy blanket woven from pure evil.

Hair—*beard*—everywhere David looked.

The infant smiled at him, its crooked yellow teeth smeared with Kate's blood, and its tiny eyes glowed with a satanic black light.

It blinked at David, before turning to feed once again.

Kate stared at her husband as the thing's teeth went back to her nipple. Stared at him, licked her lips, and started laughing.

"Moloch!" she sang through her shrill laughter. "Blessed be! He's here! He's heeeeeeeeeere..."

"Mo-loch," said the baby through its mouthful of Kate's nipple, and its voice was innocent, sweet, but far beyond its years.

CHAPTER 69

David awoke from the dream gasping for air, his heart beating so hard in his chest it felt as if it might explode.

"Jesus," he wheezed.

He couldn't get that awful demon baby out of his mind, the child who had looked so much like Christopher at first until it turned to look at him with those terrible, burning eyes. That matted, never-ending beard.

David took a deep breath, let it out slowly. Again he said a silent prayer, thanking God that it had only been a dream.

He gazed upon his surroundings, realized that he was in his own house. This wasn't George's place. At some time during the night he *had* returned home after all.

Still...he wasn't entirely sure. He could barely remember anything that had happened before the dream. The last thing David could remember was finding that Bible. That awful Bible, with God's name replaced by MOLOCH.

He stood from the sofa, forcing that memory from his head for the moment.

But then he froze as he thought he heard a noise somewhere in the house.

No way, he thought, *don't let this be another dream about psycho wives and vampire babies. I don't need this shit right now.*

This noise was different from the one he had first heard in his dream, however. Damned if this didn't sound—*holy shit*, David was sure of it now—someone was trying to break into the house!

David tensed. It sounded as if it was coming from the kitchen. A scraping sound, like someone scratching at a window. Or maybe trying to pry open a window with a crowbar.

He wished he had a weapon.

"Kate?" he whispered. "That you?"

A thump. Outside. Against the west wall of the house.

"Becca? Sweetie?"

David tensed, made a little hissing noise through his teeth. His heart skipped a beat.

"Who's there?" he called out as he entered the kitchen.

No one.

"I have a gun," he lied to the unseen intruder. "I won't hesitate to use it."

Another thump. This time it sounded as if someone was at the front door.

David turned to head back down the hallway, toward his studio where he might go for the hammer in his toolbox again, but in that split-second before the lights went out he saw in his peripheral vision the open window in Kate's bedroom, the curtain fluttering inward upon the night's breeze. It shouldn't have been open. But it was.

"Daddy!" he heard Becca scream suddenly from the other side of the house. Her voice was distant, muffled, as if she were outside. And it sounded as if her cry was accompanied by the sound of a baby squealing.

He thought of the man in the Santa Claus suit, and how the bastard had tried to steal Becca away once before.

"Oh, Jesus," David gasped, turning to run down the hall.

But then something hit him. Hard. In the back of the head.

"Moloch, motherfucker," someone whispered.

David went down.

And everything went black.

He came to, slowly, his head pounding. A burning sensation loomed at the nape of his neck, and his entire body felt as if he'd just been run over by a Mack truck.

He groaned, tried to stand, but his legs betrayed him.

Colors swam in front of his eyes. He squeezed his eyes shut, trying to wash them away, but they remained.

"My fucking head..."

He rose to his feet, but once again his knees buckled. He held onto the doorjamb, steadied himself. He touched the back of his skull, and his hand came away slick with blood.

He turned the light on in his bedroom, saw the room was empty.

No Kate. No Christopher.

He turned, calling out to them, but nearly tripped over something.

At his feet David saw the weapon someone had used to take him down. It was a heavy silver candleholder, approximately two feet long, inlaid with detailed scenes of the crucifixion in bas-relief. At its base, the metal face of Christ hung His briar-crowned head, as if sympathizing with David Little's plight. David stared for several long seconds at the thin smear of his own blood glistening upon the heavy icon, wondered how the hell he hadn't been killed.

He turned, started to stumble through the house, but nearly fell again. He caught himself, but knocked a picture of his father off the wall in the process. It crashed to the floor. The glass shattered, a spider-web pattern of cracks spreading across the wrinkled face like some hideous flesh-eating virus.

"Becca! Christopher! Oh, Jesus."

He stumbled down the hallway, through the house to Becca's room. He turned on the light.

She was gone. Gone. Her window was open too, her Barbie drapes blowing in the breeze.

Only Lucky, that fat pink bunny, lay in the middle of the little girl's bed. As if waiting for his seven-year-old companion to return.

"Oh, my God," David cried. "Becca...no!"

David pounded frantically on George Heatherly's front door.

"Come on, come on..."

Finally Heatherly came to the door. In one hand he held a .44 Magnum. Biggest damn gun David had ever seen. It shined like something alive in the moonlight.

"Damn, David, what is it? Last I saw you, you were sleeping." He glanced behind him, toward the sofa. "Like a baby. What happened?"

"They...they took Becca. And Christopher. Jesus, George, you've got to help me. I think Kate's totally gone. Moloch's gotten to her, I know that now, and I think she left with them."

George ushered him inside, comforting the younger man with a large hand upon his shoulder. He sat his gun atop the television set, allowed David to finish rambling before he said a word. "What are you talking about? What's happened?"

"You were right. She's under...she's under his influence. Moloch's got her. Kate's lost her fucking mind. I should have taken the kids...oh, Jesus, I should have taken the kids, got them out of the house as soon as I found that fucked-up Bible."

"It's okay," George said. "Calm down."

"Somebody hit me over the head, George. They took Becca and

Christopher. What are we going to do?"

"Come on," George said, moving deeper into the house. He gestured for David to follow.

"There's no time!" David shouted. "They've got my kids!"

"We can fight this thing," George said. "But we've got to go prepared."

"How the hell do you prepare for something like this?"

"Guns," George said. "Big guns."

"Guns aren't going to stop him."

"I don't know if they'll stop Moloch," George said. "But they'll damn well get us in that church. They'll damn well stop folks who bleed like you and me."

"You think they're at the church?"

"They've got to be."

"And if they're not?"

"We drive. And we find them." George placed one hand upon his friend's back. "We *will* find your children, David. You have my word on that."

"Jesus Christ, George, I can't believe this is happening."

"It's gonna be okay. Follow me. We'll get your babies back if it's the last fucking thing we do."

CHAPTER 70

The tires on George Heatherly's Ford Ranger squealed like dying infants as the vehicle swerved off of Robert E. Lee Boulevard and Morganville First Baptist appeared before them in the windshield. George had been right. Someone had painted the entire building in varying shades of red and violet. Beyond the church's stained-glass windows, a soft orange glow flickered inside the bowels of the place like long, fiery eyes blinking out at the two men as they pulled up. Otherwise, the place looked as if it had been dead for years. The property was weed-choked, crawling with overgrown vegetation, and David couldn't help it—thoughts of *beards* filled his mind, and he envisioned the whole place as strangely *hairy*.

A succession of chills cascaded down David's spine as he stared at the church. He shuddered, glanced down at the Beretta M-9 on the seat beside him. George had given it to him back at the house, and even with his kids' lives at stake David wasn't sure he wanted it. He had never been a big fan of firearms. His hands trembled as he braced himself, ready to open his door and burst from the vehicle the second they came to a stop.

"Listen to me, David," George said as he steered the truck into the church parking lot. The only sign of life in the area was a battered primer-gray pickup parked across the road. "I want you to be very careful. Stay by my side in there, follow my lead, and—"

From beneath their feet suddenly came a loud *BANG!* Then another. George barked "fuck!" and fought with the wheel, which started spinning in his hands like something with a mind of its own.

Another *BANG!* The Ranger lurched left, then right, then left again, and a *flump-flump-flump* vibrated through the floorboard and through the soles of their feet.

"Sonofabitch," George said as the Ranger slowed. It came to a stop, bumping against the sign in front of the church, the sign that had once welcomed visitors into the arms of the Lord and the fellowship of Morganville First Baptist.

MoLOCh, the sign read now. The "h" hung askew, dangled for a few seconds, then dropped onto the Ranger's hood. Below the word MoLOC read the slogan ThE TIME iS NoW...BLESSD BE PRINCE oF TEAR5.

"What the hell was that?" David asked.

"Fuckin' blowout," George said.

"Sounded like all of them."

"Yeah."

David opened his door, but then quickly closed it again. He hesitated, peering out into the darkness, toward the church. "Was someone shooting at us?"

"I don't think so," George whispered. "But stay low, just in case."

They exited the vehicle, crab-walked around it cautiously. One tire had survived, they saw now. The left rear. The other three straddled their rims, hanging half-on and half-off the wheels like giant leeches.

Both men peered out over the church's parking lot at the cracked blacktop.

"I'll be damned," George said.

Everywhere they looked, the lot was littered with nails. Thousands, perhaps millions. Nails of every size and shape. A veritable sea of them, atop the asphalt.

"Looks like we're not the only ones who came prepared," George said. "Fuck it. Time's wasting. Let's move."

They reached into the cab of the truck and pulled out the guns.

"You've got the Beretta, right?"

David swallowed loudly, held up his pistol. His hand shook as he gripped the M-9, yet he could not deny...it felt good. Damn good.

"Follow me," George said. "Let's gather ourselves."

The old Marine walked to the rear of the Ranger, opened the tailgate. He laid the guns down and instructed David to do the same.

David shifted his weight nervously from one foot to the other as George inspected the guns one by one, giving David a short, impromptu lesson in each as he did so.

"This here's an M-16. You may have heard of her. She's my pride and joy. This baby's got a thirty-round clip as well as a selector switch, giving you the options of single-shot, semi-automatic, and fully automatic. She's goin' full tonight."

George strapped the M-16 over his shoulder, letting it dangle behind his back, then picked up another gun.

"AK-47. The best overall firearm, in my opinion, when it comes to situations such as this." He handed it to David. "Use it wisely."

"Mine?" said David.

"Use it wisely," George said again.

David strapped it on, found that it did feel pretty good at his side. He was *very* aware of its presence, however, like a friend guarding his back who should only be partially trusted.

"All you gotta do is pull back the bolt and fire," George said. "You've got a fifty-round clip in there, should be more than enough for what we have to do. Be careful...but not too careful, if you know what I mean."

"Gotcha."

A single gun remained on the Ranger's tailgate. A shotgun. George picked it up and checked the chamber.

"Mossberg 500A. He's big, he's loud, he's crude as hell, but in close quarters he'll fill a crowd full of holes as fast as you can pull the trigger. I'll hold on to this one, you don't mind."

"Be my guest," David said. He started bouncing up and down on his heels without even realizing he was doing so, pumping himself up for the task at hand. Adrenaline flowed through his veins.

"You sure you can handle this stuff, David?" George asked.

"No."

"At least you're honest," George said. "Don't be scared of guns. Just respect them. Think of your kids."

"I am. That's the only thing keeping me from having a fucking heart attack right now."

George offered his friend a weak smile. "Oh. I almost forgot." The old man reached into his pants, dug around for something. He pulled out four foamy orange objects and handed a pair to David.

"Earplugs?"

George tilted his head, carefully inserted his own. He gestured for David to do the same. "You'll thank me later, we live through this. Especially when Big Daddy Mossberg starts talkin'."

David swallowed nervously again. *If we live through this.*

"Ready?"

"I'm ready," David said.

"Let's do this."

George led the way toward the church, and as they walked they avoided the thousands of rusty nails decorating the parking lot like the sharp metal teeth of the property itself.

"Fuckers got the place locked up tight," David said as they ascended the concrete steps leading up to the church's front door. In shiny silver paint someone had spray-painted MOLOCH ARISE across the width of the doorway. Above the threshold: PANNDAMONUM. A fat silver padlock hung from the door handle, and twin candles, blood red and half-melted, burned on either side of the violet door.

George stepped on one of the candles, snuffing out the flame and squashing the thing flat. David followed the old man's lead, completed the ritual by doing the same to the candle on his side.

David stood back then, a defeated expression on his face. "How are we going to get in?"

George smirked at him, hefted the M-16 in one pale arm. His tattooed bicep rippled and flexed. "I've got my key right here."

David nodded, brought forth his own AK-47. The thing looked so ominous as he stared at it, blacker than the night around it. He nervously cleared his throat, took a step back and pointed his weapon at the door.

"Shh." George's attention suddenly jerked toward the west wing of the church, at something behind David.

"What?"

"Company."

David turned, following the old Marine's gaze, just in time to see someone step out of the blackness at the side of the church. The AK-47 shook in his grip.

"Something we can do for you gentlemen?"

David's eyes were still adjusting to the darkness, but he was able to identify the man walking toward them. It was Deputy Harwood, the skinny man with greasy salt-and-pepper hair who had booked them the night Becca was abducted. He was accompanied by another middle-aged man with very tan, leathery skin and a moustache that made David think of Hitler.

Both men were completely naked. Harwood's shiny gold badge was pinned to his bare chest, just above his left nipple; a stream of dried blood ran in a straight line from that point all the way to his beltline.

"Where's my daughter—" David started, but George shot him a look.

"We'd like to get inside," said the ex-Marine.

"Too bad," Harwood replied, and now they could see that both men held guns of their own—.38 Specials. They pointed their revolvers at George and David, and their bloodshot eyes glistened wetly in the moonlight.

"Whoa." George gently pushed David out of the way. "Drop your guns, fellas."

"You drop yours," said the man with the hard leathery hide and the

Nazi moustache.

"Don't think so."

Harwood cocked the hammer on his .38, aimed it at George Heatherly's head. Fake Hitler followed suit.

The Mossberg swung from beside the ex-Marine's leg in one fluid motion, so fast that before David knew what was happening the blast had ripped open the night and the men at the foot of the steps were suddenly not there.

The shotgun's report echoed through the night as Al Harwood and his moustached friend lay dying on the ground.

"Jesus." His face pale, David stared at the dark, crooked figures sprawled in the grass. At the steaming holes in their naked torsos. One of Deputy Harwood's hairy legs flopped, like the milky-white fin of a dying fish.

"Let's go," George said. "We've wasted too much time already." He brought the .44 Magnum out of his pants and pointed it at the massive padlock on the front door of the church. "Stand back."

George pulled the trigger and the lock was suddenly gone.

He nodded toward David one last time, then reached out to push the door inward.

"You ready?"

"Y-yeah," David said.

"You'd better be." The old man took a deep breath. "'Cause it's time to fuck shit up."

CHAPTER 71

For those first few minutes after they stormed into the church, George and David felt as if they had lost the ability to do anything. Their guns may as well have been harmless plastic toys hanging at their sides. Neither of the men could move. They stood there in the dark foyer of the church's main floor, dumbfounded.

Nothing they had experienced thus far could have prepared them for this.

The interior of Morganville's First Baptist Church resembled some vision straight from Hell, a representation of the netherworld as viewed through the eyes of Hieronymous Bosch. Or perhaps the Marquis De Sade.

Four words popped into David's head: *orgy of the damned.* "Fucking insane," he murmured.

Every wooden pew inside the church had been removed, leaving a round, open space in the center of this once holy building. Battered maroon hymnals were strewn about the room like dead bats the color of dried blood, and everywhere the men looked the walls were streaked with graffiti, silver-spraypainted occult symbols and words like MOLOCH, BLESSED BE and ARISE.

The crowd gathered inside the church was naked. Every last one of them.

Some of them David recognized, most he did not.

On the stage, near Reverend Rhodes's cracked and splintered pulpit, a middle-aged lady in wire-rimmed spectacles mounted a hairy, overweight man at least twice her age. Her body glistened with sweat as she rode him, bucking and grinding violently like they were the last two people on earth with only seconds to procreate before their race was extinct. Her back was smeared with blood.

"My God," George whispered, pointing the couple out to David. "Do you know who that is?"

David shook his head.

"That's Donna Evanson. Billy Dawson's mother. And Ernest Crandell. He's a deacon here, I think."

David looked away, sickened.

No matter where he turned, however, similar scenes played out before him like some hardcore porno flick come to life. In one corner of the room, Deputy Hank Keenan lapped greedily between the legs of a woman at least seventy years old. She moaned, thrusting her hairy gray crotch into his face with an urgency David had never seen from any woman. Atop the electric organ behind the pulpit area, a skinny young man with green hair and multiple piercings all over his body pumped into a burly tattooed man from behind. David recognized the younger man as a busboy at the Denny's on Patton Avenue, his obese companion as the owner of the ABC store on Eighth Street.

All about the church, like glowing fish in a sea of decadent madness, dozens of red and violet candles burned within small holes carved three or four feet apart from one another directly into the floor.

"Un-fucking-believable," George said, watching the nude people writhe about before them in the candlelight. Their bodies seemed to merge into one crude entity, sweaty flesh undulating in a single liquid mass of sin. "I knew this thing was big, but I never thought..."

David stared wide-eyed as George pointed to a spot on the floor just a few yards away. A stocky, blue-haired senior citizen with the largest breasts David had ever seen was sitting on the face of a man wearing only a shiny red fireman's hat.

"Mavis Ledbetter," George said. "Guice's dispatcher. Man between her legs is Frank 'Beanpole' Deon. He used to work for the Fire Department."

"Christ."

But it was the object in the middle of the room more than anything else that caused bitter bile to rise in the back of David's throat. His stomach performed frantic somersaults, and it took every ounce of strength he possessed not to run screaming from the place.

No. He couldn't do that. Becca and Christopher needed him.

"What have they done, David?" George said. "Good Lord, what have they done?"

In the center of the church stood a live reproduction of the pictures in George's occult books. It was a slanted, asymmetrical effort, but there could be no mistaking the fact that the hodgepodge of scrap-metal there in the middle of the floor served as a jumbled reconstruction of Moloch's sacrificial altar. Those who had fallen beneath the demon's unholy influence had apparently melted down various metals—brass, gold, silver, copper anything they could find—in order to replicate the torso of the bull-god. In total area the thing could have measured no more than twenty or thirty square feet, but the inherent *evil* of the altar made it appear as large as the room itself. Jutting forth from the awkward angles of the monstrosity, David saw the partially formed remains of the items Moloch's cult had used to build it. From one corner of its base poked half of a silver sconce, Christ's head peeking out at His surroundings as if the Savior were sinking in a quicksand pit of molten metal. Various other items were half-buried in that silver-gold mass—chalices and half-melted crucifixes and folding chairs and even scavenged bits and pieces of long-dead junkyard vehicles. A crumpled car door. Several hood ornaments. The bent-and-folded side of a Quonset hut. Half of a grill from a Ford Fairlane. A hubcap from a '57 DeSoto. Sawblades. A grape-like cluster of rusty doorknobs. A glistening fender jutted forth from the base of the thing, still as shiny as the day it had rolled off the assembly line, though it was partially melted into the crossbars of a silver crucifix.

They had all been painstakingly molded together into a makeshift oven the size of a small gazebo.

The visage of Moloch himself, massive arms outstretched, stared down at David from atop the thing. His eyes were twin headlights, his horns crooked silver chalices, but his arms had been molded perfectly from what appeared to be pure gold, stretching down to just below his hollow stomach. The ragged dreadlock threads of an ancient soggy mop had been utilized to portray the demon's long, stringy beard.

Inside the thing's torso a small bonfire blazed. Shattered hunks of wood cut from the church's ruined pews were its kindling, and as those flames grew ever higher embers danced in the air around it like so many worried fireflies.

"They made him," David said. "Jesus, George, they made a fucking altar, just like in the books."

"I see that."

"Welcome to the conjuring," someone said, and both David and George spun toward the source of that voice.

Fred Dawson, unlike everyone else in the place, was not naked. He still wore his filthy Santa Claus suit, now more black than its original crimson, and his matted, crumb-specked beard hung down to his belly. He stank of shit and semen. He came to them from the dark stairwell to their right that led up to the church's balcony.

"Fuck you, Santa," George said.

"Shh." Fred Dawson quickly glanced in the direction of the bull-god's altar, as if fearing that his precious deity might have overheard the old man's sacrilege. "This is a house of God. Please, watch your language."

"Where's my wife?" David asked him. "And my children?"

"They are here, of course," Fred Dawson replied. "Mrs. Little is waiting for the ceremony to begin, along with the rest of us."

"And my kids?"

The man just smiled at David, steepled his fingers in front of his face as if preparing some deep, meaningful speech.

David took a step toward him, pulled the Beretta from his pants and stuck it in the Santa-imposter's face.

"Godammit, what have you freaks done with my daughter? And my baby? God so help me, if you've hurt them—"

"They are unharmed," Fred Dawson said. "For now."

"What the fuck is that supposed to mean?"

"They are waiting."

"Waiting for what?" David shouted.

"To pass through the fire. As Moloch has commanded."

David lunged at the man and pressed the business end of his pistol against Dawson's dirt-caked forehead. "Motherfucker, where *are* they?"

The man blinked at him, as if he knew he could not be harmed. "They are with Reverend Rhodes, of course."

"Goddamn you—"

"Moloch," said the man in the Santa suit.

George pushed David aside then, reared back and punched Fred Dawson in the face. Dawson crumpled to the floor, unconscious.

George wiped his hands on his pants. "That'll take care of Kris Kringle for a while."

David scowled down at the man on the floor for a minute or so, then joined George in the doorway of the church foyer once again. He stuck the Beretta back in his pants, hefted the AK-47 before him. They stared over the bizarre proceedings on the main floor, unsure of where to begin.

David swallowed, stayed close behind his friend as the ex-Marine took several steps forward into the church. The old man pointed toward an area where two men in their late twenties sat face-to-face in the candlelight, furiously masturbating one another as they hummed some unknown Gregorian-like tune. A few feet from that strange scene, four people rolled about licking and sucking and fucking one another like wild animals. Their sweaty bodies glistened in the orange light emanating from the bull-god's belly, and they plunged in and out of one another so violently David thought he saw blood mixed in with all of their other bodily juices.

"Let's get your kids," George said then, as he aimed his M-16 into the gathered throng.

"Listen up, you sick fucks!" he shouted. His voice echoed through the church, carried through the place despite the deafening chorus of orgasmic grunts and groans that assaulted the two men on all sides.

"HEY!" George shouted, even louder.

At last the unholy congregation stopped what they were doing. Their rutting abated simultaneously, as if everyone in the place were guided by a single, unified mind. They stared up at George and David.

"We've come for the baby," George said. "And the little girl."

They started laughing. All of them. Sandpapery senior citizen chuckles, insane howls, drunken redneck chortling and childish giggles merged into a single chaotic cacophony directed toward those who would dare interrupt.

"Shut up!" David shouted, gnashing his teeth. His head throbbed, and his knees felt weak. "Shut the fuck up!"

"You," George said, pointing his M-16 toward the two people closest to him. "Get up. Take us to the children. Now."

Mavis Ledbetter lifted herself off of Frank Deon's face, and even from where they stood George and David could see the shiny wet folds of her labia, could see her juices trickling onto Deon's chest as she rose. David made a sick burping noise in the back of his throat, tightened his grip on the Beretta as he tensed for a fight.

"It doesn't matter what you do, old man," Mavis said, her voice strangely masculine and somehow hauntingly seductive. "Moloch will have the children. Very soon."

"Who you callin' *old*, bitch?" said George.

"He's coming," said Frank Deon, beaming as if he'd just won the lottery. He rose to stand behind Mavis Ledbetter, and his stiff little penis bounced against the old woman's cottage cheese buttocks. "He's coming...and you will die if you try to stop him."

"You'll die if you try to stop him," said everyone else in the room. Their voices were strangely *alike*, and that sent a chill down George Heatherly's spine.

David pointed his AK-47 heavenward. He pulled the trigger, and a quick burst of deafening gunfire blew a shower of plaster from the ceiling. It rained down on them like chalky gray snow.

"Godammit, I'm sick of fucking around! Where the hell are my kids?"

George stared at the younger man, impressed.

"They have been promised to him," the tattooed fat man atop the church's organ shouted across the space between them, and a few feet away Billy Dawson's mother slid off of Hank Keenan's fat cock to announce: "He'll take them, no matter what you do. You cannot stop what has begun."

"Moloch," said Mavis Ledbetter. "You cannot stop what has begun."

"Moloch," said the crowd, as one.

"Fuck Moloch," David said.

And then something was suddenly on David's back, a horrible weight, and he couldn't breathe. He felt arms around his throat, squeezing. Tighter and tighter. He wheezed, slammed into the wall behind him. Dropped the Beretta.

"Moloch, motherfucker," said a familiar voice in his ear. "Moloch! Moloch! Moloch!"

"Blessed be," said the crowd. "Moloch!"

"David!" He couldn't get a clear shot at the man in the Santa Claus suit for fear of hitting David.

David thrashed about, slamming into the wall in futile efforts to get the man off of his back. "Get...off!"

"Shoot him, David!" the old man shouted.

David went to his knees, his vision blurring. The vice grip around his neck did not let up for even a second. He could smell the Santa imposter's breath. Onions. And beer.

The crowd around Moloch's altar drew together, inched closer.

David grasped blindly for the AK-47. He couldn't find it, though he felt its weight digging into his ass, felt it trapped between his body and that of his assailant. He elbowed Dawson once, in the gut, enough to stun him. Finally the AK was in his grip. He angled it around, pointed it toward his own head. He stared down the barrel as he brought it up, back, toward the man trying to kill him. He thought briefly how close it would be to his own head, the shot he was about to make. He hooked his thumb through the trigger guard.

He pulled the trigger, jerking his head away from the blast, his teeth clenched tightly together.

Sticky wetness splashed across the back of his head. Instantly, the arms around his throat grew slack and the weight fell off of his back.

David stood, coughing. He stared down at the man, quickly looked away when he saw the awful hole in Santa Claus' head.

"You okay?" George asked.

"I think so."

David rubbed at his Adam's apple, stared toward the front of the church, as a low humming came from behind the pulpit area.

A voice called out above the gathered throng surrounding Moloch's altar: *"In nomine Dei nostri Moloch excelsi!"*

The crowd turned from the intruders in their midst to face the church's front stage. They repeated that dark chant as one: *"In nomine Dei nostri Moloch excelsi!"*

David tensed, his grip on the AK-47 tighter even than Fred Dawson's grip had been around his throat, as he saw the speaker for the first time. It was Reverend Rhodes, but not the Reverend Rhodes who had presided over Fire Chief Randall Simms' funeral just two months ago. The pastor was nude, and his great beard hung halfway down his belly, impossibly long considering the man had been clean-shaven when David saw him last. His eyes were wild, but his mood was somber as he walked slowly out upon the church's stage. His stiff member seemed to lead the way, jutting out before him like some fleshy divining rod.

Kate followed behind the pastor, staring out at the makeshift idol as if it were the most beautiful thing she had ever seen. She, too, was nude. Her breasts hung full and pointy, her nipples hard, as she gazed out over Rhodes' gathered congregation.

But David barely even noticed his wife. She did not matter anymore. The only things he could focus on—the only things that mattered now—were his children. Their mother was leading them out, Becca softly crying as she held her baby brother in her arms like one of her dolls back home. Despite the situation, David felt a moment of pride as he saw her lean down, kiss Christopher on the forehead as if to assure the infant that everything would be okay.

Kate stood behind her daughter in the center of the stage, to Reverend Rhodes' left, her hands tight upon the seven-year-old's shoulders.

"Becca!" David shouted, running forward into the crowd of naked bodies.

"Stop him!" Reverend Rhodes commanded from the stage, pointing at the intruder among their midst.

"In nomine Dei nostri Moloch excelsi," the crowd moaned, and then they were upon him. Arms and legs kicked and punched at David as he tried to make his way to his daughter. Someone kneed him in the groin. A long fingernail barely missed his eye, scratched all the way down his cheek, burning open a deep gash along his jawline. Hands tore at his

clothes, ripped at his flesh, but all he could see was his daughter, up there behind the pulpit, silvery tears staining her cheeks like clear greasepaint in the firelight. He heard gunshots, realized George was trying to cover him, but the closer he got to the stage it only seemed to incite the crowd to pull him farther away.

"David!" George cried from somewhere far away. "Godammit, use what you've got, man!"

As David pulled out his weapons, he could hear Reverend Rhodes upon the stage, invoking Moloch. The man's voice was unnaturally loud, nearly drowning out the violent grunts of his parishioners, and David grew dizzy beneath that strange incantation.

"*In nomine Dei nostri Moloch excelsi! IN NOMINE DEI NOSTRI MOLOCH EXCELSI!*"

"*In nomine Dei nostri Moloch excelsi,*" the crowd chanted in reply as they thrashed and struck at David.

David pulled the trigger of the AK-47, roared as the weapon cut through the crowd. The man George had identified earlier as Frank "Beanpole" Deon went down with a hole in his forehead, his shiny red fireman's hat flying off into oblivion like some odd-shaped bird the color of freshly spilt blood. The tattooed man who had been sodomized earlier by the skinny young Denny's employee stumbled back as six bloody holes appeared in his flabby chest. Mavis Ledbetter went down with a hoarse shriek, a series of crimson holes polka-dotting her thigh.

Meanwhile, the fire in Moloch's hollow belly continued to blaze, crackling, popping, like the short, sharp bursts of gunfire. The room stank of burning wood, metallic gunsmoke, sweat and musty sex.

"*In nomine Dei nostri Moloch excelsi!*" Reverend Rhodes shouted, and even above the chaos around him David heard Kate echo the pastor's words: "*In nomine Dei nostri Moloch excelsi...*"

He also heard Becca sobbing frantically, and that gave him the strength to press on.

Beside him, just inches from his face, a man's brains flew out of his forehead in a thick spurt, splattering across Mavis' breasts as she rose again. She looked down at that gray mess, sopped a portion of it up with one fat finger. She stuck her finger in her mouth, grinned back at George Heatherly as if thanking him for the unexpected meal.

David glanced back, saw George covering him with the M-16, and stuck the AK-47 to Mavis Ledbetter's burly throat. He pulled the trigger. She went down with a *thud*.

David felt arms around his neck again. He gasped for air, spun around. In his peripheral vision he could see George fighting off several of those naked lunatics. He angled the gun over his shoulder, aiming it at the person straddling his back but could not get a clear shot. Hands batted at the weapon, at his chest, and he could not angle the weapon away from his own head for several seconds. With every ounce of strength he possessed, he forced the gun down, swinging it around through that sea of arms and legs. He pulled the trigger. A burst of gunfire sent red splatters across the torsos of those who had been trying to take him down from behind. Hank Keenan was one of them, as well as the two young men from the fire department who had been so infatuated earlier with one another's cocks.

"Godammit!" David shouted, still trying to throw whomever it was off his back. He tried to elbow his assailant in the face, but his shoulder screamed with agony every time he used his right arm. The AK's recoil had done a job on his shoulder, bruising it with every shot, and he briefly wished George had warned him about that.

No time to think about it now, though.

He stumbled back against the bull-god's altar, felt its heat through his shirt. Its metal body was growing hotter with every passing minute.

The person at his back screamed in his ear, and he suddenly felt her teeth in his neck.

He would know that scream anywhere.

Kate.

He howled in agony, ducked to the ground, and she fell off of him at last. But before he could grab her, she ran back onto the stage. Reverend Rhodes stood stone-still up there, watching everything with a very calm expression.

Kate ripped Christopher from Becca's arms and held the baby high.

"Accept our sacrifice, O Lord," Reverend Rhodes said above the din.

"Noooo!" David screamed.

Kate walked toward the altar, Christopher in her arms. David tried to lunge for her, but there were still too many people thrashing at him, holding him back. He tripped over a fat corpse in his path, and then they were upon him.

He could only watch as Kate laid the baby in Moloch's glimmering gold hands.

She looked back at him when it was done and grinned evilly.

"You should join us, David," her voice came to him through the din of Moloch's thrall. "You never liked my old God anyway. And perhaps you were right. He was quite boring."

Still, David thought, even as she said it, was there something in her eyes that insisted she did not believe all this? The dazed look of someone who has gone too far, but can never turn back now, a trapped *help me* look deep inside those beautiful green eyes with which he had fallen in love so long ago?

No. Maybe. David wasn't sure. All he could focus on was his infant son, lying in Moloch's arms. And *she* had placed him there. His own mother.

"You...bitch!" he shouted, flailing about beneath that smothering throng.

"Fucker!" Kate screamed at him, before running to join Reverend Rhodes upon the stage again.

The child wasn't crying. Not yet. The altar's hands were not quite heated up enough. Only its base and sides. But the fire raged on. And the heat was spreading through the thing. Quickly. It would not be long, David knew, until little Christopher was burned alive. Just like those children in the books George borrowed from the library. *Passing through the fire.* Even as David fought with the sweaty crowd he saw those worshippers who were not engaged in the fight solemnly stoking the hungry flames. Keeping the blaze going. Every few minutes they added new pieces of wood from the shattered pews all about the church. Building the fire higher and higher. Higher and higher.

Christopher started squealing.

"Jesus, no..."

Someone had his arms now. David couldn't move. Somewhere in the melée he had lost the AK-47, he realized, and he couldn't see it anywhere around him. Now he had nothing, only his aching limbs with which to defend himself.

George kicked a middle-aged man with a patch over one eye in the balls as hard as he could, then punched a red-haired teenaged girl in the stomach. She was pregnant, but George only hesitated for a second. Both members of Moloch's cult collapsed, and the ex-Marine moved forward, closer to David and the crowd atop him. A young man with a Rolling Stones "tongue" tattoo on his left bicep leapt onto George Heatherly with a cat-like squeal, tried to rake at the old man's eyes with his long fingernails, but George cut him down with a burst from his M-16. Heatherly ran toward David, pointing his gun at anything that moved, but it seemed as if for every evil person he took down, three more raving Moloch worshippers immediately took their place.

David could only watch, trapped beneath the weight of the naked bodies pummeling him with their fists, their feet, with anything at their disposal, as George Heatherly took two fists in his wrinkled face. The old man stumbled, fell back, but kept firing as a bony middle-aged woman with dirty hair and rotten teeth bit savagely into his arm, ripping a bloody chunk of flesh from his forearm. George screamed. A stout man several years younger than George ripped back on that same arm, bending it the wrong way. David heard the crack—that awful, awful *crack!*—even above everything else transpiring within the flickering room.

George grimaced, his head arched toward the ceiling and his eyes rolled into his head beneath the pain, but only for a second or two. He quickly regained his composure, aimed the M-16 with his good arm, and blew out both his assailants' throats.

George and David made eye contact.

Don't move, the old man's lips moved.

George aimed at David's attackers. Fired.

The person holding David's right arm suddenly released him. David's arm was numb, but he brought it around, punched the old woman on his left as hard as he could.

He gnashed his teeth as he felt something *pop* in his bruised shoulder. His vision blurred as tears welled up in his eyes.

But he was free.

"David, here!" George shouted, tossing him the shotgun.

David caught it, but just barely. He spun around, fired the thing without aiming, and the two men behind him fell beneath a nasty spray of buckshot. David's ears rang, like a shrill alarm inside his head. He realized he had lost his earplugs at some point during the battle.

To his right he saw a very old man sitting cross-legged upon the carpet, chewing on the earplugs as if enjoying fine chocolates. A flame from one of the candles in the floor lapped at his right leg, but the madman did not even seem to notice.

David ignored him, as Earplug Man seemed to pose no current threat.

"Get the baby!" George cried, heading for the stage.

David could not hear him, as his ears were still ringing beneath the Mossberg's report, but he didn't have to be told. He turned toward Moloch's altar and ran.

But then he stopped, pushed back as if by some invisible force. His shoulder throbbed as he stared in awe...

...as something began to *happen* up there on the church's stage.

Kate walked slowly forward with Reverend Rhodes. Becca glanced back, to the area behind the stage, squealed with terror as she too realized something *big* was about to happen. They could all feel it in the foundations of the building. A faint tremor, like a distant earthquake. Becca tripped and fell, but caught herself and ran for her father. Her body hitched with sobs as she fell into his arms.

At the front of the church, where Reverend Rhodes had once preached to the faithful every Sunday, the wall began to buckle inward. It expanded, pushing toward the gathered combatants as if made of liquid. Rippling, undulating, forming into a *shape*. The wall, like a giant bubble, swelled inward until it was even with the foot of the stage.

"He's here!" Reverend Rhodes cried, a single tear running down his face. "He's here! Come, my Lord!"

"At last!" Kate squealed with delight. "He's here! In the flesh!"

"He's here!" cried those in the crowd who had not yet fallen beneath George and David's attack.

The wall was slowly forming, David realized, into the shape of a ghastly *face*. Moloch's face. Features burst forth from the wood—first a beakish nose, its color paling from swirling wood grain to the shade of sick gray flesh, and then two wet ebony eyes the size of tractor tires blinked out at David and George. They were deeper than the blackest chasm, infinite. Two fat, bullish horns sprouted from the thing's forehead, stretched out over the length of the church just a few inches below the high white ceiling. The dozen or so fat wooden chairs reserved for the Sunday morning choir at the rear of the stage tumbled over one by one, and then Reverend Rhodes' pulpit did the same, landing several inches from Moloch's metal altar with a resounding *crash* as the creature's chin formed and stretched out of the wall. And then, at last, *hair* began to sprout from the foot of the stage, long trailing ropes of it stretching out along the floor of the church. A massive, filthy beard unrolled like some matted gray carpet until it touched the front door of the church. A dirty sea of it, everywhere George and David looked.

The church, in essence, had *become* Moloch himself.

The demon's immense mouth opened, and the sigh that erupted from within shook the building like thunder. From that black void, too, came a swarm of things that looked like brown alien babies with wings.

"What the fuck!" George Heatherly cried, running to David's side.

"Jesus, oh, Jesus..."

"Good God Almighty."

The thing stared at them, at everyone in attendance, and it smiled. As if pleased with the havoc that had transpired here tonight.

Kate and Reverend Rhodes screamed that awful chant now, louder and louder with every passing second: *"In nomine Dei nostri Moloch excelsi! In nomine Dei nostri Moloch excelsi!"*

"I've got Becca," George yelled into David's ear. "Get the baby!"

David could still barely hear his friend, but he did not have to be told twice. He kissed Becca on the cheek and shouted into her ear, instructing her to stay with Mr. Heatherly. He ran for the altar, leapt onto its base, and pulled Christopher down from those massive scrap-metal arms even as several of the terrible insect things plunged their stingers deep into him.

The baby squalled as David stumbled back, holding him tightly. David did a quick inspection of his son's body, and found no burns. But had he been a minute or two later, he knew his son might have been dead. Tears streamed down his face as he held the infant to his chest, protecting Christopher from the swarm. He stumbled back toward George and his M-16, shards of pain from the stings coarsing through his forearms.

"Give him back!" Kate screamed at David. "The master is here now! He must have him!"

"He belongs to Moloch!" cried Reverend Rhodes.

"Fuck you, and fuck Moloch," George Heatherly shouted, pushing Becca back over to her father. He cut loose with his M-16 then, Moloch's left eye bursting in a gooey mess of black and gray. Optic fluid ran down the demon's gargantuan face, onto its massive chin, and sizzled upon the carpet like acid. The monster—the building itself—made a sound resembling some massive, resounding groan. A smell like rotting meat filled the room.

Reverend Rhodes trembled as he stared at the scene, as he glanced back and forth between those who would oppose his god and Moloch himself.

"No, no," he wept. "They will pay, O Lord...I promise, they will pay..."

George fired again. This time at Reverend Rhodes. Four of the bee-things lit upon the ex-Marine, stinging his face and arms with their shiny black spears, but the tough old man barely seemed to notice. He swatted them away and kept firing.

His first few shots missed the preacher entirely. Rhodes ran across the foot of the stage, but he tripped upon Moloch's long beard. A spray of bullets struck him in the stomach, in the chest, and at last the man went down, disappearing—save for one outstretched, grasping hand— into Moloch's beard. The ocean of greasy hair swallowed the reverend's body up like a mass of squirming, hungry snakes, before growing still again save for the putrid breeze wafting through the church from the creature's open mouth.

Moloch sighed, and the sound was like a heavy wind on the highest mountaintop.

"You ruined everything!" Kate screamed at her husband.

"Bitch," George said, bringing up the gun.

David stopped him, placed one hand upon the old man's arm. "No..."

The old man lowered his weapon.

Kate ran then, as fast as she could, ran past Moloch's face and through a side door, out of the building.

"Kate!" David cried. "Kate, *stop!*"

"David," George said. "Don't you think it's best to let her go?"

David said nothing, just stared at the leviathan god who had grown from the back wall. He swatted one of the insects away from his son with his sore arm, and the thing darted back at him, stinging David in the crook of his neck right where Kate had bitten him earlier.

"I *LIVE!*" Moloch's voice boomed through the church.

"Not for long," said David.

David stumbled through the carnage to the center of the church, placed his hands on the base of Moloch's scrap-metal altar. He groaned, strained, pushed until his entire body shrieked with agony. His flesh burned, and he could hear it sizzle and pop as the heat inside the metal god's body ate away at his palms. At his back those insect-creatures buzzed and trilled. His hair flapped in the breeze created by their rapidly vibrating wings. He felt dozens of stings upon his back.

David roared, a sound derived from an equal mixture of agony and rage.

Finally, the altar teetered.

David's knees locked. His palms hissed, and his vision blurred behind a thick red fog. He pushed...*pushed*...

"Please God, give me strength..."

The altar teetered again, rocked toward the stage, toward Moloch's massive head.

And then it fell.

It crashed onto Moloch's humongous face, and the demon was suddenly *gone*, as if he had never existed. His bee-creatures vanished too—all of them, suddenly gone.

Glowing embers danced in the air, and now flames began to lap hungrily at the church carpet. The flames grew. Quickly. They trailed across the main floor of the church, up its walls in a matter of seconds like hot orange fingers reading brittle wooden Braille.

"Come on," George said, holding his bleeding, broken arm. "It's time to go."

With Becca in one arm and Christopher in the other, David looked back one last time at the mess they had caused. What Moloch had wrought. At the blackened bodies lying everywhere. At the roaring fire, spreading through the place so rapidly.

David ran from the church behind George, as fast as he could with his children in his arms, as the fire blazed at their backs. The blisters on the palms of his hands swelled and popped, but David barely even noticed as he ran with his children from that place of death.

Within seconds, the building began to fall. Creaking, groaning. A dying behemoth.

It was over.

Finally, it was over.

EPILOGUE

"Let's go, Daddy!" Becca shouted from the 4Runner. "I think Christopher's hungry."

"I'm coming, sweetie," David said.

He stood back, his thickly bandaged hands on his hips, and stared at the FOR SALE sign for another minute or so. Then at the house, at the way the setting sun framed it from behind like an old friend guarding its back. It was a melancholy scene, but David wondered why he didn't feel *something*. Anything. Though they had lived in the house for only a few months, he thought he should feel at least a sad sort of nostalgia for the few memories his family had shared at 31 Honeysuckle Lane. Because there *were* good memories, along with the bad. As hard as those were to remember.

Still, he felt only a cold sort of distance from the place, as if it had never truly been home to begin with. As if it were only a sort of dark way-station between one domicile and the next. An empty vessel, waiting to be filled by the next family who moved in with big dreams and a decent checkbook.

He glanced in the direction of George Heatherly's place before climbing into the 4Runner. He thought of his last conversation with the ex-Marine one morning a couple days after their long night at the church. He had already begun to pack up all of his family's belongings, and George had asked him if he was sure he wanted to do this, moving away so abruptly when the town felt truly *clean* now. David had assured Heatherly he was *damn* sure he wanted to do this, and nothing the old man said could change his mind.

George had nodded, moved to shake David's heavily bandaged hand, but then opted for a friendly pat on the younger man's back. One of his own muscular arms had been confined to an off-white sling. Thick red welts covered his face and arms, like David's own, where Moloch's terrible bee-things had stung him.

"It was nice knowing you, David," the old man said, "However briefly. Have a good life, my friend."

George had walked into his house then with his shoulders high, a strange expression upon his wrinkled face. It was the expression of a man who had accomplished something grand, so he could at long last retire and find some much-needed rest. Months later David would hear that George Heatherly had left Morganville himself, moving to California to live with his daughter and her husband. He would hear about the book George Heatherly wrote about their experiences—with all of the names changed, or course.

As he started up the 4Runner, David's thoughts turned from George Heatherly to Kate. He wondered if he was wrong in not telling Becca the truth about her mother. The little girl had a right to know. But he had told her that Kate had gone to Heaven to be with God. Mommy and Joel were up there right now, he said. They were looking down. And they were so, so proud of her. It was a decision he feared he might regret, a burden of guilt he suspected he would carry for years, but in the end he had decided it was for the best. Perhaps, one day, he would tell her the truth. But not until she was older. When she would understand. When *he* fully understood everything that had happened. But for now, how was he supposed to tell the seven-year-old that her mother had been committed to the asylum upstate, that Daddy had tried his hardest to talk to Mommy through that Plexiglas window but all she did was murmur incoherently about "forgiveness" and her "merciful Lord," about how she hoped He would allow her into the Kingdom of Heaven if only she could prove her worth?

How, David wondered, could he ever explain the violent twitches, the occasional guttural cry—*"Moloch!"*—that would slip out now and then like a harsh wet cough amidst Kate's ramblings about the God she had once worshipped so devoutly? How could he explain the four large brown M's Becca's mother had drawn with her own feces on the walls of her room at the sanitarium, or the MOLOCH smeared upon her forehead in menstrual blood?

He had done the right thing. He was sure of it.

For now, he would tell Becca that his mother was with Jesus. It was hard, so hard for both of them, but the truth would be even harder.

"I love you, Becca," David said as he drove the 4Runner down Honeysuckle Lane and their former home grew smaller and smaller in his rearview mirror. He wiped a single tear from his eye with the sleeve of his shirt before his daughter could see it.

"I love you too, Daddy," Becca said. She squeezed Lucky, the fat pink bunny Uncle Joel had bought for her when they first arrived—how long ago that seemed now—as if she could transfer her love through the stuffed animal into her father up front.

Baby Christopher made a "glaaabaagh" sort of noise from his car-seat, and Becca put one skinny freckled arm around her brother, kissed his tiny fingers one by one. She looked up at her father, in the rearview mirror, and grinned proudly.

David winked at her, the swollen pink scratch on his cheek resembling some crusty tear trailing all the way down to his jawline, the thick gauze bandage upon his neck a soft white tattoo. "I love you two more than anything," he said, looking back at his children one last time before devoting his attention entirely to the road before him.

The road leading out of Morganville.

AFTERWORD

Something Wicked This Way Comes (Again)

I am a child of the 80s.

Most folks these days are quick to follow that up with a disclaimer: "But I sure am glad that decade's long behind us, and ain't never comin' back!"

Screw that.

I loved the 80s. Still do. And I'm not ashamed to say so.

I can't help but think a lot of the folks who make fun of the things that were popular in the 80s—the music, the movies, the fashions (okay, I will give them that, the clothes we wore back then *did* deserve to be made fun of)—are the same folks who adore anything "retro" today. There's a saying that "everything old is new again," and I think that's especially true where the era of Reaganomics, Pac-Man, acid-washed jeans, the Pet Shop Boys, and big, poofy hair is concerned.

Maybe I'm wrong. But I don't think so.

If I were wrong, shows like *I Love the 80s* wouldn't be popular. Hair metal wouldn't be seeing the resurgence it has seen over the last few years. (Sure, many of the new bands who play that style of music today are doing it with their tongues firmly planted in their rouge-heavy cheeks; however, there's another saying that goes "imitation is the sincerest form of flattery.") 80s pop culture wouldn't take up ninety-nine percent of the merchandise racks in places like Spencer Gifts, nor would more and more entire *stores* dedicated to the "Decade of Excess" be popping up all the time.

But enough about the music and fashion of the 80s.

We're here to talk about horror.

As a child of the 80s, the books I enjoyed during my formative years have stuck with me all of my life, naturally. I still remember the first "adult" horror novel I ever read: *The House Next Door*, by Anne Rivers-Siddons (if you've never read this one, I urge you to check out this seminal haunted-house tale—but don't take my word for it, as a fellow by the name of Stephen King also cites Siddons' novel as a personal fave). After reading *The House Next Door* at the age of...oh, I must have been fifteen or so...I couldn't get enough of this stuff.

As the old Firehouse song says, "That was all she wrote."

After *The House Next Door*, I bought all the horror novels I could find. Works by Mr. King—of course—took up every minute of my free time, as well as stories by other phenomenal but lesser-known writers such as Graham Masterton, Richard Laymon, Gary Brandner, Ronald Kelly, and Ray Garton. These were the guys who made me decide early on that I wanted to do this too, one day. I wanted to be a *horror writer.*

Of course, just like anything in life, with the good comes the bad. As horror began to make serious money for the publishing houses, it soon became a classic case of *quantity* over *quality.* The big "horror boom" of the 80s brought countless generic, terribly-written novels into readers' hands, books that quickly gave the genre a bad name.

I'm not gonna name names here. I don't have to. And if I did, I doubt you'd recognize those one-hit wonders anyway. When the bandwagon crashed and burned, those folks—or should I say, their careers—went up in smoke along with a genre gone bloated and very, very tired.

You remember the cheesy covers. They were all the same: holographic demons...leering skulls...ominous-looking houses...and let's not forget the possessed dolls and/or children. Those demonic brats were all over the place! Browse your local used bookstore, pick up five yellowed paperbacks originally published in the 80s, and I guarantee you at least three out of the five will feature a leering, red-eyed kid on the cover. Even if you were to grab a title by one of the "good guys" I mentioned above, chances are the poor author would have been cursed with one of those awful, generic covers that made his or her work look like more of the same at first glance. (Jack Ketchum's *The Girl Next Door*, anyone? Those of you who remember the first edition undoubtedly recall that wretched "skeleton cheerleader"—yuck!)

The plots were interchangeable too. I'm generalizing here, in a major way, but for the most part they could all be lumped into three categories:

...stories about those pesky, aforementioned children Possessed By Evil...

...or small, picture-perfect towns Possessed By Evil...

...or a church, a school, a movie theater, whatever, that had been unwisely constructed atop an old Indian burial ground...thus, it is now

POSSESSED BY EVIL...

You get the picture.

Back then, this stuff was *product*—nothing more, nothing less. And the suits who published it couldn't have cared less about separating the proverbial wheat from the chaff.

...at least till the money dried up, and readers who had been ripped off one too many times suddenly stopped buying anything with HORROR on the spine.

I didn't start off this piece intending to trash the horror novels of the 80s. Honestly. Remember what I said at the beginning of this piece about how I loved the 80s, still do, and I'm not ashamed of that?

I wasn't lying. I adore the era, and I adore the horror stories from that era.

I even like some of the *bad* stuff, if you wanna know the truth. Even some of the badly-written stuff was *fun*, at least, and if nothing else it taught those of us who dreamed of one day writing our own tales of terror exactly what we *shouldn't* do. That's just as important, when learning your way in any craft—learn the right steps toward achieving your goal, but also learn the *wrong* way. Then you can avoid the mistakes made by others before you.

The Wicked is my tribute to those "evil in a small town" novels of the 80s. I don't consider it to be a parody, a spoof, or even quite tongue-in-cheek. At least, I never sat down to write it with those intentions in mind. Maybe it's a little bit "self-aware"—not to the extent of something like those *Scream* movies that refuse to go away—but insofar as this is a story that knows it is treading territory that has been tromped all over before. It knows it, but it doesn't care. It says, "Let's have fun with this."

Ultimately, I sat down to simply write a story that I *would want to read.* And that's what I attempt to do with everything I write.

When the timing was right for *The Wicked* to at last see release in a paperback edition, I wanted everything to be perfect. I had a vision, and I didn't want to sell anyone the rights to a new edition unless I could do exactly what I dreamed of doing with it. I envisioned a version of *The Wicked* that brought to my readers not only a *story* that paid tribute to those novels that made me what I am today, but a total *package* that would take fans back to another era.

Thank Moloch for Shock Totem Publications.

They *got it*, man. These guys really friggin' *got* it!

Kick-ass cover art, done with the classic media of—gasp!—paints and a canvas, as opposed to something thrown together digitally? Check.

Ads in the back of the book (even a cigarette ad!), just like those old paperbacks used to have? Check.

A general sense of *fun* about the whole thing, via an author and a publisher who obviously don't take themselves *too* seriously?

Check, check, check!

The Wicked is my ode to the stories I grew up with. The over-the-top, demented, but most-importantly *fun* horror novels that were all over the place when I was a teenager, for better or for worse.

There were good ones. There were bad ones. Just as there are today.

I like to think *The Wicked* is among the former.

Hopefully you agree.

James Newman
Skinny-dipping the River Styx
February 13, 2012

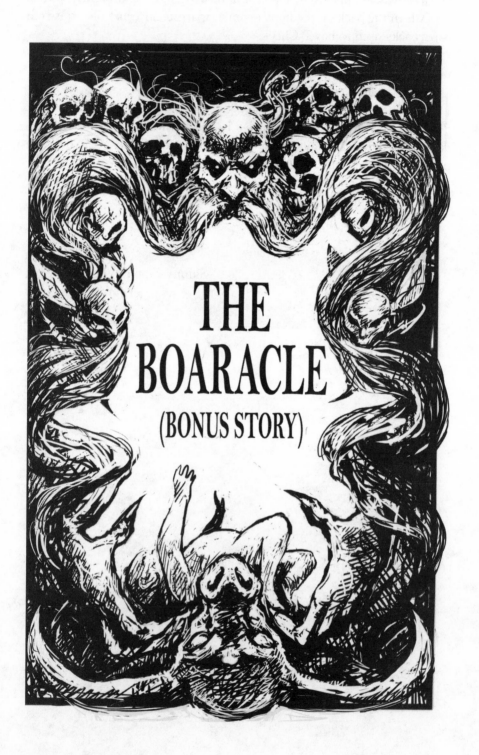

THE BOARACLE
(BONUS STORY)

THE BOARACLE

There's more than one demon in Morganville...

"Home sweet home," Paul said as he jogged up the steps of his colonial-style mansion. The Mazarati logo on his keychain glimmered beneath the security lights bordering his patio. He unlocked the door, humming a few notes from some generic techno tune that was stuck in his head, probably the last song he'd heard back at the club.

His catch of the night (what was the guy's name again? he was pretty sure it started with a "G," Glen or something) followed close behind, his fancy shoes making soft scuffling noises on the wet cobblestone walk. A light, early-morning rain hissed on the asphalt behind them and in the trees surrounding Paul's massive home. Paul looked back at the other man, winked at him as they entered the house, and Glen nervously returned his smile. The guy was wound tight. He'd been that way the whole drive home. It was obvious this sort of thing was new to him.

Paul chuckled under his breath as he ushered the other man through the foyer. "Lemme show you around, maybe we'll get a fire going a little later. I can't wait to take advantage of you."

"Promises, promises," Glen replied, but he spoke so softly Paul barely even heard him, and his voice cracked as he said it.

———

"Holy crap," Glen said, taken aback by it all. "Is that—no way! That *cannot* be an original...?"

"Wouldn't be hanging there if it wasn't." With a wave, Paul dismissed the object of the other man's attention, as if the hundred-thousand-dollar painting were nothing more than a child's scribble, something thrown together with crayons and construction paper. "Forget about that. It's nothing. Follow me...there's something *really* cool I wanna show you."

Glen's mouth hung open (*keep that up, you're gonna draw flies*, Paul felt like telling him). He was obviously struck speechless as they moved deeper into the mansion. Paul couldn't blame him. The place was amazing. Crystal chandeliers, winding staircases, works of art that put the first one Glen had admired to shame. When they had first pulled up in Paul's Mazarati, Glen had remarked that he felt like he just stepped into *Gone With the Wind*. He wasn't the first to say such a thing, and Paul had promised him, "Honey, you ain't seen nothing yet."

Glen swallowed loudly as they walked down a plush-carpeted hallway lined with golden sconces shaped like muscular nudes, both male and female.

"Jesus. This is really something. What did you say you do for a living?"

"I guess you could say...I'm independently wealthy." Paul shrugged nonchalantly as he led the way deeper into the heart of the manor.

"Ah."

The men walked down a wide corridor that seemed to go on forever. Glen held his hand out before himself, feeling his way through the darkness using the back of Paul's silk shirt as his guide.

"Could we maybe turn on some lights?"

"Shh. It's not much further now, I promise."

At last, they came to a large black door. Paul searched on his key-ring for the right key.

"If you have to know, Gary—"

"It's Glen."

"Right. *Glen*. Sorry. If you have to know, I inherited this place from my folks. They were self-made millionaires—my dad was into software, videogames, crap like that. They died in a car accident when I was thirteen."

"Oh. I'm sorry to hear that."

Glen reached out to touch Paul's shoulder, but Paul moved away, pushing open the big black door and stepping into the room.

"Don't be," he said, inviting Glen inside the room. "On my eighteenth birthday, everything you see became mine."

Finally, he turned on some lights. As if this were the only room in the manor that deserved them.

"Welcome to my favorite place in the universe. Well? What do you think?"

All Glen could say was: "Wow."

The room took up at least a thousand square feet, and hardly an inch of the maroon-carpeted wall-space lay bare.

A multitude of glassy eyes stared the two men down. Animal heads were mounted *everywhere*, along with entire bodies stuffed to perfection, trophies as if from some insane taxidermist's fantasy of paradise. Here were dozens of deer, elk, antelope, and caribou...a gray wolf, frozen in time as it howled at the moon...a sullen-looking moose...and a *zebra*. There was a huge black bear...a grinning crocodile...a slender heron with a fish in its beak...a shaggy mountain goat standing atop a slab of faux mountainside built into one wall...and a gorgeous bald eagle perched on a petrified tree-stump. In one corner a family of lions—two adults and an albino cub—cuddled together. Just inside the doorway a massive rhinoceros head glared at Glen as if he were the culprit for its condition.

"You, uh, don't exactly strike me as the 'hunter' type." Glen barely spoke above a whisper, as if this were a sacred place. As if anything louder would have been forbidden.

"Most of this was my old man's stuff," Paul explained. "He traveled constantly, when he wasn't working. Kenya, the Rockies, you name it. All over the world. He really got into that shit."

"I'll say." Glen nodded dumbly as he took it all in...

Each specimen was identified by a shiny gold nameplate beneath it, a plaque inscribed with the animal's scientific name: *Ursidae Carnivora, Aquila Accipitridae, Equidae Burcheli, Perrisodanctyl Rthinocerotidae,* and on and on...

There were surely a hundred of them in that room—*at least* a hundred.

But the single trophy that demanded Glen's attention above all else, the creature he slowly approached as Paul led the way, grinning with pride...was the *boar's* head centered along the far wall.

The thing was enormous.

The boar's great cranium was easily seven or eight times the size of most in its species. Its tusks were longer than the legs of most adult humans, and its glassy black eyes were as large as softballs. Its coarse brown fur was matted with mud, leaves, and dead insects.

The plaque beneath the boar's head was inscribed not with the animal's Latin name, but a single word in bold capital letters: LAMMASHTA.

Glen and Paul stood before the beast.

"Jesus Christ," said Glen. "Where in the world did your dad bag *that* thing?"

"Isn't she beautiful?"

"Beautiful? Not the word I would have chosen. God, it's *ugly*."

Paul shifted his weight from one foot to the other, shot what might have been an uneasy glance at the boar.

He cleared his throat and said, "To answer your question, my father didn't 'bag' this one, actually. I did. Two years ago. Not far from here. Out near where the old children's hospital used to be."

"Oh. So you do hunt?"

"No. Well...sometimes. Not really. See, it's...hmm...it's kind of a funny story. She was an accident."

"'She?'"

Paul again eyed the boar as he spoke. He pinched nervously at his lower lip with two perfectly-manicured fingers. "I...I hit her with my car."

"Ouch. This thing must have totaled your ride."

"She did. Almost totaled me."

Glen frowned, watched Paul, waiting for further explanation.

Paul seemed lost in deep thought.

Neither man said anything for several long, awkward seconds.

Then, Paul said softly, "She talks to me sometimes, you know."

"I beg your pardon?"

"I said...sometimes she talks to me."

Glen slowly shook his head. "I don't get it."

Paul's face was serious. He wasn't joking. He stared into the boar's dead black eyes, his head slightly tilted as if in reverence.

"It...*talks* to you?" said Glen.

"She. Yes." Paul reached out to him. "Here...why don't you step over here. Stand next to her. I want you to see her up close."

"What? No thanks."

"Come here." Paul's tone was impatient now. "Don't be shy."

"Paul—"

"You really should see her up close."

"Look," Glen said, "I'm starting to think this wasn't such a good idea..."

"No," said Paul. His bright blue eyes had grown cold and strangely distant. "That's not true. This was a *very* good idea."

And with that Paul pulled the long, silver blade from a secret niche hidden in the boar's massive neck. A makeshift pocket designed for holding the weapon.

"What the *fuck?* What are you—"

In a single swift movement, Paul turned, slitting Glen's throat from ear to ear without a sound.

He stood back, watched the other man die with a sad little smile on his face.

Glen made violent gurgling noises as his limbs flailed about and his blood soaked into the carpet.

After a minute or so, it was over.

Paul bent, kissed the corpse's forehead. "Thank you."

He hefted the body up on his shoulders, grunting beneath its weight.

"The sacrifice is made," he said to the boar, his voice raised but his tone solemn in respect for his hairy idol. "Please offer up thy wisdom. Speak to me now...O' mighty Lammashta, minion of Moloch."

He leaned over, allowed Glen's still-dripping blood to pool into the gargantuan boar's slightly-parted mouth.

After only a minute or two, the blood began to disappear. It gradually soaked into the creature's coarse pink tongue. Until the puddle was completely gone.

The boar began to speak to Paul then. Its voice filled his head, and at the same time vibrated through the foundation of the mansion. Yet its mouth, as always, never moved.

SO IT IS DONE. ONCE AGAIN, THY LOYALTY SHALL BE REWARDED. WHAT DOTH THOU WISH TO ASK OF LAMMASHTA?

The voice was a bizarre marriage of silk-smooth femininity and, simultaneously, a deep, demonic growl. Like two entities speaking at once. Perhaps more. It never failed to send chills up and down Paul's spine, to stipple his forearms with goosebumps.

"Thank you, great Lammashta." Paul swallowed loudly, took a step toward her. "If I may, I wish to inquire once again about the stock market."

ALWAYS WITH THE STOCK MARKET. VERY WELL. ASK, AND YOU SHALL RECEIVE.

"Someone suggested Blair Pharmaceuticals. And I've heard good things as well about Pertwee and Saint. Tell me, mighty Lammastha... what should I do? Are these worthy investments?"

The boar was silent for a minute or more. As if she were considering his questions carefully.

Paul was patient. He knew she would reply. She always did.

PERTWEE AND SAINT SHALL PLUMMET WITHIN THE YEAR. ALL IS WELL FOR NOW, BUT MANY WILL SEE FINANCIAL RUIN.

"Very well. And Blair?"

FROM BLAIR PHARMACEUTICALS THOU SHALT PROFIT GREATLY. DO NOT HESITATE. ACT NOW, AND REAP GREAT REWARDS.

"Wonderful! Thank you, beautiful Lammashta. For everything. I am humbled by your wisdom. You are truly great."

LAMMASHTA IS GREAT.

"We will speak again, within the year."

The boar spoke one last time, and her parting advice to Paul was the same as it always was: FOR LAMMASHTA'S WISDOM, THOU SHALT BRING SACRIFICE. NEVER FORGET THIS. NOW GO, MAN-CHILD...FOR THAT IS ALL.

The room grew silent once again. Only the distant sound of the rain, like the whispers of lost children in the woods, could be heard upon the roof above Paul's head.

The young man nodded, grinning widely. He let a high-pitched, almost girlish twitter slip out of him, covered his mouth, but another followed. He could not help himself. Things just kept getting better. Never again would he know the melancholy existence that had been his poverty-stricken childhood. Never again would he know what it was like to "go without."

He was better than that. From now on he would always be better than that, thanks to mighty Lammashta, minion of Moloch.

Finished with the task at hand, Paul carried Glen's corpse down into the bowels of the manor, down a winding flight of stairs lit by flickering torchlight, until he reached a secret chamber constructed entirely of stone. His soft grunts beneath the corpse's weight echoed about the high rock walls of the place, and from somewhere in the darkness water dripped constantly, as if he were exploring the cold, dark stomach of some ancient, sleeping leviathan.

Paul wasted no time in disposing of the body, tossing it into a pitch-black pit at the bottom of the stairs.

He felt a chill, but grinned nonetheless as the dead man tumbled into the abyss.

They were all so gullible. They deserved to die. Take this guy Glen. Such a fool, lured in by his own libido like a fish lured to a worm. All too easy. Truth told, Paul wasn't even gay. Hell, he wasn't entirely sure he was hetero, for that matter. He often thought the best word to describe himself might have been *asexual*.

Because the only thing he had ever truly cared about was money. Material possessions.

And Lammashta, she did provide.

He listened, waited to hear the body hit the bottom. Of course, the sound never came.

He wondered briefly how many lay down there...how many had amassed, rotting, somewhere deep down in the earth.

And how many more were still to come? How many until Paul was truly where he wanted to be, till he was satisfied that he possessed everything he had always desired?

He started back up the stone staircase, thinking about all she had done for him.

Oh, how he loved her.

One day he would show her the extent of his love.

Because Paul knew, somehow—although she had never said as much, not yet, he simply *knew*—that one day this would not be enough for her. There would come a time when sweet Lammashta would demand more from him.

And he would have no choice but to obey.

On that date, Morganville would know true tragedy. Again.

JAMES NEWMAN lives in the mountains of North Carolina with his wife and their two sons. His published works include the novels *Midnight Rain, Animosity,* and *Ugly As Sin,* the short-story collection *People Are Strange,* and the novellas *The Forum, Olden,* and *Odd Man Out.* When he's not writing, James enjoys watching college basketball and listening to loud rock n' roll ... often at the same time.

NIGHT OF THE BERZERKER

NOW A TERRIFYING MOTION PICTURE STARRING GWA SUPERSTAR NICK "THE WIDOWMAKER" BULLMAN!

AN EXPERIENCE IN TOTAL TERROR BY

ANDREW K. HOLLAND